MAGIC IN THE STARS

UNEXPECTED MAGIC SERIES

Patricia Rice

Magic in the Stars

Published by Rice Enterprises, Dana Point, CA, an affiliate of Book View Café Publishing Cooperative
Cover design by Killion Group
Book View Café Publishing Cooperative
P.O. Box 1624, Cedar Crest, NM 87008-1624
http://bookviewcafe.com
ISBN 978-1-61138 ebook
ISBN 978-1-611385786 print

OTHER BOOK VIEW CAFÉ BOOKS BY PATRICIA RICE

MYSTERIES:
EVIL GENIUS, *A FAMILY GENIUS MYSTERY,* VOL 1
UNDERCOVER GENIUS, *A FAMILY GENIUS MYSTERY,* VOL 2
CYBER GENIUS, *A FAMILY GENIUS MYSTERY,* VOL 3

HISTORICAL ROMANCE:

WICKED WYCKERLY, *THE REBELLIOUS SONS,* VOLUME 1
DEVILISH MONTAGUE, *THE REBELLIOUS SONS,* VOLUME 2
NOTORIOUS ATHERTON, *THE REBELLIOUS SONS,* VOLUME 3
FORMIDABLE LORD QUENTIN, *THE REBELLIOUS SONS,* VOLUME 4
THE MARQUESS, *REGENCY NOBLES,* VOLUME 1
ENGLISH HEIRESS, *REGENCY NOBLES,* VOLUME 2
IRISH DUCHESS, *REGENCY NOBLES,* VOLUME 3

PARANORMAL ROMANCE:
TROUBLE WITH AIR AND MAGIC, *THE CALIFORNIA MALCOLMS*
THE RISK OF LOVE AND MAGIC, *THE CALIFORNIA MALCOLMS*

Author's Note

Those of you familiar with my magical Malcolms and scientific Ives know that I'm playing with possibilities more than I'm using magic. Centuries ago, flying airplanes would have been magic and a scientific impossibility. Today, we know they aren't magic at all.

So in Theo and Aster's book, I'm playing with the possibility of precognition or "second sight"—guided by astrology. Astrology was considered a science for thousands of years and is still used today. The records of second sight go back to the Dark Ages. The accuracy of either astrology or the Sight has never been proven, but no one is working to disprove it either. So why not throw a few new planets into the equation and see what happens?

And just for the grammarians out there—as in the previous series, I know the plural of Ives is Iveses, and I don't care. If my family refers to themselves as Ives in the plural, that's how it comes out on the page. My characters are dictators!

One

LADY AZENOR DOUGALL—Aster, to her family—clutched the onyx brooch on her bodice, the one containing a lock of her much-mourned baby sister's fair hair. Even after all this time, the sorrow was a reminder of what happened should she ever shirk her duty again.

"I must not doubt my intuition," she muttered as the carriage jounced in another muddy rut and rain blurred the windows. "I *must* believe in my gifts."

"An instinct that takes you out in this storm is not very trustworthy," Aster's companion intoned in her sepulchral voice. Clad in black, cloaked in gloom, Jennet loomed large against the opposite seat. "We should turn back."

Aster had chosen Jennet for her melancholy unlikableness. She wasn't likely to become too attached to a physical representation of herself as a Prophetess of Doom. Or so she'd thought six months ago when she'd agreed to train Jennet as a lady's companion. But desperately missing her faraway family, she'd even grown fond of Her Gloominess.

"Turning back would constitute shirking my duty. The marquess could improve the future of thousands of poor children," Aster said steadfastly. "Even if I must make a donkey's behind of myself knocking on his door, he must be warned."

"He won't believe you," Jennet insisted.

Few outside her family ever did, Aster knew, so Jennet was being realistic, not pessimistic.

Unfortunately, because her family *did* have faith in her gifts, they'd been forced to cast her out of the nest and send her off on her own. Aster had proved all too painfully how correct her dire predictions could be. If only her gift would prove *useful*.

It was beyond dreadful to know when something awful would happen, and not be able to stop it. There were days when she feared everyone was better off not knowing their fate.

LORD THEOPHILUS IVES, heir presumptive to the 3rd Marquess of Ashford, teetered dangerously on a once-elegant Louis XIV parlor chair to adjust the settings on his latest telescope. The chair rested on top of a table that slanted on uneven marble tiles, balanced by several volumes from the library. The leaning tower of pieces tilted as he leaned over to check the ocular.

The downpour that had driven him out of his roof aerie also obscured any view through the three-story foyer dome.

"I need a tower," he complained to whichever of his layabout brothers followed the pack of spaniel puppies racing down the corridor.

"If you want a tower, go to Wystan." Erran stumbled over a puppy and grunted under the burden of the table he carried.

A black-haired Ives two years younger than Theo, his barrister brother had the build of a young ox. This occasionally irritated Theo, who was taller but lankier and possessed mouse-brown hair instead of the distinctive Ives black. But Erran was the more social and civilized of his brothers, while Theo preferred his quiet library, so he supposed Erran needed his handsome looks.

"Wystan is filled with expectant females," Theo grumbled, "Or I would."

The marquess of Ashford, holder of this damp estate in Surrey, was also the earl of Ives and Wystan. As earl, he owned land—and the infamous Wystan tower—in the wilds of Northumberland. Theo's glass manufactory might have been suitable there, but all his allowance had gone into building it here, so Surrey had to be his home. Besides, he still needed the notice of the Astronomical Society to sell his highly-refined telescopes, and the Society was unfortunately located in London..

"Make yourself useful for a change and stick another book under the table leg, will you?" Theo called over the yapping of the excited spaniels.

"Get your own bloody book. Better yet, get the whole damned

library before the roof falls in," Erran griped, backing around Theo's chair and dodging puppies to place a billiard table with the help of their half-brother Jacques.

"The roof and the library are Duncan's business," Theo said with a dismissive gesture. "Or maybe his missing steward's. Being the heir and the spare, they're not mine." Which had never been a sore point. Theo wouldn't have his brother's title and responsibilities for all the women in the world.

"If he can't even manage the library repair, we'll never fix that leaky pipe over the billiard room—unless I tear off the ceiling," Erran suggested.

"Absolutely not!" Theo said. "Stick with the hay baler you left strewn in the great hall. Lawyers should stick to wire and string."

Finally giving up on the telescope, he frowned as his younger brothers settled the billiard table in front of the front doors. "What the devil are you doing?"

"The plumbing was dripping on the felt. We figured if you could set up out here, so could we. It's wasted space anyway." From beneath a mop of dark blond hair, Jacques flashed an impish grin remarkably similar to his French mother's. "And as one of the irresponsible bastards around here, I have no other duty but beast of burden. Shall I start moving the library next?"

Knowing full well that Jacques was perfectly content with his side branch in the family tree, Theo ran his hand through his thick mop of hair. He winced, remembering he was supposed to have had it cut yesterday. Blast it.

He glanced out the windows at sheets of rain and decided his hair wasn't going anywhere soon. His valet had left to visit his family and never returned. Theo really hadn't noticed his absence, except when it came time for a haircut.

"It would be easier to repair the leaky roof than move the library. Didn't Duncan hire someone to work on it?" Theo climbed from the chair and made a quick calculation in his notes. He shoved the stack of paper in his waistband so it didn't end up as puppy litter.

"The esteemed Marquess of Ashford claimed he did," Jacques said. "But then his doting fiancée sent a note asking for his opinion on the summer fete, and he hasn't been seen since."

Studying the curved glass dome overhead, Theo surrendered. Even his new telescope wouldn't penetrate the thick clouds rolling in as they had for months. He needed a desert for testing his glass magnifications. He'd never persuade the Astronomical Society that there were many more moons around Saturn than the six they knew until he could actually *show* them with his new glass.

"At least Margaret knows what she's marrying into," Theo said philosophically. "She's not likely to run out on Dunc anytime soon."

Erran slapped Theo on the back, catching him by surprise and nearly bowling him over. "You should have taken your lady to Wystan instead of introducing her here, old boy. We're really sorry about that goat race."

Theo was really sorry about it, too. Celia had been tall, blond, and even-tempered—his perfect mate. It had taken him forever to woo her since they lived in different villages, and he wasn't much inclined to social occasions. But once she'd accepted his suit, he'd even sworn off mistresses in anticipation of his nuptials, so he was just a bit testy these days.

He hated hunting for another available female, but he supposed it was good to learn that Celia had been prone to hysteria *before* he married.

Wystan, however, was not the answer to anything except Erran's desire to shove Theo out of the house.

In retaliation for the unexpected slap, Theo caught Erran's muscled arm and twisted it behind his back, proving brains could beat brawn. "It was the *nude swimming* that had her fleeing for her life, sapskull, not just goats rampaging through the hall. You're all a bunch of heathens." He shoved his younger brother toward the back corridor. "Move the library or fix the roof. If you're not in London studying, you have to earn your keep."

Under Theo's careless shove, Erran stumbled against the billiard table, then tripped over Dog, his mangy Basset hound. Unperturbed, he caught himself on a door jamb, leaned down to scratch Dog in apology, then grabbed a billiard cue.

"Don't you dare," Theo warned. He was still hurting over the fiasco with Celia and wasn't putting up with more of his brothers' antics. "You're five-and-twenty and should put that thick head of yours to better use than a battering ram. When do you finish up your term at Chancellery? You don't want to arrive with a broken nose."

Erran rubbed his already misshapen proboscis. "I'm due in court next week. But I can't afford lodging in London."

Jacques hooted. "He spends all his funds on tailors and can't afford the *women* in London. Buy him a rich wife. She'll settle him down."

Always ready for a brawl, Erran swung the cue at Jacques, who was inches shorter and a stone lighter and not an adequate partner for fisticuffs. Jacques retaliated by grabbing another cue, holding it like a rapier. Hog yawned in complaint and lumbered to the side of the room. The spaniels yipped in excitement and chased each other into the fray.

Through the tumult, a door knocker rapped authoritatively. Startled, Theo dropped the puppy he'd been removing from under his telescope. Hog howled his intruder warning, and the puppies proceeded to yap in enthusiastic accompaniment.

Jacques and Erran dropped their weapons to stare.

"Who the devil would be out in this deluge?" Erran asked, grumpy at having his brawl disturbed.

"Normal people open the door to find out." Since he was as normal as any Ives got, Theo unbolted the massive carved door his great-grandparents had installed in recognition of their new marquisate.

MOMENTS EARLIER, Aster's hired carriage had lurched up to the tall portico of this massive country manor. Sheets of rain beat down too hard to fully comprehend the size or state of Ashford's gray stone fortress—but the lack of welcoming light was not auspicious.

The driver had helped her over the river of mud running down the drive between the carriage and the step. Aster opened her umbrella against the drips through the portico roof and watched the driver pound the knocker a second time.

Opening her own black umbrella, Jennet waited with her before the enormous carved doors of Iveston Hall. Inside, a racket of howling hounds, yipping puppies, and shouts of men rang over the rolls of thunder overhead.

"At least someone is home," Aster said with as much optimism as she could summon on this journey of doom.

"Savages, from the sound of it," Jennet said glumly.

Aster had had all the miserable journey from London to consider the difficulties presented by this rampantly male, officiously obnoxious, and thankfully distant branch of her wide-spread family tree. She was well aware of the futility of the task ahead of her.

And still, she could not back down. She nodded at the driver to knock again. He pounded with vigor.

One panel creaked open. The light from the foyer illumined a shirt-sleeved, well-built, almost ascetic-looking man with a thick head of unruly brown hair. He loomed over Aster's below-average height, which made him large enough to be a footman. But no footman—or gentleman—opened a door in such dishabille while wielding a billiard cue, with a giant basset hound on his heels.

His hollowed, unshaven cheeks were softened by a curl of brownish hair across his wide brow. She had been led to believe that all Ives were black-haired, tall, and broad like oxen, so this must be a servant. She dipped her umbrella to cover her face.

"I must speak with the Marquess of Ashford immediately," she said in her coldest, most formal tones. "It is a matter of life and death."

LIFE AND DEATH? Theo shoved Hog aside and peered around the door.

An enormous blue umbrella painted with—*Egyptian hieroglyphs?*—met his gaze. Umbrellas were generally waxed canvas, black, and weighed enough to make a grown man think twice about carrying them. Judging by height—or lack thereof—and the pair of small, feminine boots planted on the doorstep, he assumed the visitor to be female.

What the devil would a *lady* be doing here? In a howling storm?

Pushing back a yipping puppy, Theo lowered his eyes to peer below the canvas edge. A luscious bosom covered in a shimmering iridescent waterfall of silk rewarded his curiosity. He almost salivated like Hog over a sheep shank. He'd definitely been without a mistress too long.

A damp draft wafted a light floral fragrance around him, stunning him into near paralysis. After the noxious odors of his brothers and the moldering manor, their mysterious visitor was literally like a breath of fresh spring air. Anxiously, he awaited the umbrella's tilt to reveal its owner.

She took her damned time.

"May we come in?" a melodic voice inquired from behind the blasted canvas, revealing nothing. "We've come from London and must speak with the marquess on a matter of urgency," she repeated more insistently over yapping dogs and his brothers' attempts to hush them.

Damn, another of Ashford's mistresses? Or another desperate female determined to trick the dolt into marriage? Most generally, decent women did not show up on their doorstep without invitation and escorted by no more than a carriage driver.

Intrigued despite his cynicism, Theo stepped aside and ushered the iridescent peacock into the war zone that he called home. "Ashford isn't here, but come in and dry off, Miss..."

"Lady Azenor Dougall." Unfazed by the excited puppies rushing at her, she crossed the threshold, leaving the umbrella dripping on the covered porch.

Azenor? Despite a tingling warning at the odd name, Theo was distracted by the petite female marching into the zoo he called home as if she owned it. Lighting the gray gloom more brightly than the foyer's gas lamps, she glanced around at the billiard table, his precariously perched telescope, the romping spaniels, and his half-dressed and staring brothers as if she visited Bedlam on a regular basis.

An enormous hat adorned in vibrantly-hued peacock feathers concealed her hair and her expression. Theo ached to sweep the eyesore away, but he couldn't drag his gaze from the shimmering rainbow of fabric encasing a figure so curvaceous, he forgot to breathe.

Damn Duncan for claiming all the good women.

"When can we expect Ashford home?" she demanded, tilting her head just enough for him to see beneath the hideosity that concealed her hair.

Huge, dark-lashed eyes shimmered with the beauty of midnight—he could almost see stars against a dark blue sky. Pert nose, plump rose lips, soft oval face—she was all curves everywhere he looked. He was having a hard time *not* looking. As were his brothers, their arms now full of wriggling puppies.

If a heavenly body like this inhabited his home, he'd come down from the roof more often.

"Lady Azenor." He belatedly remembered to bow. "I'm Theophilus Ives, Ashford's brother." He jerked his head inelegantly at his gawking siblings. "Erran Ives and Jacques Ives-Bellamy, who were just about to order tea, if you would like some."

Theo shot the dunces a telling look. Any tea in the kitchen would be stale, since they never drank it, but someone had to perform the niceties—and remove the damned yapping dogs.

Theo hoped he'd phrased the introduction appropriately. His mother had died only a few years after Erran's birth. His father had never remarried, and the social graces hadn't been high on Theo's list of lessons or interests. He preferred stars to people.

A black-gowned scarecrow behind the shimmering angel grunted a warning, startling him into realizing the lady had accompaniment.

In response to the grunt, Lady Azenor sparkled, even as she frowned. Theo couldn't stop gawking like a looby.

"Lord Theophilus," the lady purred with satisfaction, apparently placing him on the family tree despite his incomplete introduction. "This affects you, also. I repeat, when do you expect the marquess?"

"Not at all this evening, given the weather. And if his fiancée has anything to say about it, probably not the rest of the week."

Her plump lips pursed in what might have been displeasure on any other woman. On this one—she seemed posed for kissing. Theo couldn't unscramble his addled brain from wanting to hustle her somewhere private, back to appropriate behavior.

If she was Dunc's mistress, could she be persuaded to desert his brother's riches in favor of a man without wealth or title, a gentleman who wouldn't let her travel the roads in a storm?

"Is there a fire where my lady might warm her hands?" the black-garbed servant inquired with a hint of acidity.

So much for impressing her with his nonexistent charm and thoughtfulness.

"Of course, this way..." Theo finally tore his gaze from the angel to note that Jacques and Erran still stood there as frozen as he. "Tea!" he ordered, before offering his arm and wondering where in hell he might find a fire.

A woman who didn't run screaming from her first sight of the Hall was a treasure worth pursuing, even if it was his damned titled brother she wanted.

Two

AZENOR HESITATED at taking the gentleman's offered... shirtsleeve. Lord Theophilus, like his brothers, was garbed most inappropriately in loose linen, doeskin breeches, and scuffed boots. She was almost terrified to look closer—she could see bare chest. With hair.

Lord Erran at least wore an expensively embroidered gold waistcoat—not so his brothers.

They were all big men. Of course they were big, she scolded herself, taking a deep breath and delicately placing her glove on his... muscled... arm. They were Ives, after all. It was to be expected, even if Lord Theophilus wasn't quite the bear of a man his younger brother Erran appeared to be. The heir had more of the lean, studious look of a monk, except for the waves of hair. And the unshaven jaw.

"I do apologize for disturbing you in such an inopportune manner," she found the words to say, while trying to curb her awareness of his lordship's masculinity. His broad shoulders and trim hips ought to be declared one of the seven wonders of the world. Or perhaps she simply lacked sufficient knowledge of male anatomy, given that *most* gentlemen wore coats, waistcoats, and neckcloths to cover themselves.

"No disturbance at all, my lady," Lord Theophilus assured her in an acerbic baritone.

Without explaining the presence of a telescope and billiard table in the rotunda, he led her through a dreary corridor with unlit lamps and frayed carpet. The air smelled of mold and damp ashes. If it were not for the labor laws the marquess supported for poor overworked women and children, she'd be thinking twice about the worth of saving Ashford and his household. She did sometimes wonder if interfering with the universe's design was interfering with the hand of God. But she simply could not in all good conscience let anyone suffer if it could possibly be prevented.

"As much as we appreciate your company brightening our dreary day, you really should not have come out in this beastly weather," his lordship said bluntly. "A servant would have sufficed."

"As if you would have paid heed to a servant," she retorted, recovering a little more of her spirit. "Or that I should send servants out in weather I wouldn't venture into myself. Besides, given the position of the planets, we would have to stay inside all summer if we feared a little rain. We are in for a few miserably wet months."

"Indeed." Without any other acknowledgment of her prediction, he indicated that she enter what appeared to be a study. The illumination of the gray day through tall, uncovered windows revealed piles of books and papers scattered across a threadbare rug, several wing chairs, and an imposing desk.

A wealthy marquess really ought to have servants lighting fires and lamps—and answering doors. Azenor recalled the chaotic scene greeting her earlier of half-dressed men, stacked furniture, and barking dogs. Perhaps all sane servants had fled the premises, or at least the female ones had. An all-male household would undoubtedly be a trial.

Not that she knew about such things. Her baby brother had barely been toddling when she'd seen him last. All her other siblings were girls.

Lord Theophilus lit a lamp on the desk, then stirred the embers in the grate until a small blaze warmed the room. He glanced around until he located a worn leather chair. He unceremoniously dumped off a stack of papers and tugged the chair closer to the fire. When he didn't provide a seat for Jennet, Azenor neatly gathered the books on a second chair and removed them to the floor, gesturing for her companion to pull it next to her.

His lordship hastened to help Jennet lift the chair—a belated polite gesture, as if his skills were rusty.

With a little time to recover from the shock of his proximity, Azenor studied Ashford's heir. There was steel and grace in Lord Theo's movement—but he did not sport the bronze coloring of an active outdoorsman. He would look sleek and sophisticated in proper attire, the kind of man one would expect to be a courtier or politician. But the sheaf of papers in his waistband revealed his true calling of absent-minded scientist.

His features were angular and striking but not overtly

handsome. His most distinguishing characteristic, aside from the unshaven square jaw that made her squirm uncomfortably, was a pair of exceedingly light blue-gray eyes that seemed to pierce her innermost soul.

She realized she was staring and hastily took the seat offered.

This wouldn't get any easier. She gestured for Jennet to hand her the tapestry valise she used to carry her charts.

"I could wish Ashford were here as this most concerns him. I must rely on you to convey the urgency of the situation," she explained, rummaging through the valise for the appropriate scroll.

"Had you sent word—" He cut off his criticism with the arrival of a footman and tea tray.

Not a maid, she noted. Probably a wise choice on the part of the housekeeper. A household of virile males and no female authority would be ungovernable around young women... which ought to make her nervous and didn't.

If she could not have a family, she must dedicate herself to duty. Given the eccentricity of her family's habits, the Malcolm librarian could not afford to be of a nervous nature.

From what she remembered, Lord Theo's chart showed a man who ignored authority, who acted without consideration of others, but who was also capable of charging at challenges like an idealistic white knight. In other words, he was a difficult, complicated man but not a violent one.

It was the marquess's dire chart causing her the most concern.

She waited until the tea had been poured and the servant departed before continuing with what she had to say. "I apologize for abruptly appearing on your doorstep. I do not always have the advantage of adequate time to send polite notes. It is not as if I spend all day studying charts of every member of the family. I would need a tribe of astrological scholars, and as far as I am aware, I am the only one in the kingdom."

His lordship choked on his tea.

His reaction was not unanticipated. She had fretted all the way here over how to make the marquess understand the dangers he faced. Scientific men simply refused to accept what they couldn't measure and tuck neatly into a tract or treatise.

She unrolled her scroll and launched into her practiced speech.

"I have been working diligently at creating the zodiac charts of all known Malcolms. Since the Ives family started marrying into ours eighty years ago, we've also had to include all your births. I must say, that has caused more work than one person can conceivably handle."

"Perhaps you need a tribe of scribes," he said, studying her artwork from beneath a sardonically lifted brow.

"I need another librarian," she said acidly at his absurdity, "but so far none of my cousins have seen fit to produce one. That's beside the point."

It wasn't as if *she* would ever be able to marry in hopes of reproducing herself. She smoothed out the vellum and tapped the fourth house at the bottom of the chart. "Your brother has dangerous transits to half a dozen points that suggest catastrophe, possible death, and secret enemies. And *all* are in the fourth house of home and family."

She glanced up at Theo, narrowing her eyes. "And *you* also have disruptive transits to points that indicate possible death of a sibling and a change in your occupation. I *cannot* overstate the danger of this next month or two to your brother, you, and your whole family. Remember that if your brother dies, your life will change beyond measure."

Lord Theophilus stared at her blankly. She understood his confusion, but there was so much she had to explain...

"And to escalate the extreme danger to your house, there is a very odd conjunction with my family's, in the parts of catastrophe and assassination. I need further study to understand, but to all indications, whatever happens to your brother will disastrously affect mine and multiply both our problems."

"And why am I to believe this bird-witted claptrap?" His tactless question was moderated by what appeared to be genuine curiosity.

Azenor drew a sigh of exasperation. She had known this would be difficult. "Because I am *very* good at what I do. If you care to wait, you will see for yourself. According to my charts, the king will die in this next month. We have plummeted into a period of change that will cause more rioting and unrest before the planets re-align. Possibly because of the extremely rainy weather, this summer will be particularly distressful. But I don't recommend waiting for those things to happen to act on my warning."

"You're predicting the king's death?" he asked in incredulity. "Isn't that treason?" He spun her paper around to study the intricate pen sketches.

She was rather proud of her charts, and this one in particular. She'd even used watercolors, to emphasize the importance of the planets for the less enlightened. "Fact is not treason," she said prosaically.

"A prediction of what *might* come true is *fact*?" He pointed at the graphics she used to chart the position of the heavens. "Those are planets?" he asked, not hiding his mirth.

"Not all," she said patiently. "They represent the heavenly bodies most associated with the Earth and its inhabitants because of their size and proximity, so we include the moon and sun. The houses, here..." She pointed out the marquess's. "The houses represent fields of experience where the planet's energies are most focused at the time of birth."

"You have the planets circling the earth?" he asked with palpable scorn.

She yanked the scroll away and reined in her frustration. "A chart is a map of the sky at the moment a person first draws breath. This one is about your brother's life. And it will *end* right here—" She jabbed her finger on a harsh black line. "—*this month*, if we do not find a way to protect him."

Three

HAD THE LADY been one of his brothers, Theo would have howled in derision at her prediction. Duncan—dead because a misplaced planet said so!

Her *charts* were preposterous, but he very much wished to know more of her considerable *charms*. If she didn't belong to Duncan...

Theo entertained himself by imagining removing the absurd feathers concealing Lady Azenor's hair. In this dim light, he couldn't tell the color of the dangling curl at her nape. He was partial to blondes, but he was willing to make an exception for a glorious peahen. She wore one of those transparent frilly collars to conceal her luscious breasts, but he was taking absurd pleasure in watching them rise and fall with her indignation—probably proof that he should get out of the attic more often.

"You are saying the stars predict Duncan will die?" he asked, just to watch her suck in a breath of outrage.

"The zodiac is a circle of space containing the orbits of *heavenly bodies*," she explained with less of the musical tone of earlier and more acerbic authority. The fluffy morsel contained a hint of steel. "I am saying there are dark aspects over these next months. There will be worldwide wars and rebellions over which we have no control. My concern is more immediate. A whole quiver full of arrow points are being triggered by transits in our family charts, but most particularly Ashford's."

"Arrow points?" he asked, his appalling curiosity and sense of humor drawing her out when he really shouldn't. "Shall I buy him a shield?"

Her lips set a little more grimly. "Arabic parts are mathematically calculated points specific to an individual's chart. Your brother's points are sitting on those of assassination and catastrophe, as I said, but they also show danger to occupation and other negativities. He could *die*."

"And you used the planets to make these mathematical calculations?" he asked, maintaining his gravity.

She didn't miss his sarcasm. "Even *Newton* used these calculations," she insisted. "Consult his theorems if you don't believe me. But my charts *work*. Perhaps because the marquess is working with my uncle—at the behest of my mother and aunts—to reform the labor laws, my family's fate is inextricably entwined with his. We cannot predict or direct fate, but we can alleviate the result to some extent if forewarned, and it is positively *essential*, in Ashford's case."

She stroked an ugly black brooch marring the beauty of her magnificent... bodice. Theo had to stop thinking of the plump bosom beneath the cloth.

"We can't keep the king from dying but we can make him comfortable?" Theo suggested, fighting lust by checking the layer of clouds out the window. If the rain didn't stop soon, he'd have to wait another month to test his new telescope glass on Saturn's moons.

She waited until she had his attention again before speaking.

"Telling a king he'll be dead in a few weeks isn't *comfortable*," she said with a degree of acidity that didn't belong on her pouty pink lips. "King George steered his own fate by indulging in excess his entire life. It's too late for him, but not for your brother. I recommend that Ashford not go out without a companion over the next month. Whatever this is showing in his charts can't be stopped—but if he's injured, he'll have someone to help him, which could save his life."

As much as he enjoyed watching the flashing midnight stars in her eyes, Theo regretted that she was another over-excitable female. He wasn't interested in hysterics these days, one with a misguided mania at that. He finished his tea cake and searched for an appropriate dismissal.

Instead, he couldn't help asking, "You mentioned that this also concerns me?"

"Of course," she said flatly, rolling up her chart. "Your chart shows you are in the part of *death of siblings* and danger to *occupation*. Practically speaking—if your brother dies, you will be the next marquess. As a Sagittarius, you will make a *very* bad marquess. You tend to act first, and ask questions later, don't you? Diplomacy is not exactly your distinction. As I've been trying to tell you, these next years will be ones of political and economic turmoil. We will need powerful leaders to guide us, but your head is in the stars."

"And yours is in the planets?" he retorted ungraciously, just a little annoyed at her assessment of his competence, or lack thereof. "A tactless man would inquire why a lady named Dougall would claim to know about my witchy ancestors," he pointed out—possibly tactlessly.

"As a descendant of Malcolms, you ought to know the answer to that. It is just this sort of ignorance we strive to prevent by keeping a library that can explain our sometimes extraordinary gifts. But do you or your brothers ever consult us? Heaven forbid. I can't believe you still call us *witches*." She rose abruptly and dropped a calling card on the desk. "I wish you would listen, but I must warn my family next. You'll know where to find me when the time comes."

Now that he had succeeded in driving her away, Theo almost regretted it. "We can't send you back out in this weather, my lady," he admonished, rising with her. "Let us have our housekeeper make up a room for you."

He tried not to wince. The housekeeper would be well into the sherry by now.

"Nonsense," she said frostily. "I have done what I needed to do for family and country. The task is in your hands now. I would not presume to inflict you with my presence longer than necessary. Come along, Jennet."

"I did not mean to offend," Theo insisted. "It's foolishness to travel on a day like this. It will be dark before you reach London." He hurried after her, unable to prevent admiring the sway of her skirt.

"My cousins are right down the road—one of the advantages of large family. You would do well to expand your circle of acquaintances instead of limiting yourself to your carousing fellows." She swept down the corridor as if she were familiar with the maze of old chambers.

"We motherless sorts have only our school chums to expand our acquaintances," he countered. "It's not as if we can introduce ourselves to women unknown to us."

Was that a delicate snort in reply? Devil take it, he shouldn't be so fascinated with a woman he'd never see again.

"You have neighbors. Your friends have sisters. You simply do not bestir yourself to seek feminine company for any purpose but carnal."

Well, he'd give her credit for being right there.

Arriving in the now abandoned foyer, she turned and offered her gloved hand. "I bid you adieu, my lord. And I wish you and your family well. Do not hesitate to call on me should the need arise."

The need would arise when Saturn fell into the sun. Ives took care of themselves. But Theo politely took her fingers and bowed. "We shall take your counsel under advisement, my lady. Thank you for thinking of us."

Her beautiful midnight eyes narrowed as if she heard the lie in his voice. "I shall see that Ashford receives a report of our conversation. You might wish to send a servant to accompany him home, starting tonight."

Lacking the presence of a footman, Jennet had already opened the front door. She tapped her foot impatiently until her ladyship swung in a swirl of petticoats and walked out into the damp wind.

Theo started to shove his hand in his pocket... and realized he wore no coat. Swearing under his breath, he let the door close on the strangest visitor the house had welcomed in decades. It would probably be a good thing when Duncan married and they had a woman around here again.

With no further distraction available, he packed up his telescope to carry it back to his room. There would be no stars tonight.

Planets might affect each other's orbits. The moon might affect the tides. But the sun did not dictate death. A pity the lovely lady had wits to let.

Late June, 1830

USING THE BILLIARD TABLE as a sturdier base for his telescope, Theo adjusted the settings on his glass and directed it at the broken pane above the door.

"What the devil are you doing?" Duncan Ives, Lord Ashford,

yanked on his riding gloves as he strode through the foyer. Tall, broad-shouldered, black-haired, and fitting the description of a villain in an old gothic romance in his billowing capes and tall black hat, he halted his progress to glare at Theo.

"Saturn is in near-perfect alignment with the earth tonight. If my new glass proves Saturn has more than six moons, my fortune is made, but the bloody rain won't stop," Theo grumbled. "I don't have enough circumference from the guard tower but the angle from the front might work at this hour."

"If this is your way of protesting that your observatory hasn't been built, it's not helpful." Duncan yanked on his other glove. "Until Margaret has settled on an architect, and we've worked out plans for renovations, there is no point in adding still another awkward structure to this monstrosity."

"I sank everything I own into the glass manufactory on your promise of an observatory. I can't earn it back until I prove the worth of my glass. Without the observatory, I'm bloody well hamstrung," Theo protested. "I've been waiting years for your damned nuptials."

Instead of adding his usual eloquent gripes about Duncan's delayed marriage, Erran merely lined up a shot on the billiard table to aim around Theo's boots. He'd barely spoken since his return from London and his first court case—a detail someone ought to ask about but hadn't.

"If you want a tower, go to Wystan," Duncan repeated Erran's earlier suggestion.

"Wystan is full of females," Theo said bitterly, climbing down. "You bloody well let every aunt and expectant second and third cousin fill the place, then tell me to exile myself there?"

"What am I supposed to do, bring them here? It's Wystan they want, and they can have miserable cold Northumberland. But it has a tower you can use."

"Right-o, a medieval fortress in the north is so very useful for scientific study and selling telescopes. I need an *income*." Theo grabbed a whip from the rubble accumulating beneath the table. In a gesture of frustration, he lashed it at his damnable older brother's boots, striping the polish before handing the whip over. "At least take the whip and watch out for the bridge when you come home.

The stones are coming loose, and I'd rather remain the spare heir. The king *did* die, as the lady predicted, you'll remember."

Theo really didn't take the lady's predictions seriously, but he damned well resented Duncan's fiancée ruling the roost before she lifted a hand to help—or even produced an heir to get that monkey off his back. Lady Azenor had been right—Theo would make a damned poor marquess.

As expected, Duncan had ignored the lady's warnings. Occasionally, Theo fretted, wondering if he should insist a servant accompany his brother. The Captain Swingers currently inciting riots and setting barns on fire across the countryside reminded him a little too uncomfortably of the lady's predictions of unrest.

Duncan yanked the whip away and cast him an evil eye before striding off down the corridor to the stable.

"The bridge?" Jacques asked, chalking up his cue now that Theo was out of the way. "I thought he was heading off to Margaret. That's the other direction."

Theo grabbed another cue. "If you haven't got the brains to work that out, we'll have to hire you out as a coatrack. Do you really think he's spending his nights with Margaret?"

Catching Theo's drift, Jacques set about knocking random balls into Erran's. "While Dunc is dipping his wick, we could just fix the window and roof."

"Not... my... job." Theo set about knocking every ball off the table, in mathematical precision.

Northumberland, it would have to be. He'd chase all the witches out of the castle and claim it for himself.

Four

LATER THAT EVENING, Theo stood on the roof, adjusting his telescope to focus on the heavens. The rain had finally let up enough to see through the clouds. All he needed was the final calculation and a sighting to confirm it—

The hatch door over the stairs squealed open. "My lord, my lord!" a groom cried from the opening. "Zeus just returned without his lordship!"

Theo's first mulish thought was that this was the first clear night he'd had in a week to track Saturn's moons—and now he'd have to spend it hunting his damned brother, who couldn't keep his trousers buttoned. If Ashford wouldn't insist on visiting his village mistress while betrothed to another, he wouldn't tempt fate.

Although Duncan was a damned good rider and Zeus was a superior horse.

That realization provoked the unwelcome memory of Lady Azenor's doom-and-gloom prediction. Theo didn't believe in hocus-pocus. His mother had left a journal of vague prognostications that had been a source of amusement when he was younger.... But as far as he could remember, they all made as much sense as assassinating planets.

Theo cast a stoic eye to the immense belt of glittering stars overhead. Selfish bastard that he was, he didn't want to be left with Ashford's responsibilities if anything happened to his damned lordship. Saturn would return in a month, but he had only one older brother.

"Saddle horses," Theo told the groom, "I'll fetch Erran and Jacques. You wake the stable hands." With resignation, he closed the telescope.

Hours later, as men carried the bloody and unconscious marquess in on a stretched canvas, Theo suffered a sick sensation in the pit of his stomach. He'd just cursed Duncan earlier in the evening, had wanted to punch him outright. And now...

He hadn't hurled since childhood, but acid ate at his midsection at the sight of his omnipotent older brother rendered helpless.

He didn't want to believe in foolish superstition. Everyone fell off a horse sooner or later. But...

Duncan was a bruising equestrian who should have had no trouble in weather as clear as it was tonight. But impossibly, the marquess now lay comatose, head and face bloodied beyond recognition, with a bone sticking out of his twisted arm. His big body appeared lifeless, not stirring even as the servants bumped him over the threshold.

Biting down his fear and self-contempt, Theo damned prophecy as superstition, swallowed his anxiety, and concentrated on what needed to be done.

"We've sent for every physician we know," Jacques said worriedly, following the litter in.

How long had Duncan been out there before the horse returned and while they'd hunted over acres of estate? How much blood could a body lose in the hours he'd been lying alone and untended?

"How bad is it?" Theo asked, holding Jacques back while the servants scurried about with hot water and bandages. "Broken bones?"

"Broken head," Jacques said, his frown deepening. "Broken arm, but it's the head that's bad. Looks like Zeus took a fall and Dunc sailed right over his neck. It happened down at the bridge, where all those rocks line the path."

"The bridge" was no more than an ancient stone trestle across a deep creek that flooded in the spring. The path was a short cut from the village to the house, not a public road. Had the horse broken its leg and not returned to warn them, no one would have found Duncan for days. As marquess, he had many responsibilities and often spent weeks elsewhere without leaving word. They would scarcely have noticed his absence.

That's when Theo's gut really took fire. He still didn't want to believe that planets foretold fate—but the lady had been right in too many respects.

"Zeus is too old to startle or bolt easily," Theo said, dismissing illogic. "What would make him throw Duncan?"

Jacques' eyes widened. "Dunc quit taking Zeus hunting because he started spooking at gunshots."

Would angry farmers *shoot* at Duncan? That was more logical—and uglier— than blaming planets. "I can't think like that," Theo decided, rubbing his head to clear out the superstition and panic. He was a man of books and science and not cut out for imagining villains. "Send for Margaret and her maids. We need women to tend him while we wait on the physicians." Theo headed for the stairs and his brother's chamber.

"He should be safe with women," Jacques agreed, trotting for the door.

That hadn't been what Theo meant, but safe was good, too. There was no reason to believe anyone had intentionally harmed Duncan, but Theo damned well wouldn't let anything else happen to him.

Standing over Duncan's unconscious form a few minutes later, gazing in horror at the gash opening his brother's head from temple to jaw, Theo froze inside. He and Duncan had argued over everything from the best time for breakfast to the size of the observatory. But in his own selfish way, Theo loved and admired his successful brother, and he'd never *ever* wanted the overwhelming responsibility that Duncan relished wielding.

Lady Azenor had been right in one more thing. Theo belonged in libraries and under the stars. He would make a perfectly rotten marquess.

Early July 1830

THE CHILDREN ARE CRAWLING under the looms, sweeping up stray cotton for their scoundrel employers, and losing <u>limbs</u>!!!! Wee children—<u>armless</u>!

Aunt Gwenna had underlined *limbs* and *armless* three times, forcing Aster to shudder at the images conjured of such a horrible injury—to a *child*. She read on, wondering what her mother's youngest sister expected her to do about this tragedy. It wasn't as if the zodiac predicted an end to mankind's cruelty.

Your mother says you are determined not to marry, which is a most excellent idea if you are able to use your time helping others instead of pandering to a husband. I have heard that you have been to see the Marquess of Ashford. He has responded favorably in the past to our desire to outlaw child labor. You must convince him the need is <u>immediate</u> *and* <u>vital</u> *to the welfare of the country's children and future to stop these depredations for the sake of a few pennies profit.*

Gwenna lived in the north country. She had apparently not heard of Ashford's grievous accident. But this reminder of how their families were connected rumbled uneasily through Aster's instincts—the danger signs connecting their families through *her* were particularly troubling.

She read on.

Are you able to train six-year-olds for safer work? Ones missing a hand? The situation is beyond deplorable. The workhouse is full of the injured and disabled and the parish is threatening not to take more.

Aster wiped angrily at a tear. She wanted to be useful, but how did one train a six-year-old, much less one missing a limb? Her heart tore knowing those children were doomed to starve otherwise. She wanted to take a big stick to the evil men who allowed this to happen.

And given the latest news from Surrey, she knew the injured marquess already had more problems than he could handle. She would fare better asking the new king to help—which was to say, she could do nothing.

Thinking of the six-year-old brother she hadn't seen since infancy, she forced back a need to cry. She had learned grief could be assuaged by acting on the more practical needs of the moment.

She resolved to petition the king *and* the marquess. She could develop a plan for training servants more quickly than she did now. She would ask Cook if children could be used in the kitchen or if that would be too dangerous.

She made notes of all she could do. Then realizing she was putting off what *had* to be done, she reluctantly summoned the woman who had been her stalwart companion these past months. Jennet hadn't been the mother that Aster desperately missed, but her companion had kept her from feeling too alone in the world. She hated to see the morose lady go.

When Jennet arrived, Aster settled back in her blue damask desk chair and regarded her large, black-clad companion with approval, even though her heart sank at what she had to say.

"Jennet, you have done an exemplary job these last months. Not everyone learns to guard their speech *and* dress in a manner becoming a lady in such a short time. I have no hesitation in recommending you as companion for Lady Hamilton's youngest daughters." Well, yes, she hesitated at sending a damp blanket to a schoolroom, but that was beside the point. "I believe by the time they're of an age to come out in society, no one will mistake you for anything less than their aunt."

"I would rather stay with you, my lady," Jennet said stiffly.

Aster fought a forlorn smile and tried to be positive. "I understand the comfort of familiarity. I, too, would prefer to keep you. But we all know the rules we must abide by. I cannot become too attached to anyone. The danger in my chart is very clear."

"Yes, my lady," Jennet said with just a hint of defiance. "But I would rather face danger with you than leave you."

At this example of her servant's steadfast loyalty, Aster wiped away another tear. She would become a watering pot if she did not toughen up. "Mary said the same, and I dared to let her linger. You know what happened. I cannot bear to let anyone else suffer her fate. Please don't ask it of me."

Jennet bobbed a curtsy. "Of course, my lady. Although I'm not young and foolish enough to let my skirts near a fire."

"I know you're not. That's why I chose you. That doesn't mean a carriage won't run over you or the plague won't strike you." Which made her worry about any orphans she might take in since she attached to children quickly, but Aster could only confront one obstacle at a time.

"I've already grown too devoted to your company," she continued, "so it's safest if you depart swiftly. The timing is propitious. With everyone mourning the king's death, there will be no activities these next months. All society will depart from town, and I'll not have an immediate need for a companion. Lady Hamilton is a generous, kind employer. I would never send you otherwise."

"Of course, my lady," Jennet said properly. "But I am still willing to take the risk of staying with you."

Aster's soft heart lurched at this loyalty—a certain sign that she was doing the right thing. "Let's just think of it this way—there are thousands of other good women in desperate need of help to achieve their goals. My aunt has already found another likely prospect for training. Would you deny someone else the chance you were given?"

Jennet's eyes widened at this perspective. "No, my lady, certainly not. You have saved my life. I just hope your next student is as grateful as I am. And should you ever have need of me..."

Aster smiled gratefully. "I appreciate that, thank you. I believe in spreading one's good fortune. So, should you ever have the opportunity, remember that sometimes all it takes is a helping hand to change a life."

With that larger goal to occupy her mind, Jennet dropped a deeper curtsy and hurried off to pack.

Aster sighed and jotted off a note to her Aunt Daphne, accepting the responsibility of training a new ladies' maid. Often the women her family rescued from workhouses weren't suitable as companions. But she could always use a maid.

And then, reluctantly, she wrote Aunt Gwenna, saying she would take the children in a month, to help in training a governess. She simply could not see how she could employ small children in any occupation that wouldn't be dangerous.

She supplemented the small stipend her family provided for her support with astrology readings. She could stretch her income to feed a few children. Perhaps she could let out a few of the upper rooms... if she did not become attached to the tenants.

Shiva, her black feline, leaped into her lap, prodding Aster's hand for a rub. "I'm glad my chart allows cat friends," she murmured, scratching behind a kitty ear. "It would be dreadfully lonely otherwise."

Shiva purred agreement. Tabby raised his striped head from the hearth to see what he was missing, but he was old and lazy. Once he'd ascertained no treats would be forthcoming, he settled back into the jewel-toned Turkish rug he called his own.

Afternoon sunshine peeked through the white lace curtains she'd installed behind the heavy gold damask draperies. The light caught on lamp prisms and darted rainbows around the room. Brass from her father's Indian adventures multiplied the meager sunlight, and she let the familiar pleasures ease her turmoil.

She was fortunate that her grandmother had deeded this house to her when it became apparent Aster's presence was too dangerous to her family for her to remain in Edinburgh. She might never have family or close human companions, but she'd always have the serene beauty of her surroundings.

She shuddered in memory of the smelly, anarchic Ives' household and wondered how they had coped since the marquess's mishap. She hoped her warning had helped to some extent, and that Ashford would recover. Perhaps she should write and ask how he fared. If she opened a conversation about Aunt Gwenna's pursuit of the new law, would that complicate the danger between their houses?

Usually, she had an awareness of these things, but the only impression she experienced was of something wrong in the connection between the marquess's family and hers. She could not put her finger on specifics. "Danger in the part of family" simply wasn't enough to issue warnings, especially since Ives were only very distant family, and she wasn't at all attached to them.

Nick, her footman, scratched at the door. Nick was a sturdy young man with a thick neck and broad shoulders. She'd rescued him off the streets when she'd seen him fling a bully into the gutter for kicking a street urchin. His preference for his own sex was so perfectly suited to her all-female household, she hated to let him go when the time came.

She took the card from the salver he offered and laughed in delight—then grimaced at the difficulty the visit caused. Emilia was one of her favorite cousins—and thus in danger in Aster's company. "Take Miss McDowell to the parlor, please, and have Daisy bring us some tea."

A visit from her cousin Emilia should brush away an impending fit of dismals, if her cousin remembered not to linger too long. They were of a similar age, both still unmarried, and both independently established outside the family home—for different reasons, of course. Emilia did not live in dread of endangering all her loved ones.

Today, Emilia had draped her tall, slender form in dramatic black and violet, displaying her mourning for the late king. With her black hair, fair skin, and high cheekbones, the effect was regal, leaving Aster feeling like a plump, dowdy hen.

She rushed to kiss her cousin's cheek anyway. "You look positively daunting today! What dragon are you about to tackle?"

"None. I have come to tell you I have surrendered. I'm going home to meet a gentleman Mother insists is perfect for me." She sighed and settled gracefully into the rattan peacock chair, arranging the turquoise and orange pillows around her full skirt.

"Your research?" Aster asked, taking the long wicker settee with its parrot green cushion.

"I need money," Emilia admitted flatly. "The equipment required to continue is extremely costly. A microscope alone is so exorbitant..." She sighed in exasperation. "If the university would only allow me to use their laboratories, this wouldn't be necessary."

"I know. I cannot persuade the Astronomical Society to accept astrology as a science so I might have access to their records. Men do not approve of what they do not understand, and women are incomprehensible to them. At least you are in a position to choose your spouse," she said reassuringly. "It is sad that your grandfather insisted that you be married before you receive your inheritance, but it does give you more options than most women have."

"I know." Emilia picked restlessly at her black lace gloves. "But no man will accept that my research is more important than sitting about the house, entertaining society. Even your charts haven't found such a creature."

"It's not as if I've charted every bachelor in England!" Aster waved the maid to set the tray on the low table she used to provide a distance between them. "I have found several who are at least temperamentally suited to you, but you make it difficult," she added, caustically. "It's challenging enough to match an intelligent woman, but your stubbornness and lack of interest in all things feminine, and the fact that you spend twenty-four hours a day either researching or gardening, makes husband-hunting impossible."

"Not *all* things feminine," Emilia said demurely, sipping her tea. "I do like men. They simply don't like me."

"There's no accounting for male taste," Aster agreed, swinging the other direction. "You are beautiful, well-spoken, and wealthy. You should be able to stand in the middle of a ballroom and draw men like flies to honey. But then you open your mouth..." She sighed in despair. "I don't suppose I could persuade you to play a mute?"

Emilia laughed. "Not likely. Whereas you babble incessantly of absurdities, and men flock to you proclaiming undying love. Perhaps the trick is to *not* want men, although I have tried that. It doesn't work for me."

"It's not that I don't *want* them..." Aster wrinkled her nose. "I just don't dare care for one. Perhaps I should just take them as men do mistresses, then dismiss them before we become emotionally involved. It would be lovely to have a man escort me occasionally, to have someone who listens and understands... Which is preposterous, of course."

Emilia looked sympathetic. "Have you tried drawing another chart for yourself? Surely the stars do not say you must live alone forever."

"I draw a solar return faithfully every year. It's as if the heavens want me to invent another planet. The calculations show me as indecisive and argumentative, when we both know I'm pragmatic and a problem-solver. Why can I chart everyone else correctly but not myself?"

"It could be that your gift is to read others, not yourself," Emilia said reflectively. "Our Malcolm gifts are not always clear. You could be wrong about your danger to others."

"I am *not* wrong about my dangerous propensities. According to my tallies, my predictions have been proven true over eighty percent of the time. Even my own mother agrees that it is best if I live elsewhere. Georgina *died* in my arms!"

"She was born just a year after Finnian and your mother is no longer young..." Emilia said hesitantly. "Perhaps she wasn't meant to survive."

Wiping angrily at her eyes, Aster shook her head. "I appreciate the thought, but that last episode with the carriage and my sisters and Finnian proved otherwise. If we'd lost my father's heir because of my presence..."

Aster shuddered in horror and caressed the onyx brooch. "I miss all of them terribly, but it was my arrival that stampeded the horses. They could have *all* broken their necks!"

"Admittedly, that was an odd episode, but it was over five years ago. Surely your fortunes will look up soon. One may hope mine will do the same." Emilia looked more miserable than hopeful.

"I will go over your chart again," Aster agreed. "Perhaps I missed something. And then I will dig deeper into our library. I'd thought someone of Malcolm ancestry would be best, but I could go through DeBrett's and see if any other eligible gentlemen catch my eye."

In some ways, it was excellent that she must live alone. It meant she had time to do all the research her family needed and to help with their various charities. She must remember to think constructively. "Perhaps a gentleman who will simply be happy to have an income and won't mind barely having a wife—"

Nick appeared in the doorway with his salver, hovering until Aster signaled him to speak. "A gentleman, my lady."

Reading the rather battered card, Aster raised her eyebrows and tried not to fret even more. "Thank goodness you're here, Emilia. After today, I'll have to stop accepting gentleman callers until I find a replacement for Jennet."

Even with Emilia present, she wondered if she should allow the gentleman entrance. He was not likely to be carrying good news. But then she remembered Emilia's predicament and brightened. "Perhaps your sun is finally in the right house! The caller is Lord Theophilus Ives, heir to the Marquess of Ashford. He might be just the solution for you."

And if she was very lucky, he might help her to approach the marquess about the child labor law. Surely his brother was recovering by now, or at least bored with lying about. She had her doubts about bringing members of her family into the marquess's circle, but where did she draw the line between caution and progress?

"Do please send his lordship in," she said, trying to be decisive.

Unlike the last time she'd seen him, the marquess's heir had chosen to dress properly today. Lord Theophilus was wearing a green coat so dark that it was almost black, as well as a proper gold waistcoat, and linen cravat. The style was a few years out of fashion, perhaps, but he would still look every inch the proper gentleman—except his coat was unfastened, his waistcoat hung by a dangling button, and he was loosening his cravat as if it were a noose around his neck.

Aster bit back a smile and noticed what a perfect pair he and Emilia would make—both tall, slim, handsome, and bookish. She fought the selfish desire that she could say the same of herself.

"My lord, I hope you have brought welcome news." Judging by the stormy gray gaze he focused on her, she knew he had not. Her fear increased, but taught hospitality from an early age, she eased him into the company. "Emilia, may I introduce Lord Theophilus Ives, heir to the Marquess of Ashford, Earl of Ives and Wystan. Lord Theophilus, my cousin, the Honorable Emilia McDowell."

Emilia gave him her most splendiferous smile, the one that should bring grown men to their knees. She even reined in her tart tongue for a vaguely pleasant "My pleasure."

With surprise, Aster noted his lordship merely gave her beautiful cousin a cursory glance before swinging his attention back to *her*. She shivered a little at his baleful intensity.

Had the doom in his chart already arrived? Surely he didn't blame her!

Five

THEO TRIED NOT TO GAPE at the lady's parlor. He'd stepped out of a gray London day into a jungle of greenery, complete with cats hiding in the foliage—although admittedly, they were of the domestic kind and not tigers or lions. Across from the window full of ferns and flowers, a mural of what he assumed were palm and banana trees adorned the parlor wall. Interspersed among the mural's vegetation were giant orange, red, and yellow flowers, not to mention a few painted monkeys and parrots.

And the most striking creature of all was perched on the edge of a wicker chair stacked in pillows to match the jungle. Lady Doom was spreading her plumage today in a brilliant yellow-and-green striped gown with just a frail bit of translucence covering her splendid bosom.

And her hair was a fiery copper. He could scarcely drag his gaze away from her riotous stack of curls. In his rage and despair, Theo railed at the fates. It was as if he'd just discovered a new comet shooting across the heavens—while his telescope was falling apart.

"Have a seat, my lord, join us in a cup of tea. Nick, have Cook send up some biscuits and a fresh pot, will you, please?" She followed this command with a gesture to take a seat near her other guest.

Theo wished tea and the other guest to perdition. He had spent his entire journey from Surrey to London rehearsing what he would say when he arrived. Finding polite conversation under this sensory bombardment was beyond his limited social skills.

Rather than take the seat indicated and offer the usual flummery—he'd already forgotten the other lady's name—Theo paced across the salon to examine what appeared to be a mask painted on a fibrous shell.

"My father, and his father before him, journeyed extensively in India and South America," the witchy lady explained. "They sent home many rare examples of native artwork. Miss McDowell's mother is my father's sister. She added to my collection with the artifacts they sent her as well."

The skinny female in black laughed. "Mother emptied the attic in relief when Aster set up housekeeping. She had no idea how to use elephant tusks and coconut shells."

"It is inspiring," Theo reluctantly admitted, wishing he could be in darkest Africa about now. "One almost wishes to visit jungles to see these specimens in nature."

"Exactly!" his hostess exclaimed in delight. "I have tried growing palms and various other plants my father brought home, but I have no conservatory, and there simply isn't enough light from a single window."

"We have a conservatory," Theo said, wondering how he could ask the other guest to leave, then pondered where Lady Azenor's rather daunting companion had gone. Awkwardly, he realized he could not stay if the other lady left, not without risk of compromising his hostess. Devil take it. He hadn't ridden all this way to turn around and leave without making his damned foolish request.

He could only conclude that desperation had driven him here. It certainly wasn't logic.

The maid carried in an extra teacup and a fresh tray of biscuits, scones, and tea. Theo eyed the delicate straw contraption he was expected to lower his heavy weight on and chose to remain standing. The feminine frippery confined him, and he fought the urge to just grab the lady and haul her outside where he could breathe freely. He tasted a biscuit rather than speak.

"How is your brother?" Lady Azenor inquired gently.

He had expected a glint of defiance, a "told you so" or two—especially since she'd been right about the king's death, the wet weather, and the rioters as well—but she seemed genuinely concerned. Theo swallowed without tasting. "That's what I've come to see you about."

The other lady smothered a laugh and stood up. "Keeping mute doesn't work either, Aster. It appears your prattle is more a case of knowing exactly what to say. I don't possess your gift. I bid you good-day, my lord."

Aster sounded far more approachable than *Azenor*. He'd done a bit of research into the lady's family, confirming his fears—she was from the unpredictable Dougalls, a Scots branch of the eccentric Malcolms, the ones with all the queer alphabetical names. *Aster,* he could almost live with.

Theo bowed but otherwise didn't acknowledge the other lady's departure now that he had his hostess alone. *Alone.* She'd let her guest leave. He was relieved and anxious at the same time.

"I won't trouble you with—" Reluctantly, he started to excuse himself.

"Sit, my lord." She pointed at the wide wicker chair her guest had vacated. "I have heard Lord Ashford was injured. How does he fare?"

Wanting to crush something but not wanting to smash furniture, Theo hesitantly sat on the edge of the straw piece. It wobbled. He sat deeper among the welcoming pillows. A few of the chairs at Iveston could use pillows like these—if the dogs didn't eat them.

His fingers were too large to wrap around the handle of the fragile teacup offered. He'd never managed the art of holding china. "Ashford's arm and ribs are mending. They suspect a crack in the leg bone that is causing him to be laid up longer than he likes." Even though he'd practiced his speech, Theo had difficulty reciting it under her concerned gaze. His gut churned, and he suffered an insane longing for the days before she'd entered his life.

He'd like to curse her for a witch and demand she remove her wicked spell. Unfortunately, modern science rejected magic.

"That is good to hear," she said with what seemed like genuine relief. "I had feared his chart predicted much worse. Lord Ashford really should hasten to marry and produce heirs. That would free you of the considerable burden you've been suffering under."

Her sympathy almost undid him. Theo refused to believe she'd *predicted* Duncan's fall or the king's death using charts based on an imaginary cosmos. But he selfishly wanted to believe she understood the burden he'd carried all these years so that she would accept his mission now for what it was.

She just sat there like a mysterious flower that would be gone tomorrow—but still sliced him straight to the quick today, letting all his guts spill out.

"He's blind," Theo said bluntly. "Ashford is totally blind. He smashed his skull. The physicians don't know if he'll ever recover his sight, and I despair of him recovering his right mind."

She paled, revealing a sprinkle of rusty freckles across her nose. Her cup rattled until she set it down.

He'd been unreasonably cruel, but that was how he felt—cruel and miserable and ready to inflict his selfish rage upon the world.

"I see," she murmured, although she wasn't looking at him as she said it. A black cat crept from behind a drapery to leap onto her lap, and she stroked it absently, as if it were truly a witchy familiar offering comfort.

"No, you don't," Theo said angrily. "He has told Margaret he releases her from their betrothal because he is no longer the man he was. She *accepted* his release! They've neither of them ever considered any other since they were in school!"

Well, except for Dunc's mistresses, but that's what bachelors did if they could afford them.

"That was very wrong of her," the lady acknowledged sadly. "Now that your brother's chart has reached the part of severity and destruction, and yours is on the part of family disaster, they are closely followed by the part of marriage. She'll regret her decision someday."

Destruction? He'd rode all this way to talk to a bedlamite?

Theo set his lips and ordered himself to keep an open mind. "Well, I regret it right now."

This wasn't at all how he'd meant to do this. Slamming down the delicate china he'd just picked up, Theo rose to pace the intricately woven green-and-gold carpet. The complex design distracted him until he practically fell over his feet. Was that a representation of the planets amid the curlicues?

Another feline peered from beneath a curiosity cabinet and ducked back under at his approach. Theo rubbed his brow and tried to focus. "Ashford has ordered *me* to marry, produce heirs, and carry on in his place, putting me in charge of his holdings." He spat out the words as if hammering nails.

"Oh dear. That is not good," she said. "A man with his head in the stars cannot be expected to grasp the nature of earthly objects. Surely you have a steward to attend the estate, at least?"

He was irritated at how quickly she accepted his limitations, but she wasn't saying anything he hadn't already told his damned brother. "Our steward disappeared months ago. Dunc never found a better one and hasn't been in a hurry to do so—until now."

"Disappeared? Do you generally have valuable staff vanish?" she asked in perplexity.

Theo waved his hand in dismissal of Iveston's perpetual state of abandonment. Of course Margaret had left. Women always did. She'd just picked the wrong damned time—if there was ever a good time to walk out on friends. "People come and go. That isn't the point. Ashford's responsibilities encompass far more than just the land. As you should be aware, our family indulges in industry. For generations we've invested in coal and canals, and these days it's steam engines and foundries and more. Our entire widespread family depends on Ashford."

Her beautiful midnight eyes widened and he could almost swear they sparkled.

"That is extremely heroic of you," she said in what sounded like awe. "You must set aside all that you are to become all that your family needs. Not many men are capable of such selfless sacrifice."

Theo wanted to snarl. "I assure you, I'm not in the least heroic. Without the estate, I have no home and no income. I need estate funds to develop the manufactory for my telescope glass. Although I'm not sure what the point is now since I'll barely find time to continue my observations. I cannot possibly manage everything."

"And you tell me this because...?" she asked with that acerbic tone belying her fluffy peahen appearance.

This was where he made a complete and utter nodcock of himself, but desperate times and all that.... "Because if I must marry to produce the heir Ashford will not, it has to be someone who understands about running businesses and estates. I cannot do it all myself. I don't *want* to do it all myself. I am a scientist, not an industrialist or a farmer."

He swung around and faced her directly. "I don't believe in astrology, but if you can use your foolishness to convince a useful woman that we suit, I won't care if she's plain as a door or frumpy as an old maid."

***

TAKEN SOMEWHAT ABACK, Aster sipped her cooling tea before answering. She was accustomed to men rejecting her charts. That this highly intelligent, eminently respectable gentleman who understood the heavens chose to reject her observations hurt more than most. But there was no sense arguing over his disbelief.

"I'm not a matchmaker," she told him. Except she could be, possibly, had it ever occurred to her to look beyond her family. She knew which zodiac signs complemented each other.

"Surely, you must know someone suitable," he insisted, pacing like a caged tiger. "Your family is full of eccentrics who must have some agricultural knowledge."

She winced. "It's true, my family contains many intelligent, capable women," she corrected, thinking aloud. "But none of them are farmers. As I told Emilia, I do not normally chart many people beyond family. I need specific information as to birth date, time, and location. I suppose I could sort through my library, but right off hand, I cannot imagine a suitable candidate. You would do better to hire a steward."

Lord Theophilus rather resembled a sleek, muscular leopard pacing her parlor in search of prey. She had the feeling she might be his quarry and that he might pounce at any moment.

"And then, should the new steward desert us like the last one, we would be right back where we are now," his lordship exclaimed with a frustrated wave of his arm that nearly decapitated a fern. "Duncan could run the estate with one arm behind his back. He only employed a steward so he could spend more time with politics and the steamship business. But he insists if he can't ride and see the fields or even the ledgers, that we will be robbed blind unless I stay on top of business."

"And your other brothers? I recall there is a pack of them." That was perhaps not the politest way of stating it, but the agitated gentleman didn't seem to object. It was rather refreshing to speak as bluntly as he. "Is none of them interested in the estate?"

The marquess's reluctant heir ran his hand through his hair—recently cropped, Aster noticed. His lordship had at least attempted to appear respectable for this visit, which gave her a visceral thrill. She didn't think the self-absorbed, absent-minded Lord Theophilus often tried to impress people.

"Not a one," he groaned. "Every marquess since the first has provided for his progeny, legitimate or not. We all receive equal allowances from the estate to establish ourselves in our interests. We have uncles and cousins running mines, canals, factories... You name it and there is an Ives behind it. Duncan has been the only Ives interested in the land. Perhaps in another generation... but not now."

Aster perused her mental list of his family but concluded much as he had. "Land is scarce. Unless one inherits a vast amount, farming is not a profitable industry. I understand."

"But women often run small farms, don't they?" he asked with a plea in his eyes.

She gestured helplessly. "We grow roses for perfume, herbs for medicine, but we do not often have the land required to run sheep or grow wheat, nor the wealth to have tenants. Perhaps a widow who has helped manage her late husband's estates. It will take some research. How long will you be in London?"

If nothing else, she had to respect a man who accepted that women could do more than look pretty.

"I can't waste a moment," he said in despair. "Erran's business is in London. William is only home a tenth of the time. Jacques is currently standing guard, dealing with farmers and merchants, but he has no head for more. The rest of the lot are schoolboys. We have a cousin who promised to help at harvest, but I need to produce my glass orders *now*. And there are still the shipping and mining ventures needing attention. I feel like a jester juggling too many balls."

"You are not very good at juggling yet," she remarked. "You dismiss everyone as inconsequential when, with a little planning, each person could take up one small piece of the load. Perhaps what you need is a *managing* female."

His glower didn't perturb her. His eyes were a glorious experience. Today, the gray had lightened to a sky blue shadowed by lashes as long as her own. Aster wanted to smile at his frustration, but this was not a laughing matter. His situation was serious—with the potential to endanger her own. Her charts had been quite clear on the matter.

Ashford's blindness was alarming. The marquess had been a potent force for change in the Lords. His loss would be felt in wider circles than the estate—like Gwenna's bill to help child laborers.

Losing his support could be catastrophic to their goals. Aster's instincts failed her on the proper action now.

"I will stay in London long enough to learn of available stewards," Lord Theo said frostily. "Then I must be off to interview them."

"Suitable women do not grow on trees, my lord," she countered. "It will take time. Your glass orders will have to wait. And might I remind you, my charts are complex and time-consuming. I do not produce them on whims or for free. Just as you must make your own living, so must I make mine. You would do well to have a few women in mind as a starting place."

That caught his attention. Apparently, if she was to cost him money, she became a little more worthy of his interest.

"You didn't charge us for the warning," he said, halting his pacing.

"I'd drawn your brother's chart for my library. The warning was for the good of the country and possibly my family. Finding a wife is a selfish pursuit and entirely a different matter."

"It's not a damned chart I want, but a wife. Is the cost the same?" He appeared to be clenching his teeth as he asked.

"It is not always a matter of money," she answered, thinking quickly. "In your case, a successful request to the Astronomical Society to accept astrology as a science would earn you half a dozen charts."

Lord Theo's jaw tightened. "Astrology is not a science. It is a female affectation I'm willing to endure in hopes of getting what I need. Real scientists would not be so polite. They would tear your charts apart if you attempted to present them."

"My charts are very scientific!" *Female affectation*! She should smack him, but she'd encountered this type of opposition too often. She simply needed to convince him otherwise. "To what purpose do you seek the stars if not to enlighten human understanding? We use the same mathematics, share the same interest in the placement of the planets. We should be *communicating*!"

"But no two astrologers could ever achieve the same results," he said scornfully. "Have you ever read an almanac that correctly predicts the weather? Science is based on empirical evidence, and you have none. I do not believe star charts predict compatibility, but you *know* women. Tell me how much it costs in pounds and cents for you to find me a wife who can manage estates."

She'd stupidly hoped this man was different because their charts seemed so compatible—another example of how badly she read her own chart. Still, she refused to let him deride her abilities.

"Ten pounds per chart, once you have provided exact birth date, time, and place," she retorted, refusing to admit she had no idea what *empirical evidence* might be. She would look it up as soon as he was gone.

"I am to walk up to women and ask when and where they were born?" he asked in incredulity.

"If you want anyone other than the Malcolm descendants in my library, you will. I can go over my charts and make lists. I can call in a few friends," she said, rising. His virile presence was too intense for concentration. She needed him to leave before she said anything else ridiculous for him to scorn.

"I cannot guarantee you will find the perfect mate within my circle," she continued, taking his arm and leading him to the door. "You have just met Emilia. She is looking for a husband so her grandfather's executor will release her rather considerable inheritance. She would be perfect for you in all other respects—but like your family, she has other interests, and they don't include estate management."

With a puzzled expression, Lord Theophilus glanced at the doorway as if it would summon the memory of the woman who had just passed through it. "Perhaps you could introduce her to Erran. He's a peacock who always comes up short on his tailor's bills."

"Perhaps," she said noncommittally. "But the task now is to find *your* match."

He studied her with despair. "I don't suppose *you* know of estates? You seem the managing sort."

Her insides clutched with the desire to shout *Yes, yes, my charts say we are all that should be compatible*, but she shook her head. Because her own chart was always strangely skewed and that *doom* in her family sector was much too accurate. "I am a city girl and know nothing of rural estates. Besides, my charts say I must never marry. It is much too dangerous, and your family doesn't need any more tragedy."

"If I don't find a wife soon, I see nothing *but* tragedy in the months to come. Either I will kill Duncan, or he will kill me." Lord

Theophilus slammed his hat on his head and strode out—leaving the peaceful serenity of her parlor shattered.

How did one find a *safe* wife for the man for whose stars crossed with her own in dangerous incompatibility?

Six

STILL GNASHING HIS TEETH in frustration, Theo sought his uncle's home near Hyde Park. Uncle Pascoe used the name of Ives, although Theo's widowed grandfather had sired him late in life and never bothered to marry Pascoe's mother. Theo thought he ought to look at his marriage-shirking ancestors as warning, but unlike Lady Azenor, he didn't believe in portents.

Pascoe was the youngest of the uncles, in his thirties. He'd been married once, produced twins still in the nursery, and had poured his energy into developing various forms of transportation so that fabrics woven in Manchester could reach London, Paris, or Boston in the shortest possible time. The process involved considerable government and political interaction, thus his residence in London.

Pascoe greeted Theo's arrival with a slap on the back and an offer of brandy. "You look as if you've just buried both parents and your favorite mistress. Come in, sit down, and tell me what I can do to help."

Taking a sturdy leather chair in the gloom of his uncle's study, Theo gratefully accepted the brandy. He tried not to contrast this dark room of heavy furniture, scattered books and papers, and dead animals on the wall with Lady Azenor's sunny, colorful, and well-ordered parlor, but the vivid image was emblazoned on his mind.

Women were an entirely different breed from men, that much was obvious. He'd never suffered from the lack of female influence but he did wonder about the changes ahead.

"You've been married," Theo said, leading with the most pressing subject. "Do all women keep a house orderly and tightly feathered like a birds' nest?"

Pascoe laughed. "Lily was never home. She ran half a dozen charities. Our housekeeper does her best to clean the clutter, but as you see—" His gesture swept the stack of paper and dusty objects on his desk. "—housekeepers are limited in scope. I shouldn't think I'd like a feathered nest much. Are you planning marriage?"

"If it's possible to *plan* marriage, I might be amenable. But I have a suspicion it will take a little more than specifying my needs as if I were choosing a horse." Theo sipped his brandy and contemplated living in a home feathered like Azenor's. He didn't think it possible, and his imagination gave it up to contemplate the more interesting picture of the lady's delicious figure in his bed.

He ought to have *something* pleasant to contemplate in the midst of total, irrevocable disaster. But the lady had been unequivocal in insisting that they would not suit. And although he did not believe in her fated doom, he knew a city girl with ridiculous notions did not meet his requirements for a wife. He needed a good, practical country woman—but not Margaret. He shuddered.

"The closest one can come to planning a wife is to attend the season's events and compare the various available misses. That wasn't for the likes of me," Pascoe said with distaste. "I literally ran into Lily in a very bad section of town. She wouldn't have been caught dead in a fashionable salon. But I don't recommend searching back streets for rare gems as a practical policy."

"One might as well rely on searching the stars," Theo acknowledged gloomily.

After a few more brandies, Pascoe dragged the story out of him. Rather than bother with the formality of the dining room, they ordered supper set up before the fire.

"Much as I hate to say this, Duncan is better off without a woman who flees at the first sign of trouble." Pascoe leaned back in his chair and contemplated the fire after hearing the sorry tale. "Perhaps your lady friend could search for the right wife for him while she's looking for one for you."

"Duncan is wallowing in self-pity," Theo retorted. "It will take time before he'll accept that he's still a valuable commodity."

Pascoe snorted at this description. "Put it in terms of profit, and perhaps he'll listen. But you're right, not just yet. He'll be hoping his sight will return, and who knows, maybe he's right. Most physicians are quacks. Is there any chance someone really tried to kill him?"

Theo shrugged. "Duncan would know better than I, and he claims not. He's not very clear on what happened. The blow to his head scrambled his memory. He just thinks the horse stumbled while his bosky mind was elsewhere, and that it was his own fault."

"It's possible." Pascoe peeled an apple as a servant cleared the dishes. "If you've seen no evidence of wrong-doing, you have no reason to believe otherwise."

Other than the lady's warning, and that hadn't been specific, but Theo's questioning mind kept picking around the idiocy as one does a scab. "I don't want to marry and bring a lady into danger."

"You want an excuse for not marrying," Pascoe pointed out cheerfully.

No, he wanted an excuse to marry managing, manipulative, colorful Lady Azenor so he didn't have to make an ass of himself bumbling about parlors.

Theo squeezed the bridge of his nose. "I hate this. I trust finding a steward will be simpler."

FINDING A STEWARD wasn't simpler. Theo stopped at one of Duncan's clubs to make inquiries and ran into the Earl of Lansdowne. The earl appeared to know him even if Theo didn't recognize the distinguished older man until they were introduced.

"Ashford took a fall, did he?" Lansdowne asked, fastening his coat buttons in preparation for leaving the club. "Will he be back for the September session?"

"One assumes," Theo answered edgily, having no idea what the answer ought to be. "I'm just here to inquire about the names of likely men for the position of steward."

The earl shrugged and donned his tall hat. "Everyone's out of town. Surely one of your bastard brothers can look in on the tenants."

At the deliberate insult, Theo rolled his fingers into fists, but even he knew better than to punch an earl. "The bastard who is training the royal hounds, perhaps?" he asked coldly. "Or the one engineering the Manchester railway? We're all such layabouts, I'm sure you're right."

He strode off, leaving the earl and his companions to glare after him. So much for asking the help of his so-called betters.

He managed to collect a few references from more helpful men and left word in several places without biting anyone else's head off. But too many people asked after Duncan, and he had nothing to give them. He had a vague notion he was supposed to pound men on the back, make jokes about Ashford spending time in bed, and assure everyone that the head of an industrial fortune was right on top where he belonged.

But Duncan was flinging shoes and tea trays and Theo couldn't speak such a massive lie.

After following up every lead he'd been given and finding himself near Lincoln's Inn Field, Theo rewarded his perseverance by stopping in to see if the library of the Astronomical Society had any new treatises. John Herschel was writing at a table and glanced up at Theo's appearance.

"Still think your lens can find more than the six moons on Saturn mine can find, Ives?" Herschel asked, setting aside his pen and rubbing his brow.

"Certainly," Theo said with a shrug. "I just need better weather." He rummaged through the pamphlets on display.

"If we're to win the royal charter, we need to produce a discovery of sufficient magnitude to gain His Majesty's recognition. I've been promising his highness he'd hear from us by September. If you can't produce your new glass, we'll have to call on someone else."

A chance to display the achievements of his new glass had been Theo's goal ever since he'd developed the new lens. But he needed more time to test it and write up the report and produce more... Theo wanted to raise his fists and howl.

"It can't rain forever," he said in surly acceptance while he scanned Herschel's latest tract.

"Your name will be ruined with the society if you can't produce," Herschel warned.

"I have the glass," Theo insisted, fighting his panic that he'd never *test* the glass at this rate. He waved the pamphlet he'd been reading. "*Inductive* reasoning?" he asked in incredulity. "You would infer a scientific principle based on what... *intuition*? Have we all gone mad?"

"Don't question the premise until you've been married for a year as I have," Herschel said dryly. "We can often see probable evidence that women think differently than men, but it is impossible to provide deductive or empirical evidence of the theory—as just one example."

Thinking of Aster and her insane theories of the universe, Theo considered punching his own eyes out. "You would prove astrology true?" he asked irritably.

"Unlikely," Herschel agreed. "But we do not always have the instruments to measure what is obvious from observation. Take the tract and study it. There is more to science than mathematics."

"I really don't want to hear that," Theo grumbled, shoving the pamphlet into his coat pocket. "Next, you'll be asking women to join the Society."

Herschel snorted and bent over his pen and paper again. "Why do you think I'm here and not at home? Not a chance, my boy, not a chance."

Weary in mind and soul, Theo stumbled back to Pascoe's to find an invitation waiting for him from Lady Azenor to join her and a few guests for tea. Theo stopped to examine his reflection in the hall mirror and tried to determine if his rumpled cravat and the gravy stain on his waistcoat might pass muster.

"You need a valet," Pascoe said, wandering down the corridor from his study.

"I don't need a valet to make glass or study the stars. Can I hire a temporary valet?" Theo asked.

"Most likely not. And my Merritt is not available. He's invaluable as far more than a valet. He can even keep books. The problem with most servants is that they're uneducated and only trained in one task."

"Not a problem I'm inclined to tackle," Theo acknowledged. "Iveston is filled to overflowing with untrained, uneducated Ives progeny. Maybe I should marry a schoolteacher and keep the brats home."

"A schoolteacher who will train them to be stewards and valets?" Pascoe hooted. "Ives don't make good servants."

"Outlaws, pirates, and potentates," Theo agreed in frustration. "We're useless."

"Leaders and men of science are always needed. We're just worthless for domestic purposes. Have Lady Azenor find a match for me while you're at it. One who can tell stories to the demanding fiends in the nursery."

"I'd rather be an outlaw," Theo growled. Realizing he was late, he hurried off without hunting for more starched linen.

Upon reaching the lady's street, Theo swallowed a lump of panic. Three carriages were unloading a wave of women in enormous silk sleeves, bell-like skirts, and frippery from head to toe.

The lady had been busy. If he weren't so terrified, he'd be impressed. His future could be in one of those carriages.

He hurried to assist the women emerging from the last vehicle. Enveloped in their silks, laces, and perfumes, Theo was too overwhelmed by femininity to notice if the occupants were fair or young. They chattered to him and each other as Lady Azenor's surly footman held the door open.

Theo entered last and the footman winked at him. Taken aback, Theo absent-mindedly clung to his hat and followed the ladies into the colorful parlor.

Azenor was garbed in peacock blue today. Unlike the others, she wore reasonable sleeves and a simple skirt that didn't require voluminous frills. Short, compared to her guests, she still stood out like a beacon of rationality and a star in the night sky. Theo wanted to grab her and carry her off and be done with it.

Which was utter nonsense and probably a product of panic. This marriage business required a good deal more...*sensory stimulation*...than his solitude-loving brain could handle all at once.

He remembered to bow politely at introductions but didn't remember a single woman's name while he watched the footman carry off his hat.

"Miss Jenkins," Lady Azenor reminded him, catching Theo's arm and turning him toward a voluptuous woman wrapped to the chin in lavender. "Lord Theo is an astronomer. He says I must find empirical evidence to prove my charts are accurate."

"As an astronomer, you should be able to duplicate Lady Azenor's charts mathematically," Miss Jenkins said in a voice deeper than Theo's own. "I have done so, although I cannot deduce more than when the planets are aligned with the sun."

"You are a mathematician?" he asked, more aware of the interesting mop of copper curls at his side than the Juno he faced.

"I enjoy numbers and equations but find little use for them in dealing with my younger sisters. Do you find astronomy useful?"

"Miss Jenkins is raising her sisters after their mother's death," Lady Azenor whispered. "You might marry off all your younger brothers as they come of age."

"That will happen when the moon is discovered to be made of green cheese," Theo murmured in his hostess's ear. The dainty Lady Aster pinched his arm in retaliation.

He forced a smile for Juno. "Perhaps Lady Azenor should teach a class in astrology so others could learn to do what she does."

"An excellent idea," the lady in lavender said. "Those of us of a mathematical persuasion could form a society."

"We need the findings of the Astronomical Society to keep our charts updated," his hostess said with an emphasis aimed at him.

"Teach your class to repeat your findings on their own and build a case for astrology as a science," Theo suggested, more or less facetiously. Lady Azenor did not seem to require simpering blandishments, so he felt comfortable speaking to her as one of his brothers. "Are all the ladies here of a mathematical sort or are some familiar with agriculture or other pursuits?"

Lady Azenor smiled frostily at this reminder of his needs and squeezed his arm to steer him. "If you'll excuse us, Miss Jenkins, I should introduce his lordship to the baroness."

"A baroness in her own right? If it means she owns land, that sounds promising," Theo said, studying the parlor filled with milling females and fighting an urge to flee for his life. There weren't sufficient chairs for sitting, so the women sipped tea from dainty cups and circulated in eddies, much as leaves did in a stream. He couldn't distinguish one from another any more than he could identify leaves.

"Could I really catch the attention of the Society if I taught others to duplicate my charts?" she asked in a low voice that mirrored her doubt.

"Only if they all read the same results into them as you do. If every one of them could have predicted the king's death and Duncan's accident, the Society would have to listen." Theo doubted the Society would *care*, but then, he doubted her predictions could be duplicated any more than his mother's vague prophecies could be proved.

Inductive reasoning, his foot and eye. Marriage must rot a man's brain if Herschel's new theory was any example.

"I would love to have the information and understanding of the planets' movements that astronomers possess. Do you produce periodicals I can peruse?" She didn't wait for an answer but brought him to a lady of average stature, whose nondescript coloring wasn't enhanced by the swathes of beige draped over her less-than-prepossessing figure. Judging from the wrinkles in the corners of her eyes and the slight sag of her jaw, the lady was older than Theo. Not entirely a bad thing if it meant she had the experience he required.

Theo wondered if he could interview prospective wives in the same manner he would interview a steward. Not that he knew how to interview a steward either.

"Baroness Wilkins, Lord Theophilus is the gentleman of whom I spoke. My lord, the baroness owns lands in the Lake District. She is familiar with sheep. I will leave you two to talk. I wish to see if there is any interest in an astrology class."

Lady Azenor abandoned Theo to his own devices.

"You need help with sheep?" the baroness asked in a guttural accent that revealed her foreign origins.

"My brother does. His estate is extensive, and his managers aren't doing the job they should." Theo wasn't good at fabricating, but Duncan wasn't ready to reveal his blindness to the world. "We need a good steward," he added.

"There are no good stewards," the lady said harshly. "You must know your herd personally. I go out with the stock each spring and take note of all the lambs. It is the only way," she insisted.

Theo damned well wasn't counting sheep, even in his sleep, but if the lady wanted to... He had to keep an open mind. Perhaps Duncan would be interested in her.

Swallowing his pride and an entire humble pie, he circulated the room. Lady Azenor had provided a wide variety of females to choose from, he had to admit. Unfortunately, they all blurred together after a while, and he couldn't remember if the one with buck teeth knew how to play chess or if the one with the mole on her upper lip was the one who kept ledgers.

The image of his lovely, serene ex-fiancée having a hysterical, weeping fit over his household's ramshackle behavior stood out starkly in Theo's memory. He didn't wish to reduce any of these pleasant ladies to similar seizures or himself or his family to the ensuing unpleasantness.

He shuddered in memory of screaming hysterics requiring sal volatile, physicians, and the shame of racing for the neighbor ladies for aid. The scolding afterward had been endless. *No more fainting ladies on his doorstep*, he decided. If he must marry, he would be firm on this point.

He worked his way back to Azenor. He had been aware of her presence at every instant, even though almost everyone in the room was taller than she. The ladies seemed to circulate around her as planets did around the sun. Understandable, he supposed, since Azenor was brighter—or at least more colorful—than any of them.

"This won't work," he murmured for her ears alone. "I must introduce them to Iveston."

Her eyes widened, as if in shock at his suggestion. Then she vehemently shook her bouncy curls. "No, no, and *no*."

"Why not?" he asked, prepared to insist.

"That is a recipe for disaster," she exclaimed in horror. "If my visit to your home represents its usual condition, you would do better to marry and make Iveston a *fait accompli*."

"I don't want to have to chain a wife to a wall to keep her," he argued. "She needs to know what she faces."

"I'm a librarian, not a matchmaker," she grumbled in return.

"You are a naysayer," he said. "Every time I make a suggestion, your response is *why*?"

"And every time I tell you no, your response is *why not*?" she retorted. "I am not being unreasonable. These are busy women. Most don't have time for jaunts into the country. And if my recollection of your home is correct, you aren't prepared for house guests."

"Perspicacious," he muttered. But his relentless brain had found a new angle and hope surged. "Help me hire servants to prepare the house. Surrey is not far and the road is good. The ladies could attend the village fete and sit down to tea with us before returning to town."

"*Hire servants*... I am not a lion tamer either!" she protested angrily. Then she narrowed her eyes as if a new thought had occurred to her.

Theo feared he ought to be wary, but he was too desperate. "Once we have a woman in the household, we can hire regular servants. I ought to present Iveston as it *could* be."

"That will take planning," she said, the wheels visibly turning behind her bright eyes. "I trust you're not in a hurry."

He wanted this done yesterday. He might be the selfish lout Celia had called him, but he'd learned his lesson. He couldn't ask a wife to be a sacrificial lamb to his brother's melancholia. Or his family's anarchy. He bowed. "I must prepare a paper for the Society and hire a steward. That should give you time to find a few maids and footmen who can spruce the place up a little. The fete is two weeks from today."

"You will provide me with the latest material from the Society so I may update my charts?" she demanded.

"I will find copies of every report the Society's members have produced and the articles that have been written this past year," he vowed.

"All right, then. Each to their own expertise. That seems fair," she acknowledged with a dip of her copper curls.

Theo walked back to his uncle's house with no memory of any of the women he'd just met but feeling lighter than air because he'd tricked the managing Lady Azenor into straightening out the madhouse he called home.

Seven

"THINK ON IT, EMILIA!" Aster insisted, pacing her parlor the day after Lord Theo's visit. "The *Marquess of Ashford*—the nominal head of all Ives. He has wealth and power to spare! You could build a laboratory on his property and never worry about funding again. He won't require anything else of you except to give him an heir. We could hire all your mother's displaced widows and Aunt Gwenna's orphans!"

Even a day later, she was still a trifle shaken from Lord Theo's masculine presence in her feminine household, so much so that she'd actually dared ask her cousin to visit again. Aster took deep breaths and tried to cleanse her mind, but the sensation of his lordship's muscular arm beneath her hand wouldn't go away. Nor did the way he leaned in to murmur outrageous comments in her ear. *Why not*, indeed. She shivered at just the memory.

She forced herself to focus on Aunt Gwenna's plea for the maimed children. If Emilia married the blind marquess... The entire family would have access to his powerful connections. They could accomplish a great deal of good—

If she wasn't bringing them into imminent danger. Her Libra mind danced back and forth between opportunities and caution.

"I won't need a husband's funds if I marry," Emilia pointed out, piercing Azenor's bubble of hope. "I'll have my own. And it sounds as if he needs someone who can act as his secretary and helpmate. That isn't me."

Aster sighed and straightened the mask on the wall. She wished she knew if Lord Theo had been admiring her decor or laughing at it. She would like to believe he did not consider her completely laughable.

"You are so narrow-minded! Not in a bad way," Aster added hastily. "I understand that you must focus on your projects. But you would have land for your herb gardens. You could expand your *Pharmacopoeia*, build your own hospital, carry out experiments..."

"Do you think your Lord Theophilus could help build a better microscope?" Emilia asked wistfully.

"I'm sure he could," Azenor agreed, not having any idea how a microscope compared with a telescope, but determined to help both his lordship and Emilia. "But Lord Theo needs help with the estate that you can't give, and the marquess's chart is a better match for yours. If you were the marchioness, you could *hire* the secretaries he needed. And I could train orphans as servants in the household without becoming too involved with anyone. Iveston Hall could use an army of help!"

"It would be better if *you* could marry Lord Theo," Emilia said. "Besides, you said the marquess isn't looking for a wife."

"*Yet*. He might be persuaded in time." There was the other fly in her grandiose hopes. Aunt Daphne needed help for her widows immediately, as did Aunt Gwenna's orphans. Could they wait until the marquess was ready to face Parliament again?

Perhaps she was getting ahead of herself. "All right, if we must concentrate on Lord Theo, we really should offer choices from our family first. I'm convinced we have the most to offer." Except for that conjunction with Mars, she corrected mentally. It was just so *unlikely* for such distant families to affect one another that she thought surely she had read her charts wrong. "We need to organize his household so we might introduce him to our family."

"We don't have time to bring in any of our unmarried relations," Emilia pointed out. "Only Briana and Deidre are in London right now, and Deirdre is already affianced."

Their younger sisters had their own pursuits and weren't any more inclined toward household duties than Emilia, Aster knew. Sometimes this planning business put her mind in a whirl. She changed direction again. "I'm not certain our sisters are safe going to Iveston, even if I didn't go with them. And they know nothing of organizing households on their own."

"They're the only ones old enough and available. We don't want any chance of matching an Ives to the younger girls! So I think that lets our family out of the equation." Emilia set down her teacup firmly.

Aster sighed. "This sounded like a good idea at first. Iveston really could use a raft of your mother's workhouse women and perhaps even some of Gwenna's disabled children. And the chance to influence a powerful marquess is priceless."

"I'm not averse to considering one of the younger brothers as a husband, even if it is not Lord Theo," Emilia admitted. "But if you intend to hold a formal tea at Iveston for your friends, you will need help. Is it safe to take Bree and Dee with you?"

"If they'll consent to help, I'll try to stay out of their way as much as possible," Aster reluctantly agreed, pondering how this might be done without her presence endangering her family. She was hoping the older girls knew to stay out of *her* way as much as she knew to stay away from them.

Could she actually *prevent* the danger she saw in her charts if she was at Iveston? It didn't seem likely, but...

Normally, she wouldn't even consider being in the same house as her family. But so many things rested on taking this chance! She needed to marry off Emilia, find positions for her aunt's impoverished women, somehow obtain Ashford's help for Gwenna's legislation, and obtain Lord Theo's astronomical aid to improve her charts.

In addition, if she helped Lord Theo find a wife, that would enhance her reputation as an astrologer. Surely a matchmaker would be a valuable commodity? If only she could foresee what trouble she might cause in less than a fortnight!

"I suppose arranging a house party at the last minute does present complications," Emilia said with a sigh. "This really is not one of your saner expeditions."

"I would fare better if more of us were of an age or personality to be managing types, or at least available on short notice," Aster admitted. "Still, Bree and Dee and you will give us a good chance of capturing Lord Theophilus's interest. Or maybe... if we're really good... Ashford's."

Emilia crinkled her nose. "I should think it would be too soon if he's suffering from his fiancée's rejection as well as his injuries. But I should like to have a look at his head. Phrenology has developed some wonderful insights into the human mind."

"You would make a marvelous marchioness," Aster insisted, burying her anxiety in favor of a positive outcome. "But if I am to do this, we need to organize. I have two footmen, two trained maids, and three almost-trained maids. If you'll bring your housekeeper, we can call on your mother's collection of untrained women, and possibly have nearly a dozen warm bodies at our disposal. If we're only preparing for an afternoon tea, we don't need to tackle the upper chambers, just the public rooms."

"You cannot expect me to organize a housekeeping crew!" Emilia exclaimed. "I'll send Mrs. Barnes, but you're on your own until the day of the fete."

"Emilia, I need a chaperone! Maids aren't enough." Aster tried not to shout her distress. "These are *Ives*! The object is to enhance my reputation, not lose it, and I most certainly don't want to be trapped in a compromising situation requiring marriage. It would be disastrous."

So disastrous it could easily explain the conjunction of Mars in both their charts on the part of peril! She shivered at just the thought. No matter how much she enjoyed looking at Lord Theo, she wasn't crashing the heavens down on their heads for a set of manly shoulders.

"You should re-do your chart," Emilia said stubbornly. "If you are any kind of astrologer at all, your chart ought to say you're perfect for an Ives household."

"Wait... right... here." Aster marched off to her study, pulled out the well-worn scroll, and marched back to the parlor. She spread the paper open across the wall mural, tacking it with a hammer and small nails.

"There, right there." She tapped one of the zodiac signs. "The transiting planets in my chart are currently on the Part of *Peril*, coupled with *Private Enemies*, there is no mistaking the menace I present."

Aster did not mention the part of desire and sexual attraction in her ascendant. She feared that part almost as much as the others, because desire could distract from her goal in staying away from relationships. And Lord Theophilus was a very desirable man whose chart matched hers in *perilous* ways.

Emilia studied the chart with doubt. "It would help if I had any idea what you were talking about. I'll have to take your word for it. You have been remarkably accurate in all your other predictions."

Emilia politely did not mention the times Aster had ignored her own predictions and disaster ensued, but it was uppermost in both their minds. Aster never, ever wished to have a baby die in her arms again. She no longer ignored her intuition. "Prophesying from the stars is my Malcolm gift. I would have preferred being a healer like you."

Emilia said wistfully, "I only wish you could perform real magic and produce a match for me."

"Perhaps if I knew more of the planets and their moons, I could expand my understanding to find suitable people. I am working with an Arabic student to translate the original Arabic texts explaining the zodiac parts. I'm hoping there are errors in the translation, but her records are centuries old. I have only just begun to explore recent scientific discoveries. Information is extremely hard to find. Men like to keep it to themselves." Aster rolled up the scroll again.

"I'll ask Deirdre to attend," Emilia said, caving in to Aster's plan. "She is moping about the house since her fiancé went off to Africa to look for gold. It would do her good to get out. But she is betrothed and not one of his lordship's candidates!"

Since her immediate family, except Briana, was in Scotland, Aster had hoped that at least one of her cousins might join her in this project. Briana and Deirdre would keep each other occupied, leaving Aster to manage all else. "I would love to have Deirdre, thank you! But she's younger than I am, as is Briana. I still need a chaperone. Perhaps I should ask Great-Aunt Nessie to meet us. She lives right down the road from Iveston."

"It will do Nessie good to get away from all those heathen nieces and nephews of hers," Emilia agreed. "She can't hear a thing, but she's respectable enough."

"Good," Aster said in relief as their plans fell into place. "I've already had acceptances from half a dozen of my more practical friends to the tea. Perhaps we'll conquer all of Ashford's brothers!"

"Mother has already informed me that they are a ramshackle lot, but that matters little to me. You had best warn your other guests and your maids, though." Emilia picked up her parasol and sailed for the door. "I am almost looking forward to the circus!"

After Emilia departed, Aster floundered between the pressing need to train her aunt's orphans and the wish to hide under the bed rather than face the intimidatingly intelligent, annoying Lord Theophilus again. If anyone could activate the part of desire and attraction in her chart, she greatly feared it would be the astronomer who refused to believe her charts but was all too happy to accept her domestic help.

HAVING SPENT another exhausting day talking to fusty old men, bored landowners, and a few of Duncan's political friends in search of recommendations for the position of steward, Theo stopped outside a noisy tavern and debated joining the din.

A ruffian stinking of ale staggered from the tavern, tripped over his feet, and fell into Theo, clutching at Theo's already wrinkled waistcoat. Considering this old ploy the last and final insult of his London sojourn, Theo bent back the bony fingers wrapped around his watch. The would-be thief shrieked in pain and swayed backward, howling and releasing his prize.

Drinking himself into a stupor held promise. Doing so in the company of strangers did not. He'd always had his brothers to watch his back, in the days when they'd indulged in such revelry. He damned well missed Duncan at times like this. Together, they would have dumped the thief in the Thames.

Disgruntled, Theo tucked his watch back in its pocket and found his way back through the gas-lit dark to Pascoe's house.

He needed an observatory. He needed a glass grinder that would perfect the magnification of his new refractor.

He needed a bloody damned wife and steward and maybe a new life in the Americas, he decided, upon finding Jacques sitting on their uncle's doorstep.

His half-brother leaped up with a beaming grin. "I knew someone would show up eventually."

"The footman wouldn't let you in?" Theo pounded the knocker.

"He doesn't know me, and Pascoe is apparently out alley-catting."

"That will teach you to come to town and socialize with family more often so the servants recognize you," Theo said dryly. As the footman opened the door, he gestured to their unexpected company. "This is my scoundrel brother, Jacques," he told the servant. "It's best not to let him in unless we're given warning but don't leave him out in a blizzard."

"I'm not likely to travel in a blizzard," Jacques protested, trailing Theo into the house. "Why shouldn't I have entrance if you do?"

"Because it's not my house. Tell stories to Pascoe's demanding offspring, and he will grant you entrance for life. What brings you here?" Shrugging out of his confining frock coat, Theo hid his alarm at his brother's unexpected arrival and led the way upstairs. "Dunc is well?"

"Dunc is still moping and throwing fits and refusing to leave his chambers. The field laborers have gone on strike for fewer hours and more pay. Duncan says they may all go to hell. I'm thinking that's not the best solution."

"You couldn't send a note rather than abandon our churlish brother to the servants?" Theo flung open a few doors until he found a bedchamber that appeared ready for guests. "Do you even have baggage with you?"

"Only the things I carry in my saddlebag. I was planning on riding back tonight except no one knew where to find you. What servant would you suggest I send who could find you any better? I doubt any of them know their way around London."

"One of us really ought to try visiting more often," Theo acknowledged, "And it won't be me. The city's sooty murk hides the stars. Where's Erran?"

"In Brighton, looking for work. He's been acting oddly since he won that court case. I thought he'd be insufferable in triumph, but now he's considering giving up being a barrister. And William took his hounds to Oxford for some reason or another." Jacques dropped back against the bed and stared at the ceiling. "Perhaps your astrologer should read all our charts. The household is descending into more chaos than usual. The twins are home from school, and the rest are expected at any minute. The housekeeper is drinking again."

Theo refrained from exercising his considerable vocabulary, knowing the havoc their various younger brothers, cousins, and Duncan's twins could cause. A jungle would be more peaceful. "I've found a temporary solution. Lady Azenor has offered to bring a cadre of servants down to straighten up the place in time for Margaret's fete."

Jacques sat up again. "Why? Does she have more death, doom,

and agony to inflict?"

"Not that I'm aware of." Theo tossed his coat over his shoulder. "Maybe I should ask if she knows any farm laborers. She has a prodigious list of people for all occasions."

"That would be most exemplary!" Jacques unfastened his cravat. "Every time we drive off another servant, we could just call on her to provide another. Where has she been all our lives?"

Hiding from intimate relationships would be Theo's guess.

Remembering the lady's suggestion that he share some small part of the mountain of tasks he faced, Theo asked, "You wouldn't be interested in interviewing stewards, would you? They're scattered over half the countryside, and if I need to return to Surrey to settle the strike, I can't be everywhere."

"Have them come to Ashford," Jacques suggested carelessly. "I know nothing of farming but surely Dunc can manage an interview."

"Perhaps." Theo remained noncommittal. Dunc hadn't been amenable to seeing anyone but family since the accident, but there was always a first time. "Get some sleep. We'll talk in the morning."

But the thought of sending stewards to Iveston so he could return to his work had Theo humming on his way to his room. If Dunc wouldn't interview them, maybe he'd have Lady Azenor do it.

Pity she wasn't a country girl who understood farming, but maybe she could look up a steward's astrological chart. That would be about as useful as an astronomer asking about crop production.

Eight

"WE REFUSE TO SHARE the carriage with Mrs. Barnes," Briana hissed as Aster attempted to arrange the various occupants of the berlin and the baggage wagon Lord Theo had provided. Briana retied the strings of her bonnet over her fair curls. "She smells of camphor and vinegar. You *must* ride with us and leave her in the wagon. Besides, if we became separated, who would introduce us at Iveston?"

"They are expecting us. It's not as if you would be stranded," Aster retorted desperately. "You, of all people, ought to understand the problem of my riding in the same carriage with you."

"We can't be more than a few hours from Iveston, and it's a beautiful clear summer day. Lightning won't strike." Deirdre added her insistence. She wore a flirtatiously up-tilted hat brim that flaunted the thickness of the mink-brown hair at her nape. "You must tell us all about the estate so we are prepared. We won't go unless you ride with us."

"I was counting on the two of you to be *sensible*," Aster wailed. "How will I explain to our mothers if anything should happen to you?"

"You travel with us, or we'll not go," Briana said adamantly. "Once we are there, we will attempt to leave the room when you enter it, we promise."

Aster glanced back at the wagon packed with servants patiently awaiting orders to move out. She had three potential maids and two footmen to train for service. They would be horrifically disappointed if they couldn't find positions. Her entire house of cards rode on this visit.

Recklessly disregarding potential catastrophe before they even started invited the worst sorts of peril.

Lord Theophilus chose that moment of indecision to ride up on a magnificent roan gelding. Today, the preoccupied scientist almost looked the part of elegant aristocrat in his tailed coat and knee boots—except for his unstarched neckcloth. His horse pranced restlessly as he lifted his tall hat in greeting. "All ready to go?"

Without waiting for her reply, he waved the wagon on and nodded at the carriage driver to assist Aster inside.

"I detest being bullied," she protested, taking a seat as his lordship rode up to give instructions to the coachman.

"He is not bullying. He is taking charge. That is what men do." Deirdre settled back against the seat cushion in satisfaction. Not quite as tall as her sister Emilia, Deirdre had a softer, rounder face and a cherubic smile which she employed now. "Thank you for inviting me on this adventure. Town is much too dull this summer with everyone in mourning."

Aster took the rear-facing seat across from her sister and cousin and fretted at her gloves while glancing out the window at Lord Theo guiding the team's horses into a busy intersection. His riding breeches pulled tight across muscled thighs, and she swallowed hard and dragged her gaze back to the girls.

"I fear Iveston will be the exact opposite of dull. You may wish to run screaming for the safety of town before the first day is over. I am counting on you to be brave and patient and help me make order of anarchy."

Both girls were foolish enough to look intrigued. Aster sighed and regaled them with the tale of her arrival at the marquess's derelict estate.

"A billiard table in the foyer?" Briana asked with laughter when Aster was done. "Really, they had no servants at all?"

"If they have them, they were in hiding. You must understand that this is an all-male household. The last Lady Ashford died over twenty-five years ago. If the public rooms are any evidence, not a thing has been changed in a quarter century or more. All those years of dogs and boots will take its toll on the best of carpets and floors. We cannot possibly work miracles. We must concentrate on emphasizing possibilities."

"We need Moira," Deirdre said with a sigh, referring to another of their cousins. "She can simply look at a room and know exactly what needs to be done to make it presentable. Her bedchamber is fit for a princess."

"We haven't time for pretty. We must settle for tidy and not-so-frayed, and we must do that with untrained staff. This is not a house party."

"But we get first glimpse of the amazing Ives who never circulate in society," Briana reminded her in satisfaction. "I'm so glad I'm not in Edinburgh this summer."

Aster frowned at this foolishness and dug through her valise to present her list of plans. "This is only a quick sketch of priorities. We'll know more once we arrive."

Briana glanced out the window at their escort. "If there are more of him there, I cannot promise my mind will be on clean windows."

Aster suffered a twinge of jealousy at her sister's freedom to choose a husband—or to admire the choices available. She had accepted long ago that she would never be able to do so.

"Lord Theophilus is in search of a *useful* wife," she reminded Briana. "Prove you can handle his household, and he may overlook the fact that you've never lived outside a city and that your grasp of mathematics is appalling."

Briana brightened. "But I like dogs. We should go on quite swimmingly."

Aster sniffed. As if a love of dogs was a basis for marriage! "Perhaps I should work harder at discovering the romantic parts of our charts," was all she said in acknowledgment.

As the high-sprung berlin rolled over the newly improved highway toward Iveston, Aster began to relax and enjoy the journey. She wasn't much of a rural sort and couldn't identify the trees or crops that they passed, but the fresh air and sunshine improved her spirits. The countryside looked much more cheerful in sunshine than in a downpour.

An hour later, they were well outside of the city, and were traveling a rural lane. She recognized a milestone and knew they weren't far from the manor. She wondered if any of the fields they passed belonged to the marquess. They seemed orderly enough.

The wide berlin slowed to traverse a narrow curve. She glanced out to see what Lord Theo was doing but couldn't find him. The hedge was too close for him to ride next to them, she supposed. Or perhaps he rode ahead to warn the household of their arrival.

She peered out the window to the road behind and noticed a

cloud of dust. A moment later, the dust parted to reveal a phaeton drawn by a team of two chest-heaving, galloping bays racing up behind them.

Nervously, she heard their coachman cursing as he hauled on the reins. Remembering another day and another disastrous carriage accident, she turned and strained to see the road ahead. A slow-moving farm wagon eased to the far side of the lane into a small opening in the hedgerow made for a stile.

"The phaeton driver is quite mad!" Briana exclaimed, looking out the window. "He means to race between us...."

Always primed for danger, Azenor flung aside her papers. "Hold the straps and brace your feet," she shouted, grabbing the leather holds with both hands. Making certain the others obeyed her order and were holding on for dear life, she closed her eyes and prayed frantically.

Pulled as far to the edge of the road as possible, the berlin lurched when one tall wheel slid off the road. The phaeton barreled past in a billowing cloud of dust and pebbles. Aster's heart lodged in her throat at seeing the brink of the ditch out the far window. One slip to the left and...

The rear wheel hit a stone, bounced, and struck the gulley. Briana and Deidre screamed and clung to their straps as the entire high-slung berlin tilted.

Cursing herself as much as the phaeton, Aster leaned her weight toward the road. She prayed that with enough leverage, the driver could right the vehicle before they hit the farm wagon.

Instead, the horses screamed their panic and picked up speed. Aster watched in horror as another sideways bounce tossed the swearing driver into the hedgerow. Shrieking their terror, the berlin's team broke into a run, dragging the driver until he was forced to release the leathers.

With a loud crack, one of the slender wheels broke and the unbalanced berlin toppled on its side, half-dragged by the frantic animals.

In a tumble of skirts and petticoats, Aster crashed into a tangle with her sister and cousin on the carriage's door, bumping with every rock the splintering wood hit.

***

HAVING RIDDEN AHEAD to let his family know the ladies were arriving, Theo panicked at the scream of frantic horses. Seeing a phaeton flying past as if the hounds of hell were on its tail, Theo kicked his gelding into his racing stride.

The sight of the driverless berlin overturned in the ditch conjured visions of hysterical bloodied females. Theo's panic escalated to outright terror. With the horses straining against their traces, dragging their hapless burden, he had to act quickly. He shoved his deepest fears into a dark hole and bolted the lid.

Reaching the stalled farm wagon, Theo threw his gelding's reins to the helpless farmer clinging to his own frightened cattle. Searching for the team's leathers in the tangle of frantic animals, he leaped off his horse and ran for the carriage traces.

Theo didn't know the two younger women well enough to distinguish one's screams from the other's, but he recognized Lady Azenor's curt commands over the crash of the carriage against rocks. He prayed that meant they hadn't all broken their necks yet.

With the overturned carriage a dead weight and its giant wheels dragging the ditch, the team couldn't escape. They had just reached the frightened rearing stage when Theo dodged between their hooves to cut the traces. "Jack, where are you?" He shouted for his driver.

"Over here, milord," he heard Jack call. "M'leg seems out of order, but throw me them reins."

"The beasts know where to run. I'll let them loose," Theo called back. "Don't move until we find someone to look at you." He cut the last unbroken strap and set the team free. The berlin finally stopped bouncing. Thank all the heavens the ditch wasn't deep. The roof of the carriage rested against the hedge.

"Lady Azenor!" he called, trying not to imagine the condition of the ladies inside but fearing every disaster his overactive brain could summon. "Have everyone hold still. I don't think I can right the carriage. I'll have to lift you out."

He took his gelding's reins from the farmer and motioned the cart on. "No point in blocking the road," he said. "We'll have help shortly."

Even as the wagon rumbled away, the berlin's wheel shifted

deeper into the ditch. "Don't move!" he shouted again. "I need to prop it or you'll just tumble more."

"I believe it's quite firmly wedged now," the intrepid Lady Azenor called. "We need help opening the door."

Theo could hear the faint panic behind her calm assertions. This was disaster beyond skinny-dipping and goat-racing. He could have *killed* all three ladies! If they were still in one piece, they'd be demanding to be returned to the safe environs of the city, and all hope would be lost. Once again, Iveston would be abandoned.

Wondering if he could take them as captives, Theo stoically climbed up on the wheel to open the door. The berlin was a wide-bodied vehicle. Petite Lady Azenor's head just brushed the side he was sitting on. She was standing on the far side of the carriage, near the front seat, leaving more room for her stunned relations to right themselves.

She'd lost her hat, and her glorious copper curls sprang from her pins in a sunset halo. She turned midnight eyes glazed with fear up to him, but without a word, she bent to help the blond lady to rise.

"The driver?" she asked in a low voice of concern—far better than the hysterics he'd expected.

"Thrown into the hedge. We'll pry you out of here and see to him next." Theo frowned and tried to work out the dynamics of hauling three ladies out a door that was now a ceiling. "Any broken bones here?"

The two young women were dabbing at their eyes with handkerchiefs and sniffing, but they shook their heads in reply. Still no hysterics. Maybe they were saving them until he'd hauled them out.

"Deirdre is the tallest of us and might climb out with a little help," Lady Azenor said, studying the situation. "Briana and I will need something to stand on. Deirdre, take Lord Theo's hand and see if you can lift yourself out."

The lady's voice was shaky, but she persuaded her companions into moving. The brunette caught the edge of the seat she should have been sitting on and pulled herself upright. She brushed off her skirts and righted her hat. She glanced dubiously at Theo's gloved hands.

To hell with propriety. Theo dropped into the center of the broken vehicle and was engulfed in sweet scents, petticoats, and other feminine frippery. Grabbing the tallest one first, he used brute force to lift her. She squealed in surprise, but scrambled to sit on the edge of the doorway and work her way down.

He kept waiting for the wailing to explode. His next victim grabbed her skirts so they did not rise as he swung her out. To his relief, she did not faint and roll off the side of the carriage into the muddy ditch but slid decorously down to the road. That left him with the ominously silent Lady Azenor.

The baggage wagon finally rolled up, much to Theo's mixed relief and despair. The maids starting crying in horror at sight of the overturned berlin, but the cart driver and two burly footmen leaped down to help.

The lady accepted the hands of the footmen, but muttered impolite imprecations when Theo caught her rump in his hands and lifted her from below. Having the meticulous lady at his mercy for that brief moment was *almost* worth his panic. Had he not been fretting about abandonment, he'd be laughing.

In minutes, the ladies were on their feet, and the housekeeper they'd brought with them was tending to Jack the Coachman. Theo waited stoically for demands to be returned to the city.

Instead, Azenor pointed her companions to the cart. "You must ride up to the house and fetch help. I'll be along shortly."

"I can ride for help," Theo corrected her. "You need to ride with the others. There's no need for you to linger on the road."

The other two women sensibly climbed into the cart, making room for her.

Lady Azenor merely lifted her deep blue eyes in stubborn refusal. "You have seen the disaster I can bring to my family. I will not repeat this mistake again."

She limped over to the stile and lifted her skirt to climb it.

Limped. The bedeviled female was injured and still prepared to walk all the way to the manor?

There was the hysteria he was expecting. *Damn.*

Nine

A STRONG ARM caught Aster's waist and hauled her from the stile. She shrieked in surprise, then pummeled the muscular limb imprisoning her. "Put me down, you oaf! You cannot keep manhandling me like this!"

The man had already had his hand on... on her *bottom*. That had been the outside of enough but—

His lordship swung her sideways into the saddle of his massive horse. Forgetting her outrage over his crude handling, Aster screamed her fear. It was a terrifyingly long way down, and the animal did not stand still. She had only Lord Theo's encroaching hold preventing her from a nasty tumble—and she really didn't need more bruises.

"I do not ride, sir! I'm not attired for this! Put me down at once."

Instead of listening, he stuck his boot in the stirrup and swung up behind her. His big hand nearly enveloped her abdomen. The strong thighs she'd admired earlier brushed her skirts—and her hip. She stiffened but she could not pull away without risking a fall.

"We will ride together to fetch help," he said in a tight-lipped command.

The horse jolted into motion with the urging of his knees. Azenor grabbed for its mane and tried not to sound like a hysterical female. "I'd rather walk. Put me down, *now*."

"No." He kneed the gelding into a canter, holding her in place although she was quite convinced she would slide off at any moment.

"Do you not think I'm bruised enough?" she asked, attempting to fight fear and maintain decorum at the same time. His hand just below her breasts created an unwanted agitation that she fought equally hard. "This is an unseemly familiarity, sir!"

When the uncivilized oaf didn't reply, she attempted to elbow him, but that meant releasing the mane. She did it anyway, and encountered a solid wall of muscle that hurt her elbow more than him, apparently. At least anger was starting to replace fear.

"I won't have more hysterical females fainting on my doorstep," he grumbled in response to her struggles.

"I am not hysterical! Although I very well could learn to be if you don't let me off this monster." *Hysterical*—the very idea was laughable.

"Walking with an injured limb when you can ride is either hysterical or stupid. Take your choice." His tone was unrelenting.

"I am not a cripple! I can walk. I cannot ride. That is not stupid. That is logical," she argued, wishing she could squirm around to see his expression but not daring to move given her current position between his thighs.

"You won't ride with the others because you think *you* caused the accident!" he shouted. "If you're not hysterical, you have maggots for brains. Did you not see Montfort's phaeton? I intend to horsewhip the lackwit the moment I see him."

"By all means, beat the stuffing out of him," she agreed through clenched teeth, wrapping her glove tighter in the horse's sumptuous mane. "But you cannot beat my planets into submission. I bring harm to those I love."

"Planets have no effect on anything!" he shouted in frustration as they cantered up the long drive to the manor. "*You* had no effect on the phaeton or the carriage or the damned Earth's movement. It was an *accident*."

"Language, sir," she scolded. "Besides, even Sir Isaac Newton believed in the effects of the sun. He studied calculus so as to better chart the planets, just as I do."

"He bloody well did not," he said, ignoring her objection to his language. "One cannot mathematically chart the fates." He hauled his horse to a halt at the portico.

She could point out that, among a number of other things, she had accurately predicted his brother's injury. But she was too breathless to state the obvious.

The massive sprawling mansion looming above her may once have been a medieval hall. It had been added on to so often that Azenor could not quite discern all its dimensions. It was all gray stone blocks, blunt square towers, and row upon row of windows.

She assumed from this angle that it formed a giant U or perhaps a square. Not a single rose bush adorned the walls. No pretty shutters or ivy lightened the heavy stone. The portico was slate and marble without a single potted tree or flower to welcome guests.

A groom came running. At least they had not misplaced *all* their servants.

"Send for a physician," his lordship snapped. "Jack is hurt. We'll need horses to haul the carriage out of the ditch and a blacksmith for the wheel. I'll send whichever of the layabouts I can find to help push it."

"Aye, milord." The groom tugged his forelock. "The team just ran in. I have fresh cattle saddled and ready."

Aster struggled to free herself, but the ground was a long way down.

Lord Theo effortlessly swung off, holding her in the saddle until his boots were on the stairs. He lifted her down as if she were a sack of flour and *carried* her up to the door. She was being helplessly hauled about in a man's arms! He might not be the size of an ox like some of his family, but surely he had the strength of two men. His hand was on her knee! Her heart pounded surely more than was good for it.

"Stop it!" she cried, beating at his shoulders. "Put me down! I am not one of your lightskirts."

He ignored her, shouldering open the front door as if he were a battering ram. "Jacques! Will! Anyone in the sound of my voice—get your posteriors down here *now* or I'll toss you out the windows."

A dog howled from the depths of the house. The billiard table still adorned the foyer, apparently serving as a convenient receptacle for outer garments, books, and assorted paraphernalia.

"Honestly, this is how you order your household?" she asked in amazement, almost forgetting that she was riding in his arms. "Do they actually listen?"

"Only when they're bored and not up to mischief," he admitted. Carrying her up the stairs, he bellowed in her ear, "There are ladies in dire need of help down the lane." The cacophony of barking dogs obliterated most of his command.

Aster covered her ears. Two spaniels and a beagle puppy raced up the stairs after them, yapping happily.

"I am perfectly capable of walking," she insisted, wriggling as they reached the top of the stairs. "I will start screaming if you don't put me down."

"I might actually enjoy that," he retorted, "so don't tempt me."

But he let her feet drop while continuing to hold her waist. Aster winced at the pressure on her twisted ankle but straightened and marched out of his hold. She glanced around at this heretofore unseen part of the house. She'd not put a great deal of thought into where they'd actually be staying in this monstrous mansion.

The first floor corridor was long and wide, the carpet as threadbare as the ones she'd seen downstairs. Gas sconces sputtered on the dark paneled walls, illuminating marble statues decorated in various forms of male outerwear apparently tossed at them in passing. She limped past the long line of carved, oak-paneled doors, admiring what she could see of the paintings hung on the wall.

"Are any of these rooms prepared for my family and our companions?" she asked, not daring to open any of the doors.

"I asked our housekeeper to open a few in the wing we don't use. You can station an army battalion in between to prevent forays by my family into your territory, but I make no guarantees. The place is riddled with staircases and bolt holes." He offered his arm.

Reluctantly, she took it. "I need to be placed in the attic or somewhere as far from my family as possible," she said. "I cannot risk more accidents."

"That's preposterous. We need a physician to look at your injuries, and you're not stomping up any stairs until he does. Mrs. Smith doesn't have time to clean up any more chambers for you." He steered her down a side corridor.

"I must insist—"

A shout and loud crash, followed by a litany of creative obscenities, buried the rest of her sentence. She thought the clamor echoed from the far end of the corridor they'd just departed. Lord Theo ignored it.

When no one responded to the uproar, Aster straightened her shoulders and pretended she hadn't heard *quailing puling fester of an ass* shouted down the hall.

"I am perfectly capable of putting linen on a bed—or sleeping in the stable if you don't show me to a suitable room," she continued without quivering. "Do you, or do you not, want us to help you stage a party for your potential wives?"

Lord Theo muttered irascibly and flung open doors, revealing beds without mattresses, parlors stacked with riding gear or telescope parts, and the general detritus of decades of neglect. Finally, he found one near the end of the hall with a dusty counterpane covering a narrow bed that might once have belonged to a lady's maid or a valet.

"And where will my family sleep?" she asked, limping over to test that no mice ran from the mattress.

"Far end of the west corridor. Take a left and limp clear to the end," he said with sarcasm, gesturing to indicate the direction. "I can't place you any further away without kicking Ashford from his chambers."

Ah, that explained the crash and obscene roars. The marquess had the rooms at the back of the main corridor. These intersecting rooms between the two wings were probably intended for bachelor guests and their servants. The housekeeper had installed Aster's family in the lady's wing. That placed Aster between his lordship's family and her own.

She glanced out the tall, narrow window into a partial courtyard between the two enormous branches of the U at the rear of the house. What had once probably been an elegant parterre garden was now a jumble of kennels, carriage parts, and rusting unidentifiable bits.

"This should suit," she acknowledged. "Just leave me here while you find help and look after the carriage and driver. I'm sure your housekeeper will show everyone to their proper places."

"I daresay she's tippling from the cooking sherry about now." He opened a brass circle on the wall and shouted into it. "Everyone, front and center! We have guests. You have five seconds before I start flinging you out windows."

Aster studied the round contraption. "What does that do?"

"Speaking tube. With luck, the sound carries further than my voice. Except that means they know I'm not near enough to catch them and they're free to slip out the back."

"I see." She lifted the brass lid and examined the dark tube before speaking into it. "I will see that you're fed fried worms and turnips for dinner unless you help my sister and cousin to their rooms. They've been badly shaken by a carriage accident," she said sweetly into the hole.

Heavy boots clattered into the main corridor and whoops rattled the rafters as they raced down the front steps.

Lord Theo scowled. "Threaten their rations, good thinking. Were you a soldier in a former life?"

"I am the eldest of six siblings." Six *surviving* siblings, but she did not bring up that painful subject. "Go lead your pack. I'll be fine here." Aster wished she had her trunks so she could begin dusting, but she'd find a cleaning closet once she drove this maddening gentleman away. His proximity muddled her mind, and she needed time to deal with the stimulating sensations created by an *astronomer's* strength in carrying her.

"The layabouts know how to find the road without my help." Without warning, Lord Theo arrogantly scooped her up again and proceeded down the corridor and toward the ladies' wing. "They can take care of the servants. I'll take care of you."

"That's the very last thing I need!" she cried in all honesty. "You have no idea how dangerous the part of catastrophe is in my chart or how wide the effect might be. *You* must stay as far from me as my family!"

WITH HIS ARMS FULL of curvaceous female, Theo wasn't inclined to be reasonable, particularly when she wasn't exactly rational either. "I thought it was only friends and family who die in your proximity?" he asked, dodging an excited spaniel to fling open the door to the bathing room. "Just call me your worst enemy and we should be fine."

"If you don't put me down, I'll call you worse than that!"

Maliciously, Theo decided he couldn't go wrong there. He could do whatever he liked, and she'd hate him. Then she couldn't tell him to go away—because she apparently only assassinated friends and family, not enemies. That was a plan he could get behind.

He deposited her on the marble floor and let her stare. He'd made certain the housekeeper had thoroughly cleaned this room before she did anything else. This was Iveston's one claim to fame— a tub that filled with hot water any time it was needed.

"That isn't...?" She touched the brass dolphin and turned it. Water gushed into the porcelain tub. She hastily spun it closed.

"A Roman bath? Almost. One of the great-grands built it for his wife, and it's been improved upon over the years. There's another in Ashford's wing my family can use. We'll leave this one for you and your ladies. You need to soak that ankle before it swells. I'll send one of your maids up when they arrive. There are linens in that cabinet." He nodded at a large wardrobe.

"You have running water, gas sconces, and speaking tubes, but can't keep the carpets maintained?" she asked, her dark eyes widening in a disbelief that made him squirm.

Theo shrugged off his discomfort. "None of the family weaves carpets or we'd no doubt have them hanging from the walls."

"I have a cousin who weaves tapestries..." she said in a dangerous tone that Theo already recognized as plotting.

He shoved the spaniel out the door and left the lady there before she discovered the risqué murals. As an afterthought, he turned the key in the lock and took it with him. That kept both the lady and his brothers from exploring until he had order restored.

She was a rare handful, and Theo had to quit thinking about her naked in the bath until he was decent enough to re-join the ladies. He blamed the long dry spell between mistresses for his illogical reaction to an irrational female.

He was not, by nature, an anxious man, but circumstances were in the process of giving him gray hairs at an early age. Instead of hurrying to help with the coach, he turned down the hall to Ashford's chamber.

The marquess was standing in the middle of the room in a clutter of spilled books and tea trays, blindly kicking any object he encountered. The puppies who'd been waiting eagerly outside the door pranced in to play tug-of-war with the papers scattered about.

"The physician said you might stand on that leg?" Theo asked dryly, since his brother's injured limb was still wrapped in tight bandages, and he wore nothing except his nightshirt to conceal the fact.

Duncan uttered a German epithet of a particularly obscene nature.

"Fine, then, wallow as you like, but keep it down to a low roar or the ladies will think we've confined a mad uncle to the attic. And these particular ladies seem more inclined to go looking for a Bedlamite rather than running from one."

The marquess swung his sightless eyes in the direction of Theo's voice. "They haven't run screaming from the premises already?"

"Their carriage overturned and was dragged half way down the lane, and they merely protested when I insisted they not walk to the house. I've locked one in the bathing room, however. She's as much a Bedlamite as you. She'll no doubt be in here as soon as she figures out how to unlock the door, so I suggest you either get in bed or put on trousers."

"Fitting," Duncan muttered, easing his way through the puppies in the direction of the wardrobe. He still limped badly. "We'd be better off hiring an army sergeant."

"I cannot bed an army sergeant. If it is now my duty to produce heirs, I need a wife. You will behave until that happens, or I'll poison you in your sleep."

Duncan snorted. "Cook is doing a damned fine job of that already. Who told him I was supposed to eat pig swill?"

"Cook quit. We're all eating pig swill. But Lady Azenor is bringing in a troop of servants. I'm hoping she'll know a cook who won't mind dogs in the kitchen."

Unable to see the latch to the wardrobe, Duncan thumped his fist against the panel until it popped open. "The solution there is astonishingly obvious," he said dryly.

"Right, build Will his own kitchen so he can raise his litters in it. My observatory comes first though." Theo slammed out, shutting in the damned hounds and leaving the marquess to dodge puppies and find his own trousers.

Not hearing screams from the bathing room just yet, he took the north stairs down, planning on cutting through the courtyard to the stable. Outside, he glanced back at the house—and saw a chain of sheets being lowered from the bathing room window.

Ten

ASTER WAS NOT so intrepid that she had any particular intention of climbing out the window. She actually *longed* to soak her bruises in a hot tub of water. Like her cats, she was a creature of comfort who preferred warmth and order and pampering.

She did not, however, appreciate being hauled about and locked up as if she were a noisome basset hound.

And she had no intention of undressing until she had clean clothing in which to dress herself when she was done. Not to mention that she couldn't unfasten her laces without help.

She smirked in triumph as Lord Theo saw her warning flag. By the time he'd stormed back up the stairs, she'd located another key on the door frame and unlocked the door. Men were so very predictable. She returned the key to the frame and stepped into the corridor as he reached the landing, breathing fire and brimstone.

"I will need a maid and my trunks before I can accept your generous offer of hot water," she said amiably, limping down the hall. "I would like to check on the rooms assigned to my family."

"You need a keeper," he replied in a surly growl, stalking ahead of her to throw open doors. "Maids." He gestured at a narrow room.

"Your sister." He opened the door on an elegant four-poster covered in what appeared to be a fading medieval tapestry.

"Your cousin." Another poster bed. A slightly more frayed tapestry.

"Clean linen." A lovely closet crammed with what was probably threadbare sheets. "Mrs. Smith only tipples in the afternoon after her duties are done."

Trying to ignore his masculine ire, Aster studied the chambers he opened. "Since they did not bring their own maids, I think it would be best if Briana and Deirdre share a room. I take it you do not house maids in your servants' attic?"

"Not currently. If yours want the female dormer, Mrs. Smith

can show them where to find linens. I couldn't tell her if you were bringing ladies' maids or how many."

"My great-aunt will be joining us as a chaperone. She'll require this chamber with a fireplace. Her feet are often cold, and she likes to put them up before a good fire. We're training new girls as ladies' maids and underservants. Let's keep them near us for now. This room with the trundle beds should suffice."

She verified that there were stairs on either end of the corridor, plus the stairs on the connecting wing. Aster supposed that was necessary for safety, but she'd have to find means of keeping out male intruders. Great-Aunt Nessie was for appearances only. Practically speaking, she was half-deaf and would be useless as a chaperone. On the other hand, Nessie wasn't likely to fret too much over howling dogs and inexplicable explosions.

A commotion of crashes, curses, and howls from below indicated new arrivals.

"Don't!" His lordship warned, catching her arm before she could hurry to greet her company. "You will ruin that foot if you hobble about anymore. I'll send everyone up to you to order about as you please."

She sighed in exasperation and gazed up at her tall host. Lord Theo truly had amazing silver-blue eyes, but his brows were drawn down in vexation, giving him a most uncongenial expression. "Perhaps if you will accept that I can take care of myself, and you would better spend your time taking care of your brothers, we might swim along a trifle better."

He scowled even more but gave her suggestion some thought. "I don't want to lose your help before the guests arrive. I am trying to protect you from the worst of Iveston's elements and show off the best. If you will promise not to run screaming into the night once I turn my back, I will attempt to do as you say."

"Do I look like someone who runs screaming into the night?" she asked with asperity.

"Yes, actually you look like a ball of fluff. But so do Saturn's rings and they're not, so I'll accept that you're tougher than you look. Hie yourself to the bathing room, and I'll have your trunks and maid sent up."

Aster didn't know if a *ball of fluff* was flattering, or what Saturn's rings might be. She didn't know how to take his lordship's seeming agreement when he was still ordering her about. She tried very hard not to think about Lord Theo at all after he'd departed. Instead, she mentally rearranged rooms for her servants. When her muddled mind deemed that impossible—his hands upon her had left an indelible impression on her thoughts as well as her person—she decided to be irritated at his arrogance. She would be very glad to send him about his business while she went about hers.

Perhaps he was right. Perhaps if she despised him, they could work together.

Her cousin and sister arrived battered and torn and not precisely happy—until she introduced them to the bathing room.

They gasped in wonder and began darting about, examining the linen wardrobe, turning up the sconces—and revealing the naked mural. Even that didn't disturb them greatly. Their family homes contained Roman statues and even an ancient mosaic or two.

"Oh, this is marvelous! I shall marry Lord Theo just for his tub," Briana declared worshipfully, running her hand over the tiled enclosure.

"You know nothing of mathematics, farming, animals, or tenants," Aster reminded her sister, perhaps a trifle waspishly. "And you enjoy the city too much and lack the patience to endure living in this rural outpost surrounded by heathen Ives."

She wasn't any better, Aster reminded herself. She *needed* the city and its libraries and lectures. She had to quit behaving like a bird-witted miss because a strong, handsome scientist had swept her across the threshold in his arms.

"Emilia would love that courtyard for her herbs," Deirdre said loyally. "Perhaps if she marries an Ives and gains her inheritance, she could hire people to manage this place."

"Emilia won't be of much help to Lord Theo," Aster warned. "She always has her head stuck in a book or her laboratory. But the marquess might be a convenient match for her. From the sounds of it, he throws things. She could ignore him."

Limping, she left to direct the new maids in their duties. Fresh from her Aunt Daphne's rural village, the maids might know how to milk cows, but they'd never seen wardrobes of the size and elegance of Iveston Hall. Azenor explained where things went, had them press out fresh gowns under the tutelage of Mary and Molly, her two trained maids, and sent them to carry the garments to the bathing room for Briana and Deirdre.

Her ankle ached so badly by the time she reached her room, she had to sit on the bed and remove her boot. She nearly wept from the agony of her effort.

Unaccustomed to physical weakness, she persisted, finally prying off the offending leather. Studying her swollen ankle, she wondered if she hadn't bitten off rather more than she could possibly chew.

Indecision was the negative side of being a Libra, she knew. She simply had to keep reminding herself to move forward and not look back.

The riotous barking of dogs warned of a new arrival. She sighed and searched through her trunk for a pair of slippers.

By the time she'd tidied her nest of curls, hidden the worst wear and tear on her gown with a shawl, and limped into the corridor, Great-Aunt Nessie's solid square figure was bearing down on her, followed by her harried maid and one of Aster's inexperienced footmen carrying a stack of luggage.

"There you are, dear girl! So thoughtful of you to ask for me." Garbed in the full skirts and petticoats of a prior century, her iron gray hair sporting a beribboned mob cap, Nessie cruised slowly down the corridor like a massive brigantine.

Aster hugged her mother's aunt. "It was lovely of you to come. I fear the house is a bit of a hubble-bubble."

"The mouse is trouble? Always are, dear. I brought my kitties, never fear." She gestured at a mewling basket carried on her arm.

Aster knew better than to correct the lady, or she'd be in the drafty corridor until dinner time. Imagining what would happen if the adventurous kittens escaped into the dog-ridden household, she shuddered and led her aunt to the furthest chamber in the ladies' wing— her lone centurion to guard against invasions up the front stairs.

"I had the footmen make up a fire," she told her aunt. "Just sit and rest and I'll come fetch you in time for dinner."

"Your young man is a winner?" Nessie inquired, settling into an almost-respectable wing chair. "He appeared a bit beleaguered to me. Did he win a great deal?"

"A great deal," Aster repeated, pressing a kiss to her aunt's cheek and escaping before the conversation became any more torturous.

She reached the corridor only to bounce off a solid wall of embroidered blue waistcoat that she recognized rather well by now. She tilted her head to scowl up at his lordship. "This is the ladies' wing, sir. What kind of example do you set?"

THEO REGARDED his maddening guest with impatience. "How will you direct a house party if you cannot even walk?"

He lifted her fluffy skirt to examine the ominous swelling of her ankle. Lady Azenor cuffed his ear for his rudeness, but accustomed to much stronger blows from his brothers, Theo ignored her puny effort. He liked that she didn't run off shrieking, so he merely offered his arm rather than hauling her around. "You will soak that injury until the physician is done with the coachman and can see you."

"Now that I have my trunks, I will be most happy to soak it in one of Emilia's medicinal herbs. I do not need your quack, who will want to suck my blood or something else inordinately obnoxious."

His ball of fluff limped irately—but obediently—down the corridor with him. "We only use the most modern of physicians, I assure you. If you keep track of our family, you will recall that we have members all over Northumberland and Edinburgh who know the finest medical students. Dr. Joseph probably saved Duncan's life."

"But not his eyesight. I've changed my mind. I'll be happy to speak with him—after I've bathed and soaked my ankle."

"You will not read his stars," Theo ordered. "Joseph is a man of science and does not believe silly superstition."

She released his arm and stalked ahead of him, limping as fast as her lovely, swaying hips could go. "Your family signs are now on the parts of peril and secret enemies. The entire summer is likely to be one immense disaster after another. I suggest that you not alienate me into leaving before you find a wife and create an heir."

"I am not reassured that I will be marrying while peril is hanging over me," he said dryly. Although he had a notion that his idea of disaster and hers might be two entirely different matters. Marrying him might be a calamity for a lady—but a blessing for his family. A point to ponder when he didn't have a desirable pocket Venus twitching her curves beneath his nose.

"I was not looking for family and relationships at the time I perused your brother's chart," she acknowledged, dismissing his argument and apparently oblivious to his panting admiration. "I shall do so this evening. It is a complex undertaking, since our families are very large, and it's difficult to separate our parts from those of the ladies I'm bringing out here, some of whom are also distantly related."

Lady parts often looked alike in Theo's experience, but he was quite certain this lady's parts would be easily recognizable. He actually bit his tongue on that comment.

"Good to know that your scientific journey is as difficult as mine," he said instead. "I left the reports you requested in your room—a little night time reading to put you to sleep."

He enjoyed her expression of delight and approval—which meant he needed to annoy her again so they could remain enemies. "I don't expect you to understand a word of the treatises, but I always keep my promises."

That returned her glare. She knocked peremptorily on the bathing room door. "It is my turn," she called to the occupants. "You must keep Aunt Nessie entertained and the maids in order and the kittens out of the halls until I'm done."

Kittens? Theo shuddered.

Two laughing nymphs emerged with damp curls, followed by two young maids carrying armfuls of frippery. Theo swallowed hard at the mountains of delicate lace and cast a gaze to the dragon lady's skirts. What did she wear under that colorful swathe of exotic muslin? Not a mountain's worth of petticoats, he'd seen for himself.

But the glimpse of her ankle was sufficient to have him salivating without imagining what else she was or wasn't wearing. She had slender, well-turned ankles to match her hourglass figure.

He didn't care if their planets fell from the sky or shot through the heavens. He wanted *this* woman in his bed and to hell with any other.

Eleven

HAVING BATHED in the luxurious tub and dressed in her dinner gown, Aster allowed Dr. Joseph to examine and wrap her ankle while she picked his brains about the marquess's plight.

"So there is *some* hope that his sight might return?" she prodded, when the physician beat all around the proverbial bush.

"Some, just as there is some chance he might keel over dead tomorrow. I do not expect either result. I believe the brain swelling is reduced, but it has damaged the optic nerve," he said stiffly.

Dr. Joseph was a man in his early thirties, disguising his youth with a prickly brown beard and wire-rimmed eyeglasses. Aster noted he peered over them most of the time. She wondered if he might be a good match for Emilia.

What to do about the blind marquess loomed larger in her mind than marrying off Emilia. Aunt Gwenna's parliamentary bill to help the children was even more important than keeping Iveston from descending into chaos—although Lord Theo might not appreciate that sentiment. How could she force a blind marquess to acknowledge his duties?

"But just as my ankle will recover, Ashford's optic nerve might," she suggested. Before the physician could argue, she asked, "Were you born in January?"

Dr. Joseph began putting the tools of his trade back in a satchel. "I was. How did you know?"

"Capricorn. Stubborn, serious, and cautious. Probably Cancer rising, so you're also empathic and a caretaker. Around the fifteenth, perhaps?"

He smiled gently, patted her knee, then stood up. "January 15, 1799, to be precise. Theo explained your predilection for astrology. You would do better to create a better almanac than to predict human behavior."

"But I was right, wasn't I? I have a peculiar ability for

interpreting what others cannot." Which might be the reason others could not duplicate her results, she realized uneasily. Her Malcolm gift gave her an extra advantage. "You are still unmarried?"

"I am. I have been too busy studying and building my practice to dally with the ladies."

"Exactly," she said in satisfaction. "Ambitious and hardworking."

He regarded her with amusement. "Will you find a match for me too?"

"Not if you continue to look upon me as some sort of fanciful child," she retorted, taking his hand to stand up. "But if you'll listen instead of judging, then you are invited to our tea party the day of the village fete. You should find the company agreeable."

"I would be delighted to join the company," he said, offering his arm to help her from the room. "I am not as certain I am delighted to eat anything served unless you have found another cook."

Aster muttered an improper word under her breath. "They have no cook either?"

"The last one booted the dogs out of the kitchen, and Will booted out the cook in retaliation. The tale is all over the village."

"Aside from his dislike of howling animals underfoot, was this cook worth keeping?" she asked warily.

"Probably the best in the county," Dr. Joseph said, watching her with curiosity. "He can't find another place that pays as well around here, so he is looking in London, although he claims to hate the city."

"Will you carry a message from me to this cook?" At the physician's expression of interest, Aster continued, "Tell him the dogs will be removed to a more appropriate area, and I will give him my mother's secret to a perfect soufflé if he will return."

The physician's lips curled in appreciation. "I will do that, my lady. It's been a pleasure talking with you."

"Likewise, I'm sure." She nodded and waited for him to take the stairs down.

Then, with determination, she limped in the direction of the Marquess of Ashford's chambers. She could not operate without his express permission. And she needed to be certain a man with so many astrological knives hanging over his head wasn't a danger to her friends and family.

And then... She might consider one of her more audacious plans, one she dare not admit even to herself, not until she had at least met the elusive marquess.

She could hear vile profanities emanating from behind the door before she even knocked. Crunching china was followed by *loathsome bampot* and a loud slam of an object against a wall. She supposed she ought to come back when the marquess was in a better humor, but she had a suspicion that would be after he was dead and buried in his grave.

She'd rather prevent that.

She knocked. More curses greeted her.

"I shall come in at the count of ten," she admonished. "And if you lock the door, I will tell the housekeeper you have killed yourself and ask for the key."

"She won't know where it is," a deep voice grumbled. "Come in. Theo said you'd be here."

Pleased that his lordship was so perceptive, Aster waded into a wonderfully spacious chamber that appeared to have been struck by two hurricanes and a cyclone. Heavy green velvet draperies hung crookedly over any evidence of sunlight. Tilted glass wall sconces gleamed dully on the walls, even though it was five in the afternoon of a reasonably sunny summer day. The usual threadbare carpet adorned the wide-planked floor, ripped in places where booted feet had caught on the threads and yanked the holes wider.

Papers, books, broken china, clothes, boots, and various items of sporting equipment were strewn everywhere she looked—on floors, tables, chairs, and desk. The broad, towering marquess with his waistcoat badly buttoned and his cravat undone resembled a bear standing in the center of chaos. His dark hair looked as if it hadn't been cut since the accident, and his thick beard hadn't been shaved in weeks, at best.

Neither long hair nor thick beard disguised the jagged healing scar disfiguring his handsome visage from partially-shaved scalp to jutting cheekbone. Ashford's stature alone was intimidating. He made two of her at the very least. The raw wound would scare small children into tears.

Azenor approved. Her newly hatched scheme took on momentum.

The marquess desperately *needed* a wife to take him in hand and direct him to do his parliamentary duty. She had resigned herself to never marrying, because she could not accept endangering a man she loved. However—she could never love a growling bear of a man like this. But with a little experience, she *could* manage him.

She needed more time to compare their charts. It was possible this scheme was the disaster hanging over the heads of both their families. She hated having to balance all possibilities. Life would be easier if she could simply do what her head said was best.

"Are you trying to kill yourself?" she asked with interest as he stumbled over a tea cart that should never have been placed where he could run into it.

"What do you want?" he asked in a surly tone. "If you just want to stare, get the hell out."

"I can find more attractive views if staring was my goal. I want to know that I have your permission to change your public rooms in anticipation of the tea party during the fete." Unable to tolerate the untidiness, she shoved the cart against the wall and began gathering papers.

"What are you doing?" he asked in suspicion. "I didn't ask for your help."

"I am the family Librarian. I am compulsively tidy. If these papers have been placed here in some kind of order, I shall happily return them to their original state. Otherwise, I see no reason not to pick them up before you trip and break your neck."

"Breaking my neck would solve a great deal," he agreed. "But I'd rather wait until Theo is wed and his wife bedded. He has a habit of losing women before he makes it to the altar."

"As you lose servants? Have you tried a smaller household?" she asked acerbically.

"Marry them all off!" he roared. "Find them all good homes, along with the damned hounds."

One of the maligned creatures crept out from beneath the bed, tail wagging.

"If you'll give me permission to make changes...?" she asked again.

"Burn the place down, I don't care. It's not as if I'll see what you've done." He swiped his foot at a broken teapot and stumbled his way back to the bed, limping far worse than she.

"May I also make some changes in here?" she asked daringly. "That carpet really needs to go. I don't know how you've tolerated it this long."

"My great-great uncle brought it back from China. It's rare and valuable." He dropped to the unmade bed, sending another puppy scrambling from beneath the mattress.

"It *was* rare and valuable," she asserted. "It is now ready for the dustbin. There is utterly no way of repairing it. Perhaps a good weaver could cut out the solid portions and bind it for a wall hanging."

"Fine. Then the damned dogs can wet on the bare floor. That will be easier to clean." He unerringly lifted an adoring puppy from the floor and stroked its head.

"You have no valet?" Azenor sought through her mental files for the last footman she'd trained. She couldn't train a valet, but a good servant could learn.

"What do I need a valet for? I sent mine to Theo so he can learn to make himself presentable."

"Ah, that explains his buttoned waistcoat. I am grateful for your thoughtfulness. It would be most difficult to find him a wife if he continued about in shirtsleeves. Thank you for this opportunity to allow me to train a few more servants and introduce my friends to your household. It should be an enlightening experience," she said primly, bobbing a curtsy even though he couldn't see it.

"I still don't believe in planets charting fates," he growled. "For all I know, you sent someone to scare my horse that night just to prove your predictions were right and worm your way into my household."

"Oh, very good, my lord. Stay on your toes and be wary. I shall send the stewards up to you for interviews, shall I? Would you like your valet back?"

"That's enough impertinence! Get the hell out and get Theo married or leave!" Ashford roared—just like an injured bear. Even the puppy in his lap ran for the covers.

"I shall *not* introduce you to his potential candidates," she said thoughtfully. "But I do wish to discuss my Aunt Gwenna and Uncle Harry's labor bill at another time. Good evening to you, sir."

Satisfied that she'd done her duty as she'd been taught, Aster limped toward the stairs. Her ankle did feel much better now that it had been soaked and bound. She had too many tasks to carry out to laze about like an invalid. A household without a cook was a *disaster*. As she knew from her own very large family, food was the glue that bonded disparate personalities into working together.

Although food hadn't bound these quarrelsome Ives together, it seemed.

"What the devil are you about now?" Lord Theo demanded, coming up the stairs with books and a walking stick in his hand.

"Asking your brother's permission to do as I please," she said haughtily, raising her nose in the air at his tone. "You said you have a conservatory, correct?"

WHAT THE HELL did the conservatory have to do with Duncan? Theo glanced cautiously in the direction of his brother's chamber. When he heard no lion roar of fury, he glanced back at the demure miss in...

His heart nearly stopped in his chest as he thoroughly absorbed the lady's evening attire. She was wearing another of those iridescent gowns that shimmered with blues and greens and grays, but it was the décolletage that held his eye and nearly caused another tongue-swallowing episode. There was nothing *demure* about the display of ripe, full curves pushing against the frailest wisp of silk, without a ruffle in sight. But it was the heart-shaped freckle nearly hidden in her cleavage that had his brain spinning in his skull and all his blood rushing southward.

He gulped and lost track of her question. Stupidly, he held out the walking stick he'd uncovered in the debris of the study. "Use this to keep your weight off your foot. Not that you have any weight..." He sighed and returned his gaze to her narrowed eyes so he could think again.

"Thank you, I think. Perhaps you should offer the stick to the marquess?"

"He had one. He used it to smash everything on his washstand the first time we offered it. Fearing he would use it to smash our heads, we hid it." Theo refrained from offering his arm as she tested the cane. He had to quit looking at her... and touching.

Not looking or touching made for difficulty in wooing, but he'd already faced that challenge. How did one woo a woman who had to hate him before she would marry him? A conundrum he meant to conquer. Could he make her hate him by touching her? Experimentation was required.

She swung the stick and used it to limp down the stairs. "Try imagining being unable to look at the stars," she said, thankfully following her own train of thought and not his. "Then perhaps you can appreciate the level of your brother's frustration. For a Scorpio, particularly, it will take an enormous will to re-learn manipulating his surroundings."

Theo skipped the weird bit and concentrated on imagining life without stars. An emptiness gaped inside him, followed by unreasoning panic and a need to *do* something to prevent such a catastrophe. And knowing it was impossible to prevent what one couldn't foresee, he grasped some of his brother's fury.

He muttered a bloody oath. "No wonder he says he'd rather be dead."

"Exactly so. So you must find things he *can* do until he has found a role that suits him. Interviewing stewards will be a start. Prying him out of that cave so he might mingle with others is probably too much to ask right now, but a goal for the future. The conservatory?" she asked imperiously.

"Is your father a general?" he asked, leading her down the stairs. "Really, the army missed an opportunity in not recruiting you."

"My grandfather was a general in India. His service earned him an earldom. My father grew up in India, explored various continents, then became a professor in Edinburgh. You must meet my mother sometime," she said with a smile that made him wary—

And thoroughly excited him. He was officially a lunatic.

"What do you want with the conservatory?" He kept his tone rude so as not to let her think they were friends. "It's food for the minions we need now, and you can't cook plants."

"Well, yes, one can, if they are the right plants. But I am more concerned with the puppies. If you want your cook back, you must find a better home for the dogs. I assume they require warmth in winter and that is why they end up in the kitchen, even though the weather is perfectly fine now."

"Will crossbreeds rare varieties of creatures. The hounds are bred for their extremely sensitive noses, and he trains them to find people. The spaniels are water dogs, capable of dragging drowning victims from ponds and canals. His work is more important than the damned cook," he said irascibly, itching to haul her down the stairs so she needn't hurt herself. But he was attempting to pretend he possessed decorum.

"Yes, but the cook is responsible for his workers, and tripping and pouring boiling soup over a spaniel's head is probably not good for dogs or servants. Is the conservatory in good repair?"

"The last I looked," Theo said grudgingly, trying to recall the ancient glass room. "One of the greats had it built to his specification with two layers of glass and windows that can be held open on warm days. There's a coal grate, if someone remembers to stoke it."

"If Will wants to keep his puppies warm, then he needs to learn to stoke it, and to open windows on warm days," she said dryly.

"If Will were here two days out of ten, that might work," Theo agreed. "But he trains animals all across the kingdom and cannot be in two places at once. Whereas there's always someone in the kitchen to feed the hounds and fire the grate."

Theo opened the door into the desolate glass room that smelled of ripe earth. With the delicious Lady Azenor inside the privacy of the conservatory without a chaperone, temptation raised its ugly head. Dirt blotted the windows, preventing anyone from seeing inside. Instead of broken-down, barren tables, there ought to be orchids dancing above her sunset curls. From the way her face lit with an irresistibly delectable delight at the emptiness, he could almost believe parrots had flown out of a jungle to land on her shoulder.

Did she not see the filth?

Well, if he meant to woo her and make an enemy of her at the same time, he couldn't find a better place to start.

Twelve

ASTER SMILED IN DELIGHT at the lovely glass room that would be filled
with sun even in winter. She could almost see the dangling purple
orchids and green bananas that belonged in here. A flowering lemon tree
would smell heavenly. She longed to start cleaning the filth—but there
was too much to be done to indulge her need for order.

She turned to speak to Lord Theo, but she nearly bumped her
nose on his linen when she did. Before she knew what he was about,
he had hauled her from the ground again, enveloping her in his
strong embrace.

Instead of beating him with her stick, she dropped it in surprise.

"Wha..." The rest of her words were swallowed as his mouth
descended on hers.

Oh my.

She had been kissed before. One did not reach the ripe old age
of twenty-five and escape male mauling. But all prior efforts were
not *kisses* compared to this.

Lord Theo consumed her. His mouth was gentle and forceful at
once, reassuring, warming, seductive... and *demanding*. She gasped
and wrapped her arms around his neck and let herself be seduced by
his need as much as she had been seduced by his wonderful
conservatory. He engulfed her in the earthy scents of the jungle she
imagined. His arms tightened, and she felt them as a shelter, not a
danger. She parted her lips beneath his insistence.

Oh my, again.

Eyes closed, Azenor gave herself up to the bliss of a possession
that roused hungers she could not name. Her formidable brain shut
down, and she surrendered to the pleasure of pure sensation. She so
seldom had the opportunity to indulge all her senses in such an
exciting manner....

This was better than the paradise of his bathing room. In fact, if
she could combine the two...

His lordship's tongue swept across hers, stealing her breath and creating very physical longings she didn't know how to satisfy. Her breasts *ached*. She dug her fingers deeper into his masculine shoulders, and he crushed her against his chest, which stirred wicked sensations much lower than her breasts.

For a lean man, the astronomer was amazingly strong. Without removing his mouth from hers, he set her on the edge of a table, shoving aside empty pots. In her current state, it seemed the most amazing feat of magic to be consumed and carried at once. She craved more of whatever enticing nectar he was feeding her.

And then his big, competent hands lifted her breasts, and the spell was broken by a spike of desire so strong, it generated an explosion of alarm.

She *wanted* that touch too much, and she knew better. Fear shoved him away.

Hiding her heated cheeks, she righted her bodice, then pushed at Lord Theo's encroaching presence when he did not immediately release her. This was *not at all* how she'd planned this visit to go. "No, no—stop. Stop this instant. We cannot *do* this."

Amazingly, he did as told. "Why not?" he asked, brushing kisses to her hair that made her shiver with desire. "We both like it."

"Is *Why not?* your answer to everything?" As if she could think when he stood over her like a conquering god. *No* seemed like a good and simple answer. "If the king told you to jump off a cliff, would the answer be *Why not?*"

He looked amused instead of offended. "Quite possibly, if I was allowed to design wings that might lower me safely."

Argghhhh! Men! She struggled to find better words.

"I cannot become attached to you," she protested desperately, knowing how weak that sounded. "It will not suit at all. Now help me down, please. This is most inappropriate. I had no idea..."

She knew she was chattering mindlessly, but she was too shaken to find a coherent argument a man of science would accept.

HAVING JUST TOUCHED those heavenly plump breasts, Theo was in no condition to be rational. He could no more hide his arousal than Lady Azenor could hide her red curls and blushing cheeks. He stepped closer to where she sat, wrapped his arms around her waist, buried his face in her hair, and his lower half in her skirts, dangerously near his goal. "I can make you hate me," he said helpfully. "What if I make you hate my house as well?"

The fluffy witch battered his upper arms with her useless fists. "Just put me down. Put me down, *now*."

Steeling himself, he lifted his irate guest from the table and set her down in front of him so that she faced the door and not him. He still kept one arm around her waist, because once one touched a heavenly body, it would be insane to let go. He was quite confident that she would drive him mad with lust before her irrationality overtook him and he lost his mind completely. "Look at all the trouble we'd save ourselves if we found each other compatible," he whispered in her ear.

She didn't lean into him as he'd hoped, but broke free. She bent over to retrieve her stick, and limped for the door. "That is not happening with disaster hanging over us. You need a helpmate, not a *general*." She added this last with distaste.

So, he'd succeeded in irritating her with that reference. Fine. He'd keep irritating her—and seducing her. She kissed like a choir of angels. Probably a stupid metaphor but he was an astronomer, not a poet. He wasn't about to give her up.

"You haven't proved to me that you aren't in my chart," he insisted, taking her arm to irk her more. "I don't want to have to kiss every woman you introduce to me if I'm perfectly happy with the way you kiss."

"Marriage isn't about *kissing*," she said, jerking open the door to return to the house. "It's about compatibility and responsibility and helping each other and..."

"Making babies," he said with a leer she couldn't see since she was marching ahead of him—like a general off to war. "Kissing leads to making babies, and that's uppermost on my mind these days."

She hissed in alarm before replying furiously, "Any young female can make babies." She thumped her stick against the floor. "Don't be ridiculous. Go find a new star or moon. I must see if there is anything edible in your kitchen or you will have rebellion on your hands."

For the first time in his memory, Theo had no interest in finding a new star—because he'd found one right here on earth. He was amazed at how this shimmering creature could fascinate him as much as Saturn's moons. Could he be the gravitational pull to make her orbit him? How?

"I'll have to show you where the kitchen is," he said, looking for more ways to vex her. "There are more stairs involved, and I think I should carry you."

AGITATED, Aster attempted to escape Lord Theo's overwhelming proximity. After what had just happened, the simple awareness of his presence threatened to set her aflame. The mention of *babies* had her nerves on fire.

With the danger signs in her chart, she daren't have babies—the thought would make her cry if she let it. Just holding a baby had killed one already—and she had *known* the danger and ignored it. Never again.

She preferred to keep busy rather than dwell on what she couldn't have. "Don't you have stewards to interview? Brothers to berate? Go away and leave me alone. If this should happen again, I shall have to leave."

"Stewards to interview arriving tomorrow," he said, with a cold formality unlike his earlier warm flattery.

Perhaps she'd finally convinced him to retreat from his pursuit. Stupidly, she was rather disappointed that he gave up so easily. *Babies*, she reminded herself. He wanted babies.

"Call for your minions if you cannot be trusted with me," he continued with what sounded like arrogance. "I'll not have you falling down the kitchen stairs. Or expiring of horror once you're there."

That was better. Anger and disdain, she could handle. "Fine, then. I shall sit in the salon while you summon servants so I might inquire into the kitchen's needs. What time do you generally dine?"

"Whenever we're hungry." He led her to the front of the house. "Cook usually leaves cold platters on the buffet. I'm assuming whoever he left in charge will do the same. You had no need to dress for dinner."

"If I am to set an example, I most certainly do." Still uneasy after her shocking surrender to temptation, Aster shook off his attempt to hold her arm. "Order does not emerge from chaos overnight."

"If only people operated on the same gravitational principles as the moons and planets, we might orbit each other in a more organized fashion," he retorted.

Aster cast him a look of disbelief, but Lord Theo actually seemed to be considering this theory. *Orbiting people*, indeed! But while he worked out his philosophical notion, he didn't argue or attempt to distract her. She chose a dog-hair-covered sofa in the dusty salon and propped her injured foot on a battered stool.

"Orbit elsewhere," she told him crossly when he paced, looking tall and more scrumptious than any gentleman should in wrinkled linen.

Being attracted to the lanky scientist would be a serious complication if she decided she should marry his brother.

Would his brother want babies? It would be safer if he would settle for a general.

"The universe would appear to be a riot of erratic objects," Lord Theo expounded with the wave of an ink-stained hand. "But gravitational forces prevent the earth and moon from bouncing off other objects like billiard balls."

"I don't believe mathematics or gravity will separate your brothers from my friends and family," she said dryly, hearing masculine voices and feminine laughter on the stairs. "If you will be so kind as to fetch them, we can descend on the kitchen and terrify the inhabitants into producing dinner."

"Better yet, let Lady Briana and Miss Deirdre go to the kitchen while you sit here and rest your ankle. I believe *you* were the one who suggested we share duties," he said with condescension.

Lord Theo marched off in a huff of brown-gold locks and rumpled broadcloth, leaving Azenor to sink into the cushions with weariness. Her ankle throbbed, but... not as much as her lips and heart ached, one from desire and the other from loneliness.

She so much wanted a family of her own.

For years, she had kept hoping her chart would open up and free her to love again. She had only just recently resigned herself to the shelf. She didn't need a bossy astronomer knocking all her vows cock-a-hoop simply because he was too lazy to court anyone else.

Bree and Dee fluttered in, exuding excitement and trailing three males. The blond one Aster knew as Jacques. He was accompanied by an unfamiliar Ives gentleman in rough country clothes, and a young boy who was no doubt an Ives as well, although he had yet to grow into his ears and nose.

"Tell us what we are to do in our expedition to the kitchen," Bree said cheerfully. "Lord Theo said we are to terrify the occupants, but I'd rather scare up food. I'm famished."

Ignoring her sister's effervescent foolishness, Aster held out her hand to the unknown Ives. "It is common in good company to introduce one's self, as my sister has plainly forgotten. I am Lady Azenor Dougall, astrologist and eldest daughter of the Earl of Lochmas. I take it you have met my sister, Lady Briana, and my cousin, the Honorable Deirdre McDowell."

Younger than Theo, with burly shoulders and square features framed by burnished bronze hair, the unknown Ives bowed over her hand. "William Ives- Madden, at your service. I believe I've been labeled the guilty party in Cook's departure. I beg your pardon, my lady, and will do all that I can to rectify the situation."

"My word, a Pisces Ives, the world will never be the same." Aster settled against the cushions and studied another of the late marquess's illegitimate sons. They were far more interesting in person than in her charts. "You may remove your animals to the conservatory, where they will be much happier surrounded by earth and sun. I recommend finding a servant to tend them. It is not a job for kitchen staff."

"We haven't staff enough to keep the conservatory warm in winter, my lady. The dogs are trained to use the back doors in the one room that always has people about. But I shall remove them for warmer months," he offered gruffly.

Aster looked from this tweed-and-leather dressed, very masculine Ives to her wide-eyed and fascinated female relations. "His intentions are not honorable. You will steer our guests away from him."

"I will happily leave the respectable ladies to Theo," William agreed with a shrug. "But do not trust Jacques, either." He elbowed the blond, amiable gentleman who had entered with him. "He may seem simple, but he's devious."

Making a dramatic bow, Jacques gestured for the boy to step forward. "And I don't believe you've met Hartley Ives-Weldon."

Dark auburn with a sprinkle of freckles, Hartley bowed formally over Aster's hand. "A pleasure, my lady." He couldn't be much more than ten, but he behaved with more dignity than his elders.

"Ah, this one shows evidence of a mother." Aster vaguely recalled an actress on the marquess's charts but couldn't recall the specifics. And Hartley was only one of a pair of twins if she recalled correctly. She would have to be wary that they didn't attempt to fool her with their appearances.

"Very good. Hartley," she said. "If you and William would begin removing animals from the kitchen, we might have some hope of retaining kitchen staff. Bree, you and Dee see if the staff needs any help in putting together dinner, please. How many of us are there? I will see what I can do about setting up a table."

"There's just us," Jacques said cheerfully. "Dunc eats in his chambers, and Theo has gone out to deal with rioting farmers. Hugh is never to be found. And I'm not simple or devious. I just lack that exhausting Ives ambition."

"You're Aries. That's to be expected." Aster gestured dismissively, focusing on the more important topic with a frisson of fear. "Rioting farmers? Is this an occupational hazard in the country? I don't wish to invite guests if there is any danger."

All three Ives shrugged as if riots were a daily occurrence, like the sun rising at dawn.

"Theo just needs to find the instigators. Foraging for food is a better use of our time," Jacques said cheerfully. "Ladies, if you'll follow us, we'll hold our own private riot in the kitchen."

Aster desperately wanted to follow them. She also wanted to run after Theo and warn him again of the assassination parts in his family sector.

But as usual, she was good for nothing except as a Prophetess of Doom.

Thirteen

SIR, THIS IS TO ADVISE YOU and the other Parson Justasses to make your wills. If your threshing machines are not destroyed directly we shall commence our labours. CAPTAIN SWING

Theo cursed the notorious message carried to their door by a neighbor lad who had been handed it at the tavern. He cursed the bloody-minded farmers who hated change and forced him to ride out in the damp night when he'd rather be at his telescope. He cursed them for obliging him to leave the lovely Lady Azenor to his brothers. And he cursed Duncan for getting himself injured so he didn't have to deal with these bafflewits.

And he cursed even more when Duncan's eldest twin cantered up half way into the village. "What the devil are you doing out here? Shouldn't you be home with your mother?"

"She has a new beau," Hugh said cheerfully. "She says we are to learn to be rich men."

The twins' mother was an actress and the daughter of an actress. They lived in a society between classes, choosing which rules they wished to obey. With the burden of duty weighing on him, Theo admired their freedom.

"I trust that means she wants you to learn to work hard," Theo said dryly. "I don't think it means you are to follow me to the tavern."

"If I do what you do, won't that teach me?" he asked with the aggravating simplicity of a ten-year-old. "I used to follow Father, but he's not much fun anymore."

Devil take it. Of course the twins were accustomed to Duncan telling them what to do. It must be even more confusing for them than it was for Theo to have Duncan living in a sour cave.

"I doubt your father takes you to the tavern. Where's Hartley?"

"He's following William. He likes animals. I don't. Father says I'm the eldest and should learn to run the estate." Hugh darted him a look from beneath an overlong hank of auburn. "I know I can't have a title, so don't lecture."

"The bloody title is nothing but a headache anyway," Theo muttered. "But I can't teach you what I don't know. You should be back at the house eating dinner or irritating your father."

He rode into the inn yard and scanned the lights in the tavern, seeing nothing unusual. But spying a phaeton in front of the stable, his irritation escalated and he swung down despite the lack of activity. "You don't belong in a tavern or around disreputable rogues," he warned his nephew.

"I want to see how you stop a riot. Will you hire men to shoot the farmers?"

"Bloodthirsty ghoul. There will be no shooting on my watch." He didn't have time to fling the boy over his saddle and take him home. Hugh would have to learn the hard way that Theo was a lousy teacher. He had no idea how Dunc would handle the wretched farmers. He just wanted to rid the world of vermin so he could return to his studies.

Of course, the vermin he had his eye on now wasn't a farmer but the person who had driven that phaeton earlier.

Striding into the dim tavern and spotting his drunken sot of a neighbor in a booth as expected, Theo almost forgot the damned farmers and the murderous Captain Swing.

But conscious of his duty and the brat on his heels, Theo approached Samuel, the innkeeper behind the bar, and signaled for his usual ale.

"Who's the instigator this time?" he asked. Duncan had dealt with the Swing rioters last summer. Theo hadn't paid the incident much attention then, but he remembered Samuel as being on Duncan's side.

"Outsiders," Samuel replied, understanding without explanation. He pulled a tankard and glanced at Hugh. "That Pamela's whelp? Is she back in town?"

"My mother is in Oxford," Hugh replied with pompous politeness—a product of repetition since his mother was invariably an object of village curiosity. "I am staying with my father, the marquess of Ashford."

Samuel snorted. "Even the ginger can't hide Ives' arrogance."

Theo thumped the boy's shoulder. "He's teaching me to farm.

Are the outsiders staying here?"

"One or two. The rest..." Samuel glanced toward the drunk in the booth. "They be staying with tenants here and about."

Theo understood the innkeeper's inference—*with Montfort's tenants.*

Lord Henry Montfort owned the land north of Iveston, but it was his lackwit son, Roderick, who lived in the manse. Duncan had told Theo that Roderick had harbored the criminals last summer. He attracted the desperate sort because decent folk wouldn't pay the ridiculous rents he charged for unrepaired cottages and poor farmland.

"Well, look, and if it isn't the milksop and the cub," Roderick chuckled drunkenly from his corner. "What drags you out of your books to see what real men do in the evening?"

Theo was no stranger to the insults for his preference for books over fisticuffs. He placed a warning hand on Hugh's head. "Bullies never grow beyond adolescence," he said loudly, for Montfort's benefit as well as the boy's. "True gentlemen needn't denigrate others to make themselves feel better."

Obviously too drunk or ignorant to grasp the insult, Roderick raised his tankard. "They're burning your fields as we speak. The Ives pedants will have to give up changing the way things are always done and do it like the rest of us, or go broke."

"Or go broke like the rest of you?" Theo asked idly, concealing his alarm. It wouldn't do to ride off in a panic over gossip from a sot. Besides, he had another interest that came first. "Exhausting your fields is how you paid for that phaeton?"

"Won that in a race," Roderick said proudly. "That's how a gentleman does it, not by grubbing in the dirt."

That was all the confirmation he needed.

"Go outside, Hugh," Theo warned in a low voice. Insults rolled off his back, but now that he'd verified the phaeton's ownership, justice was required. "It's about to get ugly in here."

"How am I supposed to learn to be a gentleman?" Hugh asked indignantly. "I'll just stand here and watch along with these other blokes."

Theo was aware that other men watched. If he put his mind to it, he might even know their names. But Montfort was the source of his anger.

Leaving the boy under Samuel's protection, Theo carried his mug over to the booth.

"Now, yer lordship, we don't want no trouble in here," Samuel called.

"No trouble," Theo said, glaring at the fair-haired rogue in the booth. "I just see a grinning toad who needs a lesson. He ran ladies off the road today and nearly destroyed a good team and my coachman by racing that phaeton and leaving them injured in a ditch without even stopping to offer aid. Don't you think that requires a lesson?"

He heard grumbles of assent, and chairs pushing back as some of the cowards ran from trouble.

"I did no such thing," Montfort said, too drunk to see the danger. "Your fancified excuse for a carriage isn't balanced. Told you it wouldn't hold up."

"The carriage isn't at fault when a nodcock forces it into a ditch. And when said nodcock fails to stop and help the injured, he deserves a good horsewhipping. Pity I didn't bring one with me. I don't suppose any of you gentlemen have a whip at hand?" Theo asked, keeping his eyes on the baron's son.

Finally grasping the insult was directed at him, Roderick glared through bleary eyes. "Bookworms don't have the guts to whip a dog," he said scornfully.

"You haven't the wits or the guts to know dogs don't need whipping," Theo snarled, expecting the man to come out fighting.

When Montfort didn't even attempt to come after him, Theo realized the dolt was too drunk to stand. Already frustrated beyond measure to be here instead of where he wanted to be, he grabbed Montfort by the shirt front and dragged him from his seat.

The sot swung wildly, landing a weak blow on Theo's ribs. In disgust, Theo released his grip and let his opponent slide to the floor. Once Roddy was sprawled across the boards, Theo upended his nearly-full tankard over his head. "I'll wait until you can stand before thrashing you properly."

Dirty blond hair dripping, Montfort clenched his fist and scrambled to stand. "Why, you—"

"Upstart?" Theo suggested, walking away. "I can't think of a better epithet at the moment. Come along, Hugh, we need to feed a few farmers."

Montfort staggered in Theo's direction, but Theo merely stepped aside, letting his neighbor fall against a table. "Sorry about the mess, Samuel." He threw a gold coin on the bar. "That should cover the cost of tossing out the rubbish."

Before he could reach the door, horses galloped into the inn yard, accompanied by warning shouts. Gut clenching, Theo stepped outside.

"They're torching the hay shed!" one of Duncan's older tenants yelled. "And marching this way."

Wanting nothing more than his quiet study, Theo dashed for his horse with Hugh on his heels.

If he hadn't dallied with Roderick... If he'd known where to go or which farmer to talk with... But he didn't. And now buildings were burning and men could be hurt.

He didn't personally know the hardworking men in the fields— but he *had* grown up around them. He couldn't believe they'd burn their crops without coming to Duncan with their grievances first.

Of course, if they'd come to Duncan recently... They'd probably been thrown out on their ears. Which was why they were trying to get his attention. And Theo was failing them.

"Ride back to the house," he shouted at Hugh. "Tell them I won't be home soon. And tell your father he'd better hire a steward with a big stick and spine of steel."

"Can't I watch the fire?" the boy called in disappointment.

"No," Theo said firmly. "It will burn out, then there'll just be a lot of drunken shouting. The ladies have probably fixed a nice meal by now. Get something to eat."

As Hugh happily rode off with that thought, Theo realized that Azenor had taught him one thing already—boys could be bribed with food.

ASTER WAS DIRECTING one of the new maids in how to properly remove the plates from the right side of each person at the table when Hartley's sturdier twin rushed into the room, brimming with excitement.

"The farmers are setting fire to the shed! Uncle Theo dumped ale over Mr. Montfort's head."

With a more adult swagger than his twin—who was under the

table with the puppies—Hugh snatched a roll from the buffet and shoved cold ham and cheese between the layers as he talked.

Jacques and William pushed back from the table, and Azenor tried not to panic.

"Surely that's only boasting," she protested. "Why would they burn sheds?"

"Hartley, run up and check Theo's telescopes. Tell us where the fires are," William ordered the twin beneath the table. "Hugh, sit and eat and pretend you're civilized."

"I want to see the telescopes." Aster pushed back from the table without waiting for the new footman to assist her. "Bree, finish directing Sally and James on how to clear the table. Sally, find a plate for Hugh."

"It is nothing to worry yourself over," Jacques said, stopping to offer his arm. "There is always tension when Dunc encloses a field or changes a crop or introduces a machine. Without Ashford riding out to explain, people become anxious."

"I brought my family and servants here," Aster said crisply, hiding her fear and concern. "Torching a shed is not *nothing*. I will not allow my guests to stay if there is danger. Who is this Montfort and what does he have to do with this?"

Limping, she followed the two men up the stairs. Hartley had already raced ahead and disappeared into the upper reaches.

"Montfort is a lazy sot who has naught to do but spend his allowance and watch corn grow." Jacques indicated a dark parlor at the head of the stairs. "There is a telescope in there. Hartley will run up to the roof where he'll have a broader perspective."

Understanding she was holding him back, Aster nodded. "Go, do what you need to do. Please be careful."

"Haven't heard that since my *maman* left for Paris," Jacques said, lingering after Will's departure. "Hartley will show you how to use the glass when he comes down."

At her nod, Jacques strode off as if eager to attend a boxing match or horse race. Their neighbor was not the only one bored with watching corn grow. *Men!* she thought in frustration, finding her way through the salon with only a candle and the last rays of evening. They were all overgrown children believing themselves invincible.

Which meant Lord Theo was doing what? Beating up bullies? Or threatening mobs? She was far better off never marrying and putting herself through this.

Hands behind her back, she peered into the glass eyepiece. It was focused on the stars, of course. She gasped in awe at the wondrous spread of diamonds across the velvet sky that had been invisible to the naked eye. No wonder Lord Theo was fascinated. He had the entire universe at his fingertips.

But hearing the clatter of boots and shouts of men as they ran down the back stairs to the stable, she reluctantly attempted to focus the glass on the earth instead of the heavens.

Hartley joined her long after the horses rode out of the yard. A spaniel trotted happily on his heels and settled across her toe. "The shed is ashes. There are torches in the lane coming from the north," the boy said, adjusting the telescope's position and fiddling with the dials. "The hedges are too high to see much. I suppose I should talk to Father."

Aster prayed she wasn't the harbinger of doom that had brought disaster on them. Surely the three or four generations separating them kept Ives from being close enough to consider them as Family on her chart. She swallowed her fear and tried to remain unruffled for the boy.

"Why don't you take your twin with you? Hugh will know more since he's been out there. Lord Ashford will need you to be his eyes, so don't leave the house unless he tells you to."

Hartley nodded. "I'll tell Hugh. He'll want to be out there otherwise."

She really had no business interfering with how the Ives operated their estate, but her heart went out to these lost boys. Their mother had essentially abandoned them into the care of a man who had too many problems to even look after himself. Really, the faster Theo married, the better off everyone would be.

Unless he married someone like Emilia, who wouldn't notice the boys' existence. Oh dear.

Fourteen

ASTER HAD SPREAD her charts out on a game table in the upper salon by the time Lord Theo and his brothers returned. After determining from the telescope that a raging fire wasn't spreading across the fields and that she couldn't see anything else, she had abandoned watching and turned to the zodiac that spoke to her more clearly. She hadn't realized how terrified she'd been until they returned safely, if soot-covered and unhappy—*this time.*

Her charts had not left her optimistic about the dangers on the horizon—all of them focused on the family sectors of the brothers. It was akin to seeing large rocks balanced precariously above the path they walked. She wished she didn't see these premonitions so clearly.

She glanced up when Lord Theo entered. The others continued on to their chambers. He carried his coat over his arm and stood there in waistcoat and shirtsleeves, his discarded neckcloth leaving his shirt open at the throat. She had to avert her eyes from his exceedingly masculine chest.

"It is late," he said with a weary growl, wiping grime from his perspiring brow. "You should be sleeping. Where is your maid?"

"Aunt Nessie kept me company for a while, but I sent her off to bed." She didn't want to admit—even to herself—that she'd stayed up to see that everyone returned safely. That was what one did for *family*, and these charts were proof enough that joining her disastrous destiny with that of a family who had dozens of knives hanging over their heads would be a very bad idea. She ought to have gone to bed—but she wouldn't have gone to sleep.

He helped her roll up her charts. "Did you find more doom and gloom in our futures?"

"Yes, I'm afraid so, but I also see your soul mate on the horizon," she said guardedly, trying not to feel the hurt forming around her heart.

"Really?" He looked interested. "What does she look like?"

"I can't tell that," she replied in annoyance. "It would be far easier if the planets wrote names across your life line, but they don't. There is a good chance that one of our guests will become your wife."

"If I live long enough?" he asked with a trace of irony. "What disaster do you foresee this time?"

"I do not mean to be a Cassandra." She knew he had every right to be skeptical about her prophecies, but it still irritated that he couldn't accept her warnings now that she'd proved her accuracy. "I cannot live with myself if I do not warn you when danger is in your future."

"Maybe I'll marry someone who will kill me? Or do you think your charts will let us know if the Hall is about to burn down?" he asked wearily.

In the lamp light, his tired smile was still able to turn her lonely heart upside-down. She ought to visit the marquess and have objects thrown at her to end this tendency toward sentiment.

Aster concentrated on tying her scrolls. "Charts are not precise. My intuition sees fire and hatred but not targets. I watched through your telescope to be certain no fields were set ablaze. How did you prevent that?"

"I invited several of our more substantial tenants to help interview stewards," he said, helping her tie the ribbons. "They know I'm useless for their purposes, and they were worried."

"Smart of you, stupid of them to underestimate you."

He halted his ribbon tying and studied her with an interest that made her squirm. "As you yourself have pointed out, I am an absent-minded scientist with my head in the stars. I let them burn down a whole damned shed and half the harvested hay while I was trying to figure out what to do. I have no idea how to interview stewards. They were *not* underestimating me."

Aster sent him a scathing look meant to put him in his place. "You stopped a riot, did you not? Could your brother have done better?"

"Undoubtedly, and before we lost a shed and all its contents. I did not even know half our tenants' names. I lack the patience to spend the rest of my days dealing with troublemakers, so do not make of me something that I am not." He sounded almost angry at her compliment.

Accepting that men did not think as she did, she asked, "What happened to the fire-starters?"

"I told them Montfort was at the tavern, buying ale for all," he said, apparently willing to be distracted. "It won't teach Montfort not to cause trouble, but it gave the hotheads something better to do."

"For now." She gathered the scrolls into her valise, stepping away from the all-too-tempting scent of raw male. "There are parts of your chart I cannot properly understand. I need to study your scientific tracts to see what I am missing in my calculations."

"I think I shall just pick one of your more efficient maids and marry her. At least she might organize the household," he said in resignation. "We are wasting our time on this tea party when we know none of your ladies will possibly suit. Half of them will no doubt run in terror once they meet the hounds and the goats and my brothers."

"Goats?" she asked faintly. Besides sweat, he smelled of smoke and ale, but she took his arm to limp down the corridor to her room. His masculine proximity made her much too aware of what they'd done in the conservatory, and she wished he'd go away. And despite his interesting dishabille, he was a gentleman, and she knew he wouldn't. "What goats?"

"You don't want to know," he asserted with unusual coldness. "And do not think that you've seen all my family. The boys are all out of school for the summer, and after visits with their mothers, will soon fill the house. We don't hold on to women, but the boys are permanent."

"There are a few girls in your charts," she said with indignation. "What do you do with them?" As the Malcolm family librarian, she had become inured to the fact that this branch produced more illegitimate offspring than legitimate. Given Ives intelligence and ambition, it hadn't held them back much in society.

She had deduced that women of low birth chased Ives because they knew, even if they were dishonored, that with the marquess's title and support their positions would be better than before.

She would rather the marquess spent his wealth on providing education for Daphne's factory laborers and Gwenna's orphans than in producing more bastards.

"What would we do with *girls* around here?" Lord Theo asked in surprise. "We can't teach them drawing or etiquette or needlework. They stay with their mothers."

"Where they belong," Aster said dryly. "Charming. I suppose I should be glad that you haven't installed their mothers in the attic or I would never persuade a single lady past the portal."

"Few dare cross the threshold as it is," he said, grimacing. "You are a rare specimen. Unless you can find me a woman as intrepid as yourself, I foresee a future of hysterics, and not the help I need."

"You do not know the right sorts of women," she said in scorn, although her lonely heart cried out for the comfort the gentleman offered and needed. "My friends and family are not so faint of heart. There is a woman perfect for you in your chart. But I am thinking the challenge is too great for any one woman. We need to think about marrying off your brothers as well."

"And while you're at it, will you feed the hungry and bring peace on earth?" he asked, opening her chamber door for her.

She almost laughed at his cynicism. But perhaps that was just nervousness at his proximity.

"I will see you in the morning," he continued without waiting for a reply, "and you can tell me of these Amazons who will run the household, keep the books, terrify rioters, and produce heirs at the same time."

When put like that... Aster winced as the door closed behind her.

She would have to be a magician to produce what his lordship needed.

"I NEED YOU THERE to interview the stewards who have traveled miles looking for this position!" Theo shouted at his boneheaded older brother. "I haven't the faintest clue of what to ask."

"I suggest—*how much do you expect us to pay you and for what*?" Duncan said grumpily, groping at his trousers, apparently in search of the placket so he could put them on straight.

"I'll send your devilish valet back to you. He's about to drive me mad. You'll look all proper and lordly and the stewards will never know the difference." Theo paced up and down his brother's chamber, kicking books and papers and china out of his way.

Duncan had thrown out one of Lady Azenor's maids after she'd dropped the china this morning. In fairness, Dunc's roar for her to leave the damned tray where he could find it had frightened half the household. The maid didn't have a chance.

"You need to look decent to woo a wife. Get used to it. It's not as if he can shave this ugly scar or needs to." Duncan shoved his bandaged leg into the opening he'd found.

"No, you'd rather prove that you can't do what you used to do and bellow the house down. This is an abuse of power, Dunc. You can't force all your duties on me. I've reached my limits." Theo kicked one of his brother's favorite novels and nearly wept, knowing Dunc would never read it again.

Lady Azenor had made him painfully aware of the loss his brother suffered. He wished she hadn't.

"It's about time you tested your limits instead of fiddling your nights away watching the moon. Get out and lock the door behind you." Duncan attempted to put both legs in one trouser hole, realized his error, and swore a mighty oath.

"I warn you, I'm bringing the stewards straight up here unless you come up with a better solution." Theo slammed out, leaving the marquess half-dressed and swearing like a sailor.

Theo bit back his own stream of profanity when he discovered Lady Azenor intrepidly swinging down the hall, using the walking stick as if she'd held it all her life. She brightened at seeing him.

Her smile made him feel ten feet tall and produced the nonsensical need to shelter her from all life's travails. Or at least carry her to a chair so she didn't harm that curvy little ankle. He could probably envelop it with one hand.

"There you are," she said. "The first of your stewards has arrived. I've had Barton put him in the downstairs office. Will that suit?"

"I don't suppose you can give me a list of questions to ask him?" Theo asked gloomily. Stars did not expect anything of him. People inevitably did. Lady Azenor wasn't any better than the rest— probably worse if he gave it any thought.

"I am not a miracle worker. Your farmers should be here soon, shouldn't they? Will they know what to ask?"

She peered up at him as inquisitively as a little wren, but there was nothing wren-like about the lady. Today, she wore what was most likely supposed to be her housecleaning, taskmistress gown. It had no lace or ruffles, but instead of a drab brown or gray, it appeared to be a gleaming bronze that set off her riot of copper curls as if she were some rare metallic object.

And she had made it clear that he could not have her. Nothing like rejection to put a man off his feed.

"The tenants will *listen*. They never talk," he grumbled. "And they'll choose the gaffer who says what pleases them most, and not what's best for all. I'll ask our potential stewards if they know their multiplication tables." Theo offered his arm to help her back downstairs.

"Does your brother have an office up here?" She glanced down the hallway, where, from the sound of it, Dunc's current fit of fury seemed to involve slippers and possibly hounds.

"Next to his chamber," Theo told her. "He turned a sitting room into a library and office. But I won't find anything any more helpful there. Ledgers are meaningless to me. Obviously, I took the wrong sorts of mathematics."

She tapped her good foot and studied the corridor for a moment. Theo watched with interest. He had full confidence in his brains and his achievements, but he had never applied himself to as many different sorts of tasks as this petite whirlwind. He couldn't help but wait with anticipation to see what fantasy emerged from those deliciously rosy lips this time.

"Tie Ashford up, if you must," she said slowly, apparently plotting as she spoke. "Have his valet clean him up. Seat him in a corner of his office near the desk where you'll be sitting. Pull the draperies and don't light any lamps. Provide chairs for your farmers. I will tell the interviewees that you are occupied, until you send word that you are ready, and then I'll send them up here."

"To what purpose?" Theo asked, intrigued despite himself. "The task you've assigned is Sisyphean. Duncan is likely to take off all our heads."

"Knock him unconscious and prop him up then," she said without a qualm. "Just as long as he's awake when we show the stewards up. Give me a minute to think this out. Fetch your valet and hot water and whatever. Ashford is a Scorpio, so he's difficult. Is he involved in any competitions that you know of?"

"Endlessly. He always wins. Or did. That's half his problem now. He can't best anyone while blind."

She offered a smile that would shame the sun. "With a mind like his? Don't be foolish. Is he decent?"

"Not in weeks," Theo said dryly. "Don't you dare go in there."

"Send the valet, please." She wriggled her fingers to signal that he was dismissed.

Theo wanted to wring the lady's pretty little neck when she marched down the hall and knocked on Dunc's door. She had to knock several times before the roar decreased to a level where she could be heard.

Theo leaned against the wall and crossed his arms. She shot him a glare. He waggled his fingers at her as she had at him. She stuck her nose in the air and knocked again.

"Lord Ashford, it is most urgent that I speak with you," she said clearly over the angry mutters from the other side of the door. When she received no reply, she spoke more loudly. "I have received a message from a friend who knows Miss Caldwell. You do not wish me to shout what it says to the world, do you?"

Theo pursed his lips in a silent whistle. The lady was devious beyond any politician or snake oil salesman he'd ever encountered. No way could Duncan deny her entry after being reminded of his ex-fiancée.

Sure enough, the door jerked open. Duncan had managed to don his trousers but not his boots or stockings. And his shirt was still untied. Theo wanted to rush down the hall and grab the lady before the dragon devoured her, but she didn't even scream when Dunc hauled her inside and slammed the door.

Thoroughly improper and beyond outrageous, but she'd done what few others had accomplished these past weeks. She'd made the dragon open his door.

Theo hurried in search of the valet so he could rescue her.

Fifteen

"YOUR FRIEND SAYS that sapskull *Montfort* is courting Margaret?" the marquess bellowed.

Aster glanced nervously at the ceiling, expecting the plaster ornamentation to rain down on her head. The marquess had a reverberating bellow.

"It has something to do with field production?" she said tentatively. It wasn't as if she had any idea if crops or sheep or whatever could be measured, but she was looking for a goal that he would understand—and that would return his interest in farming.

"Roddy doesn't even know what grows in his fields," Ashford said in disgust, fumbling with the ties of his shirt. "Your friend is ill-informed."

"It's not as if I am a farmer who understands this sort of thing," she retorted. "Perhaps this Montfort has a relation who knows what should be grown? It did seem as if there were expectations that his income will exceed yours, which interests Miss Caldwell's father."

Azenor did not *like* to outright lie, but she had learned that the more she knew of the situation, the more accurate her predictions. She had read Ashford's chart—it was littered with danger and earth. She knew exceedingly little about farming. But she understood people. So she fed him what little she knew and let him take it the rest of the way.

"Roddy's father. And Margaret's," the marquess said with disdain, grasping for something on the floor. Apparently not finding it, he flung what appeared to be a dog's toy at the wall. "Two peas in a pod. Where are my boots?"

She found his shoes on a shoe tree and handed those to him. He growled in protest. She moved quietly out of his way in case he chose to throw them.

Really, she could never care for Ashford as she cared for her family, but she could care for him as one does a querulous patient.

Would that be sufficient to prevent the danger in her chart? He really did need her.

Except then all the Ives would be family—which practically spelled Doom and Disaster in capital letters.

"You are saying that Montfort's and Margaret's fathers have some means of improving field production?" she asked with interest.

"If Roderick marries Margaret, their lands would be joined and they could use threshing machines for harvest, as just one small example, especially if they enclosed their fields. They'll reduce costs, tear down those ramshackle cottages, put the tenants in the workhouse, and improve their profits—while starving people who've worked for them for years." He yanked on his shoe rather than flinging it.

"Oh, that doesn't sound good for the tenants. Is that what you've done and why the farmers are rioting?" She hoped that his pulling on shoes was a positive sign.

"We're the largest estate in the shire. The Swingers are just picking on us because the instigators steered them in our direction. I can't believe Margaret would actually let that drunken ass court her." When he couldn't pry the other shoe on properly, he flung the shoehorn against the wall, and slammed his foot in with sheer force.

"Perhaps she has no choice? I don't know the lady. But I must see to training the maids. While you and Lord Theo go talk to the farmers, we'll tidy up this chamber." She hastily backed out of the room before he could locate her voice and use her as a target.

Lord Theo was still leaning against the wall, apparently waiting for her to be heaved bodily from the room. She marched up and pointed at the office. "I'll send footmen to arrange the chairs, shall I? He is almost dressed, but he requires a valet. I'll assume you can manage that much?"

She could swear the silver blue of his eyes laughed as he unfolded from the wall.

"I think I'll keep you," was all Lord Scientist said before he loped off, presumably in pursuit of a valet.

Aster didn't know what he meant by that. She didn't intend to be *kept* by anyone. Irritated, she clumped the stupid walking stick down the stairs in search of footmen. The Ives household had a few, although they seemed to be exceedingly dilatory. She nabbed one slinking down a back corridor and sent him upstairs.

The cook and Mrs. Smith, the portly housekeeper, were waiting for her in the downstairs office, their faces stern and unhappy. Aster sighed and prepared herself for the diatribes to follow. The Ives' servants really were not well trained.

The housekeeper vociferously registered her complaints about Dee and Bree's interference in rearranging the formal rooms for their anticipated guests. The cook demanded the perfect soufflé recipe if he was to prepare meals—but at least he was back on the job.

Aster resigned herself to not charting anyone or anything until the household was organized. That must be her first goal, preparing Iveston Hall for a tea party so she could introduce Lord Theo's prospective mates without them running screaming into the night.

Training a few footmen and maids in the process was an extra benefit, although it had been much easier in her small London household. Here, the house was so large, she tended to lose track of who was doing what.

She sent two maids and a footman up to Ashford's chambers to clear out the ratty carpet and debris. Then she led Mrs. Smith, the Ives' sherry-tippling housekeeper, into the drawing room with Mrs. Barnes, Emilia's lofty London housekeeper, to discuss what needed to be done.

The room was immense, apparently running the length of the medieval hall. A massive stone fireplace heated this area as well as the dining hall. Two huge iron-wheel chandeliers hung over two large sitting areas, with various game tables and side chairs scattered around the edges.

Aster gaped at the two-story walls of framed oil paintings above the wainscoting. The Hall's entire history was probably up there on those walls—coated in centuries of soot.

The footmen had already rolled up the threadbare carpets in the sitting areas under Mrs. Barnes' direction. Aster ordered them to haul the musty, insect-ridden wool to the dustbin, then settled into a grubby wing chair to consider the hodge-podge of furniture.

She studied an odd contraption of rusted metal and wire on the hearth, surrounded by tools of various sorts. "Is that a work of art?" she asked skeptically, nodding at the... *machine?*

The housekeeper shrugged. "Lord Erran tinkers."

Deirdre lifted a stack of musty old cloaks off a once-elegant

Chippendale chair and dropped them to the floor. "We will never have this place ready in less than a fortnight," she said in despair. "The draperies are ready to rot off the windows."

"They've been cleaned regular, they have," Mrs. Smith insisted indignantly. "And so be that carpet. What will go there now, I ask?"

Aster scowled at the lighter square of wood flooring where the carpet had once been. Then she studied the heavy maroon velvet blotting out most of the summer light—except through the moth-eaten holes.

"I'm certain the draperies have been cleaned as they ought," she said to the housekeeper. "But would you like to venture to guess how old they are?"

Mrs. Smith opened her mouth, thought better of speaking, and narrowed her eyes as she studied the ancient fabric. "Before my time," was her reply.

Since she looked to be sixty, Azenor would rather not calculate how old that made them. "What condition is the under-drapery in?"

"Stained with damp and mold," Briana announced, lifting the velvet. "The panes appear to leak and there is rot in the wood."

"His lordship said we was to wait until his lady wife decided what to do with them," Mrs. Smith said stiffly. "This room ain't much used these days."

Except as a receptacle for storing old schoolbooks, game boards, dog bones, and tennis racquets, if she was to judge by the clutter on the furniture that Mrs. Barnes was sorting disdainfully through. She had donned gloves to do so.

"Is there a seamstress in the village?" Aster asked, examining the size of the windows.

"But his lordship—" Mrs. Smith started to say, before catching Aster's pointed stare and shutting up.

"Lord Theophilus expects us to give his guests an idea of what this place could be like. Let us burn the moldering draperies along with the carpet. If there are workmen who can begin work on the panes, call them in. And I'll send for some fabric if we can have the seamstress out immediately." Aster put her aching foot up on a stool and returned to contemplating the bare floor.

Enthusiastic clapping in the doorway behind her forced her to peer over her shoulder. The blond Jacques and bronzed William stood there, hats in hand, looking—and smelling—as if they'd just come in from a bruising ride.

"Could we have the panes in the library repaired as well?" Jacques asked with interest.

"And the leak over the billiard room?" William added.

"Only if you put yourselves in charge. Get bids on the work, compare references, have Lord Theo approve the expenditures. I know my limits, and they extend to two rooms only." Aster studied the floor again, then added reflectively, "Unless you know where carpets of that size can be found in the next week."

The half-brothers studied the large bare spots with frowns.

"Don't suppose painted canvas would do?" Jacques asked.

"Or we could ask at the re-sale houses in London," William suggested. "Carpets take a long time to make, don't they?"

"Exactly," Aster said. "It would take me forever to inquire of all the carpet-makers if they have any ready that might suit, or to buy away one being made for someone else. It is a very large undertaking."

"Beans," Jacques muttered.

"Or Froggy," William added. "Let's measure it."

"Does that mean you know of carpets this large?" she asked in suspicion, since *beans* and *froggy* sounded more like infantile torture than a solution.

"Does it matter what color?" Jacques wrinkled his usually smiling visage into a thoughtful frown.

"I can't order fabric until I know the color. We don't have much time."

"Give us a day to inquire about color," Jacques said. "We should know by then. May take a little longer to haul them down here."

"I'll take bids on your window panes while I'm waiting. I'm counting on you," she warned. "And have your brother Erran remove this contraption outside!"

They saluted and loped off like over-grown puppies after a treat. She hoped they remembered to measure the two sitting areas.

Marrying Lord Theo off to one of her maids might be the easiest of all possible choices, she decided with a sigh of despair.

***

"WHERE DID YOU FIND this string of idiots?" Dunc growled from his dark corner of the study, pouring himself a tumbler of brandy. Apparently, even though he'd learned almost nothing else, he'd learned to *hear* how much liquor he poured into a glass, Theo thought cynically.

The two farmers who had joined them in the steward interviews earlier had given up in boredom and wandered to find their dinners. To Theo's disgust, they hadn't added much to the conversation when they'd been present.

"A little early to start drinking isn't it?" Theo muttered back, sitting at the desk and finishing up the notes he'd taken from the last candidate.

"My head feels like an anvil being pounded by all the demons of hell, and that racket they're making next door isn't helping. If you want me to continue sitting here, making an utter ass of myself, I need fortification."

Aster had sent all her maids and footmen to shovel out the master chambers while Duncan was occupied in the study. Theo hoped to hide on the roof after his brother tried to find his way around the remains later.

"Not one of the men we've interviewed suits your needs?" Theo asked in exasperation. "At least that stuffy one told us where our last steward went."

"Puling coward," Dunc grumbled. "He could have told me he received one of those damned Captain Swing notes."

"I assume his gossip about those threats are the reason we're attracting the dregs of the barrel. It's as if someone *wants* us to fail." Theo sighed and shoved his hand through his hair. "If this is the last of them coming up the stairs now, it's only half the men I invited."

The ensuing knock on the office door wasn't as loud as the earlier ones. At Theo's call to enter, Hugh opened the panel.

"Lady Aster says I'm to sit in on this interview," the boy said a shade too brightly.

"Lady Aster? You get to call her Lady *Aster*?" Theo had spent these last hours concentrating on taking meaningless notes rather than wonder what the lady was doing—while this infant was cozying up to her in his absence. Damn.

"She says that's her fairy name and only people smart enough to believe in fairies are allowed to use it." Without waiting for reply,

Hugh stepped aside for their next prospective steward. "This is Mr. Reuben Browne."

Theo did his best not to gape as a grizzled, stout old soldier lumbered into the room wearing a rough military coat, a crumpled cravat from the last century, and battered leather breeches and boots.

The other stewards he'd interviewed had been younger, educated gentlemen, born to landed families, capable of wielding authority and demanding respect.

This old man had only one arm. Theo cast Hugh a questioning look, but the boy merely grinned and settled into a chair in a corner opposite his father's.

"Mr. Browne, welcome," Theo said uncertainly. Realizing Duncan couldn't see what he was seeing, not knowing how to explain, he merely introduced the stranger to the marquess.

"If you mean to abscond the instant you receive one of those infamous Swinger notes," Duncan snarled, "then you may as well turn and leave right now."

"If you been casting your tenants outta their homes and putting them into the poorhouse with your machines," Mr. Browne retorted, "then I reckon I'll just turn around and go."

Before Duncan could return his injured leg to the floor and wring the man's neck, Mr. Browne continued speaking. "But I took a good look around this past day and you ain't one of them kind."

Theo took a breath of relief. "Go on, Mr. Browne." He was learning to make meaningless noises that gave Duncan time to recover his temper and conjure more infuriating questions.

The old soldier crushed his ancient cap in his one good hand. "I been around long enough to know that there are three things certain in this world: death, taxes, and change. If a man don't learn to bend himself to new things, then he'll get knocked down and rolled over and left in the mud. You've got them new threshing machines, but you also built drainage culverts to open more fields. I reckon you put the labor you saved on the machines to repairing and digging those culverts. Good men ain't got no right to complain about making improvements for the good of all with your profits."

Somewhat pacified, Duncan demanded, "Tell us why you left your last post."

Theo crinkled his brow, trying to puzzle out the reason Duncan wasn't asking about turnips and fallow fields as he had been.

"'Cause I was let go," Browne said without an ounce of defensiveness. "I don't look or sound like them swells that go to meetings to find new ways to cheat the working man. And the new master wanted me to lie to the tenants and consort with other landowners for him. I don't truck much with talk. I'm a man who gets out in the fields and does the work what I'm paid to do."

Uh oh. Theo swallowed and cast a nervous look to Duncan. His brother *needed* someone to attend meetings for him, to talk to the tenants and other landowners. There wasn't any way Duncan could ride into the village as he once had. But this man didn't know Duncan was blind.

When Duncan remained silent, Theo threw out one of the questions his brother had asked repeatedly about field drainage. The answer wasn't any more clear to him than before, but Duncan didn't argue with it. In fact, his brother sat there silently while Theo scoured his notes for other questions. Browne had answers for them all. Whether they were the right answers, he could only assume by Duncan's silence.

A cloud of gloom descended on Theo when he'd finished and Duncan still did not say a word. They needed a steward, dash it all. He'd have to put all the names in a hat and pull one out if the bloody damned marquess didn't speak.

"Thank you, Mr. Browne," Theo said dismissively. "We'll be—"

"I need eyes and ears in the field, Browne," Duncan finally said. "I want you reporting to *me*, not to the other landowners. You don't need to attend meetings. I will. How good are you at reporting production by field?"

"I ain't much at writing it all down in neat little columns," Browne said warily. "But I can tell you to a farthing how much each field earns."

"That's a start, Mr. Browne. Theo, show him to the steward's cottage, see if it's to his liking. Hugh, go with them, please, and report back." Rather than rise from his seat and display his weakness, Duncan sipped his brandy.

Theo didn't feel the relief he'd expected. If Browne couldn't write the figures down in "neat little columns," who would? And he was pretty damned certain there was no way in Hades Duncan would ride into town or anywhere else for discussions over future community-wide improvements.

It looked like they had just hired a one-armed steward who couldn't hoe the fields, keep the books, or wield authority.

The weight of Duncan's thousand responsibilities would break Theo's back. He'd have to give up the stars and study the earth, after all. Or find a wife who could be farmer, maid, bookkeeper, mother, and general of all things household.

Sixteen

ASTER SIGHED in pleasure and stretched her tired limbs in the relaxing heat of the enormous Roman tub while watching one of Nessie's kittens tackle a hanging towel. The warm water lapped at her breasts and soaked the tension from her shoulders. Living alone as she had these last years, she hadn't realized how difficult it would be to deal with so many people at once— while keeping her distance. Unlike Lord Theo, she was unfortunately gregarious by nature.

She sipped from a glass of wine. Candles along the edge of the tub improved her light, and she'd filled the water with fragrant herbs from Emilia's collection. For the first time in a long time, with warm water lapping around her, she was almost at peace with the world. If no one was near, she didn't have to worry how her planets might be affecting them. She breathed deeply as the heat seeped through her.

A pounding at the locked door jarred her from her sensual trance. The kitten hid beneath a cabinet and Aster scowled. "What is it?"

"Lord Theo says as you're to come immediately, my lady," one of the untrained maids said nervously.

"Tell Lord Theo I only work a dozen hours a day, and I'm now off duty," she retorted.

"Yes, my lady."

She could almost hear the girl bob a bad curtsy. She really shouldn't put the child between her and his selfish lordship, but the wind would have to blow off the roof before she could be stirred from this rare pleasure of heated water and fragrance.

Reading one of Lord Theo's pamphlets and mentally calculating whether the addition of Saturn's moons might affect her charts in any way, she jolted from her contemplation at a loud rap rattling the door.

"I am not leaving this bath until the water cools," she told the noisemaker. And she added more hot water to the tub to be certain it did not cool before she finished reading.

"Will's prime spaniel and Hartley have gone missing." His lordship's deep male voice penetrated the wood without shouting. "There are half a dozen dam... dashed carpenters prowling the ground floor. I cannot find the blood...blasted receipt books anywhere. And Will and Jacques are nowhere about to help with anything."

"At least your priorities are straight," she said, refusing to move from her lovely hot suds. "Will told Hartley that his spaniel needed some kind of training. One assumes that's what they're doing. The question becomes—why are you asking me?"

"Because you're the one with all the answers!" His frustration was growing evident. "I need to talk with you."

"No, you don't," she retorted emphatically. She could already feel her muscles tensing at the thought of his lordship's handsome presence. "You are merely looking for someone to share your burdens. You're not paying me enough for that. Whatever the problem, it can wait until tomorrow."

"By which time it could have evolved into a dam... blo... *wretched* disaster!"

With alarm, Aster heard the key turning in the lock. She hastily blew out the candles and grabbed a towel. "Don't you dare come in!"

She might as well shout at the wind. The door opened, and Lord Theo backed in, covering his eyes. He closed the door, keeping the steamy warmth inside.

She flung a wet sponge at him. "Of all the audacious, obnoxious, irresponsible..."

"Yes, yes, and yes," he said impatiently. "But I don't intend to shout my problems through a closed door." He turned off the gas sconce, plunging the room into near-darkness. "There, is that better?"

"No, it is not. I was enjoying the peace and quiet. Unless you're broken and bleeding in three places, you need to remove yourself instantly!" Aster didn't know whether to hunt for her robe or to remain hidden in the tub. Just his presence in the small room forcibly awakened carnal sensations she'd prefer to leave slumbering.

His selfish lordship was the one she'd been trying most to avoid by hiding in here.

In the light from the narrow window, she could see his tall shadow slide down the wall as he took a seat on the tile floor. Even sitting, he looked big and broad-shouldered, probably because she was sunk in the tub and feeling vulnerable. But he exuded an air of sadness.

"I think I *am* broken in three places," he said dejectedly, scratching at the kitten's ears when it emerged from hiding. "Duncan hired a one-armed steward who can barely read or write. I need to start another search for a man to do what he cannot. And I don't fancy a bookkeeping sort will ride out and deal with these Swingers, much less fight with the complaining mine owners, or handle magistrate duties, or propose agricultural bills for parliament. I just had to send a man to Assizes for beating his wife, and I'm not even entirely certain it's against the law."

"Well, it certainly ought to be," Azenor said tartly. "At least you've given his poor wife time to pack her bags and leave. Although she probably has nowhere to go. Forget agricultural bills. We need someone proposing legislation that protects the weak and innocent."

He snorted. "And I'm just the man for that. I'd have to take one of Dunc's pocket boroughs, and no matter how much I bribed the voters, I'd still lose because I can't say what people want to hear. I might have the responsibilities of his position, but I lack the legal power or the finesse to do anything. And it's not as if I have any interest in harvests or tenants."

"Did you just come in here to complain?" she asked. "Because I can return complaint for complaint, if that's all you need."

"No, I need someone to *listen*. I'm no good at thinking these things through on my own. Give me a good mathematical challenge, and I can whip up an answer in instants. Ask me about the gravitational pull of Mars, and I can offer an informative treatise. I can most probably do so in Latin and Greek, if requested. But I cannot tell you how many servants we employ or where my brothers spend their time."

"That's a lie." Aster used her toe to let in more hot water. The tub would soon overflow, or she would wrinkle into a prune, but shamefully, she was rather enjoying this intimate interlude. Obviously, she was a wanton. Her nipples were pearling up at just the sound of his voice.

"You knew where to look for the marquess when he was injured," she continued. "You knew where to go when you heard about the rioters. You can't expect to know where Jacques and Will spend their time if they are only here occasionally. They're grown men and you shouldn't need to track them."

"And Hugh and Hartley?" he asked, sounding angrier. "They're just boys. Someone should know where they are. As you've said yourself, we're surrounded by danger. They shouldn't be roaming alone."

Aster sank deeper. "Don't bring me into this. I live far from my family for a reason. Do you have any idea how difficult it is to stay away from Dee and Bree while knowing what a menace this household is to them? Your nephews need a tutor or someone to watch over them. Dee and Bree are like your brothers... adults. We cannot lock them in towers. That never ends well."

"We live with peril every day of our lives," he said, still sounding angry. The kitten scampered back into hiding. "You cannot simply predict danger, then hide in a cave and pretend that will keep everyone safe. Montfort would have driven the coach off the road whether or not you were in it. Your sister and cousin could fall down wells if they were on the other end of the world. You have nothing to do with their safety."

"You cannot understand how our stars cross," she said impatiently. "I don't intend to explain myself again. Now go so I may dress and return to my room. This is totally improper."

"Not if no one knows about it," he argued. "We're adults. We make our own choices."

Aster wished she had another sponge to fling. "And I've made mine. Get out or I'll leave in the morning."

"If I make you hate me, will you stay?" he asked, pushing his way back up the wall.

He didn't give her time to answer that idiotic question. He slipped out, leaving the room much colder than she liked.

ASTER SPENT the night debating whether or not she should leave Iveston Hall, but the next morning, she dressed and went down to breakfast as if nothing had happened. She couldn't even explain to herself why she chose to stay, despite his lordship's completely inappropriate behavior.

Or perhaps because of it—because she had felt his loneliness in the same way she felt her own, ached with his need in the same way as her own.

It was an impossible situation, so she turned her mind to the tasks that had brought her here in the first place. Iveston Hall could hire the servants she trained, and for the sake of their livelihoods, she stayed on. Or so she told herself.

By the end of the first week, she had employed men to repair the windows in the public rooms. William and Jacques returned with two enormous blue-and-cream Axminster carpets that fit almost perfectly in the withdrawing room. She hid some minor stains and damage in the wool with furniture, then ordered simple cream muslin and blue taffeta for the windows. The draperies were not as elegant as the heavy velvet, but on a summer's day, they would appear light and airy and prevent the rooms from being oppressive.

The new maids learned from the two housekeepers how to scrub and wax the wooden floors and polish the elegant old furniture, some of it obviously from Queen Anne's time. Aster appreciated the gracious curved elegance of that earlier period. Iveston Hall was a drastically different environment from her exotic townhouse.

By keeping William and Jacques running back and forth to London, she distanced them from Bree and Dee, who were cheerfully reading their way through the enormous library in their spare time. Aster felt guilty for not doing the same. As the Malcolm librarian, she really should be searching for more old journals from her ancestors.

While her sister and cousin were occupied in the library, she was reading Theo's astronomical texts and pelting him with questions. She avoided the bathing room at hours when he roamed the halls. Only, every time she settled in the newly cleaned withdrawing room with a fire, a book, and her charts, he tracked her down.

She didn't precisely feel *safe* in the same room with him as he prowled the floor and expressed his frustration about the battles he'd lost and won that day, but the space was larger and less intimate than a bathing room. At least, she was dressed.

On this particular evening, she hit him with her major concern the moment he entered. The lanky scientist was looking wonderfully disheveled with his hair falling on his brow and his coat unbuttoned again, but he listened when she asked, "These objects the Astronomical Society calls Ceres and Pallas... are they planets?"

She had been nearly shaking in panic since she'd read the treatise. Her charts were based on the teachings of the ancients and the lessons from her ancestors. It had taken the better part of her life to update them for each new birth in the family. She'd found Arabic scholars to help her understand what she already knew, but she had only just begun to explore the new world of astronomy.

Until now, she really hadn't had access to scientific discoveries. Those were a man's world, and they did not share with women. She had not understood how astronomy might affect astrology.

It had never occurred to her that telescopes might find new planets! Such a discovery would throw her charts completely out of order. She'd have to consult with experts beyond her acquaintance.

Everything she'd done could be *wrong*.

"Herschel calls them asteroids," Lord Theo said with a shrug, as if he didn't discuss something momentous enough to destroy everything she knew. "There is some argument that Ceres is large enough to be a planet."

He took the pamphlet she waved at him to thumb through it to refresh his memory. "Our calculations indicate there should be a planet between Mars and Jupiter, but we've not found anything larger than Ceres." He handed back the pamphlet.

"Someday, I would like to see them through your telescope," she said, biting back a relieved sigh. She charted *large* heavenly bodies, not minor ones. So far. "I need to understand if they might affect the pattern of the other planets. It's very unsettling knowing there might be more out there than we know about."

"It's *exciting*," he countered. "Just think of the possibilities! Someday man might sail from planet to planet. There could be minerals out there that can cure disease! Once the clouds clear, I'll be happy to show you."

Aster imagined standing in the dark salon with Lord Theo behind her, holding her as he taught her to use the eyepiece... A ripple of excitement warned that was the wrong path to take.

"So, the new steward is settling in?" she asked, hastily changing the subject.

"With a wife, two daughters, and a grandson," he said with a sigh, pacing. "More responsibilities. They'll need transportation to church on Sundays. And they're inquiring about schools."

"But the marquess is speaking with him?" Aster set aside her reading and admired his lordship's prowling masculinity. She rather enjoyed the pretense that she belonged here and might do something about schools and church. She leaned over and stroked one of the brown-spotted spaniels lying at her feet and wished for her cats. Nessie's kittens were lovely but couldn't be trusted out of their room.

"Dunc sits like an emperor on his throne and interrogates the poor man every evening, if that counts. But it's an improvement." Lord Theo wheeled round to face her. "You've accomplished wonders in a week. Where did these carpets come from?"

"I am not precisely certain," she admitted, admiring the thick wool rather than let him know she'd been watching him. "It seemed to involve individuals named Froggy and Beans, and you are to thank William and Jacques for their aid."

"Repairing the windows in the library should be thanks enough," he grumbled, pausing to examine the newly sealed panes in here. "The plumbing in the billiard room will require a new ceiling. You are the one who inspired them to act on their own, so my heartfelt gratitude for that."

"Your new wife may wish to completely redecorate," she warned. "I have only provided temporary solutions."

He crossed the room and placed his hands on the chair arms on either side of her, trapping her in her seat. "Marry me, and you can paint the walls crimson, if you like."

Taken aback—as much by his proximity as his demand—Aster didn't know how to respond. The delicious scent of his shaving soap had her breathing too fast. Muscled arms so close to her breasts didn't scare her so much as excite her. And his lips, his lovely, sensual lips—

Covered hers without warning. Aster closed her eyes and absorbed the bliss of heated, *personal* contact. Before she could shake free of the spell, Lord Theo groaned at her eager response, grabbed her arms, and hauled her to her feet. His kiss did not break for a moment, but deepened, until she thought she floated on air.

He wrapped his arms around her, pressing her tight against hard masculine muscles. And appallingly, rather than push him away, she caught his lapels and kissed him back, kissed him as if he were the last man on earth and everything she desired. Her lips tingled and softened, and his curved to take her in as if she were a luscious fruit.

Then he invaded her open mouth with his tongue in a carnal demand that even she understood—and succumbed to. She couldn't inhale enough of his masculine scent, the rough brush of his whiskers, the hard arms holding her. She wanted this so very badly...

He lowered his hand from her waist to her bottom, and she nearly swooned from pleasure. *This* was why women married.

And why she could not.

She struggled to stop. She needed to push away. But his kiss— his kiss sent desire to parts she hadn't known existed. She needed to explore this amazing universe of sensation he opened to her. His hand cupped her buttock and squeezed in acknowledgment of their shared path to knowledge.

The spaniel barked a warning.

Aster hastily shoved away. Theo reluctantly let her. A dark blur raced across the new carpet—too small to be even the smallest puppy.

Behind the blur raced one of Great-Aunt Nessie's kittens. And the hound puppies. And Bree. And Jacques—all shouting and wielding nets and various instruments of capture.

Aster grabbed the paper she'd been reading earlier. Flustered and overheated, she pushed a straying curl from her eyes.

"No," she said to herself as much as to Theo. "No, no, and no. It is impossible."

He narrowed his eyes at her, and she saw nothing resembling resignation in his expression. But he swung on the anarchy, grabbed a net from Jacques, and brought it down over his brother's head in an immature fit of frustration.

Jacques shouted and swung wildly at his brother.

Before two grown men could end up rolling on the floor in fisticuffs, Aster bent and grabbed the kitten racing for her skirts. "Bree, upstairs. Let Lord Theo chase the rats."

Just like that, she'd remembered her place. What Lord Theo wanted was not just a general for his undisciplined household. It had a great deal to do with creating heirs—and she did not dare have children. Not until the planets realigned or the universe exploded.

He had his soul mate waiting for him out there—and it couldn't be her.

Holding her head up so no one could see her tears, she marched out, clutching the howling cat, leaving Lord Theo to the chaos of his home.

Seventeen

THE DAY OF THE FETE dawned cloudy—to suit Theo's mood. Mr. Browne, the new steward, arrived with a list of tenant complaints that began with the wet weather ruining their cottage gardens.

Theo wondered what they expected him to do about the rain—build glass houses? And then he began pondering the expansion of his small glass manufactory to include sheets of glass that might protect plants from the elements more cheaply than a conservatory.

He lost interest in the tenant complaints and began calculating the type of glass needed and was deep into specifications when the vicar and local squire arrived. To his irritation, they demanded that he attend some fete event that Duncan had promised to officiate—back in the day when he was still appearing in public.

"Perhaps you ought to ask Montfort to do that," Theo suggested maliciously, rubbing his brow to gather his scattered thoughts. He didn't *do* public occasions. He had no ability to demonstrate bonhomie and slap people on the back.

"They're expecting the marquess," the vicar insisted. "It's a rare honor for the village folk to have his lordship in their midst. To them, you are even more exceptional. It's not as if they see you in attendance at church."

Ah, retribution. Theo understood the concept. He'd generally punched the nose of anyone attempting to get even with him, but that had been back in school. These were men of authority, and he respected them, most of the time. If they meant to get even with him for neglecting the church, he couldn't very well punch them in the nose.

"I don't suppose I could read them a lecture on how the moon phases affect the tides and possibly the weather?" Theo asked without hope.

"Just hand out the ribbons," the squire said. "You'll do fine."

"What time?" he asked in weariness, consulting his pocket watch. The tea party was still half a day away.

"At noon," the squire said in satisfaction. A portly man who'd raised his children and now had time to interfere in all things related to the village, the squire folded his hands over his ample belly. "If you are to act in your brother's place since his tragic accident, we must introduce you around."

Theo wondered what gossip rampaged that they were already considering Duncan out of the picture, but he wasn't interested in encouraging the conversation. "We are expecting guests, but I shall be there at noon, as promised."

After their elders left, Hugh and Hartley hurtled into the study with two spaniels and a hound on their heels. "May we go to the village?" they asked in unison.

Theo raised his eyebrows in surprise. "Since when do you ask permission?"

"Lady Aster said we must, so you know where we are. They're to have an archery contest and a sack race and they'll have Bath buns and sausages," both boys shouted excitedly, their various choices of fun intertwining into one whole.

Theo had a vague recollection of making himself sick by stuffing a quantity of fete food down his gullet, then rolling down hills in some mutant form of racing. He supposed he could hope the twins would considerately heave into the bushes before returning home.

He removed some coins from a drawer and handed them over to the boys. Remembering Lady Azenor's words, he warned, "Do not interrupt the ladies' party this afternoon unless you are bleeding and broken in three places, understood?"

They cheered and ran out without making any promises. He tried to remember if he'd had tutors or anyone with him when he and his brothers had run wild at that age, but he couldn't recall any. He'd trust that the squire or vicar or someone would see they didn't cause too much trouble.

By noon, he'd worked his way through stacks of invoices and ledgers and was almost ready for a walk in the fresh air to clear his muddled brainpan. About the only person in existence who had not crossed his threshold was the one he most wanted to see... Lady Azenor.

But after he'd committed the mortal sin of kissing her until they were both embarrassingly hot and bothered, and asking her to marry him, she'd disappeared. He ought to resent her rejection, but it only made him more determined.

He prayed she had not left for home as she'd threatened earlier. He was reasonably certain if there was any perfect match in his stars, it was the annoying little general, not some unknown stranger.

She'd asked him about *asteroids*—then listened to his reply without yawning. Even living in his lonely outpost, he recognized that a woman like that was rare—even if she did believe in illogical superstition.

In desperate circumstances, he could overlook a little madness.

After traversing all the main rooms in hopes of seeing the lady, Theo headed out into the damp wind. The twins had said she was about. He would have to wait for the party.

Hoping to hasten the tedious duties ahead, he rode his horse into the village. Mobs of people roamed the square, chatting and laughing and eating unpalatable food. To his surprise, there were a surprising number of fancy London carriages lined up along the church grounds. The lady's guests were apparently as intrepid as she to brave the weather. He hitched his gelding to a post and hurried toward the tent where the judging was usually held.

It hadn't occurred to him to dress for the occasion until Lady Azenor intercepted his path by holding up her dainty gloved hand. She was garbed in filmy blue frippery from the fabric holding down her enormous straw hat—hiding her bountiful curls—to the frills at her bodice concealing her delightful bosom, and even at her hem, covering her neat ankles. He hated that gown.

She glanced disapprovingly at his untied cravat. "Your guests are here. They are gathering in the tent to watch the cow judging, along with everyone else. Where was your valet this morning?"

"Hiding." Theo hastily twisted the wrinkled—and probably spotted—linen into some semblance of order. "All the ladies are here already?"

"Of course they are! We invited them to attend the fete." She buttoned his waistcoat while he fumbled with the linen. "You do own a hat, do you not?"

"Not one as ugly as yours," he countered, having already gathered that the broad brim made it impossible to tease her with more kisses. "No time to return for it. I take it I am late."

"Is there a reason your valet is hiding?" She stepped back so he could finish his buttons. When he didn't immediately fasten his frock coat, she tugged it impatiently.

He really shouldn't like her fussing so much. "Jones? I am not accustomed to anyone caring what I wear, hence I am an insult to his profession, and Dunc threw a shoe at him. He'll probably go missing shortly. Want to find another old soldier to polish my shoes?" He finished buttoning and yanked a few wrinkles out of the fabric.

"My uncle was the one who recommended Mr. Browne. Our family has a bad habit of rescuing good people from the workhouse. Uncle Calum is quite pleased that the marquess had the exceptional good taste to hire a hardworking man, even if he has only one arm."

"Remind me to look into your family before they start sending prostitutes to tend the nursery," he said dryly. "You did say your father was an earl and not a bishop, didn't you?"

Unoffended by his language, she stepped back to admire her handiwork. "My father is a Scots earl who grew up in India—not precisely your traditional English sort. The uncle in question is his younger brother, who manages the family mining interests and what little farming is done on the estate. I believe Mr. Browne served in a regiment with him at one time."

Theo rewarded himself with the pleasure of placing a hand at her back, just above the supple sway of her hips as they hurried toward the tent. Fat drops of rain began to splash the already muddy grounds. "I don't know one cow from another. I trust all I'm expected to do is hand out ribbons."

"And look like a marquess," she said in a dry tone he did not mistake.

"My boots are polished to a fine shine," he said. "Who can ask for anything more?"

"I dislike to mention this—but your fine shine has acquired a distinct odor. I wouldn't look too closely if I were you. This *is* a cow pasture, after all."

Flashing him a smile that had the power to bowl him over had she not just grounded him in reality, the lady hurried into the milling crowd inside the tent, leaving him on his own.

Amused, aroused, and irritated, all at the same time, Theo hastened to shake the hands of the dignitaries waiting for him.

As chairman for the fete, Margaret was on the dais as well. Even though Theo was perfectly aware that she had once hoped to stand up here in the marquess's reflected glory, he scowled and took the far side of the platform from her.

***

ASTER CIRCLED among her friends, welcoming them, giving them directions to the Hall, admiring frippery—while keeping the corner of her eye on Lord Theo on the ceremonial platform. She had already learned the dark-haired sylph on the dais wearing a pleasant smile and a London gown was the woman who had been affianced to Lord Ashcroft. She should have made more effort to discover the lady's birthdate. In person, Miss Caldwell didn't seem as unlikable as Aster had expected her to be.

A roped-off section in front of the dais separated animals from the crowd, but rough men laying wagers on the contestants pushed and jostled the ropes. Always wary of potential disaster, Aster watched and stayed to the rear of the tent.

Having spent most of her growing-up years in the Edinburgh residences of her mother and father, she had very little experience with country fetes. She'd attended a few church festivals where the women baked and knitted and showed off their handiworks, but that didn't involve smelly sheep and cows in a tent. If it weren't for watching hatless Lord Theo awkwardly hand out ribbons and shake hands, she'd make her excuses and head back to the house.

Realizing her heart raced a little too fast while watching his lordship, Aster pasted on a smile and began edging toward the exit. She patted hands and reassured everyone they were welcome to arrive at the Hall whenever they were ready.

As she reached the tent entrance, a loud crack of thunder preceded a precipitous cloudburst of rain, and she groaned in dismay. A gust of wind caught the canvas overhead, and the crowd glanced anxiously at the swaying tent poles. But warm and dry, most people returned to watching the highlight of the fete—although Aster assumed it was the presence of the rarified aristocrats providing the entertainment, not the cows.

Hoping this was just a shower, Aster waited at the exit for a chance to run for the covered carriage she'd had the wisdom to order earlier.

Outside, fete attendees raced for the church or their own homes. She watched the twins roll under a farm cart, still devouring their sausages as if they were starved.

Inside, the nervous animals lowed and bleated. The humidity increased the stench, and she almost wished she dared brave the rain to escape. At least her family was back at the Hall, so her presence wasn't endangering them.

A streak of lightning followed immediately by another loud clap of thunder warned the storm was directly overhead. Aster turned worriedly to check on the proceedings on the temporary raised platform where Lord Theo and the other dignitaries continued handing out ribbons.

As she watched, a fistfight among the gamblers broke out near the rope. The crowd shuffled out of the way. The animals shifted, and Miss Caldwell looked uneasy, holding out her hand to steady herself on the nearest male arm, which happened to be Lord Theo's. How had she worked her way to that side of the dais?

Rather than comfort the nervous lady, the ungentlemanly astronomer leaped off the platform to break up the combatants. Aster rolled her eyes at this typical Ives behavior, but admittedly, stopping the fight seemed smarter than escorting a fainting female. He *had* said he was done with hysterical women.

She admired the muscular strength of Lord Theo's punch that laid flat one of the irate gamblers who swung at him. With the swiftness of expertise, his lordship shoved aside a blow from another swinging fist and popped his assailant's nose until it bled scarlet. Apparently living in a brawling family taught one boxing skills.

Pushed to their limits by the yelling and shoving, the cows abruptly broke free of their enclosure. With bawling *moo's*, they yanked on ropes and scattered sheep.

Frightened, the entire herd of animals fled in every direction— including into the makeshift platform. As one large steer smashed into a prop holding it up, the whole deck listed to one side. The no longer dignified dignitaries slid sideways into the trampled filth.

Appalled, Aster covered her mouth with her palm as Miss Caldwell and her fancy gown hit the mud along with the vicar and squire. She was pretty certain the lady's screams were more furious than terrified.

She searched for Theo in the melee of muddied farmers and gentlemen flinging punches below the collapsing platform. To her relief, she spotted him rising from the mayhem, shaking the drunken gamblers by the back of their coats.

That's when the other half of the herd burst through the ropes in his direction—and straight at the tent pole.

Aster's screams joined those of all their guests and the villagers.

TEMPER ROILING, Theo dropped the drunkards and grabbed the tent pole. Cows and sheep milled and trampled the crowd—including his lady guests—driving them into the storm. The wind tossed the soaked canvas, and rain poured underneath, turning the trampled grass to a sea of mud.

So much for his polished boots.

With despair, Theo watched Lady Aster open her ugly umbrella and hasten her friends to a waiting carriage. She no doubt blamed her damned stars for mad cows and Englishmen. The rest of her guests would just have hysterics and leave.

He was almost convinced his own planets were crashing from the heavens, telling him marriage wasn't in his cards, that he'd be forever alone. He had been fine with that when all he knew was the stars, but now that he'd been burdened with the weight of the world, he understood that he'd only been half living.

One sturdy lady in silk and lace dared the trampled cow pen to pet a few animals and calm them down. Remembering his vow to marry any woman who could help him with his hated chores, Theo tried to memorize her features so he might pay attention to her should she survive the storm.

She smiled at him but didn't attempt to push through the herd to help him hold the pole steady. He couldn't blame her there. Besides, he supposed ladies didn't speak to gentlemen to whom they'd not been introduced. He couldn't remember being introduced to her anyway.

The storm blew off as hastily as it had arrived. The tent pole sagged from the weight of the dripping canvas and the sloppy mud, but the farmers were leading out the last of the cows. Lady Azenor had apparently rescued her friends. And the rest of the crowd had dissipated.

Theo looked for the lady who had petted cows but she was nowhere about.

Envisioning a lonely future of miserable village fetes, rioting farmers, and a servant-less household, Theo slopped through mud to his horse, wondering if it was too late to run off to Africa. He shook his head in disbelief as his soaked nephew ran up—carrying an umbrella.

"Lady Aster sent the carriage in case it's still raining," Hugh announced, handing him the umbrella. "She says you're to go in the back way and change first." He fretted at his lip as they walked, apparently attempting to remember all his instructions.

She hadn't run away, taking all her guests with her?

"Oh, and she says thank you for being a hero and holding up the tent and that she'll be certain all the ladies know how brave and strong you are," Hugh finished triumphantly. "Although I think any of us could have held a tent pole."

How did the damned woman do it? She had air for brains if she thought he was a hero or she was the impetus for catastrophe, but she still miraculously held the damned tea party in her dainty hands. He was almost ready to believe in magic.

Theo ruffled the boy's hair. "Go try it and see what happens when the next storm blows through."

"Maybe next year." He ran off toward the merchants closing up their food carts.

A hero. The lady thought he, the socially inept bookworm, was a hero.

Or a sapskull who would believe her flattery—the lady did tend to embroider the truth upon occasion.

In either case, he knew his duty. If she'd gathered the party, he had to attend and do his damndest to choose a wife.

Africa was looking more promising. What would the stars look like down there?

Eighteen

STANDING IN THE REFURBISHED drawing room, surrounded by elegant guests waiting for their host, Aster felt her smile falter at the introduction of still another Ives gentleman—who wasn't Theo—into the party. This gentleman brought two small children.

Apparently Iveston had few footmen guarding the doors because the household welcomed anyone at any time. She refrained from rolling her eyes at this insight.

Her female guests eagerly assessed the handsome older Ives standing in the entrance—they were there because they were interested in marriage, after all. And admittedly, the curly-haired tots were adorable.

Uninterested in acquiring a husband, Aster more pragmatically checked for a wife, a nanny, or a nursemaid to handle the children clinging to the newcomer's boots—but of course, there was none. Ives simply did not keep women about. She was starting to accept their peculiarity.

Distinguished, with just a touch of silver threading his black hair, the uninvited guest smiled deprecatingly as Aster broke free from her guests to greet him.

"My apologies for interrupting Theo's tea party, but the nanny quit, and I've an important appointment in Brighton on the day after tomorrow. I was hoping there would be a maid who could look after the twins for a few days."

Aster opened her mouth but words failed to emerge. After the muddy fete fiasco, she'd just spent the last hour frantically preventing her guests from fleeing to the city. She had instructed maids and housekeepers in the fine art of cleaning silks, drying shawls, and scrubbing slippers so her guests could converse in comfort. And now he wanted a *nanny*?

She didn't even know who he was!

As if summoned by her distress, Jacques materialized at her

side. "Pascoe! Come to look over the bride selection? Lady Azenor has provided some prime choices. I might even consider the wedded state, if they weren't all smarter than me."

Aster didn't believe in having vapors, but she thought she might acquire the talent if she must deal with Ives impropriety for much longer. It seemed far simpler than instructing the heathens on basic etiquette.

Rather than introduce herself, she crouched down to take small hats from the silent, wide-eyed children. "Do you like biscuits?" she asked.

At their eager nods, she summoned one of her new footmen to lead them to the kitchen. Theo's younger brother Erran sauntered up to smack the newcomer on the back in male greeting. More elegantly dressed than any of the other brothers she'd met, Erran had an odd habit of not speaking. He stayed true to form now.

Having caught her breath and recovered some of her equilibrium, she rose to the occasion. With the men looking on her in bemusement, she held out her hand to the stranger. In her haughtiest teacher tones, she announced, "I am Lady Azenor Dougall, daughter of the earl of Lochmas. Lord Theophilus asked me to hostess this party for him. And *you* are?" she prompted when no one seemed inclined to do more than gawk.

"Our Uncle Pascoe Ives," Jacques hurried to explain. "He exports and does something official in government."

Ah, another one of the illegitimate branches. She recognized the name.

Mr. Ives bowed over her hand. "My pleasure, my lady. I've heard much about you. I don't suppose you produce nannies by magic?"

Sigh, another reference to her witchy ancestry. What was it with these rude men?

Thankfully, Lord Theo *finally* descended the front stairs—at a dangerously masculine clip—before she had time to compose a retort. Theo's hair was still damp, but he'd apparently located his valet. His brown muffler was precisely tucked into his chocolate brown coat, which fit impeccably to emphasize his naturally broad shoulders and slim hips.

Aster thought her eyes would roll back in her head at sight of the tight-fitting buff trousers accentuated by his high-waisted frock coat and gold waistcoat. She had to forcibly drag her gaze down to inspect his polished black pumps, complete with small spurs. He was appropriately dressed for an informal country afternoon in a manner that would make any red-blooded woman swoon.

While she wondered if one could recommend valets for medals, the men were tossing greetings over her head. And the ladies in the drawing room had quit any pretense of sipping tea and were riveted by the spectacle of so many Ives males gathered in one place.

Taking a deep breath to steady herself, Aster led the gentlemen into the salon, offering tea and introductions. Dr. Joseph was already there, along with one or two other gentlemen whom Theo had suggested. Congratulating herself on averting the disaster the storm had almost wreaked, Aster separated Theo from the herd so he might meet his prospective brides. She simply wouldn't think about *nannies*. That wasn't part of the task at hand. She must stay away from children at all cost.

"There was a stout female wearing something green," Theo whispered. "She petted the cows and didn't run screaming. Which one is she?"

"Besides my Aunt Nessie?" she asked in exasperation, gesturing at her aunt, garbed in green stripes, sitting beside the fire, gossiping with the other companions.

"Half a dozen guests are wearing green, including me, and I don't recognize *stout*." Probably because she herself wasn't of the graceful slenderness of women like her cousin Emilia. Once upon a time she had fretted over her looks, but now that she knew she wasn't destined to marry, her shape seemed no longer relevant.

Aster gestured at a woman casting them interested glances. "Elizabeth might be cow-witted enough to pet a rampaging wild animal."

"Cows are placid beasts, not wild animals. And she seemed to be calming them down, which seemed like a better reaction than screaming." He shot her a pointed look.

Aster shrugged off his disapproval. "I scream when people are stampeded or I am in jeopardy of being buried alive in a collapsing tent. If Hugh did not tell you, you are my hero for averting *that* disaster." She led him toward Elizabeth, a lovely young woman with big eyes and a gorgeous complexion, if not a stylishly skinny figure. "I am not accustomed to rustic pursuits."

"I'd rather not be," he said grimly. "Cows are Dunc's interest, not mine."

He smiled and bowed as Aster introduced him. "Miss Warrington's home is near Oxford," she continued after the introductions. "She is an animal lover who has provided me with some of my lovely kitties."

Aster discovered she was gritting her teeth and tried to smile as if she were actually pleased that Lord Theo had finally expressed an interest in a more suitable candidate.

"The cowth were motht lovely, milord," Miss Warrington simpered, batting her lashes. "My father raitheth pigth."

It was at that disastrous moment, as Theo struggled to suppress his horror, that Aster recognized the error of their ways. Lord Theo might claim he'd marry any Friday-faced female who could help him with his duties, but the intellectual scientist had failed to mention that he really did not wish to spend his life discussing farm animals. And she had learned that despite his social unease, he enjoyed articulate conversation, which even she must admit, was not easy with Miss Warrington, whose affected lisp intensified with nervousness.

What he *needed* and what he *wanted* were of opposing qualities.

Daunted by the discovery, Aster searched the room for someone who might better suit his conflicting needs. Her cousin Emilia had arrived a little while ago and was now talking animatedly to Theo's impoverished—mute—lawyer brother. Emilia was an excellent conversationalist—when she wasn't buried in her studies. But she had even less interest in cows and tenants than Aster.

Deirdre was already affianced. Briana... was simply too young and effervescent. Theo and his burdens would crush her happy nature. Surely they must have older guests who were articulate. Desperately, Aster began counting through them for the most suitable....

Until she saw Aunt Nessie petting her kitten by the fire. Theo's aging basset had taken its favorite place on the hearth, and Aster's lungs quit functioning. She held a hand to her chest and tried to catch her breath and not panic.

Always on the alert for catastrophe, she recognized the potential straightaway. She had foolishly involved too many of her family in this occasion and allowed them too close to her. What on earth had she been thinking?

She couldn't leave. She had to send her family away before the roof caved in. Surely, Bree and Dee would understand. They had been willing to stay away from the fete. Emilia... would have to decide for herself. Her cousin really did need a husband.

First, she must deal with the imminent disaster of Nessie and the kitten. Leaving Theo looking lost and harassed, she hurried across the enormous medieval hall...

But not in time. A squeal of toddler excitement echoed through the door of the dining room on the east side where the buffet was set up.

Boyish laughter and puppy yips resounded from the corridor through the north door.

By the fire, the kitten tensed in Nessie's lap. The hound looked up warily.

Aster couldn't divide herself into three pieces and rush three different directions.

In their slightly damp and bedraggled silks and laces, her guests appeared oblivious to impending pandemonium. They were chattering with handsome, eligible gentlemen, and sipping excellent tea. They were enjoying the feast produced by a happy cook—who had been assured his meal would inspire a new mistress to organize the household. Even the servants were praying for Theo to find a wife and return stability to a home that had been upended by the marquess's tragedy.

And the whole charade was about to descend into the usual Ives anarchy that would drive their elegant guests screaming from the Hall, never to return. It only needed goats.

Aster swallowed her panic and acted quickly. She snatched the anxious kitten from Nessie's lap just as two pairs of twins raced in two separate doors, hands full of food, chasing after escaping spaniels and puppies—and a tiny *goat*. At least, Aster thought it was a goat as she clutched the terrified kitten and froze in horror with utterly no idea how to halt a herd of rampaging creatures.

The aging basset howled a protest at the intrusion on his private domain and trampled the frilly hem of Aster's gown.

Locating this new source of amusement, the other dogs

instantly raced toward the fire and the basset....

And Aster. And the kitten.

THEO WATCHED in abject dismay as the polite party exploded with the force of a celestial supernova—playing out his worst nightmare. Hysterical ladies screamed, dodged, and spilled their tea onto their fancy gowns as the dogs and brats—and damned *kid*—crashed past them. William, of course, was nowhere in sight to rein in his pack of howling hounds. And Pascoe was on the wrong side of the room to stop his giggling tots from chasing the puppies straight toward Lady Azenor... and the fire.

Theo dropped his cup and dashed across the new carpet, shoving aside his guests as Hog howled and leapt from the hearth— knocking over his hostess with the kitten. At the same time, the baby goat leaped for her arms and apparent safety from the dogs.

Assailed on both sides from dog and goat, Lady Azenor toppled, wailing as she hit the floor. The kitten leapt free and ran for the new draperies, followed by the pack of puppies and spaniels. The goat lingered to nibble a bit of lace. Theo feared the lady had skipped hysterics and gone directly to fainting when she did not immediately arise.

Appalled at the sight of embers from the fire igniting Azenor's frilly hem, he leapt over Hog and a spaniel in his effort to reach the far side of the room, while her aunt screeched and stamped her feet futilely from the chair.

Horrified, all the adults froze in place. Or so it seemed to Theo as animals and children raced past him in the wrong direction.

Apparently conscious but dazed, Azenor rose up on her elbows, as yet unaware of the expanding fire. Dodging the goat, Theo shouted a warning as she grabbed the arm of a chair to pull herself upright... and her frilly blue skirt swirled, feeding the fire.

Spinning around to see what he shouted about, she shrieked. All the ladies around her shrieked. Her aunt dumped the dregs of her tea on the flames. Azenor attempted to rip off her hem, succeeding only in setting her aunt's knee robe on fire. The flames inched toward her stout aunt, who shoved back her armchair to escape the encroaching conflagration.

Reaching the hearth, Theo caught Azenor's waist and held her still while he ruined his new pumps and fancy trousers stomping flames. More ladies rushed to dump their tea on the last embers.

Aware that Pascoe and his brothers had grabbed crying toddlers and shouting twins, Theo angrily dismissed the lot of them once he had the flames out. Let the whole damned house come down on their heads. Let Duncan crawl out of his cave to find out if they were being massacred. Theo had what he wanted—shivering and shaking—in his arms, and he didn't intend to let go this time.

He'd even take the hysterics. He was done with hunting a bride.

Azenor pounded his shoulders as he carried her and her scorched skirts away from the fray and up the stairs. She wasn't screaming anymore, he noted with satisfaction. She was swearing and trying to beat him into pulp. He could handle that better than weeping and vapors.

Let his damned brothers manage the guests and the dogs and their own damned brats. He was learning that handling responsibility was all about priorities, and right now, the lady was his.

She'd told him once that he was a man who acted first and thought later. Theo was damned fine with that. He carried her into the upper salon at the top of the stairs, slammed, and locked the door.

Then, while she struggled in his arms, he held her tight in relief that she was safe—and with a desire that he no longer meant to control. He kissed her beautiful soft lips until she quit beating him up, grabbed his neck, and kissed him back—as if she really needed him as much as he did her.

Theo closed his eyes and absorbed the heavenly bliss of lush curves and passionate lips. She smelled like apple pie and spice, and he wanted to eat her up in lewd ways that would undoubtedly send her shrieking into the sunset. But for just this one moment, he lost himself in pleasure and let the thunderous chaos of his home fade away.

The beautiful, wondrous lady clung to his neck, making him feel *necessary*, a notion he'd never encountered. In joy and relief, he dropped her feet to the floor so he could crush closer. She let him press her back against the door and explore her silky skin with his kisses. And when he finally cupped the perfect curve of her breast, she moaned and eagerly pushed into him, until his trouser placket threatened to pop its buttons.

He had her burnt skirts rucked half way up her delightful leg, revealing dainty lace garters and muddy stockings, when heavy fists resounded against the door.

"What the devil is going on down there?" the marquess roared.

That blind, lame Ashford had deigned to totter out of his suite and traverse the entire corridor shocked both of them into parting.

The din of barking dogs, crying children, and shrill female voices clamored in the distance. But it was the man pounding the door who demanded their full attention.

Azenor's big blue eyes were shining with pleasure—and dimming with growing awareness. "How did he know where we are?" she whispered.

"It's the only door not too warped to slam," Theo said with regret. He hadn't realized it would finally drag Duncan out of his lair.

Theo wouldn't let the lady shoulder any of the blame for his appalling behavior. He caught her waist, and holding her possessively at his side, opened the door.

Both of their stunned families and half the guests streamed up the stairs, summoned by Duncan's bellows.

Theo's heart sank to his gut—until he remembered the rest of his useless company was probably rushing for the front door and safety. Theo glared at the slender female in purple shooting him with accusation, then at his brothers and Pascoe, who appeared intrigued now that they knew the marquess wasn't in any danger.

"I am choosing a wife," Theo told them with as much dignity as he could summon considering his current disheveled and aroused state. "The lot of you can go hang yourselves." He slammed the door and locked it again.

This wasn't how he'd planned marriage, but after today, word of Ives anarchy would spread through half the kingdom. He'd tried the socially acceptable method of choosing a wife. Now he'd try it his way.

Azenor yanked from his hold and hurried to put the length of the salon between them. Not precisely the best start for his proposal.

She held her elbows as if she were about to fly to pieces. "I *cannot* be your wife," she asserted angrily. "That is inviting disaster. Has this day taught you nothing? I thought an Ives would be safe enough from me, but..."

"But you *care* too much, correct?" Theo asked in triumph. "You only harm people you care about, you said." He swung his arm to indicate the cacophony of barking dogs, shouting men, and crying children. "And this is how I live. This is not disaster, it's my *life*."

"You are supposed to meet your soul mate!" She looked as if she would weep.

He didn't want her to cry, but he understood the desire. His brothers were just outside the door, damning him, arguing with each other, and generally doing what they always did, while the ladies slipped away and the servants quit.

"Listen to them," he continued, gesturing at the door. "Do you really think you and your planets caused that? You want to blame my family's maladjusted behavior on your *existence*? Because we've been like this since well before you were born. Unless you're insane enough to claim god-like powers, I will have to disagree with your chart. Tell me you won't marry me because you hate me and my family and want us all to go to hell. I can understand that, but do not blame yourself for one precious second."

Her lips parted as if she'd reply, but he'd stopped the little general's words. Producing a linen square from her voluminous sleeve, she sank into a gilded chair that tilted unevenly and wiped her eyes. Theo wanted to go to her, but she hadn't given him that right yet. He couldn't press her.

The clamor outside the door was doing that for him. She was well and truly compromised. He'd not left her a choice.

"Marry me," he said. "If my family is doomed, at least I'll have the opportunity for a brief interlude of pure pleasure before I die."

Nineteen

ASTER STARED at his lordship with wide-eyed incredulity. Her heart was beating so fast, she thought she might actually faint. After weeks of work and the utter *fiasco*... then his proposal on top of his kisses... How could she begin to think?

No, impossible! was her first reaction to his proposal.

"If my charts are wrong, and I'm *not* the danger, then everything about my life is *wrong*," she cried, ignoring more pertinent problems pounding at the door. "I thought perhaps the asteroids unduly influencing some of our behavior caused the differences I cannot see in my charts, but they cannot change what *houses* we're born in!"

She wanted back in Theo's arms again. The world went away when he held her. He'd bravely stomped out flames and ruined his beautiful clothes and saved her from being Roast Stupid. She'd always been the Prophetess of Doom who protected everyone else—but her pathetic cowardice longed for a strong man like Theo who could provide courage when hers failed.

She wanted to be a normal woman who could kiss a man without fear—a woman who could have a family. *And she wasn't*. No kiss could change the day she was born.

"The asteroids are chunks of rock and ice," Lord Theo said disdainfully, dropping to his knees at her feet and ripping off her charred flounce, while unnecessarily holding her ankle. "They float between Mars and Jupiter and have no effect on anything whatsoever. You may as well blame Saturn and Uranus and the other planet we know is beyond them—if only our telescopes were stronger."

"Uranus?" she asked faintly, leaning over to watch him remove the smelly fril l. "What is Uranus?"

"A planet," he said in irritation. "And there are undoubtedly more of them we can't see. Your charts are based on ancient astronomy. It's your instincts you need to heed. What do your *instincts* say about me?"

"There is another planet beyond Saturn?" she asked in utter awe and a new kind of horror—one of changes so immense that she thought her world might explode.

"Probably dozens. That's irrelevant."

Dozens? Irrelevant? Before she could scream her dismay, he continued.

"You predicted Duncan's accident without *need* of Uranus or asteroids or moons. Perhaps it's *you* and not your charts that matter. My mother predicted an angel would fall out of the sky meant just for me, and you're that angel. Would you dismiss my mother's predictions?"

"You are funning me," she said, withdrawing the foot from which he was stripping a stocking. Too confused to argue about her charts when her whole world was cracking open, she fell on the unrelated topic. "I'm hardly an angel, although *falling from the sky* might explain the cloudbursts that follow us."

"See?" He yanked off her other shoe and stocking. "Your instincts figured out what I couldn't. I was waiting for you to land on my head."

Was he actually agreeing that she might have an unusual gift?

On the other side of the door, voices rumbled. Aster feared they'd be removing the hinges shortly. Her family might not be loud and noisy, but they were quietly practical—most of the time.

"Another planet changes *everything*!" she protested, unwilling to submit without understanding—or escape Theo's soothing touch. He was rubbing her bare foot now, searching for damage. She'd never known how erotic bare feet could be. She tingled in places that shouldn't be thought about.

She couldn't think, and she desperately needed to think.

"Fine then, you'll have an entire lifetime to change all your charts. But right now, we're going out there and telling them you've accepted my suit so your sister and cousins don't stab me while I sleep. Duncan is *out of his cave.* Do you have any idea how huge that is? We have to either rescue him or your guests. I'm asking again—what do your instincts say about you and me?"

"But... my family," she cried, "And yours! I can't endanger—"

He stood up, placed his hands on the chair arms, and leaned over her, all but breathing fire and brimstone. "Us, my lady. Us, first. Tell me about *us*."

His broad chest with its silky scarf and pretty waistcoat filled her vision. Beneath the clothes beat a heart that matched hers. Without their clothes, without their responsibilities...

"Setting aside our disastrous families, our charts are perfect for each other," she whispered, revealing what she'd tried so hard to conceal. "But they don't include Uranus and asteroids."

He drew her out of the chair and held her close again. She didn't fight him. She leaned against his strength. He was everything she'd ever dreamed about—and this was all wrong. And so right.

How could she throw out a lifetime of beliefs?

How could she not?

"To hell with Uranus and asteroids. Marry me, my lady." He kissed her hair, and brow, and ear, and worked his way down her cheek while he waited for her response.

"Aster," she finally said. "You had best call me Aster if we are to marry. My family would think it very odd otherwise."

She couldn't believe she'd said that. She needed to take it back. But everything she knew had been spun on its head, and all she could do was what *felt* right. And Lord Theo—with his bookish tendencies and scientific mind and masculine ability to sweep her off her feet—felt so very, very right.

He crowed his triumph and hugged her closer.

She tried to push away. "But only if you will introduce me to the Astronomical Society. I cannot remain ignorant of current discoveries for one moment longer."

He stiffened. "You will not like them," he warned. "Men of science know that the planets do not revolve around the earth."

Aster closed her eyes and let doubt sweep over her. No matter how right his arms felt, no matter what sweet words he murmured in the heat of the moment, she had to remember he didn't believe in her or her charts or abilities.

"I cannot marry a man who does not believe in me," she insisted. "That means you are not accepting my warnings and you are unnecessarily risking your family.'

"You cannot go out there with anything less than a betrothal," he argued, pointing at the door where voices were growing louder. "You've admitted your charts agree we will suit. Let me accept responsibility for any further disaster."

"You are the risk taker, not me!" she cried in horror. "I will agree to a betrothal, no more, until we settle our differences. We could be endangering the twins and all your brothers and—"

Theo grabbed her and kissed her so thoroughly that she forgot what she was protesting. How could he do this to her so easily?

When he finally dragged her over to open the door, she was afraid to face the people on the other side. She wasn't the same person she'd been a few minutes ago. Could they tell?

"Theo," he whispered as he turned the key. "I am Theo to my family. And you are my family now." He opened the door wide.

With four large intimidating Ives men scowling down at her, Aster was not entirely certain she wished to be family. Even the marquess, in stocking feet and with his coat askew, managed to glare sightlessly at the squeak of the opening door.

"My betrothed, gentlemen," Theo announced with hauteur. "Stand back and let us pass."

Wordlessly, Cousin Emilia swatted the men out of her way, grabbed Aster by her arm, and swearing under her breath, dragged her barefoot through the upper corridor.

"Have you lost your mind?" Emilia asked after Aster directed her to the proper room and they'd closed the door. "Those men will eat you alive!"

"I am not a fluffy meringue," Aster protested, hunting through her meager wardrobe for an unburnt gown. "I don't have time to argue this under the circumstances. Are any of the guests left?"

"Bree and Dee can see them off. Your Ives savages most certainly won't. Instead of looking after children and guests, they were fighting over who got to break down the door!" Emilia rummaged through drawers, looking for stockings. "You cannot mean to marry that brute who carried you off and compromised you as if you were naught but a maid!"

"He told me there's another planet I know nothing about." She was too agitated to even begin to understand what that would mean to her legions of charts.

Presented with the ugly stocking she had to draw on, Aster

sighed in confusion. A lifetime of a man massaging her toes... might almost be worth living with savages.

But she had vowed never to endanger anyone again by ignoring what the planets told her.

"And you *believe* him? Men will say anything to get what they want!" Emilia handed her a pair of ankle-high walking shoes. "I think we need to take you directly home."

Aster looked up in alarm as reality sank in. "Oh, the party is over! I do need to go home. But the marquess has just come out of his room, and there's so much more to be done—"

But Emilia was right. She couldn't stay here. It was only a betrothal, after all.

As much as she longed to be with Theo, to manage his unruly household, to hug all the twins... She didn't belong here. She might never belong anywhere except alone.

ONCE THE ENTERTAINMENT was over, their guests scattered back to the food, the fire, or their carriages to spread the gossip. Theo dragged his hand through his hair and watched forlornly as Aster escaped with her cousin.

"Now that little contretemps is over, I need to talk with you, old chap." Pascoe broke up the remaining crowd by pounding the marquess on his back and steering him down the corridor with a friendly arm around his shoulder. Both men were similar in height and looked to be good friends out for the evening—even though Dunc was only half-dressed and Pascoe was keeping him from bumping into statues.

Still shaken by the enormity of what he'd just done, Theo simply watched them depart. Having just turned his entire life on its head, he wasn't certain what he should do next. If he couldn't kidnap Aster and carry her off to an altar, he needed distraction while he fretted over what Aster's family was telling her right now. Not having to deal with Duncan left him empty-handed.

He turned back to Jacques and Erran. "Who's minding the brats now that their fathers are squirreling themselves away in a cave?"

Instead of answering, his brothers regarded him with something akin to awe. "You talked the lady into marriage? After we nearly set her on fire?" Jacques asked.

"With goats involved?" Erran added, shocked into speaking.

"Are there any more where you found her?" Jacques demanded with interest.

"Downstairs." Theo started in that direction—until he winced and glanced down at his crisped shoes. "And the wealthiest one just escaped with my betrothed. Keep your eyes open, idiots. Which ladies fled and which ones didn't?"

"Wealthy?" Jacques glanced after the ladies, who were already out of sight. "She was about to pry the hinges off with a fire poker. She's a *lady*?"

"Viscount McDowell's eldest. Maternal grandfather left her a fortune, if she marries." Theo tottered toward his room, holding the more damaged part of his feet off the ground.

He thanked the heavens that Aster had not noticed his burns, or she'd blame herself for bringing more *danger* to his doorstep. Kissing her into mindlessness had been well done on his part, he thought in satisfaction. And if he thought too long about her kisses, he'd forget his brothers and hunt her down for more.

Learning to deal with a wife could almost be as intriguing as studying the stars, if his damned family would leave him alone.

"Two more of them downstairs," Jacques said helpfully. "A bit young, but pretty."

"One of them is already betrothed," Theo warned, assuming Azenor—Aster's—companions were brave enough to linger. "But someone ought to be down there seeing off our guests and rounding up the nursery set."

Erran threw a longing look down the corridor and muttered, "Termagant."

Theo ignored that idiocy and returned to his chamber to the horrified cry of Jones, Duncan's valet. He thought the man would have hysterics before he got him out of the damned tight trousers and into something more comfortable and less charred.

Theo was pondering how he would pull boots over his damaged feet when a light knock rapped at his door. The valet answered it, wearing his best disdainful air. Theo began to consider hiring one of Aster's footmen in Jones's place. He didn't like feeling he was sartorially challenged and less aristocratic in comparison to his own damned servant.

He debated rising at the murmur of a feminine voice on the other side of the door, but Jones closed the panel before Theo could summon the energy.

"The lady sent an unguent for your burns," Jones said, nose high in the air. "Shall I dispose of it?"

"Bring it here." Theo sniffed the concoction and decided it stank bad enough to be useful. He rubbed some on the worst sores and wished he had Aster here to do it for him. He might never forget the bliss on her face when he'd rubbed her feet.

How fast could he obtain a marriage license and have her to himself?

First, he'd have to convince her to actually marry him.

And then he'd have to convince himself that sharing a lifetime with a doomsayer and believer in magic was worth the creature comfort she might provide. He was desperate enough to believe anything—but her demand to be presented to the Astronomical Society would destroy his credibility with the men to whom he wished to sell his telescopes.

Twenty

ASTER SPREAD her chart and Theo's on the floor of her bedchamber while Bree and Dee looked on. Nessie had retired to her room after all the excitement. Emilia had gone back to town with the last of the guests, unable to persuade Aster to leave with her.

She had not fulfilled her duty and found Theo a *suitable* wife. She simply could not abandon him until she'd had a chance to consider his insane proposal.

Although her wicked heart screaming *yes, yes, yes*! wasn't helping rational thought.

"Uranus complicates everything!" she wailed once she'd examined her calculations, even knowing her sister and cousin had no idea what she meant.

She shook the pamphlet Theo had given her explaining the mathematics of the new planet's position. "There are only twelve months in our solar year. We cannot add a *thirteenth* house to the Zodiac just because we've discovered a new planet. Mercury rules both Gemini and Virgo because it goes around the sun so rapidly. I cannot substitute a slow-moving planet like Uranus. *Why did no one tell me about Uranus*?"

"Because you were using old journals from the last astrologer in the family and none of us are scientists?" Bree suggested. "It's not as if any of our family is likely to obtain scientific tracts on astronomical discoveries much less *read* them."

"Theo says there may even be more planets than we have seen, ones even slower to orbit the sun than Uranus," Aster said gloomily, glaring at her no-longer relevant charts. "Nothing computes anymore."

"How about marriage?" Dee asked helpfully. "You seem to have calculated nicely into that. Why not roll up your charts and think about weddings? Will his lordship have banns called or go to town for a license?"

"But I must be certain marriage is safe!" Aster stabbed her finger at all the danger signs in her chart. "How does Uranus affect these?"

"The same way it affects everyone else in the world who can't read charts," Bree said impatiently. "You are betrothed. You must write our parents and make plans. You must have a *life* for a change, instead of worrying about what *might* happen!"

Aster didn't know how to have a life anymore, not one that included people she cared about—*more* than cared about. The power her scientific lordship exerted over her was beyond frightening... and well into thrilling. But marriage to him meant that she'd have to give up everything familiar—her snug nest, her friends in the city—and move even further from her family, for a dangerous household bordering on madness.

Marriage meant babies.

Which was why she was wildly attempting to find reassurance in her charts. The change he asked of her was so immense...

Change. Uranus could explain the inexplicable gap in her chart *here....* If Uranus affected her sun at...

As her instincts kicked in, she scrambled to make the calculations, forgetting Bree and Dee and the world beyond the scrolls on the floor.

She was still at in the wee hours of the morning, well after everyone had yawned and wandered off to their beds after an exhausting day.

She needed to tell Theo about these new points, here and here and here. They showed up on all the charts of Theo and his brothers! What an extraordinary conjunction of sun transits and Saturn. All pointed toward accomplishment, allegiance... *love of brethren*!

If she took that into conjunction with Uranus as an influence...

But Theo still had Catastrophe conjuncting with Commerce— would that be his glass manufactory?

She almost had all the new lines drawn when she heard a horse thundering from the stable. *From* the stable? She glanced out to see a large man in an old caped redingote ride a mighty steed down the drive.

It couldn't be the marquess. Theo's uncle then? And he'd left the children here?

Realizing she ached all over from sitting stiffly on the floor all evening, she debated leaving her final calculations until morning.

The *instinct* Theo had said was more important than her charts said she was on the right track, and her heart was immeasurably lighter with hope.

If her mathematics were correct, Uranus was an *enormous* factor in her life. No wonder her chart and her life were in such conflict! Her new chart opened up endless possibilities—not necessarily of the good kind.

She must have all the information the Astronomical Society possessed before she agreed to any dangerous commitments. What if she was still misreading the charts and there were more planets of doom affecting her or Theo or their families? She needed to know *everything*.

But Theo had promised to help her, which relieved a huge part of her burden. Just having knowledge within her grasp, she felt bolder. Instead of crawling between the covers, she wanted to head for the bathing room in the middle of the night. That wasn't all she wanted, but until she was married...

Her pulse accelerated at just the thought. *Married*. If she had drawn the lines correctly... she might marry. And maybe have children. She was too afraid to consider all the potential interferences just yet.

One change at a time—did she wish to live here in this foreign territory with madmen? Well, not madmen. Stability simply wasn't in their charts. Their stars were littered with bravery and valor, individuality, and discord—elements that disrupted stability, if nothing else. She'd need the courage of a pride of lions to survive.

Deciding to follow her brave new instincts and take advantage of what might be her new home, she gathered up her robe and candles with a vow to make use of the beautiful tub. She deserved a good long soak in warm water.

She almost retreated the moment she stepped into the corridor.

Barefoot and in shirtsleeves again, Theo leaned against the wall across from her room. He looked fatigued and worried, but he smiled with such delight at her appearance that she didn't have the heart to scold. She halted, clutching her clothes to her chest, waiting for explanation.

"Pascoe just left," he said, as if that explained everything. When she waited, he sorted for the clarification that didn't always come easily to him. "He and Duncan have heaped more work on my incredibly limited abilities. I watched the light in your window the whole time we talked and wondered if you were packing and planning on abandoning me come dawn."

"I was recalculating our charts," she whispered, not wanting anyone to overhear. "Your glass manufactory may be in danger in this next week. But studying all of you together has been enlightening. If I am correct, you can defeat all these terrifying knives hanging over you by working together. Your aspects are in perfect alignment for allegiance to lead to accomplishment."

He raised a skeptical eyebrow. "Allegiance? With my brothers? You *have* met them, haven't you?"

She sighed, taking his point. "My head is tired and my instincts confused and I thought I should take a break."

"And bathe," he agreed with a wicked grin. "We could save on hot water and do so together."

Shocked to her core, she simply stared at him. His words made no sense in her sheltered world, but her *instincts* clamored to heed him.

He caught her elbow and steered her around the corner. "I think I shall take advantage while you're not slapping me. We are both of age. I only need ride to the bishop and obtain a license in the morning. We can be married the day after... unless you wish a grand ceremony with all your family around you?"

"This is a betrothal only," she said in alarm, attempting to pull from his hold. "I need more time to study—"

"And dither yourself into old age," he argued. "Marriage never comes with certainty. You have the rest of your life to study your charts and pinpoint every discovery I hear about and fret over every circumstance. In the meantime, let us have a little pleasure."

"Pleasure," she murmured with a sigh. "A nice bath is a pleasure. Your household... not so much."

"And me?" he asked in that seductive baritone that turned her thoughts to mush.

Butterflies swarmed in her middle, and she was certain she walked through a tropical heat. "You... You are dangerous," she acknowledged.

He chuckled wearily. "That is not what people usually call me. I know you believe I act without thinking, and I fear you never act at all if you can avoid it, and that we have immense differences to overcome... But they are *interesting* differences, aren't they? It's not as if we dislike each other. And even your charts say we suit."

"I can't know that until I chart Uranus," she argued.

Outside the bathing room door, he wrapped her in his arms and held her tight. She could hear his heart pounding against her ear. "Follow your instincts and marry me, my general."

Her heart beat in tandem with his. He had said she would never act at all—she wasn't like that, was she? She had to decide, to quit her Libra dithering and actually say yes or no so he could go on with his life. She clung to his greater strength, his familiar masculine scent, his seductive voice... and wanted to be as selfish as he and marry him without regard to consequences.

A wedding. Did she dare plan a wedding? It seemed so very impossible that everything could change in a day....

"I would rather go home for the wedding—if I can prove to myself it is safe," she acknowledged cautiously. Just saying the words created excitement at the possibility of seeing her siblings and beloved parents again. "Is there a rush?"

He pulled back to look at her. In the gaslight, his grin was almost diabolical. "You know there is. Besides, we could not ride together to Scotland unless we were married without offending everyone concerned."

"Perhaps just a simple ceremony here," she suggested, still uncertain of such an enormous step, one she had never considered. She could not deny that she longed for a family again. But a family of her *own*?

And this particular family of madmen? She took a deep breath and shut out that thought, recognizing a challenge she wasn't quite ready to face. She had difficulty enough making decisions about herself. Making ones that affected countless others... She needed time.

He wasn't giving her time. He was telling her she was wasting time. And maybe she was.

They entered the bathing room, and Theo lit the candles she'd left around the tub. Aster shivered—not with cold but anticipation. His large presence in the lovely little room enhanced the sensuality of the flames, the erotic murals, and the steaming water he turned on.

"Perhaps I should let you soak first," she said hesitantly, uncertain if he really intended what he seemed to be doing. Sometimes, with Theo, it was difficult to follow his thoughts.

He found the scented salts she'd left on the rim and dumped them in, letting the aroma of apple blossoms fill the air. "Now I see why you always smell so good."

She was truly out of her element. Before she knew how to respond, Theo removed the bundle of her robe and nightshift and deposited it on a chair. He kissed her hair, turned her around, and started unfastening her gown. "You cannot do this yourself, can you?"

She'd donned a simple gown after removing her burned one, but it was still easier if someone else unfastened it. "We should not," she tried to protest, but he kissed her bare shoulder, and a shudder of expectation wracked her. She *could*... if she was prepared to allow herself to care. She swallowed and her heart pounded erratically.

"*This* is how we know if marriage suits us." He peeled off her bodice and pushed her skirt to the ground, leaving her clad only in her shift. She hadn't seen a reason to wear a corset in her own room.

"By undressing?" she asked uncertainly, wanting clarification in words when he so obviously preferred deed.

"That's a good start." He turned off the water tap, then divested himself of his silk waistcoat.

Torn between grabbing for a towel to cover herself and the tempting lap of warm water, Aster did nothing. Sometimes, her Libra worked against her. And well, sometimes... instinct worked in her favor.

Seeing her hesitation, Theo pulled her into his arms and reassured her with his blazing kisses. She sank happily into the mindlessness he'd taught her earlier.

His arms had become a safe haven that she trusted. His kisses promised the world and beyond. She desperately wanted to believe she'd found a home and a man who accepted her as she was, that she could have a normal life like any other woman.

And she knew all the fallacies such mindless belief concealed, but she didn't care, not when her hero was kneeling at her feet, peeling off her old stockings as if she were a princess and he, her gallant knight.

She should have been shocked when he stroked her bare limb, but she wasn't. She was grateful that he lowered her into the tub without removing her old shift. She wasn't ready to reveal how ungraceful she truly was. She simply stretched in the welcoming water and admired her betrothed's broad shoulders and the intensity of his gaze as he leaned over to kiss her again.

"You are so beautiful," he murmured, soaking a sponge for her. "I cannot believe I am so fortunate as to find a woman who is beautiful, brave, and wise beyond all measure. When I turn angry and forgetful, I want you to remember I mean this with all my all heart."

He boldly applied the soapy sponge to her bare shoulders, untying the ribbons of her shift as he did so.

"I am none of those things," she protested dreamily as she held her soaked linen across her breasts. "You should join me so I can stroke away your anger the way you're easing my weariness."

He chuckled, and the intimacy of that warm sound in her ear aroused her as much as his caresses.

"I don't want to frighten you into not marrying me," he said. "Besides, should I join you now, I couldn't restrain myself. I don't want there to be any chance of leaving you with my bastard should I fall off my horse on the way to London tomorrow."

Oh, that was where mindlessness led... She was *almost* glad that he cared enough to be careful.

"That is something we really must discuss..." she tried to tell him. She wasn't brave enough to risk children yet. Marriage was terrifying enough.

The sponge dipped lower, daringly caressing her breast. Aster caught her breath at the piercing sensation shooting straight to her womb.

She didn't want to think or talk at all. She wanted to rely on instinct, and instinct said this was a good man who even now meant to take care of her.

"We'll share a tub after we're married?" she asked from her blissful haze.

"Even if it must be at this hour of dawn to avoid all the demands on our time, we will share this tub as soon as possible after the vows are said," he promised.

The sponge floated away, and his bare hand cupped her breast, shoving aside the wet shift. She cried out when he caressed her peaked and aching nipple.

When Theo leaned over and took her nipple into his mouth and sucked, she shuddered with desire. The scrape of his beard, the delicious scent of maleness, the caress of rough fingers that possessed strength he refrained from using...

She would surely die if she never knew this man's bed. She knew there were ways of preventing children. She had simply never thought to study them.

Except he needed an heir...

"Please," she begged, not knowing what she asked.

But he knew. He kissed her hungrily, and slid his big hand lower, brushing aside the barrier of her shift to caress her thigh... and higher.

"No matter what the day brings," he murmured, "if I know I have this waiting for me come night, I will survive." He touched her between her legs.

Aster nearly rose out of the tub in shock, but he returned to kissing her into submission again.

She was ready to agree to anything he said, no matter how inane. How did he do this to her? She was the Prophetess of Doom. She should see all the obstacles ahead of them. And Theo simply erased them with a caress. Was it because he was so large that he made her feel safe? Because the hank of hair falling across his brow tugged at her heart? Because he was so smart and as lonely as she and he never gave up?

She purposely looked for obstacles. He accepted them and climbed over. That, alone, was worth more than she knew how to give.

"I know nothing of cows and tenants," she insisted, without knowing what she was saying. His fingers were stimulating tissues even she'd been afraid to touch, and her body had developed a mind of its own.

"I've decided that's not important. *You're* important. You're the star I can hold and study and touch, and I want you to pull me into your gravity and hold me. I promise that you'll be the center of my universe and I'll never let you go."

A vow that impassioned required more from her. From deep within her, Aster recalled the vows of her ancestors. Even as she gasped when he pushed two fingers inside her, she murmured helplessly, "I vow to love, honor, and take thee in equality for so long as we both shall live."

Wordlessly, he kissed her, pushed his fingers deep inside her, and shattered her universe, all in one motion.

Twenty-one

TORTURING HIMSELF by behaving like the gentleman Aster deserved, Theo carried her to her bed rather than ravish her while she was ripe, ready, and willing.

He was looking forward to having a passionate wife in his bed, but that didn't comfort him now, when he'd been inches away from heaven. Lying in bed recalling Aster's lush curves—and insane promise to love and honor him—didn't satisfy his hunger or his roiling thoughts.

He refused to believe his betrothed's insistence that her charts spelled doom for their families, but after Duncan's accident... He wanted a more logical explanation of how his brother could have fallen off a horse he'd ridden a hundred times before in far worse weather, while twice as drunk.

Pascoe's admonitions of foul play afoot, on top of the farmer's unusual unrest preyed on Theo's mind. Bringing a wife into this insane asylum...

Shrieks, laughter, and the patter of little feet woke him much too early. Theo groaned at the dim light, thought to turn over and go back to sleep, then remembered the day's task—a marriage license.

He was not a man who gave up or changed his mind easily once he'd decided on a course.

Pascoe's warnings, Duncan's demands, and a household of children took second place to obtaining the piece of paper that would tie the fairy general to him for the rest of their lives. He ought to be terrified at the notion, but after almost losing Duncan, Theo had a dread of mortality and a need to share his life with someone who understood what he was and wasn't. To hell with the damned estate.

So, call him self-centered. He'd found a courageous woman who wouldn't abandon him, and he meant to keep her, even if she was slightly mad. A woman probably had to be mad not to run fleeing from this household.

He grabbed bread, bacon, and a cold egg in the breakfast room while Aster's sister and cousin and a maid hustled the brats into seats. He noticed Aster wasn't down yet, and her family was shooting him suspicious glares, so he left before they could formulate an attack.

At the stable, he encountered Erran and Jacques looking concerned. Theo ordered a horse saddled and tore into his bread and bacon, refusing to ask for the bad news so obviously on their minds.

"We think the dogs scared off an intruder at the glass manufactory last night," Jacques finally said. "We found footprints in the mud outside the windows."

"And a charred stick beside some kindling." Erran added what Jacques was hesitant to say, reining in his normal fiery temperament to speak neutrally. "It was too wet to burn."

Hadn't Aster warned last night of catastrophe to his manufactory? Theo refused to live with superstition.

"Hire sharpshooters," Theo said callously, knowing Pascoe had brought rumors of more Swinger incidents, although his manufactory shouldn't be of concern to unhappy farmers. "Ask Browne if he can call in any of his old soldier buddies. Leave the hounds to run loose at night. Have the men pack up the most important equipment and finished inventory and take them home at night. Fill pails with water all over the building. I'm going to London."

Previously, he would have been horrified at the idea of anyone striking at his livelihood. But money couldn't buy him sanity. Right now, his focus was on one thing only—obtaining the license that would make Lady Azenor Dougall his and his alone. After that, maybe he'd worry about glass and idiots and sheep—preferably a long time after.

Maybe they should take a honeymoon to the Outer Hebrides.

He liked that thought entirely too well. Wondering if Duncan had ever considered running away from his responsibilities, Theo urged his horse to the vicarage to begin the arrangements for a marriage.

***

"YOU ARE REALLY considering *marriage*?" Bree asked in whispered horror over the breakfast table. The children had been whisked away by a maid-in-training who had decided she might like working in the schoolroom.

Aster added jam to her toast and dreamily contemplated what other women normally spent lifetimes planning. She had never indulged in marriage fantasies—or not for long, leastways.

"There are planets out there not in my charts," she answered obliquely, more interested in thinking about what Theo's hands and kisses could do.

"Does that mean that everything you've told us about our charts is wrong?" Dee demanded. "Is Edward *not* the right man for me?"

"Astrologically, Edward is the ideal man for you," Aster said, puzzling out how she could know this without charting Uranus into her cousin's chart. "There might be slight differences if I apply the mathematical calculations I used last night, but would you give him up over slight differences? If so, then you had best not marry him."

Dee slumped in her chair and glared at her teacup. "I want certainties. Do you even love Lord Theo?"

Aster shrugged and sipped her tea. "I don't know that love can be charted or predicted. He needs me. We enjoy each other's company." And more, but she wouldn't try to explain the physical bliss he'd taught her last night. "Is there a better basis for marriage?"

"Aster!" Bree nearly shouted, horrified. "You cannot just take the first man who offers simply because he asks. Marriage is forever! One needs love to smooth over the difficulties, and heaven only knows, this household is simply bursting with difficulties."

Aster smiled over her teacup. "And here I believed everyone thought me compromised and that I must marry. Tut, tut, my dears, you are showing your eccentricity."

Bree glared back at her as only sisters could. "If all those guests were your friends, they wouldn't say anything."

"People talk. It's what they do best. Father's allowance is modest and not sufficient for clothing and feeding the servants I train. If my reputation is ruined, my additional income will dry up. But here..." Aster sat back and admired the enormous dining hall they'd cleaned and refreshed. "Here, I could train an army, and the Ives fortune won't even notice the dent."

"That's not what marriage is about," Dee grumbled unhappily.

"Edward is off making his fortune so he can afford to keep you in the style to which you are accustomed," Aster pointed out. "Marriage is about many things, some of them unpleasantly financial. You may dream of love and romance and hearts and flowers, if you wish. I've never had that opportunity. To find a man who knows about my disastrous chart and is willing to brave it to have me... That's romantic enough for me."

She'd almost convinced herself that marriage was the best choice. If she could simply concentrate on all the positive arguments and avoid the negative ones, her Libra need for balance would happily take vows.

She'd already given her vow.

Inhaling sharply at that memory, she wondered what had inspired that moment of sublime commitment. Or insanity. She'd barely realized she'd known the words. Had she actually said she vowed to *love* Theo?

He hadn't said the same—but then as she well knew, Theo did not always speak his feelings. Although the things he'd said last night—had been said in the heat of passion. In the cold light of day, he hadn't even waited around to kiss her good morning.

There she went again, waffling. It wasn't as if she actually believed she was in love with Theo. She was much too practical for that. Her concern needed to be whether it was *safe* for her to marry. She didn't want to bring more danger into anyone's lives, and unfortunately, she didn't see how she could close her heart to Theo and his family so they'd be safe from her unstable chart.

She fretted over that far more than the realities of marriage to a man of science who didn't believe in the zodiac.

As they finished breakfast, Jacques entered, seeming diffident.

Of all the Ives men, he looked and behaved least like an Ives. He was blond, slight, and possessed a smile that was almost boyish in its charm. Of course, he was only twenty-three, if she remembered his chart. He wasn't smiling now as he waited for Aster to acknowledge him.

"Is something wrong?" she asked, gathering up her shawl and thinking she needed to send for more clothes. And a wedding gown! She'd burnt her only good day dress.

"Dunc won't answer his door, Theo has gone to London, and we have a problem Mr. Browne isn't suited to handle." He shoved his hands in his coat pockets and frowned at Bree and Dee.

"And you have some odd notion that I can?" Aster asked in astonishment.

"It involves women," he said bluntly. "And if something isn't done quickly, one of them will kill the other, and Theo will have a real problem on his hands."

"Women? If they're some of the marquess's mistresses or the like, then I would just take a broom to them. That's most likely not the best solution," she said pertly.

"Tenants. They're fighting over a cow. It was just words before, but it's escalated to fists and hair pulling. I fear it will grow worse."

Puzzled, Aster donned her shawl. "I cannot imagine what I can do. Are they very far off? I don't ride."

"Not far, but the gig will take us faster than walking, if you don't mind." He seemed relieved and worried at the same time.

"I trust neither of them has a knife." Hoping the morning wasn't too cool, she hurried toward the stable exit. She wasn't wearing boots, but her shoe wardrobe was as limited as her gowns. She really needed to send for more if she meant to stay.

She did mean to stay, didn't she? To live in disorder and chaos and abandon her beautiful city nest? Panic clawed at her insides, but action allowed her to hide it.

"Agatha has a rake that she swung at us when we tried to interfere. If William were here, he could probably grab her, but I don't think I could take on either of them without causing grave insult. Assaulting tenants is probably not the done thing." He hurried her out to the yard where a stableman was hooking up the traces to a polished low-slung gig.

"And hauling women about is the only way you can contrive to settle a fight?" she asked in disbelief.

"If they were men, we'd just wade into the fray and pop them one until they saw stars," Jacques asserted. "I'm not bad at fisticuffs. But I've never hit a woman."

"Thank goodness for that." She allowed him to hand her into the gig. "Where are their families?"

Jacques shrugged. "I do not keep up on the tenants, but from some of the argument, I gather a father or son is involved. But there were no men about while we were there."

"You live here but you do not know the tenants?" Aster tried to fathom how that might be, but the inhabitants of her father's rural lands were more family than tenants. It was a very small estate built mostly on rocks, after all.

"Dunc deals with them. And the steward. I didn't really grow up here. I know the men who hang about the tavern on a Saturday evening, but I have enough problems without hanging about their daughters." He scowled.

That was the first time she'd seen him scowl. There might actually be depths to the pretty boy. "No scattering of more Ives' bastards?" she asked cheerfully. "That must be hard on you."

He shot her a look of incredulity. "You do not mince words, do you?"

"Do you think I'd have any chance of surviving here if I did?" she asked.

He accepted that without argument and continued bluntly, "I send most of my allowance to my mother to keep her in fripperies so she can look the part of wealthy lady. I am hoping she'll find a protector. Supporting a mistress isn't in my cards."

Aster compared his words to what she recalled of his chart and shook her head. "That's not all, is it? You have a dream that you're hiding from your brothers."

The dappled mare clip-clopped a half mile before he reluctantly replied. "She knows theater people and brags about my plays to producers. I've even had one or two accepted, although they've made very little money. I've vowed if I have no success by the time I'm twenty-five, I'll take over Theo's glassworks. He can use the help, and I'm not totally incompetent."

"No, you're just an Aries, with dreams bigger than you are. You need to be in London, rubbing elbows with dramatists, making yourself known. I believe most successful men become so by knowing the right people."

Before he could respond, they heard the furious shouts of the fight over the hedge, and Aster gestured for him to stop. "Best not to let the mare too close to a brawl. I can walk from here."

Jacques tied the animal to a tree and followed her over the stile into a field apparently used as an animal pen. A few bored sheep munched a patch of clover, and a cow and her calf lay in a brief patch of sunlight through the clouds.

At the edge of the enclosure, two women reached across the stone-and-hedge wall, yanking each other's hair and trying to drag one another across the barrier. Fists had been engaged and blood had been spilled, but so far, the rake and hoe nearby did not seem to be in play.

"He gave the bloody cow to me!" the tall, black-haired younger of the two women yelled. "You have no right to steal it. I'm going to the marquess, and you'll see who gets what."

A stouter, shorter woman with salt-and-pepper hair flying down her back did her best to smash the taller woman's head into the wall. "It's my cow and he had no right to give it over. I raised her since birth. She feeds my young 'uns. And you'll take her over my dead body."

"Women ain't got no rights, you old biddy! He gave it for services rendered, all proper and square. I *earned* that cow!"

"I begin to see the problem," Aster whispered as they approached. "Is the older lady married and the younger one not?"

"I believe the younger is a widow. I've seen her in the tavern, entertaining several of the men. I know naught of the other." Jacques held her elbow to assist her over the rough field.

Perhaps this was the kind of problem Aster could help Theo with. She knew little about cows, but she knew people. Eager to prove to herself that she wasn't making a mistake by marrying Theo, she studied the situation.

"I'll come up on their near side," she suggested, "if you'll come up on their far side and remove their weapons, please. I'd rather not be smacked in the face with a hoe." *Before her wedding*, she didn't add. That still seemed a little ephemeral with the groom missing. With her luck and planets, Theo had probably broken his neck galloping to the bishop.

"Hello, ladies," she said cheerfully, lifting her old skirt and approaching from the nearest side.

Caught up in their fury, neither woman responded.

She really wished she knew if they fought over husband or son. Barring that, she wished she had a broom. Or a bucket of water. She glanced around, noted Jacques had purloined the weapons, and saw a bucket by the water trough. She nodded in that direction. His eyes widened, but like all Ives, he was smart and caught on quickly.

"The marquess sent me to see what the quarrel is about," she said more loudly. "I do believe he is the magistrate. Shall I take your grievance to him?"

"Who the devil are you?" the younger woman demanded, yanking harder on the older woman's long hair.

"Lady Azenor Dougall, affianced to Lord Theophilus. If you don't cease your fisticuffs, I shall have to resort to drastic measures. Wouldn't it be better to state your case rather than decapitate each other?"

The younger woman swung her fist at the older's jaw, sending the matron staggering. But neither released their holds. So much for reason and logic.

"Well, Miss La-di-da," the younger sneered. "I'm Mrs. Maeve Higby and this here cow stole my cow. I want it back. You tell the marquess Maeve wants Agatha arrested."

Aster was developing a strong dislike for the bigger of the two. "And you're Agatha?" she asked of the older woman.

"My Harvey did not give that cow to the whore," the presumed-Agatha shouted. "She's lying!"

Ah, they were coming closer to the core of the argument. Still, she didn't know if they were talking husband or son. "And who might Harvey be? If you would please release each other, we might reach the bottom of this faster."

"The witch got him drunk!" the older woman shouted. "My Harvey never strayed afore." Infuriated at just stating this aloud, the wife used both hands to slam Maeve's head into the hedge.

With a sigh, Aster nodded at Jacques, who stood by with a bucket. Granted permission, he happily flung the water over both women.

They shrieked and jumped apart, wiping at the foul-smelling slime dripping down their faces. Aster hurried to place herself between them. "Cooler heads prevail," she informed them. "Mrs. Higby, I would have your tale first."

Before either could speak, young Hugh galloped up on a restive mare. "Mr. Browne says I'm to take both ladies to the office," he shouted.

"Browne can go to hell!" the belligerent Maeve retorted. "It ain't none of his business, and none of your'n either." She swung her fist at Agatha, who dodged.

The blow struck Aster squarely on the cheek, and she staggered. Shocked, Jacques and Hugh jumped into the fray as the two women went at each other again.

Appalled, Aster drew back as the irate widow grabbed a loose stone from the wall. With a furious swing, the widow aimed at her adversary.

The stone flew from Maeve's hand and slammed into Hugh, who dropped to the ground. Blood spurted from the blow to his brow.

Feeling the crushing of doom to her faint hopes, Aster fell to her knees besides the boy, weeping and trying to staunch the gash with her gown.

Twenty-two

WITH THE LICENSE tucked in his coat pocket, Theo galloped for home, trying not to imagine all the potential disasters he'd left untended. Instead, he fretted over whether purchasing a special license instead of a regular one had been a wasted effort. Would Duncan actually come downstairs if they married in the Hall?

He had hoped to marry this evening. Waiting for morning seemed to just ask for trouble. He would become as superstitious as Aster at this rate.

But the vicar was busy and claimed the morning would be better. The special license would allow him to come to the Hall. That had been the best Theo could arrange. He need only hang on to the lady another eighteen hours or so, and she would be irrevocably his.

Perhaps he ought to feel a little guilty about not asking her father for Aster's hand, but as she'd said—Theo was inclined toward action first, and Scotland was a long way away.

By the time Theo saw the Iveston carriage and the baggage wagon loaded with boxes rumbling toward him, all his doubts and fears coalesced into shocking reality.

Once again, he was about to be abandoned—*Aster was leaving.*

What had his brothers done this time?

Which made him so angry, he couldn't think at all. Aster knew better than to be frightened off by anything his family did. He expected more from her!

Maneuvering his gelding to block the lane, Theo held up his hand ordering his driver to halt. Ever obedient, the coachman did so.

Theo swung down from his horse and yanked open the door. Three demure young women and one confused old one stared back at him. "Where are you going?" he demanded. "Why aren't you planning a wedding?"

And then he saw the bruise on Aster's cheek, and his temper exploded. *"What the devil happened?"*

He hauled her bodily from the carriage to examine the damage, wanting to weep as he caressed the appalling purple marring her perfect cheek. He didn't think he shouted, but she winced, and her younger companions bunched their gloved fists. He held her tighter, waiting for explanation, with his heart ready to burst from his chest.

"It was an accident," she asserted, struggling against his hold. "Hugh was hit by a rock. You should go to him. Now put me down."

She spoke calmly, but Theo could practically feel her vibrations. It didn't take a mathematician to add two and two. *If she blamed herself for Hugh's injury...* she would run. She *was* running.

He added the fuel of panic to the conflagration of his fury and fear.

"How badly is Hugh hurt?" Theo's imagination had run rampant since the Prophetess of Doom had first darkened his doorstep. Alarm thundered at the thought of young Hugh lying hurt and injured as Dunc had been. But he would yank out his heart before he'd lose his little general. He clamped his arms tighter against her struggles.

"Dr. Joseph is with him. He seems to think Hugh's eye will be fine in a few days. Now set me down." She wriggled against him—as if all those lush curves squirming against him would encourage him to set her aside.

"And why aren't you with Hugh instead of in a carriage?" Theo demanded, even knowing the answer.

"He could have lost his *eye*! This is all my *fault*," she wailed, flinging her arms around his neck and weeping into his shoulder. Theo held her close and despaired of ever having what he wanted.

"I simply cannot risk endangering anyone else, so I am leaving," she announced, pushing against him again.

That's what he'd figured. Hugh got swatted—and she believed it was *her* damned planets at fault. A gentleman would let her go and try to woo her back to reason—or better yet, hunt a more rational female.

Theo had no such intentions. He kicked the carriage door closed on the gaping women. "Go fetch the lady's wardrobe. And cats, and a wedding gown," he commanded. "She's marrying me tomorrow with or without you."

Aster pummeled him with her small fists, but he wasn't having any of it. He'd pander to her planets some other day, but not on his wedding eve.

The driver was already heeding his orders about London, and the team galloped off. Theo doubted even Aster's audacious relations would leap from a moving vehicle.

All he needed to do now was persuade a madwoman to stay—which made him equally insane. They deserved each other.

Carrying his betrothed, Theo flung her into the saddle, much as he had the first day she'd arrived.

"No running away," he informed her, swinging up behind her. "I will not have hysterics. That's an order."

She choked on a mixed sob and laugh. "You cannot order me about. If I wish to go home, I shall. You cannot let me harm anyone else." She keened this last.

Hysterics, Theo thought in his fit of rage. But he meant to stay the damned course. This one was not escaping. "Unless you deliberately hit Hugh in the eye with a brick in a malicious fit of temper, I will not believe you are responsible. We cannot keep having this argument."

He urged his mount down a side lane and toward the pond. The day was hotter than Hades. They both needed to cool off, and he knew just the place to do it. Memories of last night's bath danced in his mind as one of the best moments of his appalling life.

"We *must* keep having this argument until you listen," she cried in anguish. "It does not matter how it happened—I am the *catalyst*! My chart is littered with danger. I simply cannot do this to your family. I *cannot*!"

"Because you've grown fond of them?" he asked skeptically. "That's not possible. They're an ornery lot of useless thugs, including me." Reaching the pond, he swung off and lifted her down.

"Do you mean to dunk me to see if I'm a witch?" she asked in confusion, taking in the pastoral setting of willows and sun-flecked water.

"Excellent thought." Theo removed her scarf and flung it over a laurel, then swung her around to start on her confounded hooks. "But if you drown, I drown with you. We're in this together."

She grabbed at her bodice and attempted to struggle out of his hold. "We are not! What are you doing? I can't swim!"

"Of course you can't. I'll teach you if you like. But it's shallow on this end. We're going to cool off and let the madness die down before we go back to the Hall. And then you'll plan our wedding. I am not listening to any more daft warnings." After loosening her hooks, he yanked off his coat with the precious piece of paper inside, deliberately folding the coat and hiding it under the laurel.

A scientist learned to think through a problem and come up with a detailed solution. He could do this, one step at a time. *Seduce the lady* seemed the next logical step.

"My warnings are not daft! Hugh could have been blinded!" she shouted, as if he were deaf and not just stubborn and selfish.

"Duncan could have married Margaret," Theo countered senselessly.

He slid Aster's sleeves off her shoulders when she did not undress as requested. She had beautiful shoulders, all soft and creamy. And then there was her splendid bosom, rounded like full moons above her chemise. He could just look at her and be a happy man. Well, for a while. Looking and not touching would quickly make a starving wolf of him.

"Duncan marrying Margaret would not necessarily be a disaster." She translated his senseless remark while trying to return her bodice where it belonged. "I need time to *think*!"

The pins had loosened from her hair, and copper curls sprang every which way. She brushed one from her eyes, and Theo took the opportunity to yank a sleeve entirely off her arm.

He appreciated the fact that she understood him well enough to follow his inadequate communication. "You don't need time to realize that you *leaving* us would be a disaster," he countered. "Life is messy. Things happen. Learn to take them as they come. Tomorrow, the moon might fall into the sun. You cannot live in constant fear."

"Yes, I can," she whispered as he pulled her closer to push off her other sleeve. She leaned into him, and her tears dampened his linen. "My baby sister was *recovering* from fever. I just wanted to make her feel better when she grew restless, so I picked her up to soothe her. And she *died*, right there in *my* arms. I wanted so much to make her well, and I *killed* her!

"And then, after the funeral, I climbed into a carriage with my little brother and sisters to keep them entertained. And the horses spooked and ran for a cliff! Our driver saved us, but the children were all bruised and shaken. My father's only heir broke his arm! It could have been so much worse. You have to understand," she pleaded. "Even Uranus cannot change my disastrous chart in the family sector."

Theo gathered her up and sat down on the stile with his goddess in his lap. "My mother died when I was five. We had an older sister who died of influenza when she was a baby. My father lost fingers in a yachting accident. Duncan is blind—and it's not because you told him so. *You* are not to blame. The stars and the planets aren't to blame. And if you try to tell me this faradiddle one more time, I shall fling you in the pond and refuse to listen ever again. Do you understand?"

"You're not listening now," she muttered against his chest.

"I know," he said in satisfaction. "I'm *doing* now. I'll listen later."

With that, he finally kissed her.

Twenty-three

ALL FAMILIES SUFFER TRAGEDY. Aster attempted to grasp what Theo was telling her while he was kissing her—not the best time to try to organize her confused thoughts. The accidents didn't have to be her fault?

He nibbled her lips, and her heart raced faster.

Her baby sister had died—just as his has.

His tongue played a seductive game until she parted her lips and allowed him entrance. She inhaled the ale he'd been drinking and the musky scent of sweaty male, and her insides tightened in expectation.

Desperately, she tried to recover her train of thought.

Did she dare believe that maybe the chart meant someone she loved was in danger—but she *wasn't necessarily that danger?*

Theo caressed her breast, and she nearly expired of lust. Despite her throbbing jaw reminding her of the jeopardy she placed them all in, Theo's caresses made taking life's risks seem so sensible, so possible... She couldn't think while he was kissing her like this.

She slammed her hands against his broad shoulders, shoving him off balance just enough to escape from his lap. "If it's not *me*," she said curtly, "and I am free to marry anyone I choose, then I should find a man who treats me with respect." She yanked her gown up and reached behind her to pull together what hooks she could reach.

Lord Theophilus Ives, scientist extraordinaire, sat there, stunned. And speechless, but that was not unusual for him.

Stupidly, she almost wept at his loss... and hers. They really were perfect for each other in so many ways. But not in the ones that truly counted. Her family was right.

They didn't love each other. He clearly did not respect who she was. He didn't even seem to respect himself most days. They would drift apart the instant the lust wore off.

Trying not to see the desperate man beneath Theo's towering rage, she dug in her hair for any remaining pins and began pulling it tight. "I want to go home. I want my cats. They at least accept me as I am."

It was almost like hitting a man when he was down—if he was not so much bigger than she and so very certain of himself.

Stiffly, eyeing her as if she might shift into a dragon at any moment, Theo yanked on his coat. "I accept you as you are," he said with an unusual degree of caution.

"If you did, you would be introducing me to the Astronomical Society and pointing out to them that through the positions of the planets, I have predicted everything from the weather to our disastrous family connections. You would accept that I know things that you do not. Just because I cannot always predict my own chart perfectly does not mean I am not good at what I do."

"They will not listen," he argued. "I am saving you from humiliation."

"Say you," she said with scorn. "Isn't that something I should be allowed to decide? Do you mean to haul me around for the rest of our lives whenever you don't agree with me? Or do I have permission to think for myself upon occasion?"

She had no idea where these words came from. She terrified herself by saying them. She felt as if she were ripping her heart out and handing it to him.

Not that his lordship understood that. He looked thunderous. He visibly struggled—probably to prevent heaving her over his shoulder again. Finally, he gave a curt nod. "Fine. I shall escort you back to London. I will speak with Herschel about having you present at the next meeting. And I will send a note to the bloody damned vicar that he need not officiate our wedding in the morning."

He sounded as if he'd just agreed to stand before a firing squad.

WOMEN were a calamitous, illogical, impossible solution to anything, Theo concluded—without objectivity. His mind was a stew of confusion and fury and... He wasn't certain what that other scream in his head meant except maybe anguish at losing something precious that he really wanted.

What *she* wanted was a man who would *accept* her as she was. What the devil did that mean? He accepted her! She was the witchy general who would command his unruly troops, then warm his bed at night. Wasn't that what they'd agreed?

They had, until he'd told her that she wasn't to blame for harming family. Where had that gone wrong? He ought to be like Erran and quit talking. Life was simpler that way. He didn't know what he was saying half the time anyway.

"Herschel and the other old men in the Society will shatter your zodiac with mathematics," he argued aloud. "Then you'll hate me for doing what you asked me to do!" He'd known better than to deal with hysterical females.

"That's my problem, not yours," she argued. "Let me down from this animal!"

Even though Theo knew Aster deserved a man who didn't have all his problems, he still couldn't let her go. He couldn't explain his irrational decision to carry on with the wedding. It wasn't because he was so honorable that he thought they should marry because he'd ruined her reputation. He was simply smart enough to know that if he let this miraculous woman go, he'd never find a better one.

"We have to return to the house for a gig and the horse is faster than walking," he muttered. "Maybe I should kidnap you like some medieval villain. A tower would be helpful. We have one in Wystan."

Her protest over the horse and his irascible musings ended the moment they rode up to the house to discover an unusual number of horses and a carriage in front. "I think we should leave for Gretna Green," he warned.

NOW THAT SHE'D QUIT dithering and taken a stand, Aster didn't want to be tossed back into the turmoil of deciding right from wrong, up from down. She didn't want to think at all.

Seeing the carriages, she found Theo's suggestion of Gretna Greene to almost be appealing—except she wasn't going anywhere with him. She was still angry, although she hadn't quite clarified why. "You should have let me go to London," she corrected. Eyeing the unfamiliar carriages, she added considerately, "And you should have come with us."

"Is it too late?" he asked, even as the front door swung open and dogs poured into the fading sunlight.

"Father is threatening to cut off heads again!" Hartley shouted from the porch. "Hurry!"

The marquess had come downstairs?

Under those extraordinary circumstances, Aster didn't protest as Theo swung her to the ground. Picking up her skirts, she raced after him to the open door.

Inside, a small crowd greeted their disheveled arrival. Confronted with a lady in an elegant carriage gown, a gentleman in tailored coat, and Mr. Browne, the steward, as well as Erran, Jacques, and Hartley plus a scattering of footmen and maids, Aster considered turning around and running back out again. They all stared at her unfastened attire and bedraggled hair and struggled not to look shocked.

"What the devil is this about?" Theo thundered, uncaring of appearances, as usual. Aster pinched his elbow to remind him of introductions. He performed a cursory bow for the guests and offered his version of etiquette. "Margaret, Sir George, Lady Aster."

Oh, dear, these were Theo's neighbors—hers, should she be so irrational as to wed an Ives.

Besides being beautiful, Ashford's ex-fiancée appeared calm, collected, and haughty. Sir George looked like a portly, grumpy squire, snapping his riding crop against his tall boots. They did not look very friendly.

Aster dipped a hurried curtsy, painfully aware of her rumpled, dusty travel gown. She needed to change before she dealt with whatever problem had arisen now.

If the son of a marquess could dismiss common courtesy, then so could she. "You'll forgive me if I run upstairs to right myself. I shall be right back down."

With ingrained hospitality, she gestured at one of her new maids. "Bring tea to the parlor for our guests, please."

Then, without waiting for explanations, she dashed up the stairs, feeling her face turning red enough to conceal any bruising.

She was not married yet. She had just cast aside any claim to a position in the household. With her chaperone gone, she was in a very precarious position—and the marquess stood scowling in the intersection blocking access to her room.

Ashford or his valet had tugged on his coat but not his neckcloth. He wore slippers and not boots. But his ferocious expression would blind all onlookers if he went downstairs now.

"Who's there?" he barked.

"Just me, my lord. If you would shift a little to your left, I'll be out of your way. I'm not dressed to meet your guests. Don't cut off any heads, please, until Theo can find out what's wrong."

She thought a smile tugged at his grim lips, but she wasn't in any humor for Ives eccentricity.

"Good, Theo can cut off their heads. I'll not have them accusing my steward of any wrongdoing if it's that witch Maeve who is causing trouble. I should have flung her off the property long since. Hugh is asking after you. Go reassure him."

He stalked back to his chamber with his hand against the wall. Aster winced and bit her lip as he whacked a statue of Pan in a niche. He merely halted, felt around a bit, then deliberately knocked off the riding cap adorning the imp and continued on.

The twins! How could she have forgotten them? She hurried to their chamber and peered in. "I have to save your uncle from beheading," she informed the boy in the bed. "Do I need to send Hartley up?"

"Lady Aster!" Hugh cried in relief. "I thought you'd run away. May I get up now? It's very boring lying about in bed."

Unable to tell him that she meant to flee, she studied the raw redness of the abrasion and swelling bruise on his poor face. She truly wanted to believe this would have happened whether she'd been around or not, but she was pretty certain that ordering the pail of water had been the trigger to the rock throwing.

But maybe... maybe that was just human error? And not the fault of fate or the planets or anything else? How did she sort one from the other?

"Boring is good," she said, entering the chamber to dip a cloth in the basin of cold water beside the bed while she fretted over what was best for herself as well as this family. She applied the compress to the swelling and made him hold it. "Boring is safe. Be boring for just a little while longer. Give me time to clean up, and I'll send Hartley to entertain you with tall tales of mighty mice."

"Mighty mice?" he called after her, but Aster was already hurrying off.

She came from a very long line of women who went their own way. She *could* return to London and confront the Society and live down the gossip about her reputation. It would be awkward but not impossible. The question became—what did she want most?

And what she wanted most—she swallowed a large lump—was *Theo*. She wanted a family and babies and a man who believed in her. It was that last part that remained uncertain. He wanted her. He needed her. Those things, she understood. How could she make him accept that she had an unusual gift when he wouldn't even listen?

She had to make Theo and his family and his daunting neighbors downstairs understand and appreciate her family's wayward tendencies. If she really, actually, meant to marry and live here...

That probably meant she was insane. But she must start as she meant to go on. Looking around her bare chamber in horror, she thought she might be meant to go on as a ragged hoyden. Her sister had taken her clothes back to London.

She ran from room to room, scavenging sufficient pins to shove in her hair, even if it curled in wisps every which way for lack of a brush. She adjusted her scarf to cover her wrinkled bodice. *Sartorial* disaster was not the sort of thing she looked for in her charts.

By the time she sailed down the stairs again, the grand rotunda was empty, and she slowed to listen for gunshots or screaming. Loud male voices roared from the rear office. Surely the very proper-looking Miss Caldwell would not join the men. Aster glanced at her confused footman, who indicated the drawing room door.

"Very good," she assured him as he opened the door for her. *She still had servants to train*. She must remember her goals and weigh them against potential disasters. Wouldn't the poor people in the workhouse suffer disaster if she didn't train them?

Donning the casual authority of the earl's daughter that she was, Aster swept into the drawing room as if she owned it. Her petticoats were too limp to rustle. Her traveling gown was too stiff for elegance. All she had was attitude, and though she seldom wielded it, as an earl's eldest daughter, she knew how.

"Miss Caldwell, we have not been properly introduced."

Aster held out her hand and waited for the baronet's daughter to stand and acknowledge her. She could tell it grated on her guest—who had probably been lording it over country society for years—but Aster wasn't feeling friendly to a woman who would abandon her betrothed when he most needed her—

As she meant to abandon Theo. She tried not to wince at that realization.

Jacques stopped pacing the hearth at Aster's entrance and bowed. "Lady Azenor, our neighbor, Miss Margaret Caldwell. Maggie, this is Theo's betrothed. Or I think they're still betrothed. I don't keep score well."

Aster sighed. "One of these days, I will teach the lot of you proper manners. Until then, would you fetch Hartley and send him up to Hugh, please? And I think the marquess has been diverted from beheading, but you might want to go up and see what he has to say about the widow who struck the boy. I doubt that Theo knows her."

"Maeve claims she was only defending herself," Miss Caldwell declared. "You and Mr. Browne have no right to throw her out of her home. We've settled her into a cottage on our place and have come for her cow."

Aster donned her best smile. "If that's all this is about, I shall straighten out the story myself. Do have a seat, Miss Caldwell. If we are to be neighbors, the least we can do is get to know each other over a cup of tea."

If she couldn't immediately flee back to London, she might as well make herself useful.

Jacques looked from one to the other of them warily, then escaped with obvious relief at Aster's nod of dismissal.

Aster took one of the newly cleaned arm chairs and poured the tea from a mismatched set of china. "The widow owes us a cow for nearly putting out Hugh's eye and causing such a violent disturbance that it dragged Mr. Browne and one of our tenants from their work, not to mention bruising me on the eve of my wedding. An adulteress and a woman who would sell herself for a *cow* receives no sympathy here. Would you care to explain what is really happening?"

The lady scowled and studied her teacup. She seemed to be a few years older than Aster and far more poised and polished than Aster ever hoped to be. Margaret looked the part of marchioness with her elaborately coiffed ringlets and artfully applied cosmetics. Aster wished she knew the lady's birthday, but she would place her wager on Margaret being a Virgo.

"I'd meant to take out that wall of windows and replace them with doors onto the terrace," the lady said, not answering the question.

"First, there would need to be a terrace and not a lot of broken stones and crumbling benches," Aster retorted. "Were you intending to marry his lordship for his house?"

The lady shrugged. "At least it would have been my own, to do with as I wish. How is he?"

"Furious. Beyond furious. And you score no points with his brothers. Theo is marrying me simply to return some semblance of normality. Crying off was not well done," Aster said crossly.

"I nursed my mother for years. I do not have the heart to nurse a husband and all the other Ives who will inevitably spill through here when they need help."

The lady wrung a lacy handkerchief, then continued. "Did you know that when Duncan and his brothers were very young and attending Eton that they were sent home when the school closed from an outbreak of measles?"

Aster shook her head, soaking up any information that might aid her.

"Their father was in London. Their younger uncles were at Oxford or out carousing. Their older uncles had left the household. There was no one here to greet the boys except a few footmen and kitchen staff. When Erran came down with spots, Duncan had to ride out in search of a physician. The three of them took care of each other until the physician finally realized their plight and sent for their father. Nursing Ives is a never-ending process."

Aster sat in horror trying to imagine such an appalling lack of concern for family. They had been raised like wolves! No wonder Theo was desperate for her small help.

"Do not feel sorry for those little boys," Miss Caldwell warned, reading Aster's expression rightly. "For they have grown into men who are equally negligent. They care for nothing but themselves and their own pursuits. Duncan has already abandoned parliament and the work he was doing there to nurse his wounds. Theo will ultimately abandon the Hall when denied the observatory he wants. You would do well to go home, my lady."

Having delivered her horrifying message, Miss Caldwell brightened. "Montfort's place will suit me far better than this gloomy Hall, and he said we might live in London. I think I shall enjoy that."

She didn't look as if she'd enjoy it, Aster observed, but imagining those three lost little boys, she was too sick to her stomach to continue the conversation. "You wish me to convey that message to the marquess?"

Miss Caldwell finally looked up to meet Aster's eyes. "Did you not ever wonder why there are no women in the household? They will kill you just as they've killed every other woman in their care. I think I shall take my chances on Montfort."

Well, dying could certainly be the disaster she saw in her charts—but marriage seemed far more likely to be the looming tragedy.

Twenty-four

THINKING THE TOWER in Northumberland was looking better and better, Theo settled the matter of Maeve, the Cow Deprived. "You're welcome to the witch," he told the baronet. "I fully support Lady Azenor's insistence that she be removed."

Aster hadn't told him that after Maeve had hit Hugh, she'd ordered Browne to fling the widow off the estate. He twitched his shoulders in discomfort at his increasingly tight coat. Did one just toss tenants out of their houses? How the devil would he know?

Was that the disaster she kept predicting—letting someone else handle his responsibilities led to rock-throwing and cow-stealing? *Damnation.*

Eager to prevent Aster's escape, Theo steered his neighbor from the office. "After what Maeve did to Hugh and Lady Azenor, I won't allow the woman to return to Iveston. If you wish to file a complaint against Mr. Browne—who was merely doing his job—then so be it and good luck. No tenant harms my betrothed and my nephew and remains on my land to tell about it."

"It won't do, it won't do at all," the baronet continued to protest as Theo escorted him from the office. "You need more experienced guidance."

Ah, so there was the reason for this visit. The baronet thought he could run the estate better than Theo.

"The laborers are all up in arms as it is," Sir George continued. "The widow is very popular. Her plight will stir them to rage."

"Duncan is still magistrate, is he not?" Theo asked, attempting to conceal his contempt. "If I ask, he'll have Maeve up on charges of assault. We'll send her to gaol and then there's none to incite anger. She's damned lucky we're just kicking her out. I'm wagering I could find women willing to testify Maeve engages in prostitution. You've picked the wrong cause, Caldwell."

Theo stopped in the drawing room doorway and felt his anger

diminish at sight of his maybe-betrothed presiding over the
company. She glanced up at his arrival, and he could swear she
winked. Her copper curls twisted every which way, falling on her
brow and nape with abandon. Her traveling gown was much the
worse for wear. And she still looked like royalty in the cream and
azure chamber she'd created.

"Sir George." Despite her wrinkled dishabille, Aster nodded
with the dignity of a queen.

The baronet was a large, stout man with receding blond hair
and a booming voice that fit a hunting field better than a drawing
room. He looked uncomfortable bowing over Aster's hand, speaking
polite pleasantries. As soon as he straightened, he sent a pleading
glance to his daughter, who instantly rose.

"It's been a pleasure, my lady," Margaret said in the polished
tones that Theo knew she'd learned at her expensive finishing
school.

He didn't think Margaret sounded pleased, but he was as much
in a hurry to pry their guests out as they were to leave.

"I understand there is to be a wedding?" Sir George boomed,
taking his daughter's arm. "Shall I offer our congratulations?"

Heading off any tart reply Aster might make, Theo steered his
guests toward the rotunda. "I'll accept them. Lady Azenor is a prize
well beyond my expectations."

A prize he'd stolen, coerced, seduced... No wonder she was
ready to fling him in the pond and set the goats upon him.

After seeing his guests off, Theo returned to the drawing room,
but as he'd feared, Aster had already slipped away. He'd need to put
a bell on her to keep up with her. He hurried up the stairs to check
on Hugh—and found his reluctant bride telling tall tales to the
twins—and to Duncan.

His brother had propped himself against the wall to listen. At
Theo's arrival, Duncan twisted his head as if to determine who was
there. He scowled a warning.

Properly cautioned against interrupting, Theo silently jostled his
big brother for position because he was still irritated at having the
estate's responsibilities dumped on his inadequate shoulders. Since
Duncan was merely listening to the story and not seeing the maternal
scene as Theo did, he shifted without complaint. No one had ever told

them bedtime stories. It was an illuminating experience.

Theo waited until Aster was finished and the twins were roaring in laughter before he intruded. "I'll not tell Pascoe that you know how to tell stories or he'll steal you from me."

"Pascoe can find his own damned woman," Duncan snarled, returned from fantasy land to the moment. "Did you rid the premises of intruders?"

"No thanks to you," Theo retorted now that the spell was broken." I could have used a little support down there. I didn't know who the devil Maeve was."

"If you spent less time in the library and more time in the tavern, you would."

"You're complaining because I'm not a drunk and a rakehell?" Theo protested.

"I shall have Cook send supper up here for all of you." Ignoring their bickering, Aster rose from the side of the bed. She touched her own bruise, then Hugh's. "I think Hugh and I shall spend more time in the library and less separating quarreling tenants."

That sounded as if she meant to stay. Heart thumping illogically, Theo offered his arm. "I'll be happy to lead you to the library, unless you wish to rout a few more ogres for me. Quarreling neighbors are as bad as tenants."

"We don't want mothering," Duncan protested. "And the estate doesn't need more bookworms in the library."

Theo swung around and whacked his brother's bulging bicep with all the strength of his bookworm fist. "You abdicated, big brother," he roared as Duncan staggered back in surprise. "If you want the damned throne back, I'll hand it over, and Aster and I will repair to the tower in Wystan. Otherwise, leave us to muddle along as best we can."

"Hugh," she addressed the boy in the bed, "if I see you and your brother treat each other like savages the way your father and uncle do, I shall send you both off to Wystan so you might learn civilization." Aster sailed out of the room.

Defending himself from Duncan's retaliatory swing with a lifted arm and shove, Theo ran after her.

***

ASTER WAS DOWNSTAIRS ordering a meal served in the twins' chamber when Theo caught up with her. She didn't want to be angry with a man who had been raised like a wolf and didn't know better, but she was confused and shaken and *she had no clothes.*

"You hit a blind man," she said before he could speak.

"I discovered well before he was blind that the only way to hit Duncan is when he doesn't see it coming," Theo declared without remorse. "His arms are longer than mine, and he always wins otherwise."

"He can't *ever* see the blow coming," she protested. "You must change your ways."

"If you've decided to become a bitter spinster who berates astronomers for their bigotry rather than marry me, what does it matter?" he grumbled. "I believe I shall retire to Wystan and let Erran run the estate."

"Oh, that will work very well. Erran speaks even less than you do. But I suppose he *does* know how to dress properly."

Which avoided the subject—did she wish to become a bitter spinster? Of course not. But that was a very real possibility given her ruined reputation. And if she didn't dare visit her family... She wanted to beat Theo for making her face facts.

"I *accept* that your science is different from mine," Theo said gruffly, out of the blue.

His hair flopped in his eyes, his coat was undone, and his boots were still muddy from the pond, but in her eyes, he was still the handsomest man she knew—and the most appealing. How could one resist those little-boy-blue eyes?

"I really don't want to let the Society humiliate you as it does anyone who offers theories different than their own, but I will, if you demand it," he added reluctantly.

Aster held a hand to her chest to keep her heart from leaping out. He still wanted her to stay!

Choices. She must make choices. Her stars seemed further away than ever. "You said so earlier. I believe you. Perhaps I'll wait until I have more information about planets and moons and asteroids I don't know about before confronting them."

He studied her warily. "Do you still wish to look for a smarter man than me?"

No, she wanted to fling herself into his arms and return to the pond. Or the tub. Or a bed. And she was officially out of her mind. "There are no smarter gentlemen in London or I would have found them. What I want is *respect*. If you can accept that my science is different from yours, then I will accept that men don't understand that their version of science cannot explain everything."

His beautiful silver-blue eyes flickered with hope, and he shoved a straying strand of hair from her cheek. "I accept that science cannot explain women. Do you still wish to return to London?"

"I have to go to London to fetch my trunks. I can't be married in this!" She held out her drab traveling gown.

He carried her hand to his mouth, kissed it, and nearly brought her to her knees. How could the man who yelled at his brothers and hauled her around like a sack of coal be the same man who otherwise treated her as if she were more valuable than gold? Perhaps she could find a scientific treatise on men. Or write one, if she lived long enough.

"We have a date with the vicar tomorrow. You're not going anywhere," he insisted, catching her arm and dragging her back up the stairs.

"We appear to be going *somewhere*," she corrected as she ran to keep up with his longer steps. She was definitely out of her mind, but a thousand times happier than when she'd told him she was leaving. That had to mean something.

"To the attic. There are trunks and trunks of clothing up there." He led the way to a floor with many paneled doors and hurried her past them.

"You want me to wear someone's old clothes on our wedding day?" she asked in incredulity. "Is this how Ives kill their wives— with insanity?"

"We don't kill our wives. My great-grandmother and grandmother were both still alive when I was born. No one lives forever. And if Margaret was telling you about our mistresses, they never hang about after they discover we won't wed them or pamper them with jewels. They're not dead, just gone for greener pastures. Margaret is looking for excuses for her abominable behavior."

He understood her fear and effectively dismissed it! Now she remembered why she adored this man. He was dangerously close to being the stabilizing influence her Libra indecision needed.

He flung open one of the doors they passed in the silent upper corridor. "Nursery, schoolroom, servants quarters, in case you're interested."

With curiosity, she peered past his shoulder to a linen-shrouded room, until he tugged her hand and dragged her to a new flight of stairs.

Well, almost the balance she needed.

"You wouldn't happen to know Margaret's birthday, would you?" Dragged along by Theo's haste, Aster was practically gasping for air by the time they reached the final landing.

"First of September. She throws a harvest festival early and calls it her birthday fete." The stairs opened onto another corridor of low ceilings and plain doors.

"Virgo, as I expected. I should draw her chart and see if she is right for Duncan. Perhaps we could bring them together again. She seems like the managing sort he needs."

Aster stared in curiosity at the rows of doors on this top floor. She'd never seen a house so huge that even the attics had attics.

"Please, don't," Theo admonished. "They've both led each other on for a decade. It's time to move forward, and I'd rather not do it with Margaret wasting money on silk furniture the dogs will ruin. Her only interest has ever been spending money and demanding attention."

"But someday, Duncan may marry, and his wife will be in charge," Aster argued, finding a new reason to doubt her sanity in marrying into this family.

"We'll cross that bridge when we come to it. I'll charge the estate for my services in the meantime, and we'll be rich and build our own house. It doesn't look as if I'll ever have time for an observatory anyway." He sounded resigned.

"What exactly is an observatory?" she asked, since it seemed so important to him.

"A structure for observing celestial objects. Stonehenge might be a prehistoric example for observing the sun and moon. McFarlane in Scotland has instruments that measure the stars from a specific point to create sailing maps. Sir William Herschel built a magnificent one in Slough. I want a specific point for observing the moons—a place large enough for my very largest glasses."

"A structure on a hill? Is that what Wystan is?" She tried to imagine where he might put such a building on the estate.

"Wystan is tall but the tower is too small for my scope without considerable improvement. There's a rocky hill on the south end of this estate, but all my money is tied up in the manufactory. Until it starts making a profit, I can do nothing."

Dismissing the subject, he opened the first door and lit a sconce on the wall.

The last rays of sunlight illuminated a dusty chamber of old boxes, trunks, and wardrobes. In ways, it was actually neater than the rooms below. No one had spilled books or saddles or dogs up here. The dust lay evenly between rows and rows of... *clothes*?

"Probably dating back a century or more," Theo said with a casual gesture. "I believe some of the ancestors liked to throw theatricals, but we've not had so much of that in our time."

"Jacques would have liked a drama or two," Aster said, cautiously opening the first wardrobe. But Jacques had just been one more of the wolf pack abandoned when convenient and left to fend for himself. Duncan might claim they didn't need mothering, but the marquess lied through his clenched teeth.

A cloud of moths flew out of a packed space of old velvets and wools—winter clothes. Vowing to return with lavender and cedar, she shut the door and proceeded to the next.

"Those look like they might be my mother's," Theo said, peering into the crowded closet of delicate fabrics. "They'd be the newest of the lot."

Aster gingerly removed a gown so fine, it could have been a night shift. "The embroidery is lovely," she said, holding it up to her front. "But I would look like a barque of frailty in this, even should it fit, which it won't. Your mother must have been very tall and slender. I would trip over the hem and fall out of this bodice." She eyed the narrow band skeptically, wondering how anyone except a broom might fit into it decently.

Theo held it up to her shoulders, and his eyes gleamed with delight. "Could you have a seamstress make it into a gown for just my perusal?"

Aster shivered in anticipation. If she went through with this marriage... So, maybe he didn't love her. Maybe he didn't respect her abilities. But would she find another man who would look at her like that? She doubted it. And she wanted to wear wispy gauze just to see him gaze upon her with such happiness. Theo wasn't a bad man. He deserved a little fun. So did she.

"I'll see what I can do," she said, teasingly flirting the thin fabric, "but I'm not quite so concerned with the bedchamber as I am the church."

"That's good to know," Theo said, holding the fabric up for her to admire. "But the vicar is coming here so Duncan might attend. Does that help?"

"The vicar is the same as a church." She hung the gown back and rummaged on the shelves, producing some lovely gloves—and a book. "What is this doing in here?" She opened the leather cover to read *Georgetta Ives Personal Journal.*

Theo glanced at the pages. "Ah, so that's where it got to! My mother used to scribble in this. I don't have many memories of her, but I do have a few of her writing in this book. She wrote predictions for all of us when she was ill and could no longer get about. I guess someone stored it with her things so we didn't destroy it."

"A journal! Could she be a Malcolm who isn't on my family tree?" Aster asked excitedly. "I can't think of a more thrilling wedding gift."

"If that's what it takes to persuade you to marry me, then it is yours," he said, moving on to the next trunk. "Looks like these might be my father's things." He removed a green-and-red striped waistcoat. "Perhaps I could gift wrap myself for you to open tomorrow night."

Enfolding the precious journal in a piece of cloth, Aster laughed as he lifted out a matching green frock coat. "Look at the lapel and all those buttons! It would take me half the night to pry you out."

"That won't do." He caught her waist and kissed her. "Are you sure you cannot wear the embroidered gown? Then we could go straight to bed afterward."

Flushing, she swatted at his sleeve and escaped his hold to open the next door. "You will be presenting me to your family and others as your wife. If we are really to do this mad thing, we must do it properly. I still think we should wait until I have time to run to London. Delaying another day can't hurt."

"You have no idea how much it can hurt," he said with a groan, peering over her shoulder. "I left you for a few hours and found you fleeing once already. I'm not risking that again. I like that yellow one. It's not quite as nice as those shimmery things you wear, but it would look good on you."

"I think it's supposed to be cream and has just yellowed with age." Aster drew out a gown of rich silk. "At least it has a decent bodice, I think." She held it up to examine the fit. "But I think it was meant to be worn with panniers to hold up all this fabric."

"It may have been my grandmother's. Didn't they wear those bigger gowns with all this lace back then?"

"The silk is gorgeous." Aster smoothed the billowing layers of skirt around her. "Your grandmother must have been more my size. If I had time, I could take apart the skirt and fashion sleeves..."

"No time." He began unfastening her hooks. "Try it on. You can say it's a family tradition to wear our ancestor's wedding gowns."

"I doubt that it's a wedding gown." But it didn't really matter. Aster loved the richness of the silk, and the tiny seed pearls, and the extravagant lace... She gasped at how quickly Theo removed her bodice.

"Given the choice, I'd walk you down the aisle like this," he said in satisfaction, pressing a kiss to her bare nape. "Hurry and put this on before I start looking to see if anyone stored a mattress up here."

She hastily stepped away. "You have a way with words after all," she muttered, struggling into the bodice. "The sleeves only come to my elbow. I think it needs an undergown."

Accustomed to the billowing sleeves of current fashion, Aster wiggled her arms through these narrow, short ones. Theo pulled the bodice tight from behind and began to fasten it.

It fit perfectly, sort of. Aster gaped at the way her breasts almost flowed over top of the sumptuous fabric. "It definitely needs a top layer," she fretted. "This wasn't meant for morning wear!"

Theo held up lengths of matching lace. "Can you use any of this? I prefer the top just as it is, but I suppose it isn't proper to give the vicar a fit of apoplexy."

"*That* would be one definition of disaster," Aster said dryly, fastening what appeared to be a silk collar attached to the lace and letting the whole drape over the bodice and down to the floor. "I'd rather not let my stars kill off the entire village, if it can be avoided." She examined the effect of what was more cloak than veil. "I'm not a seamstress, but it appears this was designed to be tied on, so I might fashion a shawl and train out of it."

Removing the lace, she let him drop the skirt over her head, then held it to her waist. The lovely silk puddled over her toes. She still felt like a princess.

"I am the luckiest man this side of heaven," Theo said fervently, gazing down on her. "And I'll frame all the weird star charts that brought you to me."

"I am not convinced that I am the perfect partner I see in your charts," she cautioned—although she was pretty certain she was, except for that danger problem. If there was a better match who might not burn down the Hall, she felt obligated to warn him. "You could be overlooking someone right under your nose."

"You're right under my nose, and no other, so it has to be you." He bent to steal another kiss.

When she came up for air again, Aster pushed him back. She needed air to clear her head. "Show me your telescopes."

"Taking you on the roof at night would be disastrous," he said, helping her out of the gown. "You don't know your way around."

"How do you keep from killing yourselves and each other?" she cried in despair. "I will have to lock all of you up to keep my predictions from coming true!"

"*Then* we'd burn the house down," he said cheerfully. "*We* are the disaster, not you."

Twenty-five

AFTER SPENDING most of the night preparing a marriage bed fit for his bride, Theo paced his chamber the next morning, dodging the valet's valiant attempts to straighten his stock. "Aren't her sister and cousin back yet? What the devil is keeping them? London's only an hour away!"

Sprawled across Theo's bed examining one of Aster's charts, Erran shrugged. "It takes hours to primp."

Erran had apparently widened his range to brief sentences. Theo had been enjoying the unusual silence from his brother's mercurial moods, but he supposed he should be grateful he didn't have to deal with a mute brother as well as a blind one.

"They wouldn't primp before they got here." Dodging the valet's stock straightening, Theo stalked to the window but the drive was still empty of carriages. "The vicar should be arriving, shouldn't he? Jones, get the devil out and go prettify Duncan!"

"He said the same about you," the valet said with dignity.

"Dashitall! I'll have to ride into the village and find the vicar in my wedding clothes. Does anyone know if Aster is ready?"

"One of those new little maids has been running about asking for pins and darting up and down to the attics," Jacques said. "And the twins are at the telescopes, watching for her sister's arrival. I'd say your lady won't be ready until the other women are here to approve."

"You know too damned much about women. Go find the vicar. I'm going to talk to my bride." Theo brushed off the valet and flung open the chamber door.

The twins practically spilled in, both chattering at once.

The swelling around Hugh's bruise had diminished but half his face had gone purple, making it easier than usual to tell them apart. "Two carriages," Hugh shouted.

"A huge black stallion!" Hartley added with a hint of awe.

"The vicar's gig is way behind."

"And everyone in the village is walking this way!"

Theo used an inappropriate swear word and pushed past the boys. "Why on earth is the village coming? Are they carrying pitchforks and planning on storming the castle?"

Emerging from Duncan's suite to see what the ruckus was about, William shoved one of the spaniels back inside and shrugged his lack of a good answer.

"They're hoping for a party?" Jacques guessed.

"I'll see what kegs we have on hand." Finally interested, William hurried for the back stairs.

"Kegs without food aren't a good idea," Duncan called from his doorway. "Who the devil invited them?"

A chorus of "Not I" rang out as Theo hurried toward Aster's chamber. He feared he would live in a perpetual state of panic at this rate.

He should have set her up in a suite. He should have prepared for a party. He should have done ten thousand things besides seducing her in inappropriate places. It was a miracle she was still here.

He pounded on her door. "We're about to be inundated with guests," he shouted."

"And the problem with that is?" she inquired from within.

"They'll want food." That sounded feeble. He was panicking over nothing.

He was panicking because the vows had yet to be said, and he was still terrified she'd run. Margaret had been right in that much— Ives couldn't hold on to their women any better than they could keep servants.

"Cook is preparing a feast for us," she said reassuringly. "You'll just have to share instead of keeping it all to yourselves. You might tell him to bake more loaves and add another roast to the spit." She sounded as serene and calm as Theo didn't feel.

"Are you ready?" he asked. "Do you need anything? I can have them open the wine."

He thought he heard her giggle.

"A drunken bride! That would embellish the family legends for a century."

He took a deep breath. If she meant to be part of the family legends, she wasn't running away yet. "It will be a drunken groom if you don't come out soon," he insisted, glaring at the wooden panel separating them.

"Let me know when the vicar is ready and my sister is here."

"There's a huge man on the black stallion," Hugh shouted. "He's riding up the drive before everybody."

Aster's door popped open. "A *black* stallion?"

Theo forgot words. His bride was a vision in cream and copper. The maid had somehow battled all the wiry red coils into lush, silken, upswept waves, surely adding inches to her height. Or perhaps the old-fashioned high-heeled slippers had done that. Her beautiful midnight eyes were almost aligned with his nose, and he had the preposterous notion of simply kissing her until they melted away.

That was before he glanced down and saw the creamy perfect globes of her breasts rising above a teasing fringe of lace and silk, and he almost expired on the spot.

She was wearing pearls that perfectly adorned her slender neck and emphasized the plumpness of her most excellent bosom. He should have remembered to ask for his mother's jewel case. Duncan must have thought of it.

She was marrying a brainless maggot.

"Did Hugh say there was a rider on a black stallion?" she prompted, forcing him to drag his gaze upward again.

"I'll lock you in a tower before I let a rescuing knight sweep you away," Theo declared senselessly.

"No rescuing knight," she replied with a hint of tartness. "Most likely my father, the Terror of Lochmas out to do what he does best—intimidate. You had best lock yourself in that tower."

Theo swallowed. "I thought he was a professor."

"He's a *Dougall*. He conquered Amazon tribes! He only teaches because my mother won't let him roam while the children are still young. It's summer, so he's not corrupting young minds but out causing trouble." She didn't look as concerned as Theo felt.

The knocker thundered in the rotunda below.

"Will someone answer the damned door?" Duncan roared.

The marquess had shuffled his way as far as the intersection between the two main corridors without knocking over any statues. Wearing a tailored black frock coat and starched linen, with his hair trimmed and his face shaved, he almost looked like the brother Theo knew—except for the raw red scar searing brow to temple.

"You can't hide from my father," Aster whispered. "Assist the marquess down the stairs and confront Lochmas directly. Knowing he didn't catch you by surprise will take some of the wind out of his sails."

Theo didn't know about greeting a Scottish earl bent on intimidation, but keeping Duncan from falling headfirst down the stairs seemed the wisest course of action. More than anything, Theo wanted Duncan presiding over the family and estate again so he could retreat to his scholarly corner, undisturbed. He had to keep Dunc alive for that to happen.

Reluctantly tearing away from his bride's radiant beauty—her eyes were shining so expectantly that shooting stars would dim in comparison—Theo hurried back to the main corridor.

They were really doing this. Aster was actually marrying him—provided her father didn't kill him first. He could barely breathe for fear he'd bungle these next hours.

Theo tugged at his tight neckcloth before catching Duncan's upper arm and steering him to the handrail. "Aster says it's her father," he said. "Can we lock him in the dungeon until the service is over?"

"Lochmas is out there?" Duncan asked in incredulity. "You dragged the Lion of Edinburgh out of his lair? I think just *hearing* how this plays out should be sufficient. I won't need to see it."

"You know her father?" Contrarily, Theo contemplated tripping his obnoxious brother and letting him hit the rotunda headfirst for not providing that tidbit of information.

Duncan shrugged. "We correspond occasionally."

Below, a nattily attired footman opened the door. Where the devil had they acquired livery?

"Where is my daughter?" roared the large, black-haired man shoving past the startled servant. As if possessing a second sight, the intruder stalked to the center of the circular entrance and glared up the stairs.

Theo had guided Duncan to the last landing. He pinched his brother's arm in warning. "Center floor, on the star. He looks like one of us."

"Rumor has it there's an Ives in the woodpile back a century or so ago. He may be a cousin four or five times removed, nothing to worry about," Duncan muttered before turning his blind stare to the spot where the earl stood. "Lochmas," he said genially. "We hadn't expected you."

For a moment, it was almost like having his old brother back, and Theo swelled with pride and relief.

"Obviously not," the Scots earl retorted with a load of sarcasm. "You didnae have even the courtesy to send an invitation."

"Papa!"

Theo swung around to watch his bride rushing down behind them. She'd lifted her skirt to reveal trim, beribboned ankles as she took the stairs at a reckless pace on heeled slippers.

Theo held Duncan in place, averting collision as Aster dashed past to fling herself into the earl's arms. Even the earl looked startled, Theo noted with satisfaction.

"What are you *doing* here?" she cried excitedly. "I thought you'd promised to take the little ones to the Highlands for the summer. You know it's not safe to be near me."

Guiding Duncan down, Theo listened with interest for the reply to this.

"Your auntie said you were flirting about this place, and your mama fretted, so I came to see what it was all aboot." He set his daughter back far enough to study her, and his frown blackened at the bruise on her brow. "What the deuce is this! Have the brutes been beating you?"

She tapped his brawny shoulder impatiently. "Don't be ridiculous. I got in the way of a rock. And you may get in the way of worse if you hang about me for long. But it's so good to see you!" She hugged him again.

Through eyes black as a moonless midnight, the earl glared over her head at Theo. "And you cannot protect her from flying rocks?"

"No more than I can stop the rains or keep my damned brother from trying to break his neck," Theo replied, leading Duncan down the stairs. "You want to lock her in a tower?"

The earl's expression saddened as he hugged his daughter. "You preach misfortune, lass, and now I hear ye're wedding without any of us to see you off! That's a misfortune if I ever heard one."

"We were intending to take a wedding journey north," Aster said excitedly. "It wouldn't have been proper to travel together otherwise."

Theo and Duncan reached the rotunda foyer. The earl attempted to disentangle himself, but Aster placed herself between them, holding her father's hand—presumably to keep him from fisting it.

Theo was grateful for her calming influence. In revealing his blindness to the outside world, Duncan seemed tense enough to attempt swinging back if it came to fisticuffs. If Aster handled her father, Theo could divert arrows to Duncan's pride.

Sharing, he decided, that's what marriage was about. Relief replaced his earlier anxiety. The burden he'd been carrying momentarily lightened.

"Lord Ashford, this is my father, Adam Dougall, Earl of Lochmas. Papa, may I present Duncan Ives, the Marquess of Ashford, and my betrothed, Lord Theophilus Ives. Theo is an astronomer, and he's told me there are more planets than in my charts!"

"Is there now?" the earl rumbled irascibly, glaring at Theo. "And what else does he be telling ye that you think to marry without my permission?"

"Lady Brianna Dougall and Miss Deidre McDowell," the footman announced at the door. "Miss Emilia McDowell," the servant added after studying a card. A hasty consultation concluded with, "And Lady Daphne McDowell."

"Aunt Daphne!" Aster cried, still clutching her father's hand but turning to smile toward the new arrivals. "How lovely of you to come! I so much wanted family to be here."

"What are they doing now?" Duncan grumbled in Theo's ear.

"Aunt Daphne is a dauntingly tall lady with a huge bosom draped in scarves," Theo whispered. "Even the earl looks cowed. And the vicar is hovering behind them. Announce that we're repairing to the drawing room, and we'll enthrone you by the fire. I think Aster chose the King George chair for just that purpose."

His bride had arranged it so that Duncan's raw scar would be turned to the fireplace, and the wings on the massive chair would protect him from three-quarters of the room, so people would have to stand directly in front of him to speak. Aster had a way of tending to details.

Duncan snorted in appreciation of her efforts. Theo was so

relieved that his brother wasn't throwing tantrums that he would have blessed Aster on the spot had he been a bishop.

"Let's not linger in the foyer like dolts," Duncan drawled, gesturing toward the drawing room. "Lady Azenor, place us where you will. This is your day."

"It's a shame you can't see the dazzling smile of approval my bride is casting in your direction," Theo murmured for his brother's ears only. "Or maybe it's not, because that means you won't try to steal her from me."

"Do I hear cats?" Duncan muttered in return.

Ashford's hearing had evidently improved with blindness. Theo cast a hasty look for the culprits. "I believe the lady's servants have arrived with trunks and... *cats*," he confirmed with resignation, noting baskets on the arms of several of the maids.

Dogs and cats—no wonder her charts were covered in disaster. Theo cast prayers to heaven and was grateful the fire wasn't lit.

Still clinging to her father's hand, Aster took Duncan's other arm as they entered the newly refurbished drawing room. "This couldn't be a more perfect wedding day if I'd planned it. I am so happy you came down in time, Papa. You must tell me how you met up with Bree and Dee."

She cast a glance over her shoulder. "And Vicar Matthews! You look dashing today. I told Cook to make certain he fixed those scones you like. You should have brought your wife."

The vicar had a wife? And liked scones? Theo cast his amazing bride a look of disbelief. He wanted to ask her how she learned these things, but he was afraid she'd say she'd read it in the stars.

If she hadn't been on the other side of Duncan, he'd lean over and ask her if their wedding day was fated for disaster—because he was having a damned hard time believing he could keep a goddess.

Twenty-six

UNEASILY AWARE that she was playing the part of the general that Theo called her, Aster saw Duncan seated in the large chair by the hearth. Even with the raw scar, the marquess looked impressively aristocratic and confident. It was hard to tell that he couldn't see anything. Even Emilia was casting him looks of interest, which was astonishing in itself.

Her father was not so easily disposed of. The earl was accustomed to thundering through classrooms of cowed students or around a stone castle that absorbed his roars. A polite, nearly bare, drawing room filled with women and Ives... She took a deep breath to calm herself and glanced at Theo for reassurance.

He winked. Giddiness bubbled up inside her at the intimacy of the communication, and she didn't know whether to laugh or to smack him. He solved the problem by turning to her father and gesturing at a far corner of the enormous room. "My lord, perhaps we should step aside while I assure you that I can support your daughter in the style to which she's accustomed?"

"She doesn't need a jackanapes like you for that!" the earl roared, but he stalked off in the direction indicated.

Wishing she could simply run upstairs and cuddle her pets, Aster hurried to thank the vicar for coming instead. She directed him toward Ashford so the marquess wouldn't feel abandoned. That Duncan had actually emerged from hiding to be displayed in public for Theo's sake was a wedding gift beyond anything she'd ever dreamed. She had to show him her gratitude.

She left the other Ives brothers to sort themselves out while she ran to her family, flinging her arms around her stiff and proper aunt and kissing her on her cheek. "Thank you, thank you for coming! I so wanted family with me but given my disastrous planets, I was terrified to ask."

"If these young sprouts could visit without coming to harm, I saw no reason why I shouldn't," Daphne said imperiously, apparently knowing nothing of the carriage accident. "Your mother would never forgive me for not seeing that you're marrying safely. Besides, there are a few additions to the wedding ceremony of which you might not be aware. This is as good a time as any to teach the next generation." She looked pointedly at her daughters.

"Additions?" Aster asked weakly, noticing for the first time that her aunt had directed a maid to carry in a valise.

"As librarian, you should know this," Daphne scolded. "Did you think you could marry without me? The ceremony is in all our journals."

"Oh, dear, not the druid ritual? Surely we're beyond that sort of primitive superstition in these days of enlightenment." Aster grimaced as her aunt gestured for the bag and opened it, drawing out a rowan ring.

"Do you think keeping your genealogy charts and journals is superstition?" Daphne asked indignantly.

"Of course not," Aster said. "They contain valuable information. I'm not certain *rituals* are valuable."

"Do you wish your marriage to be a success?" Daphne demanded tartly, as if that settled the matter.

Bree and Dee dug into the valise, producing short capes, another rowan ring, and green candles molded and scented to look and smell like evergreens.

"The candles are pretty," Bree said with a decided lack of enthusiasm. "Shall we set them on the mantel? Light them? Duel with them?"

"It's enough to set them about, I think." Daphne gestured at tables. "It might be dangerous to light them with so many people in the room."

"Thank all that is holy," Aster said fervently. "My disastrous planets have not gone away with a change in location. I'd rather not burn down the Hall before I'm wedded."

"And bedded," Emilia said with a laugh. "Your groom cannot take his eyes off you, even when your father is roaring like a wounded lion."

Aster turned to see if Theo needed rescuing. He didn't even seem to be listening to her father's diatribe. He was watching her with a hint of worry. Tall, lean, elegantly garbed in black and white—

although the wayward hank of golden-brown still fell on his brow—her scientist was all a woman could dream of.

She smiled reassuringly, and he took a step toward her. Her father grabbed his arm and dragged him back. Given the level of male posturing she'd seen in this household, she had every reason to be confident that Theo could handle the earl.

She took a steadying breath with that realization. She really didn't doubt Theo. She doubted *herself*. Yes, she was angry that he couldn't accept her charts. But what man would? She simply needed to convince him. Somehow.

"Did my father wear a rowan ring when he married my mother?" Aster asked as her aunt shook out a black cape.

"Of course he did. He is a Malcolm, after all. If your bridegroom wishes to marry a Malcolm woman, he must show his acceptance of our ways. We are not women to be bullied by society or limited by perceptions." Daphne placed the rowan ring over the elaborate curls so precariously pinned into Aster's hair.

"All Malcolm men wear capes?" Dee asked with curiosity. "Will our brother have to wear twigs in his hair? His bride might take exception."

"Kenan will have to make his own decision on that," Daphne said grandly. "Malcolm men do not happen often, so there is no tradition. The rowan is a vital tool of our magic, but men do not need to display their power as much as women do."

Bree and Dee grinned at the word *magic*, and Aster sympathized, but she was too nervous to argue. She'd read the journals. She knew their history better than the girls. *Magic* merely covered the inexplicable, not necessarily the scientifically impossible. Her planets *existed*. Her accurate predictions, however, defied known science.

Rowan, on the other hand, was symbolic of their ancient heritage only useful for cowing the ignorant as far as she had determined. If she intended to start as she meant to go on, wearing twigs in her hair would certainly make a statement of sorts. She just feared it was "the bride is weird" and not "the bride is powerful."

Hugh, sporting a large goose egg over his black-and-blue eye, ran up and waited for acknowledgment. Fearing he brought news of potential disaster, Aster introduced him to her family.

"That is three of you with bruised brows," her aunt said in puzzlement. "Are fisticuffs common in this household?"

"No, we simply attract trouble," Aster said as cheerfully as she could manage. "Did you have a question, Hugh?"

"The maids would like to watch the service, my lady. They ask if they can bring down the little ones if they're ever so quiet and stand outside the door. And Uncle Pascoe sent word that he'll be here shortly. Papa said we should wait for him."

Oh dear, she'd all but forgotten the little ones in the nursery. She would be a shameful mother. But if she meant to include family—no matter how huge a circle that meant—then she should start now.

"Of course they may attend. Why don't you let them know as soon as Mr. Ives arrives? Are the villagers being looked after outside?"

"It's starting to sprinkle, so Mr. Browne has opened the stable. They're setting up tables there," Hugh said cheerfully. "Cook has covered the kitchen with food. I stole a cake."

"Why don't you run down and have them put together trays we can circulate among the guests in here while we're waiting? I'm not sure anyone properly broke their fast this morning." Except the twins, who never went without food, ever, Aster had learned.

"Pascoe Ives will attend?" her aunt asked with interest as Hugh ran off. "He's well known in political circles and could be very useful in our push for the child labor law."

"I don't know him well, but he has two small children, and he can't keep a nursemaid. So if you know anyone suitable, he would be most appreciative. And since we seem to have time," Aster said with a sigh and a wistful glance toward Theo, "you should come speak with the marquess. He is very proud and does not want anyone to notice his affliction. I would appreciate it if one of you would explain what's happening to him as we go on."

As she led her aunt toward Duncan, Theo broke away from her father to join them, leaving the earl to decide whether or not to follow. Aster smothered a grin. Her bookish bridegroom wasn't in the least concerned that he'd just dumbfounded her father, who wasn't accustomed to people turning their back on him.

"Now we will see if you are up to dealing with my family without running away to Wystan," Aster murmured as Theo grabbed her hand.

He eyed the twigs in her hair with interest. "So far, I'm more intrigued than intimidated."

"Father did not nail you to the wall and torment you?" She wished she could have been a fly on that wall, but she understood men had to pretend they were in charge by having manly discussions.

"He is rightfully anxious about you. You and I know that I'm a prince among men." He flashed her one of those boyish grins that made Aster's insides flip with happiness. "But he needs it proved. I reminded him that his daughter is the most astute of women and a perceptive reader of the zodiac and would never join hands with a renegade. That oddly seemed to reassure him."

His cheerful confidence melted her just a little more. Aster wished the crowd away and wondered if she could persuade them that if Pascoe wanted to be present, he should have been here by now.

"We cannot repair to our chamber until the guests are gone anyway," Theo whispered, as if he'd heard her thoughts.

"Could we invite them all to visit your telescopes and push them off the roof?" she suggested. "That should be sufficient disaster to prove my prediction."

Instead of replying, he chuckled and took up the role of presenting everyone to Duncan. Her groom was learning proper manners quickly, if only in self-defense, to prevent their families from insulting or maiming each other before they were introduced.

Duncan pried himself out of the chair to be presented to the ladies, but Aster knew her family didn't stand on formality and intervened on his part. "As you know, the marquess is still recuperating from his accident and must rest his leg. My lord, please do not continue standing and undo all the doctor's good work. Where is Dr. Joseph anyway? I invited him."

"He has a patient in trouble and will be along later," Lord Erran offered curtly, wandering up to add to the crowd as Duncan gratefully sat down. The marquess seemed to be locating voices well, but he was still tense.

Of all the Ives, Lord Erran was the most taciturn and the most fashionably attired—which seemed at odds with his powerful boxer's build. Aster wished she'd had time to study her charts to see if her sister or Emilia would suit him, but that would have to wait until she was married. Although she had a notion her quiet, studious life of studying charts was about to end. She was starting to understand some of Theo's frustration.

She couldn't believe she was actually marrying the brilliant man she'd met little more than a month ago! Theo's charts had shown the part of murder followed by marriage. Her charts had given her no such warning. Although, she realized with a sigh, she hadn't been looking for marriage in her stars.

Or perhaps *marriage* was the danger in her family sector, and she'd overlooked that angle.

Fortunately, the servants arrived with trays of food and tea, and the crowd around Ashford began to part.

"Emilia is looking for a husband," Aster whispered in Lord Erran's ear as he shifted to grab a small sandwich. "She has a very large inheritance."

Looking mildly interested, he turned to find her tall cousin, now speaking with Aster's father.

"Brianna knows Mrs. Siddons," she murmured to Jacques a little later while pouring a cup of tea. His eyes widened, and he carried a plate of delicacies in the direction of her younger sister.

As his brothers and her family began to drift off in different directions, Theo hugged her. "Now do we get an explanation of the twiggy hair?"

Apparently smelling the sweets, Duncan declined the tray a footman waved beneath his nose. "Malcolm idiocy," he answered without hesitation. "I've heard about their ceremonies. They like to pretend they're bewitching you."

Aster filled a small plate with delicacies and broke off a bite-sized piece of a lemon bar. She popped it into Duncan's mouth before he finished his sentence. He glared but chewed.

"I like that solution," Theo said, helping himself to the other piece of the bar. "Every time he says something unpleasant, I shove food in his mouth."

"Large family, old trick," Aster said with a dismissive wave. "Aunt Daphne, you may explain to the marquess what we will be doing. If Mr. Ives does not arrive before everyone is finished eating, then I suggest we not take up more of the vicar's valuable time and proceed with the ceremony."

"Or we'll have a stable full of drunken villagers who will begin burning down the Hall," Theo added helpfully. "I'm fairly certain the kegs will have been breached by now. Whose idea was it to invite the village?"

"Mine," the earl thundered, coming up behind them to grasp a fistful of the sweets. "Marriages should be celebrated by the entire community. If you're not to do it proper in the kirk, then you must bring the congregation here. I'll not have my daughter married off in a ramshackle manner."

Aster sighed and squeezed Theo's hand. She should have guessed. Theo pressed a kiss to her brow to show his lack of concern for her father's arrogance. Her groom smelled of sandalwood and lemon and she almost licked him.

Duncan held out his hand for more lemon bar. "Then let us hurry and finish the food and get this over with before the village is staggering drunk. Are you wearing a frilly cape yet, Theo?"

"Cape?" he asked warily.

Daphne signaled for the valise. "You are all descendants of Malcolms, however far removed, and fully entitled to the appropriate symbols. I have brought black for Lord Theophilus in honor of your heritage." Aster's aunt brought out a waist-length cloak of the sort a medieval knight might have worn.

"I hope you brought brooches," Aster said, reaching for a sandwich to settle her nervous stomach. "I had to search the house up and down for sufficient pins for my attire and have nothing left to pin a cape."

Daphne held up matching gold circle pins. Aster sighed and allowed her lovely silk bodice to be covered by a white silk cloak pinned by a gold brooch. At least it didn't entirely conceal what her low-cut neckline revealed and that Theo had been admiring.

Her bridegroom frowned warily at the rowan circlet but obediently stooped so her aunt could place it on his thick hair. It immediately slid to one side, and he had to catch it.

"Theo's head is too big for the rowan," Aster told Duncan, who couldn't see the silliness but listened appreciatively.

"Perhaps we can pin a brooch to his head," the marquess said dryly.

"Very helpful, big brother. I shall remember that when the time comes. Aster, make certain he marries another Malcolm," Theo ordered, submitting to the rather dramatic black cape that worked well draped over one shoulder of his black and white attire.

"Yes, master," she acquiesced with a mock curtsy—which drew his appreciative eye to the little cleavage she now revealed. "Do you think we could break out the sherry yet? I'm not certain I can tolerate the suspense much longer. What if your uncle is leading a band of wild savages or has crashed his horse over a bluff or wild lions have leapt out upon him? How long must we wait?"

"Duncan's eaten the last lemon bar from our plate," Theo noted. "That's signal enough for me."

"I've a biscuit to go," her father said with a nasty grin. "How much will ye pay me to scarf it down?"

"Do you want me to take Aster to see her family on our wedding journey or shall we go to the Outer Hebrides instead?" Theo asked without rancor, taking the sweet and handing half to Aster.

Aster beamed happily. "See, Papa? I am marrying a master of compromise. Just don't anger him."

Theo placed a finger of warning over her lips and nodded toward the entrance. "The mob approaches."

The delighted screeches of two toddlers in the foyer spoke for themselves. The maids hadn't waited to come down—and Pascoe had apparently arrived. Nervously, Aster straightened her cape, then took Theo's hand again.

"Is the vicar still standing?" she whispered, afraid to look after all the liquor had been passed around.

"He's a good, teetotaling man." Theo gestured for the vicar to join them.

"Teetotaling?" Aster asked weakly. "Is that cant?"

"Ask the vicar," Theo said with a shrug. "He's the one who used the term. I think it means he frowns on inebriation. We'll have to send him away before the kegs are emptied."

Pascoe strode in, drenched from the rain, and carrying his young twins. "Let the party commence!" he shouted into the sudden silence following a crack of thunder.

"It's a solemn ceremony of matrimony, not a heathen festival," the vicar retorted, striding toward the hearth where the participants stood.

"Oops, we'd better look holy," Aster whispered to her groom as the vicar eyed their rowan and capes with suspicion.

"Tradition," Theo told the wary vicar in a grave tone. "You will be joining two very old families who are set in their ways. I trust you won't mind our eccentricities."

"I'd mind them less if you spent more time in church. I'll count myself lucky that you have bothered to request my presence at all." The vicar stationed himself in front of the unlit hearth and raised his voice over the growing roar of rain. "Dearly beloved, we are gathered together..."

Theo held Aster's hand so tightly, she thought her bones might break.

Twenty-seven

"I BELIEVE EVERYONE has slid under the table by now," Theo whispered, leading his bride to the back stairwell later that evening. He held up his candle and admired her now disheveled beauty. The village guests had insisted on several rounds of dancing to a fiddle. Her face was flushed and her smile—so beautiful that his heart, and other parts lower, ached.

His bride had been the toast of the party, but Theo's mind currently had only one thought in it—and it wasn't dancing.

"It's been a lovely celebration," Aster sighed in satisfaction, taking his hand and examining his bruised knuckles. "You should not have punched that silly twit. He isn't worth the bruise much less the brawl."

He couldn't remember a time when anyone had been concerned about the state of his knuckles. His selfish side relished the attention—only because it was his intriguing bride offering it.

His bride—a woman who was all his. He was feeling very caveman-ish as he led her up the stairs.

"If Montfort's father won't teach him how to behave, someone must." Theo grinned in satisfaction at the memory of plowing his fist into the pup's square jaw. "Although I rather like your father's method of lesson-teaching. Your interference may have kept us both from flinging him into the pond, and I doubt that Roddy ever exerted himself to learn to swim. I think disaster has been nicely averted for today."

He rubbed the sapphire-and-gold ring he'd placed on her finger hours ago, claiming her as his. They'd returned the capes and rowan to her aunt directly after the ceremony—which had exposed the full beauty of his bride's bosom for his admiration. He'd spent the afternoon wishing everyone would fall off a cliff so he could have her alone.

When she'd disappeared from the festivities to feed her cats, he'd grabbed the opportunity for escape. After she'd seen to her pets, he'd led her astray.

Finally, he had her alone.

"Amazingly, everyone has been on what passes for their best behavior," she acknowledged. "Ashford has retired to his room, and your brothers dragged Bree and Dee off to the dancing. I think they're all sufficiently diverted to make our escape, if only I knew where we're escaping to!" She looked up at him expectantly.

Theo kissed her quickly, just to show his appreciation. To do more would delay them where they might be found at any moment. "Come along. I've planned a hideaway. It's not much right now, but if you like it, we can improve it later."

"One of those improvements your family enjoys like plumbing rather than niceties like fluffy pillows?" she asked in amusement, following him up more stairs.

"We might even have fluffy pillows unless you take to bringing the animals to bed with us. But right now, we may need your umbrella." He led the way up to the attic level. "If it's raining, you may wish to simply stay down here. I had a room made up in the attic in case of rain. At least we'll hear anyone coming if they're looking for us."

"And what do you have that requires an umbrella?" she asked with interest.

Theo thought his heart might explode with approval at her willingness to adventure further. He could not imagine another woman of his acquaintance being so intrepid. He led her up a narrow set of stairs and pushed open a hatch door. "The rain seems to have stopped. I think I even see a few stars."

"Your telescopes!" she said breathlessly, pushing up closer to see out. "You do not fear me falling off the roof?"

"I have illumination tonight." Helping her to the roof, he hugged her and let her admire his handiwork.

He'd set lanterns along the path to his telescopes so she could see where to place her feet. Above them, clouds parted, revealing the night sky in all its diamond-sparkling glory.

But tonight, the woman in Theo's arms captured his attention more than the stars. She laughed and tilted her head back against his shoulder to admire the celestial display. "I feel so small and unimportant!"

"If you do not fear crossing the roof, I'll show you how very insignificant we are." He held her shoulders and waited, hoping he had correctly judged her reaction to his academic choice of wedding night activity.

She studied him with curiosity. "I know that it's providential the stars have finally come out in time for our wedding night. I am all in favor of visiting the stars, but would you really show me the universe before bedding me?"

"Yes," he said firmly. "I do not need to seek moons tonight, but I want you to understand why the stars are more important to me than cows. I need you to understand why—if given any chance—I'll disappear for hours at a time, probably when you need me most. And I want you to be comfortable seeking me out if you need me."

Her smile was more blinding than the sun and his heart nearly stopped in his chest. He was having a hard time staying with the agenda he'd set to make her wedding night perfect.

"Then let us examine the stars," she said with all evidence of happiness. "I must admit the real sky is far more intriguing than mathematical charts."

Theo held her in a firm grip as they crossed the flat but uneven roof, aware of the precious gift he'd been given this day. His bride was sturdy and strong, but beside him, she felt like an autumn rose capable of shattering in a wind. He'd never been trusted with a treasure to guard, and he was desperate to show that her predictions of disaster were incorrect.

Her copper curls flew about in the wind, and she brushed them away with one hand while gripping his arm in the other. He led her to his newest telescope and showed her the eyepiece. "Look in here. Close one eye until you can focus."

"It's all blurry," she said in disappointment, peering into the glass.

"Give your eyes time to adjust. It's very odd to see objects so distant up close, and it takes time to accept what you're seeing."

She placed her hands behind her back, and Theo could tell his whirlwind bride was concentrating hard. Here was the focused, intelligent woman who had drawn up those intricate charts. Even if he did not understand her work, he admired her dedication to a complicated task. He wanted her to feel the same about his pursuits.

"Oh," she finally said with eagerness. "Is that odd bluish circle a planet? It looks like a big ball!"

"Uranus," Theo said in satisfaction, circling her waist in his arms. "If you look close, you can see the brightness fades toward the outer edges. And each night, it's in a slightly different place in the sky because it is orbiting the sun at a different rate than we are."

"Uranus! That's the planet changing all my charts! It's so pretty. Can I see other planets?"

"Some other night." Theo teased at her breasts, eager for the pleasure part of his agenda now that he'd done his duty. "Tonight, we'll create our own stars."

She leaned into him with a sigh of pleasure and let him caress her as he desired. "I thought you'd never ask."

Below, the fiddle played and people laughed as the party spilled from the stable. Theo hoped that meant everyone would stay occupied another few hours. Aster's father might be a fire-breathing dragon, but he'd been right to create a celebration to disguise their escape.

"Come along, then, and see what I've so crudely thrown together. I thought if I did it myself, no one would know where to find us." Holding Aster's arm so she didn't slip in her high heels, Theo led her toward the office he'd established on the roof in lieu of the observatory he craved.

He assumed the structure had once been a guard tower of sorts. It had been expanded and improved over the centuries, but it was still very crude by any standards. He swallowed his fear of terrifying his bride into running and opened the door. "If it isn't to your taste, we can return to the attic suite I had the maids set up."

He touched his candle to a sconce, illuminating the room, and tried to see it through her eyes. The mattress wasn't ordinarily in here. He'd rigged a rope bed to hold it, and remembering her cushioned drawing room, he'd rounded up all the unused pillows he could find. He'd stolen covers from unused beds. But he hadn't added draperies to the many windows. The night sky provided decoration.

"Oh, how cozy!" she cried, to his relief. "Even though you argue and disagree with my warnings, you've still found a place so far from my family that I can't possibly harm them!" she cried in glee, flinging her arms around his neck. "You understand!"

Well, mostly he'd wanted privacy from *his* family, but he'd accept all the gratitude he could get. He held her tightly and poured kisses on her head while their hearts pounded in tandem. "I understand your fear, anyway. I'm still not saying you're right. I just want you to be happy."

"Oh, my, look at the moonlight!" she cried, spinning out of his arms to admire the windows. "It spills everywhere. I'm so glad the rains have gone. Is this your desk?" She touched the crude table covered in papers and books. "The roof must be snug for these not to be damp."

"It is the bed I wish you to admire, goose, not my papers." Finally having her alone, Theo swung her into his arms and covered her mouth with his so she could not object to his name-calling.

Far from objecting, she flung her arms around his neck again with gratifying speed. "This," he murmured senselessly. "This is what I need more than planets and stars. I feel as if I've waited forever."

"To the twelfth of never," she agreed, spreading her kisses up his jaw.

Glad that he'd stolen the time to shave again, Theo let her take the lead on kisses while he reached for the hooks at her back. To his surprise, he only found ribbons. He tugged on one, loosening her bodice, but he couldn't find the rest of the hooks to remove it.

She smelled of roses and cinnamon, and everywhere he touched was like caressing purest silk. She surrounded him in her sensuality before he even had the pleasure of her feminine pulchritude in his crude hands.

She gasped as he slid off her narrow sleeves, baring her shoulders. Still half-fastened, the bodice merely slid to the tips of her high, full breasts, framing the heart-shaped mark near her cleavage. Moonlight spilled across her ivory skin, and Theo wanted her naked.

As if reading his mind, she clasped her arm over her falling bodice and smiled up at him. "Unwrap me," she commanded, turning her back to him.

"Laces!" he crowed in delight, finally seeing what she had done. "How did you do this?" He'd never been given a gift-wrapped package. Aster was all the presents he hadn't known he'd missed receiving until now. Like a boy with a new toy, he painstakingly undid the remaining ribbons, freeing them from their hooks, so he could peel back the wrapping of her gown.

His efforts were rewarded with the exposure of her translucent shift and slender back—a gift from the heavens, one only a man could appreciate.

"I robbed your mother's wardrobe of ribbons. It wasn't difficult. Otherwise, you'd have spent all night unfastening all the beads from their loops." She shrugged off the bodice, revealing a beribboned corset.

"Gift-wrapped, just for me," he said with amusement, tugging ties all over. "I could learn to love this game." He placed kisses where each ribbon unfurled, starting with her satin shoulders, working down to her breasts as he unwound the corset.

"I shall remember to wrap all your gifts in ribbons from now on," she said in a whisper, shivering as he leaned over her shoulder and kissed just above her bared nipple.

His bride was strong and smart and everything he'd ever wanted in a woman—but she was still untouched by any hand but his. Even though she encouraged him to play, Theo still understood that she was a responsibility as great as taking on Duncan's duty. It would be up to him to teach her to want him as much as he wanted her.

If he wasn't so powerfully aroused, he'd reach for a book to see if anyone had written lessons on such an immense subject.

He couldn't stop touching Aster if someone had offered him an observatory.

He turned her around, lifted her heavy breasts, and pressed a kiss to each one. His magical bride moaned and held his shoulders to steady herself.

He untied her skirt and petticoat and lifted her from the lengths of silk and lace. Carrying her to the mattress, he pressed kisses everywhere he could reach, too thrilled to have her to himself at last to think further.

She still wore her flimsy under-shift but she did nothing to cover herself as he shrugged off his coat and began unfastening his waistcoat. Moonlight poured over her skin in a pearly radiance he could practically taste. Theo hastily struggled from the fancified waistcoat the valet had locked him into.

"I'm warning you, if they start shooting cannon down there, I'm not going out to see what's happening." He unbuttoned his breeches so he could free his shirt.

"We have enough family around to handle any emergencies, I should think," she said, with what might have been amusement except she seemed fixated on his undressing.

"Should I turn off the sconce?" he asked, aware the moonlight was as bright as the light.

"I'm not shy if you're not." She snuggled into the pillows, the very picture of innocence and wantonness combined. "Although if the lights can be seen below, you might want to conceal our hiding place."

Just looking at her was making him light-headed. He wasn't a connoisseur of women, so he didn't have the words to define his bride's lush sensuality. He simply knew he could explore her delights for a lifetime.

He turned off the lamp, then sat down beside her to rip off his shoes and stockings. The moonlight illumined the bed beautifully. He could see her rosy nipples through the transparent chemise. He wanted to remove the rest of the pins from her wayward curls, bury his hands in the mass, then kiss her breasts until she begged for more.

"I'm not a smooth seducer," he warned her. "I am not glib with words. Charm is not in my nature. But if you don't need charm and seduction, I think I can do what comes naturally without any problem."

She laughed and ran her hand up his bare arm. "I distrust charm and seduction. I trust you and your planets. *This* is safe and good and real. I think I shall start looking for the silver lining behind every cloud. If the roof crashes under us tonight, then it's a sign that you needed to fix the roof, and we discovered it before it leaked."

Theo laughed and sprawled out on the crude, pillow-littered bed with her, leaving his trousers unfastened but still in place. Propped on one elbow, he leaned over her and began kissing her again. "I will endeavor—" he said in between kisses "—not to crash any roofs."

ASTER WELCOMED Theo's heavy weight pressing her into the mattress. He grounded the giddiness inspired by his caresses—and the dizziness of believing she could actually have *family* again. She was so filled with joy that she thought she might explode into bubbles—and all because of this man, her husband.

She knew where intimacy led, understood the danger, and she still could not force herself to be her usual sensible self. She was entitled to set prophesy aside on her wedding night and simply enjoy the pleasure provided by the man she'd just promised to love, honor, and obey. Except she'd changed that vow to love, honor, *and take thee in equality*, according to Malcolm custom. The vicar really hadn't noticed. Perhaps because her family had begun humming.

Boldly wrapping her arms around her groom's neck, she pulled Theo down to cover his face with kisses. The stars were right about this much—he was the perfect mate for her.

She studied his bare chest in awe and excitement. For someone who claimed to spend a lot of time with books, Theo was well-muscled. She'd seen him knock Montfort half way across the drive, so he wasn't precisely the bookworm he claimed.

But despite all that powerful strength, Theo was careful in not pushing her too far, too fast. She appreciated his attention to detail, and relished his admiration as he opened her shift to gaze unabashedly on her breasts. But once he bent to taste her aroused nipples, the connection he'd already taught her between what he was doing and her womb drove her into a frenzy of desire.

She dared a touch to his dark nipple, and he moaned just as she had when he'd touched her. Liking that, she rubbed harder, then lifted herself to suckle as he'd done.

"Oh, gads, Aster!" Theo fell down on the mattress, carrying her on top of him. "You're a brilliant student. Tell me what you'd like."

"For you to show me what you like, then perhaps I'll know."

He suckled at her breast and ran his hand between her thighs to ply her there. Like the wanton she was, Aster spread her legs, begging for what he'd denied her earlier. She ached with need and was liquefying with lust.

Theo wasted no time in returning her to the mattress so he might remove the last bits of his clothing. Finally, she could admire all his glorious masculine nudity, although he did not give her much time to study his maleness. He dropped down on top of her, pushing her into the bed, using his powerful thighs to open her for the act she craved.

"It's time, Theo," she whispered urgently. "I won't break, I promise. I *need* this." She wasn't entirely certain what she was saying, but her womb had been empty far longer than she'd ever wanted. If she was to ever have a child of her own... Ancient magic ruled the night. "Now, Theo, please."

Their bodies shadowed his heavy arousal, but she felt the blunt thickness pushing at her slick entrance. He caressed her there, causing her to moan and lift into him in eagerness. He eased deeper. She raised her legs to surround his hips, desperate for completion. He pushed again, stretching her more.

"Oh, bloody hell, Aster. If I don't take you now, I may combust," he muttered, pulling back and surging forward again.

He still wasn't completely inside her. She feared he was too big, that she was too small or unformed. But then she remembered this was where babies came from, and she grabbed his shoulders and pressed kisses everywhere she could reach. "Do it, Theo. Make me yours," she urged.

With one final thrust, he broke her in two. She cried out her pain and delight and confusion—just as shots filled the air outside.

"Not stopping," he muttered, pulling back and thrusting again, rubbing that place that made her swoon with need.

She dug her fingers into straining masculine muscles and lifted herself into him. "It's good, Theo, it's so good, don't stop, don't ever stop."

And blessed man that he was, he filled her, he sent her reeling toward the stars, and while her body convulsed with the rapture he provided, he shouted his release and poured his life's seed into her.

Twenty-eight

THEO WANTED to sprawl forever on top of his magnificent wife and never have to leave this glorious haven again. But aware he was nearly twice her weight, he forced himself to roll over. A few more pops that sounded like gunfire split the air. "They may all shoot themselves," he muttered, cuddling her warm curves against him.

"Watch the window," she murmured sleepily. "If the sky explodes, it's just my father."

"Perfect sense," he grumbled, prying open one eye while his brain screamed for insensibility. "Looks like a shooting star."

"My father's fireworks. He's a madman." She snuggled closer, bringing all her cinnamon-roses lusciousness into contact with his waking body.

"Fair enough. No wonder we don't scare you. Go to sleep before I molest you again." He sprawled on his stomach to quench arousal and circled her waist with one arm.

"Bathing room next time," his redoubtable wife reminded him.

That wasn't conducive to appeasing desire.

They slept despite the fireworks. They woke with the gray dawn and made love again.

And then, with the snickering unfamiliarity of newlyweds, they crept down to the attic suite where the confused maids had lit a fire and laid out robes on the untouched bed. Someone had thoughtfully added the cats.

Theo studied the striped creature clinging to the ancient draperies. "We might want shutters once we choose our rooms."

"Tabby is intrepid. He'll come down when he's ready. Do we get to choose our own suite?" Aster asked with interest, gathering up a purring ball of black fur.

"I recommend installing an armed fortress to block passage to everything in the rear corridor in the wing furthest from my brothers and nearest the bathing room. All we'd need is access to the kitchen and we could forget everyone else exists." Theo tied his banyan over his trousers and wondered if his valet was wandering the halls with his clothes in hand.

"That is admittedly tempting." Aster set her cat on the bed. "I'm not accustomed to so much... interaction. May I transport my pillows and carpets from my London house?" She removed her wedding dress again, and tied on her sturdy flannel robe.

Theo scowled at the plaid abomination she was wearing. "When's your birthday? I'm buying you a better robe."

"October second, but we've better things to do than look for robes. Having all our clothes in one place might be useful though." She gathered up her silk and lace and waited for him to open the door.

His hitherto undiscovered caveman side wanted to hide her out of sight of their families and keep her to himself. But he supposed he'd have to prove that his wife still lived before her father would leave them in peace.

Who was he trying to fool? Peace did not exist in Iveston.

As if to prove this truth, the nursery rang with wails as they passed by. Aster hesitated, but hearing Pascoe pleading with his offspring, Theo dragged her on.

On the next floor, Hugh and Hartley were dueling with canes they were probably supposed to be taking to their father. Theo guided Aster down the cross corridor to her old room and pressed a kiss to her brow. "Bathe, dress, we'll tell the guests they can leave or we can, and we'll pack a breakfast and hide."

She laughed, kissed his jaw, and slipped into her room.

He really should have planned this better, but he was blamed lucky to have even arranged a marriage ceremony. He'd done it! He'd persuaded the fairy general to stay with him and she hadn't run off! Theo nearly strutted back to his chamber.

Of course, now he had to ensure that his bride would not abandon him *after* the fact. This thinking of others business was rough.

He let Duncan's valet shave and dress him. Theo resented the necessity, but if he was to act in Duncan's stead, then he must make some attempt to keep up appearances, at least while Aster's family hung about. Besides, she had seemed to appreciate his sartorial elegance yesterday and at the tea party—until he'd had to stamp out flames.

He refused to go downstairs until Aster was ready. With the new freedom of a married man, he knocked on her door and slipped past her maid when she opened it. His bride smiled in delight. Reassured by her welcome, Theo kissed her brow and finished hooking one of the gowns her sister had brought with her.

"It's raining again. Let's play house," he murmured.

She laughed and slipped from his grasp. "First, let's see if we are to be rid of my family and half of yours or if I must tell Cook to butcher a herd to keep them fed. *Then* we can play house."

"Feeding the savages keeps them occupied, understood," he said wisely.

She took his arm. "Having so many people here at once offers easier opportunities to escape," she assured him. "They can entertain each other."

The rotunda was already filling with boxes and trunks, Theo noted in relief. Aster might believe that guests entertained one another, but he knew his family better. War and chaos ensued when they were trapped in one place for any length of time.

The newly redecorated dining chamber was crammed with people in travel dress filling their plates and roaming about, reminding each other of tasks to be completed before they left. Only half of them even bothered looking up when Theo led his bride into their midst. The women, of course, swooped in with a flutter of perfumes and petticoats to hug and kiss Aster. Unused to this much femininity in one place, Theo reluctantly released her and made his way to his new father-in-law.

"The fireworks were... entertaining," Theo said dryly.

"Glad you enjoyed them," the earl roared, slamming him on the back. "Bring Aster up to see us and you'll see real fireworks! When will you be coming?"

"When Aster says the time is right," Theo replied, realizing Aster's charts made a grand excuse for almost anything.

"She'll dilly-dally if you let her," Lochmas warned. "If she says a date might be a good time, settle on it right then or she'll come back a minute later and tell ye there's a bad star on the right or summat of that sort. Take her in hand!"

Theo grinned to himself at the idea of taking Aster in hand—he doubted if his interpretation was the same as her father's. "Right you are," he said jovially. "I take it everyone is set on leaving today?"

"Pascoe's been telling me of some Luddites who want to turn back time, stop canals, close the turnpikes, and build medieval castles or lunacy of the sort. They're a danger to the likes of us. I'll be going up to London with him to see if there's aught we can do to end their depredations. He told you about guarding the manufactory, did he now?" The earl wasn't roaring, but speaking urgently, casting a glance about the room half full of women.

"He did. My men have been warned, but I can't buy an army to guard all the machinery. There can never be progress if we must constantly be looking over our shoulders! We'll just deal with problems as they arrive." Annoyed at being dragged into business on what he considered his honeymoon, Theo began filling his plate.

Aster's Aunt Daphne sailed up to join them. "I have half a dozen more workhouse girls to send down for training. Pascoe says he's stealing one of Aster's half-trained maids for his twins. You'll need to set up a nursery to train more."

Theo coughed and the earl roared his laughter.

ASTER GLANCED up to see Theo's ears turning red and her father laughing like a fool. Aunt Daphne appeared mildly offended. All was well with her world.

Her new husband had refused to don a high shirt collar, as usual, and he'd already loosened his neckcloth, but his form-fitting green coat and white trousers had her sighing with lust.

"Did you have a chance to observe Theo's brothers?" she asked Emilia, watching Theo rather than the company. "I need to see how this new planet affects my charts. I can start on the one you're interested in, if so."

Emilia answered with a verbal shrug. "They're all handsome. If all they need of me is money, then the younger ones will suit. The marquess is a demanding sort, though."

"All right, I'll look at Lord Erran, William, and Jacques." Although Aster had her doubts about all three. They didn't really *need* money, but she thought they might need women to look after them them—as Theo had. And Emilia wouldn't do it. "I'm just not entirely certain this is the best way to approach your need for funds."

"I'm not likely to fall in love," Emilia reminded her. "I don't have time. I need to be back in my laboratory today, if I could just persuade Mother to hurry up."

Now they both watched the other side of the room where Daphne had caught Theo's studious attention.

"I'm not entirely certain I can train as many servants as she wishes," Aster said doubtfully. "This house needs a great deal of attention, and I still have my charts to keep up. It would be lovely to have a few servants who actually know what they're doing, but I'd feel as if I was letting your mother down."

"Hire teachers," Emilia suggested.

"Not if I have to train them too! But I suppose I could make a few inquiries. We could transform Iveston into a school for professional servants," she added with a laugh.

"Training people makes more sense than sending them to the workhouse. Then all you'd have to do is figure out what to do with all Aunt Gwenna's maimed children." She patted Aster sympathetically on the shoulder.

"Now that I've acquired a husband, I fear that task must fall on Brianna or one of our cousins. Surely one of us has a gift for that sort of thing." Aster fretted at her bottom lip, knowing her aunts had been depending on her—but so was Theo.

She had been selfish in choosing to take this opportunity for a family instead of remaining single, but she still didn't regret it. Perhaps if she never looked at her charts again, she could live like everyone else and blithely take one day at a time.

That would be truly selfish. Her duty was to protect and aid her family, and her gift was reading the stars. Theo knew she couldn't just be a housewife. She feared life would become very complicated once this moment of happiness passed.

Hearing Pascoe coming down the stairs with his excited toddlers, Aster realized she now had more than herself and Theo and their respective families and problems to fret over. Soon, they might have their own nursery. When would she have *time* to chart the planets?

Her various duties nagged at her as she saw her family off. She cried as she hugged them and sent them away, not knowing when or if she'd see them again. She was not so very far from her London relations, but until she saw her chart clear, she wasn't certain how often she dared visit.

Theo held her as they waved farewell to the carriages rolling down the drive. Fighting tears, she clung to his strength for these few minutes. Learning to deal with each other and their new relationship was the real test ahead of them, not this parting.

As they left the portico and returned to the rotunda, Duncan's angry shouts rang overhead, a couple of the puppies escaped the conservatory, with one of the twins chasing after them, and the housekeeper awaited Aster's orders. *This* was her future.

She hesitated, overwhelmed, but Theo was made of sterner stuff. "Meet us upstairs, Mrs. Smith," he ordered, marching for the stairs. "Bring a few strong footmen and your maids with you. We have work to do."

Aster hitched up her skirt and hurried after him, heart foolishly singing. Theo might declare himself a bookworm, but he knew how to take charge when he wanted. He was a handsome man, but when his jaw set like that, he was swoon-worthy.

"We'll need carpenters," Theo declared as he led his parade down the intersecting corridor to the west wing where her female relations had stayed. "We'll add a wall and entrance door across here."

He gestured to an area half way down the rear wing. "Aster, do you want a parlor in front? I think we could knock out the bedchamber walls and extend a room across here." He indicated the area just past where he wanted the door.

Delighted with the notion of designing her own suite, Aster opened the doors to the small chambers on either side. "There won't be a lot of light, but we could add a chandelier over the entrance. These old pieces will need to be hauled to the attic. Mrs. Smith, can you direct that?"

The portly housekeeper nodded officiously and gestured for one of the footmen to begin dismantling old beds. "New draperies, my lady?"

"Yes, certainly, once the carpenters are done. We could remove these now before the mess ensues. Perhaps some of the fabric is salvageable?"

Uninterested in draperies, Theo proceeded down the corridor, opening more doors. "This one for the master chamber, I believe."

He stood aside so Aster could admire the spacious room he'd chosen. "Do you require a separate chamber or should we turn the next one into dressing rooms?"

Aster covered her mouth and thought of the immensity of what he was asking in front of all their servants. Privacy was obviously not part of the routine here. Rather than answer, she crossed to the connecting door and peered in. "This chamber would make a lovely large dressing room with small bedchambers on either side."

She'd leave it up to everyone else to decide whether one of the beds was for her or for her maid. For herself—she'd rather sleep with Theo. She glanced up and saw a sparkle of approval in his eyes. Good. She'd done one thing right today—proving theirs was definitely not a marriage in name only. She was ready to shut everyone out and return to Theo's bed, except they really didn't have one of their own yet.

He crossed the corridor to two similar rooms. "Our offices?"

Aster tried not to let her mouth drop open. "Our very own private offices where we can work uninterrupted?"

"The very same," he said in triumph. "We will lock the front entrance against all intruders and have locks for our offices as well. It will require fire and blood before anyone is allowed to disturb us."

"You learn well," she said with laughter. She swept into a peacock-blue room adorned only with an ancient chest of drawers and a vanity. The wooden floor was scarred but solid. The window overlooked the abandoned courtyard and what had once been a rose-covered stone wall. "I want this one. I shall have my charts brought down so I might start work at once."

"What about the salon, my lord?" Mrs. Smith asked worriedly, nodding her head toward the end of the corridor.

Aster followed them down to the unexplored reaches of the wing. Double doors opened onto a marvelous expanse of windows, old carpets, fading drapery, and a vast collection of ornate gilded chairs and tables apparently stored here to protect them against dogs and boys. The ceiling had been painted and plastered in the style of Adams, and the fireplace surround was decorated in the same style with blue cameos, gilded plaster roping, and hand-painted flowers.

"Oh, this must have been grand!" She raced from window to

window. "Why will this not be our parlor instead of destroying those front rooms?"

"Because this is our *private* parlor," Theo declared. "Or nursery or schoolroom or whatever you wish to make of it. Others might visit in the front parlor, but this one is for us alone."

"And the cats," she declared pertly, trying not to show how she felt about the notion of a nursery. "And Hog, of course."

"Shutters on the windows then," he agreed with laughter. "I just want these rooms to look like your London home—all neat and orderly and full of fascinating curiosities."

A *home*—he was creating a nest for her to feather. Aster flung herself into his arms and covered his square jaw with kisses.

The servants hustled out.

"When the world crashes all around us, we'll come here," Theo whispered in her ear.

When, not if.

Twenty-nine

SATISFIED that he'd given his little general a task that would make them both happy, Theo left Aster transporting her charts and cats to her new office and went in search of Duncan.

He didn't have to go far. With his host duties over, Duncan had crawled back into his cave. Theo found him stalking his chamber in boredom, apparently counting his steps from one wall to the other.

"A cane would save a lot of counting," Theo said dryly, picking up an abandoned walking stick and looking for a safe place to set it.

"And how the hell do you expect me to find the bloody things?" Duncan demanded. "They walk off on their own."

"Not if you would hang on to them instead of flinging them at our heads. Did you, Pascoe, and Lochmas come to any conclusions about our Swinger problem or do we just wait for the rioters to destroy the threshers?" Theo rapped the cane's handle against Duncan's shoulder so he'd know where to find it.

Duncan swiped the stick and used it to find a chair. "I will become old and fat moldering up here," he complained rather than answer the question.

"I am hiring carpenters to build a suite in the west wing. I can have them build you a boxing gym if it makes you happy. Or perhaps we can hang ropes out the window for you to climb up and down."

The damned marquess actually looked interested in this last proposal. "Ropes might be easier than stairs. Or a platform pulley between the floors."

"I'm glad I've given you something to think about. Now will you answer my question?" Theo gripped his fingers into fists of frustration. "I promised Aster a wedding journey, but we cannot go until I know the estate is safe. I have no understanding of the rioters' arguments."

"That's because they're not logical," Duncan said with a dismissive gesture as he took a seat. "The men behind our local riots are ninnyhammers who indulge in drunken rages based on jealousies, arrogance, stupidity, and fear."

Theo scowled. "Fine, then. Who are these monsters of depravity so I can ship them to New South Wales, or better yet, deepest Africa where they might feed hungry cannibals? Sensible Englishmen don't need iconoclasts telling them what to do."

Duncan snorted. "That's what you get for burying your head in books and scientific communities. *Iconoclasts*! Go to my clubs and talk to those so-called sensible Englishmen and see how many believe trains will be the end of civilization as we know it. Most of them think steam is the work of the devil."

"What do your aristocratic clodpolls have to do with our threshing machines and rioting farmers?" Theo asked, running his hand over his hair and wishing he could hide in his office with his telescopes and books. The passages of planets were predictable. Human behavior eluded him.

"Wealthy landowners who don't want to spend money to change their ways encourage the Luddites to do their dirty work for them," Duncan explained impatiently. "Right now, threshing machines are their target. There's similar unrest over our mining improvements. Your glass manufactory is mysterious and thus cause for suspicion, so you're next on their list. And if Pascoe is correct, we may be targeted out of jealousy and spite simply because we're Ives. You haven't made a friend in Montfort. And now that I'm no longer marrying Margaret, Caldwell is no longer inclined to stand in Montfort's way."

"What the devil do they care what we do?" Theo's fury rose with his impatience. "It's our land!"

"I told you, it's not logical." Duncan tapped his stick. "The uneducated and narrow-minded simply fear change. The more educated leaders resent our wealth, and fear us because we're more powerful than they are, which threatens the control of their petty fiefdoms. Pascoe believes my support for several Whig bills has led Caldwell, Montfort, and others of their ilk to distrust us. We are, after all, aiding and abetting the despised Cit industrialists as well as supporting labor against the time-honored traditions of the upper classes. There's nothing you can do, Theo. Browne is handling our tenants. They won't be joining the rioters. That's all I can promise."

"We should steer the drunkards toward Montfort. I'd think his tenants ought to be ready to rise up in arms given how he treats them. I can't keep hanging about, waiting for disaster to strike." Theo winced, remembering Aster telling him he tended to act before thinking. She was right.

"So, don't. Go to London. Present your astronomical papers. Visit Aster's family. William can stay here for a change and lead armies, if needed. We must go on as if all is normal."

This was his new normal, Theo realized glumly. "I never wanted your responsibilities. I don't have the right brain for them."

"I can't ask you to be me," Duncan said with what almost sounded like regret. "We'll just have to muddle along as we can. Tell me, do you love Aster? Does she love you?"

Theo blinked at this unusual change of topic. "I have no idea. It's not as if anyone ever taught us what love is about. I enjoy her company, and I think she's what this place needs. Is that not enough?"

Duncan rubbed his stick thoughtfully back and forth across the floor. "I can't say for certain. I just feel as if there needs to be something stronger than *like* to compel a woman to stay when the odds start stacking against her."

That's what Theo feared too, but he wouldn't admit it to Duncan. "Any woman who has learned to deal with Lochmas has to be strong. She'll stay," he said with a confidence he didn't feel.

Duncan nodded doubtfully and they left it at that, although worry hollowed a deeper hole in Theo's gut. If he refused to believe in Aster's astrology, then he had no right to believe foolish superstition about Ives always losing their women.

HEARING Theo's familiar boot steps on the uncarpeted corridor later that evening, Aster hastily pushed up from the charts she'd spread across the bare floor of her new office. The day had been a busy one, as she'd feared, but she'd stolen these last few hours for her work.

She petted the cats and left them in the snug nests she'd prepared for them out of old drapery and pillows. She suspected Theo wouldn't want Tiger kneading his head any more than she wanted Hog panting in her face.

She hurried across the hall to their new—shared—bedchamber.

Theo had thrown his elegant coat on a chair and was sprawled in his shirtsleeves on their new bed, hands crossed behind his head. He seemed to be studying the embroidered canopy she'd dug out of the attic for the old four-poster she'd had carried in from a guest room. He didn't glance up at her entrance but apparently recognized her footsteps as she had recognized his.

"Are those planets amid the blue blossoms?" he asked.

"They are now," she said in satisfaction, lying down beside him and gazing upward. "I'm not certain what they were intended to be, but I added a few stitches. I wasn't aiming for accuracy, just effect."

"I'm impressed. Your talents are many. I should show you what each planet looks like and let you paint the ceilings. Or the walls. Or do you know how to tell workmen to do such things?" He turned on his side and propped himself up one elbow to gaze down upon her.

Aster stroked the lines of weariness on his bristled jaw. "Just tell me what you wish, and I can find someone to do it. That part is easy. Family and tenants and keeping your enormous household accounts and that sort of thing... will take some practice."

"Just knowing you are here is enough right now." His fatigue seemed to dissipate with her stroking, which cheered her immensely. She liked knowing he needed her. She hated to add to his burdens. "I've worked on my charts some more."

He tensed again. "Do I want to hear about it?"

"Remember I told you I saw danger in the part of commerce but accomplishment in the form of allegiance?"

"And remember we laughed at the possibility of my family working together?" he retorted. "And *commerce* can mean anything."

"Not when it's on *your* chart. Your only commerce is the manufactory. And when it's in my chart as well, then it almost has to mean the manufactory is in danger. The problem is..." She hesitated, then almost whispered, "A Mars transit to both our moons is squaring Saturn. It's not just the manufactory in danger this week, but our *home*— the Hall. *That's* why I see all these knives in all our charts. Because we're all in this house when the heavens align against us."

"So all your hard work goes up in flames this week?" he asked with a hint of sarcasm. "Planets do *not* predict doom and gloom. I'll hear no more about it. Instead, tell me how you found all this flummery." He gestured at the bedcovers. "We have carpets and matching drapery? And rather impressive dressing tables."

Aster nearly wept at his dismissal of her fear, but admittedly, there was very little he could do even if he believed her. With a sign of resignation, she returned to stroking his hair. "This house has vast, uncharted depths, and no one has thrown anything out in centuries. It's just a matter of exploring and asking the servants. They're the real secret to everything. Molly has an eye for good fabric and knew exactly where to find what, even though she's only been here a few weeks. And I kept Mrs. Smith so busy, she didn't have time to tipple."

"Remarkable." He pressed kisses across her cheek. "I'll have to start thinking about installing a valet next."

"I have a few ideas about a valet as well," she said while all that temptation loomed over her. She wanted to wipe away her predictions as much as he wanted to wipe away the burdens he carried—and they'd learned a very good way of doing so.

"Will your ideas wait until morning?" He didn't give her time to answer but covered her mouth with his.

Aster was absolutely positive that valets could wait until morning. She wasn't certain her other news ought to wait, but she allowed Theo to charm and seduce her rather than add to his burdens.

IT WAS REMARKABLE how much easier it was to face a gray day when Theo had a woman to wake him with kisses—one who didn't insist on repairing her hair or asking for jewels before he tumbled her between the sheets again. He almost felt like a new man when he sprawled in utter satiation across soft linen on a mattress as fluffy as a cloud, with his wife's heavenly breasts crushed into his ribs.

"I read your mother's journal," she murmured into his shoulder.

Theo let that slide right by him. He'd given her the journal, after all. He'd expected her to read it.

"She's not on the Malcolm family tree, so I don't know if she really had a gift for prescience," she rambled, seemingly aimlessly.

Too replete to move, Theo summoned ancient memories. "Her family lived in the Americas for a long time, but her father inherited a title and brought his family back here." Theo knew he should get up and go over the ledgers with Browne this morning, but newlyweds ought to be given some leisure, he decided.

"Along with prophesying about angels falling from the heavens, your mother predicted a summer of very bad weather that would bring tragedy and danger to your family," Aster whispered. "I cannot say I yet understand Uranus, but if I'm calculating its effect correctly, we are both now sitting on the part of catastrophe. Your mother's journal agrees."

Theo winced. "*Both* of us?" That was his real fear—losing this piece of heaven at his side. He didn't want to go back to the dull days of living with his sweaty brothers in a decrepit hovel. Aster's colorful world delighted him—*Aster* delighted him. So much so that he probably ought to get up before he ravished her again. "I thought it was just commerce we affected," he said in derision.

"I told you, our *home* is in danger, which necessarily includes the entire family." She pinched him for his disbelief. "Even the twins are my family now. Perhaps we should head for Scotland and not come back until the danger is past."

"Will that help?" he asked in idle curiosity. "Are we the danger? If we leave, will everyone else be safe?" He had no objection to an excuse for heading north and escaping the estate burden, although his brothers might have something scathing to say about it.

"Together, we are part of the danger, yes," she said reluctantly. "But we cannot stop the weather—or prevent tragedy—by leaving. I'm sorry. I can't be more clear than to say the Hall and the manufactory seem to be the focus."

He growled irascibly and hugged her closer. "I don't care about your damned charts. I just want it understood that whatever we do, we do together. I will not have you leaving me as you did your family because you fear you're the problem."

She nodded warily. "It was easier when it was just me," she said. "It is very hard to protect everyone and still do my duty."

"Then worry about hiring servants," he suggested. "That's easier than wondering if we should hire an army to surround us."

"I'll need to have the rest of my things brought here," she said, apparently ready to be diverted. "Do I close up my home and bring my servants here? I will have to find a new home for my cook, if so."

"No, let us leave your house for our escape," Theo said, relieved to be discussing the mundane and not the impossible. "I like the idea that we have a place in London we can visit anytime we like. You may want to keep a skeleton staff there, and we can bring additional servants with us when we go up. I know Duncan has a townhouse, but it's large and in one of the older parts of town. I think he rents it out."

Her smile of delight erased all other concerns.

"I didn't want to seem demanding, but I like Town. So it will be lovely if we can visit. Perhaps we can go up soon and choose what to send here." She frowned again. "I wish I knew if it was better if we were not here this next week."

He ignored her reference to the planets and pretended she spoke of practical matters. "If the weather lets up, I'll go out tonight and see if the moons of Saturn are visible. Once I have my paper ready, I can arrange to meet with the Astronomical Society."

That got Theo stirring. He leaned over and kissed his perspicacious bride. "Command your troops, general. And I'll command mine, and soon, we'll have this war won."

Theo's confidence carried him through the tedious accounting session with Browne—who truly did carry the numbers in his head but couldn't write them down if a gun were held to his brainpan. Theo transcribed the information and handed it off to Jacques to put into the ledgers in proper form. Someday, he supposed, the amounts might even have meaning. For now, he felt fortunate to have them written down for reference.

"Are you keeping Lady Azenor's London house?" Jacques asked a little too casually as Theo was preparing to leave the office.

Theo froze, not completely willing to discuss their plans for occasional escape yet. "Of course, why?"

"She said I should spend more time in London making myself known among the theater community, and I realize she's right. I thought if I had a place to stay, I might learn my way around better." Jacques bent over the ledgers, trying not to look too eager.

Theo did his best not to pull his hair. He needed Jacques *here*, with Duncan. And he wanted the town house for himself and Aster. But that was his selfishness talking again.

With a sigh, he agreed. "I'll talk to Aster. It's a small place. I don't know if she'll wish to spend much keeping it open." He hoped that was restrained enough not to insult Jacques, who really did need to set out on his own. "I hadn't realized you were interested in theater."

Jacques flashed one of his grins. "Lady Azenor knew without my saying a word. Your lady is a bit spooky."

"In a good way," Theo reluctantly acknowledged. He still didn't believe in the zodiac, but Aster had inexplicable insights he was coming to accept. "You should tell the twins to let you know when their mother is in town. She might introduce you around."

"You should have Duncan open the townhouse," Jacques suggested. "Their mother is more likely to be polite if we offered something in return—like a place to stay or an occasional dinner. Now that we have a woman in the family, we can entertain more."

"If only we didn't have to stay here to be certain the family fortune isn't pillaged and stolen," Theo said dryly. "You talk Duncan into selling the London tomb and buying something more fashionable. I have to go count turnips."

Despite his discouraging words, Theo was still feeling remarkably optimistic as he rode out to discuss new barn roofs and try to decipher Browne's questions about the upcoming fall harvest. All he could do was gather information to take back to Duncan, who was probably walking the floors and smashing windows by now.

If they could pry Duncan out of the house so he could discuss these things with the tenants and other landowners, life would be simpler. But his brother had hidden in his chair through the wedding, then refused to join them in the stable party. The marquess didn't appear prepared to meet with anyone but family yet.

Pondering tying up his brother and flinging him into a carriage to cart about the countryside, Theo progressed through the remainder of the day's tasks.

He stopped at the tavern on the way home, just to wet his thirst. He knew Duncan often came here to talk with the men in town, but Theo hadn't a clue what they discussed and wasn't committed to learning. He was still pondering tying up Duncan and hauling him around. Duncan had, after all, promised Browne that he'd meet with the other farm managers so Browne needn't do so. But the inability to ride up on his big stallion—lord of all he surveyed—was no doubt painful to Dunc's pride.

Theo recognized the mayor and squire huddled at a table with other men whose faces were familiar, but he hadn't bothered learning their official capacity. He supposed they might be merchants. Since they didn't sell telescope parts, Theo hadn't had much reason to call on them.

He stepped up to the bar to order ale and felt silence fall around him. Even he wasn't dense enough not to notice.

Sipping his ale, he raised his eyebrows at the innkeeper respectfully keeping his distance while polishing his mugs. "Am I wearing a monkey on my back?"

The innkeeper shrugged. "The vicar and squire's wives called on yours today."

Theo tried to imagine how that might have gone but couldn't. Human nature simply wasn't predictable. "I assume Aster didn't poison anyone."

"No, she told them the rains were part of a pattern of disaster, or something of the sort, and that the stars say they won't clear until September." The innkeeper kept his voice low, glancing at the table of muttering men in the corner.

It was Theo's turn to shrug. "The rain has been pretty disastrous. We've lost a lot of crops already."

"The squire's lost more. He didn't install the drainage you did, as I understand it. Same as with the others."

"And this is my fault?" Theo asked, suffering an uneasy sensation in the pit of his stomach.

"There's some said your mother was a witch. With your lady wife prophesying disaster until September, they're wondering if you married one too, and if she's the reason your fields are faring better."

Theo wondered if there was enough ale in all the kingdom to drown superstitious ninnyhammers. Deciding there wasn't, he slammed down his mug and stalked out. He simply didn't have what it took to deal with muttonheads.

He had a beautiful wife to go home to... and there wasn't a damned thing witchy about her.

Most of the time. He winced, remembering her painfully accurate predictions. If she was right about the rain, would the villagers decide to burn the witch—and the Hall with it?

Thirty

ASTER WRAPPED HER SHAWL against the evening breeze on the roof and anxiously watched Theo adjust his telescope. The sky had cleared again, as if just for them, and a million stars twinkled overhead. She could not imagine how he could find a planet, much less count the moons surrounding one, in that enormous ocean of beauty. She simply prayed that he could achieve what he sought. He deserved this opportunity.

His lanky frame stiffened, and he groped for his notebook. Aster handed it over with his pencil, her anticipation elevating a notch. He scribbled hastily and handed the items back to her so he could adjust the glass again.

She clutched the notebook at his grunt of excitement. She wanted to ask questions but didn't dare disturb his concentration.

Theo whistled in excitement. "It's there," he whispered. "In the outer orbit, as I expected—the seventh moon. Perfect, absolutely perfect. I wish there were a way to record this image. I'll not see it so perfectly again." He held out his hand for the notebook.

"Seven moons," Aster repeated in awe. "I cannot imagine such a thing. If there were people living on Saturn, can you picture what a sight that would be?"

"People cannot live on rock with only gas to breathe, but one must wonder what's on the moons. Herschel will be thrilled. This means the Society could gain royal recognition. We'll be the *Royal* Astronomical Society."

He turned and caught Aster up in a hug. "I did it! I proved my scope is strong enough to see further than any other! We'll have orders pouring in once I introduce my paper to the Society."

She covered his bristled jaw with kisses. "Don't go finding any more planets until I figure out Uranus, please."

"Then hurry, because I'm pretty certain I can find another once I study the numbers." He swung her around exuberantly. "It's miraculous having someone to share this with. If we weren't already married, I'd ask you again."

Aster laughed, thrilled more than she could express, but still wary of calamity—especially calamity she might not predict since her charts were now in disarray. "Remember that when I do something that upsets your plans."

"Telling Herschel your philosophy ought to do that," he said, but his disgruntlement was buried beneath his desire to return to his scope.

He wasn't reneging on his promise! She wrapped her arms around him. "I will be very mathematical, I promise."

He kissed her, then set her down to check his scope again. "He's more inclined to scientific persuasion than the village, I suppose. You've almost convinced the village that you're a witch, and that Iveston is benefitting from your magic. If only you could wave an enchanted wand and make Duncan see again, I'd sacrifice cows for you."

Knowing his opinion of cows, she laughed—and hid her concern. Villagers generally did not see *witches* as benefactors. Her family had suffered for generations from that kind of prejudice, but this was an enlightened age. She hoped. "I'm not fond of cows, but hiring gardeners for the courtyard might keep me happy."

"A gardener, it is." Apparently satisfied that he had all his calculations properly recorded, he picked up the lantern. "You are a distraction, my lady. I should take this opportunity to search beyond Uranus, but I can think only of celebrating in your bed."

"I'm sure that urge will melt away after a week or two," she scoffed. "And then I'll spend my evenings updating my charts for the discoveries you're making alone."

"I'll fortify my office up here and provide a better bed. We'll hide here together." He helped her down the hatch. "Or once I'm wealthy enough to build an observatory, I'll install a hidden bedchamber where no one will ever find us."

"A bedchamber with a nursery," she said dryly as they traversed the stairs. "One, of necessity, leads to the other."

"Start training those nursemaids, then. There's no reason to waste these rooms." He gestured at the empty corridor they'd reached.

Aster let the idea of half a dozen children brighten her outlook, refusing to believe her chart would endanger future generations. She could be carrying Theo's child even now, and her smile widened. "You will hide when these rooms are filled with wailing infants," she predicted, taking his hand and swinging it.

"I have no idea what I'll do," he admitted. "I'm content having you all to myself. But if having children makes you happy, then I'll be happy with that too. I am supremely easy."

Aster giggled. "No, you're not, except when you're anticipating bedplay. But luckily, I wouldn't want a simple man."

William met them at the next landing. A big man with a square face that was slow to smile or frown, he appeared close to scowling now.

"Duncan said I was to leave you be, but he's not been out listening the way we have. I think there's trouble afloat, and the dogs are restless."

Aster clasped Theo's hand tighter. Here it was, the misfortune she always anticipated. "I hate this," she muttered. "Everyone was just here dancing and having a good time. Why would they cause trouble now?"

"Not the same people, dear heart," Theo murmured. "It's an outside faction rousing the rabble. Go on to bed. William and I will take the dogs out."

She couldn't ride with them. Scowling, she released his hand. "I want riding lessons."

Theo pressed a kiss to her head. "I'd rather think of you waiting for me in bed. We don't need a warrior queen."

"I could carry a torch and shout spells at them," she said disagreeably. "Go on. I'll have the twins watch the telescopes and tell me what's happening."

Theo and William hurried off, leaving Aster to her uneasiness. She found Hugh and Hartley already in the salon, arguing over who got the more powerful glass.

"Hugh, take one of the telescopes to your father's room and tell him Theo is out looking for trouble. Station a footman nearby to run messages in case the marquess wishes to communicate with anyone." Others might fear Ashford's growls, but he needed Aster too much to throw her out for audacity. Hugh could blame her for this interference, and Ashford could do naught but roar, which he would be doing anyway.

Wanting to believe her charts were wrong, knowing they were not, she could only pray the evening would bring no more than burned straw and sheds as before. But forewarned was forearmed... Danger might not be averted, but it could be diminished with planning.

Aster gestured at the second twin as Hugh ran off to annoy his father. "Hartley, if you would be so good as to man the second glass and keep me informed, I'll read your favorite story aloud while we wait."

"Robin Hood!" the boy shouted in glee. "Do you know where I should look?"

Aster dug through the stacks of books littering shelves and corners. "William and Theo will be riding out with the dogs. Follow them. I should have told Hugh to look all over, in case they're heading in the wrong direction."

She simply could not turn off her anxiety. How could she guard the Hall's inhabitants? If Saturn's alignment was perfect for Theo's moons, it was all in perfect opposition to Mars as well. How had she not understood until now that real stars and her charts were one and the same? Tonight could be the night her chart predicted. She could not think straight for fear.

"Our father's chamber has more windows. Hugh will look out all of them. Do you think Papa will ever get his sight back?" Hartley adjusted the scope, pretending nonchalance.

"When I have time, I'll consult his chart and see if there are any major changes in his health sector." Would Uranus change what she saw in Ashford's future? She itched to work out this more pleasant possibility. "That's all I can do. I'm no physician." She wished she was. It would be nice to do more than order people about and fret.

"Maybe we should go to church and pray?" he suggested tentatively.

"I think that is a most excellent suggestion. Let's see how many of your uncles we can take with us on Sunday. Your mother must be very proud of you." Finding the book, Aster settled into a chair beneath one of the gas sconces rather than pace restlessly.

It had been so much easier predicting doom and riding away to leave someone else to deal with it. Right this minute, she despised her gift.

"Mama tells us we must get good marks in school and impress Papa so we always have a home. She likes traveling to different theaters and doesn't much like staying in one place."

"You'll always have a home here," Aster assured him, hoping she wasn't lying. What would happen if the Hall burned down? "But good marks will give you more opportunity in the future, so they're an excellent idea too."

Hartley shot her a distinctly Ives scowl. "They can't teach me about dogs at school."

She couldn't help but smile at his boyish intent. All Ives had their peculiar interests. "What are they doing out there, can you tell?"

"The hounds are leading them across the north pasture. I think I see torches near the London road."

"And where are the thresher machines?" Aster chewed her fingernail and stared blankly at the first page of the book.

"They used to be in a barn by the north road, but Theo had Mr. Browne move them. But the glass manufactory is by the north road also," Hartley said worriedly, following the action. "They won't burn an empty barn, will they? There are kittens in there."

"Oh dear." Aster bit her lip. "Cats are smart. They'll run," she said for the boy's benefit. Danger in the family sector did not mean danger to the cats, she was reasonably certain. Going out there to save cats—now that would be dangerous.

But Theo's manufactory... Everything he owned and wanted was in there. At times like this, she wished she really was a witch.

Anxiously, she began the tale of Robin of Loxley and Maid Marian.

A few minutes later, a footman scratched at the salon door. Aster gestured for him to speak.

"Master Hugh says as there's horses comin' up through the east pasture, quiet-like. The marquess says we're to send word to Mr. Browne."

"Mr. Browne is gathering the tenants," Hartley said from the window. "I can see where they are now. I can ride out and tell him."

"No, we need you here," Aster said without hesitation. "James, send one of the grooms to inform Mr. Browne. Tell him what you just told us."

She didn't want to turn Theo from protecting his livelihood

until they knew what they were dealing with here. She hoped Mr. Browne knew what to do. She bit her lip and prayed she'd made the right decision.

The footman bowed and hurried off. Aster couldn't sit still. She rose and took the telescope from Hartley. "Where do I look?"

He explained and she eventually located the stealthy figures approaching the creek that fed the pond. They were some distance away and hiding in the shadow of the hedgerow, but she could clearly see their surreptitious pace. They were coming from the direction of the village and not riding boldly up the drive. Their behavior had danger knives written all over it. "Is that the bridge where your father was hurt?"

"Yes, it's the shortcut to the tavern."

Hartley didn't see her point, but Aster's instincts leaped to appalling conclusions. That was private land. Everyone connected with the Hall was riding north to the more obvious danger on the public road. Whoever was sneaking in the back way was trespassing, using the riot as a cover.

There were no houses in that direction, no witnesses to notice intruders.

Those could be the very same people who had brought down the marquess. Perhaps she was being overly suspicious, but Ashford had been blinded while planets transited on the part of *assassination*. And now they'd moved on to *catastrophe, danger, and violence*.

And the Hall and all its inhabitants were under those knives. She could not simply sit here and do nothing. Should she send grooms to Theo after all?

"Keep an eye on them. I want to talk to your father." Aster lifted her skirt and hurried down the corridor.

The marquess was pacing his chamber, twitching his walking stick angrily while Hugh ran from window to window.

"What would qualify as catastrophe?" Aster demanded, not even bothering to knock to announce her presence.

"What the bloody hell does that mean?" Duncan swung to face the direction of her voice. The scowl on his scarred visage was formidable.

"I won't try to explain our natal transits, but Theo and I are on the part of *catastrophe* in the home. I believe those are your would-be assassins coming across the bridge. Would they strike the Hall if they think they've rendered you helpless?"

Duncan glowered, but he didn't call her a bloody fool. Aster thought that might be promising—and terrifying.

"They've left one man by the bridge," Hugh reported from the big bay window. "The others are leading their horses this way."

"They're cutting off help from the village," Duncan deciphered. "If anyone wants to warn us, they'll have to go the long way or be cut down. If Theo and Browne are engaged elsewhere, they have the Hall isolated."

"Surely there is no reason to cause you more harm?" Aster asked in alarm. "Where's the sense in that?"

"If they deliberately lured Theo and the others out of the house, they could be after the Hall... or you," Duncan said with a frown of puzzlement. "Erran's in Brighton. Jacques, William, and the boys have no legal authority and are harmless. If they think they've rendered me helpless, you're the only one of importance left. You're a weaker link than Theo and an easier target."

"Me?" she squeaked. But her charts agreed. She just didn't *understand*.

Duncan thought about it. "After my injury, they expected us to wallow helplessly. Everyone knows I'm the one who runs the estate and no one else is interested. But then Theo stepped up. Worse, he dared to marry into a family nearly as dangerous as ours. If I'm right, that means the men out there are of some station, probably men who oppose my beliefs and practices—or more likely, their hirelings are out there."

"I'm still not understanding," Aster said in bewilderment. "It's not as if I can do anything." But if *she* were the target and not the Hall... then the manufactory was more important, and she was right to leave Theo defending it.

"You already have—you involved your father. He's in London now with Pascoe, both of them throwing their weight around, rocking the boat. Parliament is about to be dissolved because of dissatisfaction with Wellington's Tory party."

"My father is loud, but he's not *dangerous*," Aster protested in bewilderment.

Duncan snorted. "Your father is one of the most powerful men in Scotland, and between us, we're related to half the landed gentry in the kingdom. Pascoe and your father will be standing in my stead to lead the election. If you are correct about assassins wishing to stop me, they have learned to their dismay that instead, a double monster has risen in my place. They must be in a state of panic."

"What can they expect to do to *me* that would stop my father?" Aster cried, bringing the topic back to the moment. She was unwilling to believe civilized Englishmen would conspire against her or her family.

Her family. She—personally—was a real danger to them, even when she wasn't in Scotland! It wasn't just a figment of the zodiac. Appalled, she shut up, trying to determine how she could avert a catastrophe she couldn't see.

"If you are right that these men actually attacked me," Duncan continued, apparently using her as a sounding board, "then they did their best to make it look like an accident. Outright murder is apparently not on their agenda, yet. I assume that at the very least, they will attempt to frighten you off. Women do generally leave us, so it's not exactly a far-fetched notion." Duncan's grim tone said it all.

If the villains didn't succeed in driving her away, they might set fire to Theo's manufactory. That would guarantee he gave up and abandoned the estate. Incinerating the Hall would scatter everyone to the winds. Aster could barely contain her horror at the choice before her.

She had to leave to save those she loved. Again. She didn't think she could bear it.

"Theo and William are holding the ground between the men in torches and the manufactory and barn," Hugh reported. "The grooms have just saddled up. It will take them time to reach Mr. Browne."

While Theo battled rioters, stealthy invaders crept up on the house. It was too medieval to make sense—except in the terms Duncan laid out. With her gone, her father would abandon Duncan and any upcoming election.

"Everyone knows I don't ride," Aster said, attempting to find another solution besides fleeing. "They can't expect me to just up and run away if they start shooting at windows."

"They don't realize that you know they're there, so, no, they don't expect you to ride out. They don't want to rouse the household. They want to frighten us, perhaps do something so appalling that we'll leave and never come back. I think I'll sit on the portico with a shotgun," Duncan said grimly.

The notion of blind Duncan with a shotgun was appalling enough. Desperately, Aster sought other solutions. "If they see me leave in a carriage, would they go away? Perhaps if I didn't come back...?"

Hugh turned, looking shocked. "You wouldn't do that!"

Well, yes, she would and had. Her younger siblings had survived and become used to her absence by now. The twins would, too.

But this time, she was resisting the idea. She watched Duncan hopefully. He didn't have her family's strong belief in her gift. Surely he wouldn't believe sending her away was a solution.

"Be the mother duck who leads the predators astray?" Duncan asked with his dreadful intellectual interest. "It would be dangerous."

And Theo would die a thousand deaths if he knew what she was about. He might never forgive her.

"I don't think we can trust the difference between assassination and catastrophe," Duncan concluded dryly. "You're safer behind stone walls."

"I'll go out and sneak up on them," Hugh declared bravely. "Maybe I can tell who it is or hear what they mean to do."

"No!" both Duncan and Aster said together.

"The grooms will warn Mr. Browne," Aster continued. "He'll come back and catch them by surprise. They won't expect that."

That satisfied Hugh. She could tell it didn't satisfy Duncan, who was clutching his fingers so tightly his knuckles had turned white.

It didn't satisfy her either, not when danger and violence hung over her head.

If Uranus had corrected the inexplicable parts of her chart— altering everything she'd believed—could it mean that *she* was meant to change?

Her heart pounded as she considered this switch in perspective.

Instead of *limiting* her possibilities by staying safe and alone in her home, perhaps her chart meant she was to go out and *conquer* the dangers, not hide from them? That would be an abrupt about-face, but *acting* instead of running... She took a deep breath to steady herself.

If the Uranus in her chart meant she should take action against danger instead of running from it—what could she do? The list of things she *couldn't* do was infinite.

Thirty-one

"WHERE IS JACQUES?" Aster demanded as an intriguing notion occurred, brought on by Hugh's brave suggestion that they learn who the invaders were.

"He's guarding the back door. The front is bolted and I've ordered a guard seated at it with a shotgun and pistols," Duncan said as if he were ordering fish for dinner.

Aster wrinkled her nose at the idea of weapons in the foyer, but she would need to learn to live with male reactions to trouble—another possible Uranian change in her life. Studying men would be fascinating, if only all the changes would give her time to observe instead of causing her to run in circles of terror.

For herself, she preferred a more peaceable response than weapons. "I'll need Jacques' help. I'll send Hartley to you, and he can serve as messenger. James can take over Jacques' guard duties."

She left before Duncan could protest. He would most certainly object if she described what she meant to do. Her vague notion wasn't much more practical than sending sneaky horsemen to the house to scare her. By doing what? Burning the Hall? Shouting threats? Table-turning seemed logical, if she could think of something suitably scary.

She sent Hartley to his father, and gesturing for the footman to follow her, she hurried downstairs. She found Jacques with his boots propped on a table, reading a stack of paper. A pistol and gunpowder rested on the table, easily at hand—giving her still another idea. She really was good at adapting, wasn't she? She'd thank Uranus for that too. She should start looking for the positive aspects suggested by the new planet.

Jacques shoved the papers in a drawer and stood up. "You're not thinking of going out there, are you?" he asked warily. "Theo would cut my head off at the groin if I allowed it."

Aster laughed at his crude expression and helped herself to the gunpowder bag. She brushed right past him, knowing gentle Jacques wouldn't lay a finger on her. "I'll take care of Theo. We're about to make what I believe is a reconnaissance mission, and stage... what is it the military calls a diversion?"

"A diversion," Jacques said dryly.

"We need brooms and cloaks. James, will you gather what you can find as quickly as you can and carry them to the stable? Be very quiet, please." Aster hurried into the starlit night, clutching the bag of explosive powder. The moon was low, but the gravel reflected enough light to find her path. "I don't suppose you have any of your gas sconces out here?"

"We do," Jacques said, gazing around as if expecting soldiers to leap from the nonexistent bushes. "We used to light up the drive for parties. Haven't lit them in ages, but they operate off the same coal as in the house."

Aster smiled in delight. "Do you think you could figure out how to turn them on?"

"As boys, we turned them on so we could play outside at night— until our father caught us. I assume they're still connected. What are you plotting?"

"I noticed that while he was here, Erran was experimenting with a machine for tying hay into squares for storage in the stable." She had thought it an odd occupation for a lawyer at the time, but he seemed happier playing with wire than sitting in the house.

"Erran was trying to help out by creating a hay press. It's stationary, so we can't take it from field to field, which makes it pretty useless, but the bales are easier to haul and store. And in this wet weather, we needed dry storage, why?" He halted at the trough.

"Do you know the opening scene to Macbeth?" she asked, eyeing the lovely stacks of hay just recently hauled in and not yet stored.

"I have it memorized. Want me to find a cauldron and eye of newt?"

"That would be entertaining, too." She turned as James came running with an armful of brooms and cloaks. "But a stage production with flaming torches, brooms stuck in hay bales, a few cloaks... Those men out there think I'm a witch. Can you produce a witchy scene?"

She could almost feel Jacques light up as his imagination caught fire.

"I have no idea what it will accomplish, but I can do that," he agreed. He grabbed a handful of the fabric James was carrying and swung it dramatically. "More wind would be helpful."

"Knowing who is down the road and what they're saying would be more helpful." Aster took a cloak for herself, disguising her hair beneath a hood and draping the cloak over her clothing so she might blend in with the night. "Stage your scene with the haystacks. The intruders are coming up the bridge path from town, so make your witches visible from that direction, please. Light the torches when you hear me chanting."

"You're not heading down there alone!" Jacques cried, his delight dissipating with alarm.

She shrugged. "I'm small and quiet and they won't even know I'm there. The hedge is thick. I just want to listen, I promise."

She ran off, knowing Jacques wasn't Theo and wouldn't sling her over his shoulder and bodily haul her back to the house. She loved that her husband wanted to shield her from harm, but he needed to learn that he wasn't the only one with a duty to protect others.

And this time, she would defend her family by *meeting* trouble instead of running from it. If she had been limiting her possibilities by staying safe at home, then change meant she must go out and *conquer* the dangers instead. The ability to act filled her with excitement. No wonder Theo preferred to just *do* rather than dither as she often did. She must overcome the debilitating effect of fear.

Taking action offered exciting freedom.

The grass was lush from the summer rain. Her slippers scarcely made a sound as she hurried along, blending in with the darkness of the hedgerow, disturbing the creatures who lived there. They rustled and scattered, but her attention was more on the murmur of voices emerging from the lane. They were leading their horses, so the soft plod of their hooves in the mud wouldn't be heard from the Hall. She couldn't peer over the hedge to see more.

She should be terrified, but she was simply furious. If these were the men who had harmed Duncan and forced Theo into a position he despised, she'd like to see them drawn and quartered. She realized it was impossible to prove what had happened the night Duncan's horse had thrown him—but she could prove what was happening tonight.

When the voices rose more loudly from the far side of the hedge, she slowed down, wary of snapping twigs. But the intruders were making more noise than she was.

"They won't let me past the front door," a vaguely familiar voice whined. "You should have sent someone else."

"There ain't anyone else we can trust," a less educated voice growled in response. "Just be convincing, tell her Miss Caldwell needs help, get her out in the open. And we've got Maeve going to the back door. Even if you don't sway her, her maids will come running, and she'll believe them."

"I don't like it," the familiar voice whined. "Theo will kill me. You should have sent Margaret. They'll believe her."

"You ain't got nothin' to worry about. His lordship won't know who was at the door. You just get the lady out where we can take her. Once he talks with her all nice like, she'll run back to town where she belongs."

Aster shivered. She had no doubt they were talking of her, but who was the person meant to persuade her into running away?

"He'll never talk her out of leaving all this wealth," the whiny gentleman continued. "He's better off burning the Hall or crippling Theo the way he did Ashford."

Aster stifled a gasp and grabbed a tree branch to steady herself. She should have brought a stout hoe and beat them over the head! Who the devil was this murderous "he" who apparently wasn't with them?

"Burning the manufactory can be blamed on the rioters. Another accident would be too suspicious," another voice joined in. "We just want to discourage bringing in any more ladies with powerful families. His lordship's bewitched now, but he'll give up if she's not around. We talked it all out, and this is the plan. Don't go backing out now, Montfort."

Ah! She remembered the drunken young man Theo had popped in the nose. Most excellent. Now she had a name, and Theo could ask questions later.

She really would like to know what kind of story they'd concocted that they could possibly believe she would leave Theo over it, but she'd heard enough. Bewitched! She almost laughed aloud at that. If they believed anything of the sort, they deserved what she'd planned for them—and more.

Picking up the heavy cloak, she ran back toward the stable. A fox dashed out in front of her, and she squeaked in alarm, cursing herself even as she did so.

"What's that?" one of the intruders asked nervously.

She froze as the horses halted. An owl hooted, and she could almost hear the intruders exhale in relief. Or perhaps that was her.

"Just critters," the leader scoffed. "Come on."

She wanted to whoop and cackle and scare them more, but she was too close. Reacting instead of hiding didn't mean putting herself in danger. Now that she knew a little more, she picked up her skirt and ran.

The horsemen would have to break cover when they reached the open stable yard. She wanted to be in place before then.

How dare the monsters think they'd frighten her!

She wished she had one of Theo's telescopes so she could see where the grooms were. She had no doubt that Theo would come running if he thought the Hall was in danger, but that would mean he'd have to sacrifice his manufactory to the rioters. She'd rather catch these predators on her own and leave Theo to save his livelihood.

As she entered the yard, she observed Jacques' stage setting with approval. He had set up the hay, broom sticks, and cloaks just as she'd hoped. Once turned on, the gas torches would create as much shadow as light, and the straw "witches" would loom spookily. She smiled at the superstitious fools who had given her this notion.

Locating a pitchfork, she stationed herself at the bottom of the ladder the men used to climb up to the loft, waiting for the low murmur of male voices approaching. From the Hall, she heard a knocking and calling at the servants' door—Maeve? Aster hoped their malicious ex-tenant had a good view of the stable to frighten her into the next county.

Once she heard the clop of horses, she assumed the invaders could hear her. She summoned the Latin she'd learned in order to read her family's older journals and began loudly intoning passages of nonsense. Jacques's shadow immediately appeared at the corner. She waved at him and began climbing the ladder, pitchfork and gunpowder in hand. The climb was awkward with the cloak dragging and her skirts wrapping around her ankles, but she was furious enough to scale mountains.

The breeze was chillier on the roof, but she had the heavy wool cloak for warmth. Aster chanted louder, giving her voice depth and direction, delighting in the farce. Maybe she was meant to be a witch. She laughed wickedly at the thought—just as the small group of men and horses entered the open yard. Perfect timing! They froze at her cackle of laughter and glanced around, searching for the source.

She threw more Latin at them, just as the gas torches abruptly flared on. The flames illuminated the stable yard in flickering shadows, casting the haystack witches into threatening flares of dark and light. Jacques had set his stage with the cloaked hay and broomsticks perfectly, creating wonderfully eerie figures. For emphasis, Aster shouted louder nonsense and waved the pitchfork, as if she were truly casting spells.

The horses whickered and stamped nervously. Laughing as maniacally as she could, Aster took a handful of gunpowder from the pouch and scattered it in the direction of the torches below. Her father—with his love of fireworks—had used this prank on more than one occasion.

The powder hit the flames and popped. In a dramatic stage voice, Jacques began chanting what sounded very much like ...*toil and trouble, fire burn and cauldron bubble*. Trying not to laugh, Aster pointed her pitchfork at the men and cursed in more incomprehensible Latin, flinging another handful of gunpowder.

The torches theatrically popped and flared, and terrified, the intruders leapt for their horses. The gentleman in the tall hat led the way.

"Call me a witch, will you?" she cackled after their retreating backs.

THEO SAT ASTRIDE his horse, William beside him, holding off what appeared to be several dozen angry farmers bearing torches. He didn't recognize the blackened faces of the ringleaders shouting strident war cries about injustice.

He had a rifle and knew how to use it. He didn't want to. These could be his neighbors and tenants. They almost certainly had families. But his workers would lose their employment if the manufactory burned. They had families to feed. He was torn.

"I can sic the hounds on them," William suggested dubiously.

"They have pitchforks. I don't want dumb animals hurt any more than dumb people," Theo replied. His sarcasm seeped through.

"You sit up there in your fancy Hall, eating feasts, while our families starve!" shouted one of the soot-coated leaders.

Theo felt a chill of unease.

Aster had said both the manufactory and the *Hall* were in danger. Surely, they wouldn't...? He glanced over his shoulder to his home standing like a rock in the distance. He couldn't see more than the tower crenellations.

Her predictions were absurd... except when they weren't.

The Hall could withstand armies.

His family couldn't. His *family*. Aster. The twins. Duncan. All helpless. While he was down here guarding a damned building. If Aster was right...

Aster had been right about everything else.

Fighting back a wave of terror, Theo gathered up his reins. Superstition or not, he had to believe her. "Shoot anyone who carries a torch anywhere near the manufactory. The Hall is in danger. I have to go back."

He kicked his gelding into a gallop, slowing only to order Browne and his tenants to divide in half—half to William and half to the Hall. If he lost buildings because he'd believed Aster's prediction instead of the danger right before his eyes, so be it. He'd rather take that chance than risk losing his family.

Theo was pretty certain his heart stopped beating as he rode over the hill to see the gas torches flare on at the Hall.

He damned well stopped breathing when he saw the lone figure on the stable roof—*Aster*. He'd recognize her even if she'd been wrapped up as a mummy. He would kill her—if she didn't kill him first. What the devil was she about, flinging a cloak and pitchfork and shouting like a bedlamite? He scanned the yard, looking for an enemy.

His heart *did* stop when he saw the last fleeing horseman turn and aim a shotgun at the roof. The explosion of gunfire rattled the yard.

Aster screamed and slid down the far side, out of sight.

Panicking, unable to emit a sound, Theo kicked his lathered horse into a gallop. He couldn't breathe, couldn't think until he'd reached Aster. He traversed the final distance into the yard at breakneck speed. Heart and head frozen, he could only act. Dropping from the saddle, Theo raced around the stable, steps behind Jacques, who was shouting frantically.

He would kill Jacques another day. The huddled mound of cloak and legs sprawled on a stack of newly-delivered hay was all Theo could see now. His vocal chords and lungs returned. *"Aster!"* His frantic cry rang against the cobbles as he dropped into the hay and lifted her limp form into his arms.

"Mmpf" was his only reply as she wiped at her face.

Oh, God, she was alive. He still couldn't breathe. Every muscle in his body had tightened into knots.

"You've killed me dead," he muttered into her hair. "Tell me you're alive. If anything happened to you, it would just be easier if I died now while my heart's stopped working. Aster, for the love of all that's holy, *tell me you're alive!"*

"Straw," she murmured, brushing at the cloak. "Mouth."

"Fetch water," Theo shouted at Jacques, who was dancing around helplessly. "Tell the others to go after the mongrels in the lane."

A month ago, he would have been racing after the bloody bastards, whip in hand, with no thought to anything but his fury— because his anger would have been more important than all else. But now—all that mattered to him was in his arms. He wasn't going anywhere until he knew his fairy general would hold and kiss him again.

He hugged her closer, trying to determine if she was hurt, but she merely snuggled against him and wiped her face on his waistcoat. He wanted to weep but didn't know how. "You could have broken your bloody neck! Don't ever do that to me again. I mean it, I can't bear it. If what I'm feeling now is love, it's excruciating. I can't live through this agony another time," he whispered, before Jacques could return.

She squirmed and kissed the skin above the opening of his shirt. "Love hurts," she murmured insensibly. "It's so very painful when you want to be with someone and can't. I didn't want to love anyone ever again."

Theo gulped air and tried to steady his breathing by covering her face with kisses. When she didn't wince, he had to hope she wasn't injured too badly. "It damn well hurts when I'm with you and see you do insane things like that!"

She sighed and turned her head so her mouth met his. Theo sank into the kiss, needing the reassurance before he shook sense into her.

She placed a hand on his chest and pushed away to gasp for air. "I didn't run away," she said proudly. "I *stopped* the danger I saw in my charts."

"I'm not certain that's a better solution. I was coming to do it," he grumbled, reaching for the water Jacques handed him.

"I've sent Browne and the others down the lane. I didn't know she would climb on the roof!" his brother said hurriedly. "Honest! We were just scaring them off."

"Go away." Theo waved at him. "Go tell Dunc what's happening before he tumbles down the stairs trying to find out."

Jacques ran off and Aster struggled to sit up, but Theo wouldn't let her. He fed her water and rocked her in his arms and tried to come down out of the boughs she'd sent him into.

"You came back because of my prediction?" she asked in disbelief.

"I couldn't take a chance of losing you," he said again, because it bore repeating. He was still coming to grips with the realization, and he needed to say the words to make them real. "You nearly yanked my heart and soul out of my body just now. If I lose you, who will help me keep this place whole? Unless you want to kill me, you have to vow that you'll never risk your life like that again!"

"Can't," she said with a cough after swallowing the water too fast. "Even childbirth is dangerous."

He took the flask away from her and pounded her on the back as she coughed. "In your case, even drinking is dangerous. You're a walking, talking thundercloud. I'm never letting you out of my sight again."

She sat up and kissed his cheek. "I love you too. Now will you take me to the bathing room?"

She *loved* him. As he loved her. It was a wondrous—unutterably terrifying—realization.

Thirty-two

ASTER ALLOWED Theo to haul her from the haystack. With the wind knocked out of her from the terrifying fall—then from Theo's almost-declaration of love—she was pretty shaky.

Had he really returned to the Hall because he *believed* her prediction?

She clung to his neck as he lifted her. She pressed kisses on his bristled jaw and let his muttered curses and threats flow right over her. She was his *heart and soul*! No one had ever said such a wonderful thing to her. Her own foolish heart pounded a timpani in response. She had never expected love, and she closed her eyes and soaked up the bliss.

She would never have dragged that admission out of him had she not risked her silly neck and dared to confront danger. She'd interpreted her chart correctly—Uranus made her good at abrupt changes! Like declaring and accepting love...

She was still shivering from being shot at, but her love for Theo spilled over to warm her. She had not dared admit love, but when she'd offered him her Malcolm vows, she'd already been head-over-heels. It had been foolish of her to deny the obvious—so she would stop being foolish right now while she still had the power to speak.

"I love you," she murmured again in a break in his aggrieved tirade. "I'm sorry I scared you."

Theo carried her in the side door, kicked it shut, and kissed her fiercely—then lifted his head and glared at her again. "You terrify me. You always terrify me. I wasn't meant to take care of others."

She nibbled his neck. "That's just plain silly. Just because you never have before doesn't mean you aren't capable. You'll learn. And you can put me down now, honest. I'm not broken, just shaken."

"I don't think I can let you go," he admitted. "What if you decide to fly off the roof? Slide down banisters? How am I going to live should you leave me? It's too perplexing, so I'm keeping you right here where you can't escape."

"I don't think that will work very well," she said with amusement. "Perhaps you could just take me to the bathing room. Hot water helps, and I can't go far from there. You need to see who the intruders were. I know Montfort was one, but I didn't recognize the others. And they talked about someone who wasn't there, someone who caused Duncan's accident. You really need to stop the marauders before they grow bold enough to do worse. And what about your manufactory?"

His arms tightened around her, and his lips formed a grim line. "I will kill Montfort tomorrow. Browne can tie up the others and let them rot in the fields until daylight. I don't give a damn what William is doing to the rioters. I want to look the villain who shot at you in the eye before I lop off his head. Besides, I have just this minute vowed to put you first, before any and all head lopping."

She laughed a little against his shoulder. "You are starting to sound like Ashford. There will be no head lopping, please. But perhaps you should join me in the bath, then, and re-direct your hostility. You promised we'd share and we haven't."

Theo's grip loosened, and his mouth formed a softer line as he gazed down on her. She was learning to re-direct her action-oriented husband, she thought. His heated look took the chill from her bones without need of hot water.

"That's the best method to prevent beheading that I've ever heard. We need to find a woman for Dunc so he can try that solution." He kissed her hard and carried her up the stairs in the direction of their suite and the bathing room.

HOLDING A TELESCOPE, Hartley ran up when Theo and Aster reached the upper corridor. "William has routed the rioters! The hounds are chasing the leaders back to London, and the tenants are racing after the rest with pitchforks."

"Excellent." Theo didn't halt. "Now watch to see what happens to the ones in the lane."

Hartley cheerfully ran off, leaving Theo to carry his mad bride to the tub.

He lit all the lamps and admired her naked, in the water and out. Hot water did nothing to reduce his need as he joined her.

After making soul-satisfying love to his witchy wife in the tub, reassuring himself that she wasn't broken, Theo settled Aster in his arms and thought he'd melt and become one with the water. His beautiful bride was a creative and eager lover. He didn't know what he'd done to deserve her, but he was more than ever determined to keep her for a hundred years.

She'd predicted disaster, and they'd averted it. How was that possible?

She was nibbling his neck, and he was debating whether they could just mindlessly spend the night in the bath when he heard a scratch on the door.

"Do we have to answer it?" he murmured. Aster's wet breast was pressed into his chest, creating erotic sensations, and her bottom was positioned precisely where he needed her. "And why are they scratching instead of pounding and shouting?"

"Because I am a very good teacher." When she pushed at his arms, he reluctantly released her, and she stood up.

Admiring rivulets of water running from his wife's exquisite curves, Theo watched in amazement as she pulled a rope—and a... *drapery?*... cut off the bath from the door.

"Enter," she called, sinking back into the tub facing him.

Theo scowled at the curtain, as if it was at fault for the intrusion.

"His lordship requests your presence, my lord," a female voice said. "They have captured the..." The maid hesitated over the message. "The *miscreants*, I believe he said."

"Thank you, Molly. Have Mr. Ledbetter lay out Lord Theo's clothes, will you? My robe will be enough."

Aster dragged her toe down Theo's chest while they waited for the door to close again. He caught her foot and nibbled the predatory toe, then rubbed her feet until she groaned helplessly.

"Mr. Ledbetter?" he inquired while she leaned back and hummed with pleasure.

"Mr. Browne recommended him, said he was batman for a captain during the war. He's a bit rough for London ways, but I thought he might learn something from Jones and be more suitable for your equally crude habits."

"What the devil can he learn from Jones?" Uncertain whether to be pleased or not about her hiring another valet, Theo grudgingly released her foot to peer around the curtain. Their robes had been neatly hung on hooks that he was pretty sure hadn't been there before.

She purred happily and paddled in the water some more, stirring the scent of roses. "Jones is an unappreciated genius. That coat and muffler he dressed you in for the tea party were not only the epitome of fashion, but suited you perfectly. Ledbetter will not have his fashion sense. He will only see you shaved properly and lay out clothes as requested, that sort of thing. You can yell at him all you like, and he'll only wait until you give him sensible orders. Jones is a little more... sensitive."

"You intend to civilize us," he complained, reluctantly climbing from the tub to towel off.

"I doubt that's possible," she declared, gazing meaningfully at his partial erection. "Men are more or less animals who have learned to disguise the fact. I don't object, mind you. But the more civilized you appear, the more other men respect your disguise."

"That's ridiculous," he protested, but he had never learned to be sociable and didn't understand human nature enough to argue. He donned his robe and looked regretfully down on her. "Will you stay here so I can come back later?"

"I'd turn into a prune. I've soaked away my aches. I'll wait for you in bed, so tell Ashford to be quick about the trial. And don't attempt to haul your prisoners off anywhere until morning." She raised her legs out of the water and seductively rubbed one curvaceous limb with the other.

She was bribing him not to linger elsewhere. But now that he knew she wasn't broken, he had to return to his responsibilities. The balance between keeping his wife happy and doing what must be done was tricky, but he was smart. He'd figure it out eventually. He might be the first Ives in a generation to do so.

"We can't hold a trial without you as witness. Dunc's just wanting an excuse to beat someone up. I'll be back quickly." Theo leaned over and kissed her head, then let himself out of the bathing room.

Amazingly, clean clothes were laid out in the suite for him, and there wasn't a servant in sight to yell at. And no reason to yell. Loose trousers, an old shirt and waistcoat, and his slippers were sufficient to take him down the corridor to Duncan's chambers.

Theo could see where this business of thinking about others first instead of just pounding heads would be an equilibrium as difficult to maintain as the one between husband and wife. But if it meant keeping Aster, he'd learn. She'd hired a *valet*—one that she thought might suit him! And that drapery thing in the bathing room... Given their domestic interruptions, that was beyond clever, and one of those niceties an all-male household would never consider.

Instead of complaining, Aster sought solutions. Theo thought a woman like that might be a rarity.

Unfortunately, the ability to think and do for herself led to roof-climbing episodes. He might die of heart failure before he was forty.

Duncan's chamber was huge, but it felt crowded when Theo entered. Large sweaty men milled and filled the space with furious energy. William had had time to return, smelling of dog and horse and bunching his fists as if ready to murder. Mr. Browne hovered over his prisoners. Jacques paced. A few of the more substantial tenants whispered nervously against the walls.

Duncan had taken a chair at his writing desk and was irritably tapping his walking stick. At Theo's entrance, he actually looked up as if he could see him.

"It's about time. I want these miscreants hung." Since Duncan couldn't see the two crudely dressed ruffians cowering in the room's center, tied hand and foot, he didn't bother glancing at them.

"You're the magistrate," Theo replied, studying the pair. "Is trespassing a hanging offense? Or were they the ones with the shotgun?" He knew they weren't. He'd seen the rider wielding the weapon. He'd been a stout man with a barrel chest. These two were short and half-starved. And the gentleman in the tall hat leading the retreat—Roderick, no doubt—hadn't been the shooter either.

"We didn't do nuffing!" the older one with a bristly reddish-gray stubble shouted.

"Well, fine," Theo said equitably. "Then tell us who shot my wife and we'll just charge you with trespass."

"Big bloke," the younger one said, wiping his nose on his sleeve. "Told us we was there to keep the peace. He was afraid you'd have guards. Warn't nobody supposed to get shot."

"You simply rode onto private property under the instruction of a complete stranger without question?" Theo asked in disbelief. Duncan was the one who should have been conducting this interview, but these imbeciles had caused Aster to climb a damned roof! Theo wanted to shake the pair until their teeth rattled and information spilled out.

"He gave us coins and said a lady was in danger and we was to rescue her," the older explained. "But then he and the gent got to arguing as we rode, and there was talk of witches back in the tavern, and we got kind of nervous like."

"Did anyone go after Montfort?" Duncan asked in a voice of menace.

"We sent men over to his estate to keep an eye on him," Mr. Browne said. "We didn't see him on the road."

"He'll have cut across the field," Duncan said in disgust. "Only people who don't know the area stick to the main road."

"Which means their leader knows our land," Theo pointed out. "And Aster said someone else sent them here, the same someone who caused your horse to bolt to make it look like an accident."

That silenced the room. The prisoners began to squirm.

"We don't know nuffin' 'bout that," the older protested again. "We was just hired for the evenin'."

"As were the leaders of the rioters," William said, speaking up. "They weren't men from around here. Once we separated them from the crowd, the others protested about threshers and losing their jobs and were pacified when we told them to report to the office if they wanted work."

"And what became of the leaders of the rioters?" Duncan asked.

"They were on horses," William replied in disgust. "They got away. You think this was a conspiracy? The rioters and these dolts were working together?"

"Looks like it. Lock this pair up. Let's see if anyone comes looking for them." Having made that decision, Duncan smacked his stick against the desk legs as if pondering his next move.

Not so long ago, Ashford would have ridden into the village to question every man, woman, and child until he had answers. Theo couldn't do that. Slumping against the wall, he let Browne and the farmers lead out their prisoners. Jacques and William stayed behind.

"Surround Montfort's place," Duncan ordered. "He's our only lead. One assumes his father put him up to this. The pup wouldn't stir a finger otherwise."

Theo reluctantly imparted his last piece of information. "I'm sorry, Dunc, but Aster said Montfort mentioned sending Margaret to lure her from the house. We have no way of knowing if Margaret would have known why, but it sounds as if her family might be involved too."

Duncan nodded. "Caldwell and I have been at odds for a long time. I just can't imagine he or Montfort would act without some incentive and outside leadership. They complain, but they seldom act on their own initiative."

"Why would they go after Lady Aster?" Jacques demanded.

"Margaret tried to scare her away earlier," Theo said, remembering the visit after the Maeve incident. An idea bubbled at the back of his mind that he was reluctant to voice. It wasn't as if he understood why people did what they did. But almost losing Aster had shaken him out of his usual complacency. If he was to start believing her predictions...

Aster had said that *allegiance led to accomplishment*. "I think— and this is just a point worth pondering mind you—that they are trying to keep us from working together."

Duncan's stick quit spinning. Neither Jacques nor William interrupted, so Theo was forced to continue.

"We *don't* work together," Theo pointed out. "We each have our own interests and go our own ways and the estate pays us enough to do so. No one ever expected me to take over Duncan's chores, no more than I expect anyone to take mine."

"What does that have to do with Lady Aster?" Jacques asked, frowning.

"And Margaret," Duncan said thoughtfully. "And maybe Theo's ex-fiancée."

Theo rubbed his brow. "I didn't go after Celia when she ran. She had hysterics and I said good riddance and went back to my telescopes. Duncan practically shoved Margaret out the door. That's what we do—ignore everything except our own selfish needs. Women won't tolerate that."

His brothers stared at him blankly, although in Duncan's case, there could have been comprehension behind the blind stare. Theo couldn't tell.

He grimaced and sought the right words. "Without women, we have no nucleus to orbit, no common objective to keep us together. The children have mothers and come and go, so they're almost dispensable. But Aster..." Theo sighed and tried to straighten his thoughts. "Aster unites us somehow."

"You think thugs figured that out?" William asked with a thick layer of skepticism.

"No," Duncan said. "Margaret did. She's known us all our lives. She would have complained about us to her father. Theo's right. None of you has any interest in the estate. My enemies would naturally have thought that if they brought me down, no one would pick up the reins. But Theo not only picked them up, he brought in reinforcements. The house filled with women. We started hiring servants. The lot of you were all over London hunting carpets to please Aster, for pity's sake! Even Pascoe came down for the tea party. She *united* us."

They all fell silent, contemplating this message.

"The Greeks said 'United we stand, divided we fall,'" Jacques acknowledged. "The Bible says much the same. That's smart of Margaret, if you're right that she figured out that we were easily divided. Instead of fighting each other, we need to stand together to fight a common enemy."

"But how do we do that?" Theo demanded.

"The estate funds all of us. Without the land, we wouldn't have the wherewithal to explore other ventures," William said. "Iveston is where we must stand together."

"He's right." Duncan glanced up to Theo through unseeing eyes. "Give Aster full rein of the household. Let her turn this into a home where women and children are welcome, and the rest of us will follow. Give the family reason to defend our heritage."

Because Duncan would never marry and provide the same, Theo recognized with sorrow.

Theo's days of selfish pursuits were over. With Aster to show him the way, he thought he might enjoy the change.

Thirty-three

"I LOVE YOU."

Theo's whisper tickled Aster's ear and she shivered with desire. Unfortunately, all she could do in response was stroke his newly-cut brown hair where it flopped over his brow.

"I love your exotic nest," he continued, pulling her closer despite the crowd of people watching them from the corner of their eyes. "And I want all these people to go home so I can show you how much I want you."

Aster patted his starched white linen, leaned into his formal black frock coat, and muffled a laugh. He smelled of sandalwood and Theo, and she almost agreed to his disgraceful suggestion. "I love you and my nest, too, which is why all these people are here. You are famous. You will become more famous as you improve your telescopes and find more planets. These people will spread your fame and make your fortune. They will also take notice of your brothers—which is part of the point, isn't it? To build Ives strength into a fortress as formidable as the Hall?"

She couldn't see through the throng in her small parlor, but she knew Jacques was circulating, charming the ladies. William had refused to come to town, preferring to wait for country entertainments. Erran had been here earlier, but as the third son of a marquess, he didn't have much more prestige than the illegitimate ones. That would change, Aster knew, but these things took time. Theo's success was only a first step.

"Duncan should have been the one entertaining all these years, making these connections," Theo griped, but he hugged Aster and sipped his brandy with appreciation.

"He prefers the country just as William does." She was starting to understand the Ives brothers even better through living with them rather than just studying their charts. "It will all balance eventually now that our planets are moving out of the Mars conjunction."

"I can't think we're safe if our enemies are still hidden." Theo frowned as if he could discern their adversaries in the crowd. "The two thugs we captured had nothing useful to add about the ringleaders. I should have ridden after Montfort myself. We'll never catch him in France."

"Roderick was just a weak link. His father is probably more dangerous. If your brother's opponents are political, let your Uncle Pascoe find them. He looks dangerous enough to eliminate crime in high places." She watched Theo's uncle work his way through the crowd of well-wishers, his dark gaze always wandering past whomever he was half-listening to.

Her elegant husband snorted most inelegantly. "He has given me an assortment of secret missives to take to your father on our wedding journey. They'll out-conspire any amateur conspirators. Shouldn't we go to bed early so we'll be fresh for our travel in the morning?"

She laughed and slipped from Theo's grasp to greet Jacques. "Have you charmed all the neighbors into helping care for my plants while we're gone?"

"Your accommodating maids will do that," Jacques said with a shrug and a deprecating grin. "But your neighbors may feed me. I appreciate being given run of the household but have no good way of paying you back."

"You'll owe us," Theo said sternly. "We'll collect someday."

"Don't go compromising my maids," Aster said, equally sternly. "I have a reputation to uphold for good servants. It is the only way I'll be able to staff the Hall."

Jacques tilted his head with interest. "You both sound like Duncan. Is this what family togetherness will bring us?"

Aster smiled and hugged him. "And this." She kissed his cheek. "And this."

She indicated the party in her parlor. "And all this. With wealth, comes responsibility."

Jacques rubbed his cheek and nodded. "That's a nice trade. I'll take it." He held out his hand to shake Theo's. "Find Duncan a wife just like yours, and we'll be shaped up in no time."

"That's Aster's department. And I don't think anyone but you agrees that women are the answer," Theo said, shaking on it. "Erran has his nose out of joint over his inability to attract women without funds, William has only one use for women, and you know Duncan can't court anyone if he won't leave the damned house."

"Love will find a way," Aster said with assurance. "I'll have the servants clear the buffet. That should send your guests out the door, so if there is anyone with whom you wish to speak, do so now."

"Does that mean we can go upstairs soon?" Theo whispered hopefully as Jacques hurried off.

"Soon, and I have a surprise for you, so be very polite to our guests until we reach our bed," she replied with mischief, before departing to direct her army of servants and friends.

REMEMBERING the night months ago when she'd rode into a storm as the Prophetess of Doom, Aster almost wiggled with excitement as she handed the heavy sheet of vellum to her beautifully naked husband. She hadn't been able to wait until they were in bed to present his wedding gift.

"I am now the Prophetess of Boons," she declared happily. "Or maybe the Prophetess of Good Fortune, what do you think?" Wearing a whisper-thin night shift, she climbed into the small bed they would need to replace to accommodate Theo's large frame.

Eagerly, she studied her husband's usually non-expressive face as he read her father's letter. His ambiguously blue-gray eyes lit with inner fires, and his lips curved upward in a rare grin. He stared at the paper, then at her, and back down again.

"Really? Your father won't take this back if we must cut our visit short or he disagrees with my politics?" He shook the letter in her direction as if daring her to deny the contents.

Aster fluffed her pillows against the headboard and settled back. She noted with gratitude that Theo's attention instantly diverted from the letter to her breasts. She had never been particularly grateful for her plumpness until Theo landed in her life.

"My father has already transferred the funds," she told him. "He knows I won't renege on my promise to journey north. My mother is deliriously planning parties and dinners and probably slaughtering a fatted calf. My siblings are no doubt bouncing off walls. You will have to endure utter familial chaos for weeks. I think my father's settlement is barely payment enough for your suffering." She grinned at his expression of dismay.

"For this..." Theo took a deep breath and reverently lay the letter on the desk before climbing in beside her. He pressed a fervent kiss against her brow. "I will be able to build the observatory *and* buy that small estate farm to put it on. It has a farmhouse, and a clear view of the night sky. And I never thought I'd earn enough to actually buy *land*."

He sprawled across the sheets and dragged her on top of him. Aster covered his jaw in kisses and began nibbling his ears as he stroked her, his thoughts obviously still half in the stars.

"My father believes you're taking me firmly in hand and showing me it's nonsense to stay away from my family." She bit his ear a little harder. "He approves. And really, I'm worth every penny of that dowry."

Theo laughed and pulled her closer, now fully engaged. "You are, and more. Half of it will go into a trust for you and any children, as will the land. I can earn the rest. Duncan is paying me well to handle his duties, and the telescopes will be selling soon. But I married you for your real worth, not for your father's wealth. You are more valuable than the crown jewels. I cannot believe my good fortune."

"Prophetess of Good Fortune it is, then," she murmured as he flipped her back to the mattress and began kissing all the places where she'd sewn stars on her nightshift. "I do love an observant man," she said with a sigh of pleasure as he found one over her breast.

"And I do love a woman who brings the stars down to earth just for me." Theo raised up and covered her mouth with his, stealing the breath from her lungs.

GET A FREE STARTER SET OF PATRICIA

RICE BOOKS

Thank you for reading *Magic in the Stars*.

Would you like to know when my next book is available? I occasionally send newsletters with details on new releases, special offers and other bits of news. If you sign up for the mailing list I'll send you a free copy of the Patricia Rice starter kit. **The books average 4.4 out of 5 stars and together usually retail over $15.00.** Just sign up at **http://patriciarice.com/**

As an independent author, getting the word out about my book is vital to its success, so if you liked this book, please consider telling your friends and writing a review at the store where you purchased it. Reviews help other readers find books. I appreciate all reviews, whether positive or negative.

About the Author

With several million books in print and *New York Times* and *USA Today's* bestseller lists under her belt, former CPA Patricia Rice is one of romance's hottest authors. Her emotionally-charged contemporary and historical romances have won numerous awards, including the *RT Book Reviews* Reviewers Choice and Career Achievement Awards. Her books have been honored as Romance Writers of America RITA® finalists in the historical, regency and contemporary categories.

A firm believer in happily-ever-after, Patricia Rice is married to her high school sweetheart and has two children. A native of Kentucky and New York, a past resident of North Carolina and Missouri, she currently resides in Southern California, and now does accounting only for herself. She is a member of Romance Writers of America, the Authors Guild, and Novelists, Inc.

For further information, visit Patricia's network:
http://www.patriciarice.com
http://www.facebook.com/OfficialPatriciaRice
https://twitter.com/Patricia_Rice
http://wordwenches.typepad.com/word_wenches/
http://patricia-rice.tumblr.com/

About Book View Café

Book View Café Publishing Cooperative (BVC) is a an author-owned cooperative of over fifty professional writers, publishing in a variety of genres including fantasy, romance, mystery, and science fiction.

In 2008, BVC launched a website, bookviewcafe.com, initially offering free fiction and gradually moving to selling ebooks of members' backlist titles, then original titles. BVC's ebooks are DRM-free and are distributed around the world. BVC returns 95% of the profit on each book directly to the author. The cooperative has gained a reputation for producing high-quality ebooks, and is now moving into print editions.

BVC authors include *New York Times* and *USA Today* bestsellers; Nebula, Hugo, Lambda, and Philip K. Dick Award winners; World Fantasy and Rita Award nominees; and winners and nominees of many other publishing awards.

CPSIA information can be obtained at www.ICGtesting.com
Printed in the USA
LVOW08s1021190516

489024LV00001B/67/P